A CASE OF
DOUBTFUL
DEATH

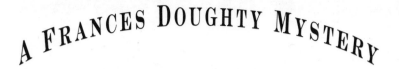

A FRANCES DOUGHTY MYSTERY

A CASE OF DOUBTFUL DEATH

LINDA STRATMANN

The Mystery Press

*This book is dedicated to the Friends of Kensal
Green and the General Cemetery Company
with especial thanks to Lee Snashfold and Henry
Vivian-Neal for all their help with my research.*

www.kensalgreencemetery.com
www.kensalgreen.co.uk

First published 2013

The Mystery Press, an imprint of The History Press
The Mill, Brimscombe Port
Stroud, Gloucestershire, GL5 2QG
www.thehistorypress.co.uk

© Linda Stratmann, 2013

The right of Linda Stratmann to be identified as the Author
of this work has been asserted in accordance with the
Copyrights, Designs and Patents Act 1988.

British Library Cataloguing in Publication Data.
A catalogue record for this book is available from the British Library.

ISBN 978 0 7524 7018 4

Typesetting and origination by The History Press
Printed in Great Britain

CHAPTER ONE

In the cooler months, Henry Palmer's most important duty was to keep the coal fires of the mortuary burning steadily. After all, as Dr Mackenzie used to say with his most engaging smile, an expression that ladies often commented was wasted on the dead, it wouldn't do for the 'patients' to be too cold. Cold was the enemy of putrefaction, and worse than that, it paralysed the living, giving them a ghostly semblance of death that could delude the most skilled physician into certifying that life was extinct. While eminent medical men were confident that cures to the deadliest of disorders were almost within their grasp, science was still plagued with fundamental uncertainties. One of these, declared Dr Mackenzie, whatever practitioners liked to claim (and where, indeed, was the doctor of medicine who would ever admit to making a mistake?) was the infallible diagnosis of death. Failure to see the spark of life in a pale still form which seemed to have given up its last breath was, in his opinion, the worst possible error a doctor might make, for it could lead to horrors almost beyond human imagination.

The causes and consequences of premature burial were something he had made his special study for many years. To Mackenzie, the establishment, of which he was both founder and chief director, was not a place of death, but of reassurance. He called it the Life House, and the new admissions, who were laid gently on flower-strewn beds, were, at his express instructions, referred to as patients, and never corpses. He even ensured that the main repository was divided by a curtain into male and female wards. It would never do for a patient to awaken and find themselves in the company of persons of the opposite sex, a shock which might have a fatal termination in someone already in a fainting state. Every patient, on first being admitted, was carefully examined, and if no sign of life was apparent, a length of thin cord was tied to a big toe and a finger, and connected to a bell, which was hung from a hook on the wall. Should any of the patients revive, the smallest movement would announce to the orderly employed to keep constant watch over the wards that one of his charges was alive, and every means of resuscitation that modern medicine could provide was at hand to ensure the speedy and effective restoration of consciousness.

As far as Henry Palmer was aware, in the fifteen years of the Life House's existence no patient had ever revived. Enshrouded by the warmth of the carefully tended winter fire, or in balmier seasons, the glow of the sun seeping through high windows, there was no answering flush on sinking cheeks, no sheen of sweat on pallid brows, only the spreading and darkening stains of decay. From time to time, the sound of a bell would be heard, but that was only due to undulations of the abdomen brought on by putrefactive gases causing a tremor, which rippled into the dead limbs. Before long it would be necessary to inform relatives that the patient had undeniably passed away, and the remains would be consigned to a coffin, placed in a side room referred to as the 'chapel', and later borne to a final resting place in All Souls Cemetery, Kensal Green.

Palmer had a great deal of respect for Dr Mackenzie, despite his employer's eccentric beliefs, and while many a man might have recoiled from the uncongenial and unrewarding work, the young orderly took satisfaction from knowing that he brought comfort to bereaved families. During the long, quiet hours spent with the dead he saw that all was neat and well kept, changed the linen coverlets, maintained the banks of fresh flowers around the silent forms, cleaned the bedsteads, and sprinkled and swabbed the floor with a solution of carbolic acid. The pungent tarry smell of the liquid, the odour of wilting bouquets and the warm nostril-stinging tang of burning coal were between them almost enough to conceal what would otherwise have been the most powerful smell in the building – the sickly odour of the decomposition of human flesh. He made a round of the patients every hour, looking for clues that life remained, and, finding none, entered the details in a report, priding himself on his meticulous and neatly-kept records. Dr Mackenzie, who lived close by in Ladbroke Grove Road, called twice a day, and his partner, Dr Bonner, daily. The third director, Dr Warrinder, was also a regular visitor, although Palmer felt that his interest was merely to supply an occupation for his retirement, something that had been forced on him by failing eyesight. The three doctors would solemnly examine every patient as Palmer gave them his verbal account of the day's transactions, then they would read and initial his record book, and compliment him on a duty well done. There were occasional visitors, strictly by appointment, who were always medical men. Mackenzie abhorred the idea of prurient persons hoping to glut their gross tastes on scenes unfit for all but the eyes of professional gentlemen, and most especially would not tolerate visits from members of the press, or females. Families wanting a last view of the departed were never shown into the wards, the body being decently laid out in the chapel.

On the day of the funeral Palmer would be there in his good dark suit of clothes, looking like an undertaker's man and assisting the bearers. It was only on the patient's final day above ground that he allowed himself to think of whom he or she had once been, and say his own farewell. His sister, Alice, and her friend Mabel Finch, to whose company he had recently become very partial, had both said, not without a laugh from Alice and a blush from Miss Finch, that he was almost ladylike in his feelings, not that that was in any way a bad thing. Dr Mackenzie was also at the funerals, with large sorrowful eyes, a man of science forever searching for the truth and always disappointed.

Although friends and relatives were known to cling desperately to the hope that their loved one might not after all be dead, the prospect of revival was not something the Life House made much of in its message to the public. The enterprise made only one very clear guarantee. No customer of Dr Mackenzie's Life House would ever be buried alive.

❧

'How very curious!' exclaimed young detective Frances Doughty, making a careful study of a letter she had received that morning. It was a single sheet, with pale handwriting very lightly impressed upon the paper as if the writer was elderly or ill, and there were little stops and starts, suggesting that the composition of the message had been interrupted in a number of places by sudden and uncontrollable floods of emotion.

Sarah, her trusted companion and assistant detective, a burly woman whose broad, plain face and stern expression concealed a world of loyalty and kindness, looked up from the drift of lacy knitting that seemed to flow effortlessly from her powerful fingers.

'New customer?' she asked.

'Yes,' said Frances, 'her name is Alice Palmer, and she will be calling this afternoon.' A small photograph wrapped carefully in light tissue as if it was a jewel, had been enclosed in a fold of the paper, and she showed it to Sarah. The sitter was a slender young man in his Sunday-best suit, looking self-conscious and clutching a hat. 'Miss Palmer's brother, Henry. Have you ever seen him?'

Sarah peered at the picture and shook her head. 'No, I can't say as I have. Isn't he the man Reverend Day told us about in his sermon yesterday?'

'Yes, Mr Palmer disappeared six days ago, and his family is very anxious for his safety. But here is a detail that piques my curiosity. For the last two years he has been working as an orderly at the Life House in Kensal Green.'

'I've heard of that place,' said Sarah, scornfully, 'and they've no business calling it a Life House when all they do is take in dead folk. Coffins in and coffins out. *I've* never heard of anyone coming back to life.'

'Nor I,' agreed Frances. 'There are stories of course, but they may be made up. But there is no denying that many people feel a great anxiety in case they should be taken ill and appear to be dead, and then buried before their time. If they know that they will be taken to the Life House it will put their minds at rest.' Frances laid down the letter and photograph and picked up a copy of the *Chronicle*. 'This, however, is the really interesting part. Henry Palmer disappeared on the very same evening that his employer, Dr Mackenzie, died.'

Sarah nodded. 'So he could have murdered Dr Mackenzie and then run away?'

'There are many ways that the two events could be connected,' said Frances cautiously, 'or it could be that they are
not connected at all. There is such a thing as coincidence, and
I do allow for that when events are in themselves commonplace and unremarkable. But, where two rare and unexpected
things happen on the same day and concern people who
are acquainted, that circumstance deserves a very close
examination. It does appear, however, that there was nothing
suspicious about Dr Mackenzie's death, although he was only
forty-seven. It says here,' she went on, perusing the *Chronicle's*
obituary, 'that he had been very ill for some time, and it was
well known that he had a weak heart. He had been advised to
rest or even give up business altogether, but in common with
many dedicated gentlemen he chose to ignore his doctor's
warnings. On the evening of the twenty-first of September,
he was making his usual rounds of the Life House when he
appeared to faint, but it was soon discovered that he was dead.
His associate, Dr Bonner, said that he died from disease of the
heart brought on by a septic abdomen, almost certainly made
worse by overwork.'

'Did Dr Mackenzie get put in his own Life House, then, and
left to go all rotten?' asked Sarah.

'Apparently so,' replied Frances. She put the newspaper
aside and waited.

❧

In the few months that had elapsed since the shocking
case of murder that had elevated Frances' reputation in the
public mind, Frances and Sarah had become quite settled in
their new home and also into an acknowledged position in
Bayswater society as ladies who could deal with any difficulty.
Frances was spoken of in hushed tones across fashionable tea
tables as a clever young woman of almost masculine mind,
while a story had recently flown about the district of how
Sarah had exposed the activities of a thieving footman by dint
of picking him up and shaking him until the teaspoons in his
pockets rattled.

They occupied a first-floor apartment on Westbourne Park Road, rooms which would, in the days when the house had been the home of a gentleman with offices in the City, have been family sleeping accommodation. There was a large front room, which made a comfortable parlour where they dined and received visitors. A smaller room at the back of the house was where Frances slept and where she also kept her late father's writing desk and all her papers and books. The compartment which connected the two must once have been a dressing room, and Frances had hesitated, because of its small size and Sarah's imposing width, to suggest that she might like to make it her sleeping quarters, but Sarah, anticipating Frances' concerns, had at once appropriated it to her sole use, firmly declaring it to be the cosiest bedroom she had ever known.

The furnishings throughout were plain and practical, since Frances liked to be surrounded by things that were useful and easily kept clean. Ostentatious decoration, she believed, was something that should be reserved for important public buildings. She had been in too many homes where the acquisition of pretty trinkets had disguised a discontented household. When her friends, Miss Gilbert and Miss John, leading lights of the Bayswater Women's Suffrage Society, had first called upon her, they had gazed upon the simple austerity of the parlour with expressions approaching panic, although they would not have dreamed of offering any comment or suggestion. Soon afterwards Frances had been sent, almost as one sends a parcel of food to a starving family, two large cushions made of maroon velvet with heavy gold fringes, one embroidered with the figure of Britannia and the other with Boadicea. Frances made a special point of always placing these on display whenever the ladies called for tea.

As to the matter of family portraits, an essential in any parlour, Frances was in some difficulty as she had only one, a study of her late brother Frederick taken on the occasion of his twenty-first birthday, and that she had placed in a prominent position. She had no pictures of her father, and if there had been any of her mother or of her parents' nuptials, those she felt sure had been destroyed long ago. Sarah had a photograph of her eight brothers, but it was felt best to place this in another room, so as not to alarm visitors.

During the day, Frances and Sarah saw clients and pursued their enquiries. In the evenings, they sat in easy chairs before the fire, enjoying a princely feast of cocoa and hot buttered toast, and while Sarah wielded her needles, Frances read aloud from the newspapers. This was not merely for the entertainment they had to offer; as Bayswater's busiest detective she must make sure to know everything she could about recent events and notable people in that bustling part of Paddington. Sarah's tastes were for the more sensational items of news, anything that might make her open her eyes wide or even declare 'well I never!' She often laughed heartily at the reports in the *Bayswater Chronicle* of the sometimes unseemly quarrels between the men of the Paddington vestry, and commented that if *she* was there she would bang their silly heads together and then perhaps they would attend to their business more and there would be fewer holes in the macadam on Bishop's Road.

Frances' first venture into her new profession had not been without some anxiety. For several weeks she had worried less about solving cases than keeping herself and Sarah fed and housed. Fortunately the success of her first case, which was not unconnected with the recent General Election, had been followed by a secret meeting with a parliamentary gentleman as a result of which she had since been in receipt of a modest salary, on the understanding that her services would always be available to the government. It would not make her a rich woman, but it provided a measure of financial security.

That summer she had been entrusted with a mission of great delicacy. An eminent gentleman had asked her to deliver a message to a lady, a message of such sensitivity that it could not be committed to paper. Tact and discretion were required. Frances had duly delivered the message, but finding that tact and discretion were insufficient to achieve the desired result she had added a few firm and well-directed words of her own, thereby avoiding a scandal. Her probity and discretion had been appreciated in the form of a very handsome honorarium, and Prime Minister Mr Gladstone, who was torn between a natural compulsion to save her from an unsuitable life and his awareness of her usefulness, had made her the gift of a prayer book in which he had been kind enough to inscribe his signature. That item, too, occupied a place in the parlour, although modesty forbade Frances to show the dedication to visitors unless specifically requested.

For the most part, however, Frances' commissions had been of a more mundane nature – discovering the whereabouts of erring husbands, enquiring after the honesty of ardent suitors, or recovering letters written in the heat of a passion that had since cooled.

The only case in which she had failed was a quite trivial one, and yet it remained on her mind. Mrs Chiffley was the wife of a prosperous tea merchant, and some months ago her husband had presented her with the gift of a parrot. Unfortunately, while her husband was away on business, Mrs Chiffley had carelessly allowed the bird to escape. She did not wish to advertise in the newspapers for its return in case her husband came to know of her error, neither was there the option of buying a replacement as the bird had very distinctive markings which Mr Chiffley had commented upon. Mrs Chiffley, in desperation, had come to Frances, offering a substantial reward for the safe recovery of her pet, but Frances could do no more than make discreet enquiries and ask her trusted associates to keep their eyes well open. The bird could have flown back to India or even China for all she knew, although she did occasionally submit to the fear that she would discover Mrs Chiffley's parrot in the windows of Mr Whiteley's emporium, its sapphire feathers enhancing a fashionable hat.

Frances could not help wondering if there were other private detectives who experienced failure. It seemed unlikely that she was the only one. Unfortunately, she did not know any other detectives and even if she had it would have been impertinent to say the least to ask them about their unsolved cases. She suspected that other detectives did not take their failures to heart as she did, but cast them aside without a trace of guilt and forgot them in a moment.

Closer to her inner soul was her indecision as to whether she should try to find her mother. Frances had been brought up to believe that her mother had died when she was three years old, and had not long ago found that the abandonment was of a more earthly nature, and in the company of a man. Early in 1864, her mother had given birth to twins, a girl and a boy, of whom her husband William had suspected he was not the father, but the girl had died very young. It was possible that Frances' mother was still alive, and also her brother – perhaps, it had been hinted, a full brother – who would now be sixteen. Frances felt sure that she was equal to the quest, but still she hesitated. She was afraid not of what she might find, but that her efforts would be met with a cruel rejection. She had lived above her father's chemist's shop on Westbourne Grove for many years after her mother's departure, and even now that she had quit the Grove, everyone there knew her new address, so if her mother really wished to see her she could easily discover where she might be found. Supposing her father to have been the obstacle to a reunion, her mother could hardly be ignorant of William Doughty's death, a tragedy which had exercised the gossips of Bayswater for some weeks, and whose aftermath was still unresolved. It was the strongest possible indication that her mother, for reasons of her own, did not wish to be discovered. All the same, every time Frances pushed the idea aside it returned, and she tormented herself with the thought that her mother might have come into the shop as a customer, and never revealed who she was, and she might have seen and spoken to her and never known it. The only other place that she and her mother held in common was Brompton cemetery where her father, older brother and sister were buried. Frances went regularly to tend the graves, but saw no signs of another visitor, and no one could tell her if another lady came there.

❧

With the hour approaching for the arrival of Miss Palmer, Frances peered out of the window. Although it was only September the weather had been shockingly inclement, and the early days of what had promised to be a delicious autumn had suddenly declined into a misty gloom and whole days of smoke-laden fog. A cab paused outside and a gentleman alighted, helping a frail-looking lady descend. Her head was bent and she was muffling her face with a woollen shawl. Frances watched them as they approached her door and then waited for them to be shown upstairs.

Frances supposed that other detectives must have offices where they saw clients across a desk, but she, having none, used the parlour table, which was always furnished with a carafe of water and a glass, so that nervous clients could moisten their throats, also a discreetly folded napkin which was often pressed into service as a handkerchief. A notebook and a number of sharp pencils were essential for recording what was said, but just as valuable to Frances was Sarah's no less sharp observation and opinions.

Alice Palmer was twenty-two but she seemed faded like a portrait badly painted and left in the sun. Anxiety lay upon her, a deadly unseen canker that consumed her energy. Frances suspected that the young woman had barely eaten since her brother's disappearance. Miss Palmer's gentleman companion, who was scarcely older, helped her to be seated and introduced himself as Walter Crowe, saying that he and Alice were engaged to be married. Frances did not normally provide nourishment for her clients, but in this case, sent for tea and sponge cake. Mr Crowe smiled sadly as if to say that nothing could tempt Alice to eat until her brother was found.

Frances knew that asking timorous clients to talk about themselves often helped ease them into a frame of mind where they could talk more freely about the things that troubled them. She invited both Alice and Walter to tell their stories, and learned that Walter was the son of a journeyman carpenter, and, seeking to better himself, was now a joiner with his own business. Alice's mother had died when she was seven, and she and her three brothers, of whom Henry was the eldest, had been left orphans when their father died in a railway accident four years later. Henry, who had been just fifteen at the time, had been the mainstay of the family, ensuring that all the children were kept clean and decently clothed, received an education and, in due course, found respectable employment. Her brother Bertie was now eighteen and worked in a butcher's shop on the Grove, living above the premises, and sixteen-year-old Jackie was apprenticed to Walter and lodged with him. Alice worked in a ladies' costume shop on the Grove, and she and Henry shared lodgings in Golborne Road.

The tea and cake arrived, and Sarah stared at Alice with an expression of savage determination, which Frances knew very well, realising that the young woman would not be permitted to leave the house without having accepted some nourishment. Alice, moved almost to tears of terror at Sarah's look, sipped milky tea and put a fragment of cake into her mouth.

The Life House, Frances was told, was situated in Church Lane not far from the eastern entrance of All Souls Cemetery, Kensal Green. Henry's duties lasted from midday to midnight every weekday after which the other orderly, a Mr Hemsley, was there for the next twelve hours. Henry had never complained about the nature of his work, or his long hours, or made any suggestion that he might seek other employment. He invariably walked home, but was careful to creep in quietly so as not to wake Alice, who was always in her bed by 11 p.m. He was a sound, reliable man, a man you might set your watch by and know that once he had promised to do a thing it was as good as done. He was the very last man to run away and put his family to worry and distress.

Tuesday the 21st of September had started showery, but as the day wore on the streets had gradually become occluded by a cold, grey fog. Alice had gone to her work that morning as usual, leaving Henry's breakfast and some food for his luncheon on the table, and returned to find that the breakfast had been eaten, the dishes cleared, and the luncheon taken. She had gone to bed at her usual time, but when she awoke the next morning she saw, to her surprise and concern, that Henry's bed had not been slept in. She was obliged to go to her work, but as soon as she was able, she sent an urgent message to Walter to say that Henry had not come home. From that moment Walter's efforts to find her missing brother had been both determined and tireless.

Walter's first action was to go to see Alice's brother Bertie at the butcher's shop, who confirmed that he had not seen Henry that day. Walter then sent Jackie to Golborne Road to see if Henry had returned home, but the boy came back with the news that Henry was not there.

Walter next called on Alice at her place of employment, hoping that Henry might have gone to see her or at least sent a note, but she had still heard nothing from her brother and was now almost out of her wits with worry. Walter then took a cab up to the Life House and found that while he was not permitted to enter the wards, which were the preserve of staff and medical men, he could be admitted to the side chapel, which he found crowded with visitors; friends of the recently deceased Dr Mackenzie who had come to pay their respects. The doctor's remains were in an open coffin, surrounded by floral tributes and sad faces. There was nothing unusual about the corpse, which looked very peaceful.

Walter was informed by a distressed and exhausted Dr Bonner that his colleague had collapsed and died the night before, indeed Mackenzie had been speaking to Henry Palmer when he had suddenly clutched his stomach and chest, groaned with pain, and fallen. Bonner and Palmer had spent an hour doing all they could to revive him, but had at last given up hope. Bonner, who was well acquainted with Mackenzie's history of ill health, was in no doubt that the doctor had indeed breathed his last. Since Bonner understood that Mackenzie's landlady, Mrs Georgeson, waited up for her tenants so she could lock the premises at night, he had instructed Palmer to call on her and inform her of what had occurred. It was by then almost eleven o'clock, so Bonner had told Palmer that after speaking to Mrs Georgeson, there was no need for him to return to the Life House that evening, and he should go home. Palmer had departed as instructed, and Bonner had not seen or heard from him since, but then he would not have expected to. He had remained at the Life House after Palmer left until the arrival of the other orderly, Mr Hemsley, an hour later, and had then gone home to try and get a little rest. Early the next morning, he had notified Mackenzie's friends by telegram, inviting them to a viewing at the chapel at ten o'clock. As far as he was aware he was still expecting Palmer back at the Life House at midday for his next period of duty.

Walter had observed but not spoken to the other partner in the Life House, Dr Warrinder. That gentleman had been very upset and was fussing about the place, constantly asking Bonner if he was sure that his friend was really dead. He had even held a mirror to Mackenzie's nose looking for the misting that would show the doctor still breathed, but without finding anything that might give him hope.

Walter had next gone to Dr Mackenzie's lodgings and spoken to the landlady Mrs Georgeson, who had just returned from viewing the body. She confirmed that Henry Palmer had come to the house a little after eleven o'clock the previous night to inform her of Dr Mackenzie's death. He had left after a few minutes' conversation and had last been seen walking down Ladbroke Grove Road. At this point in Walter's narrative, Frances fetched a directory with a folding map on which he pointed out Henry's most probable route home, going south down Ladbroke Grove Road away from the Life House, and making a left turn either down Telford Road, Faraday Road or Bonchurch Road, all of which would have led to Portobello Road, then turning right down Portobello Road for a short distance and left into Golborne Road.

It was about a ten-minute walk from Dr Mackenzie's lodgings to Henry's home, allowing for the darkness and the fog. Walter had carefully followed each of Henry's possible routes, but had seen no sign of him. He asked everyone he met on the way if a man had been there and suffered an accident or been taken ill, but had learnt nothing. That evening Walter and the Palmers held a family conference and agreed that if Henry was not back by the next morning they would inform the police.

Early the next day Walter went to Kilburn police station. The desk sergeant listened with grave attention, but took the view that Henry would have been upset by the death of Dr Mackenzie and had either taken a little more drink than was good for him, or his mind had become temporarily unhinged. Walter had found it impossible to convince him that both these suggestions were out of character. He then spoke to an Inspector called Gostelow, who impressed him as a very sensible man, and promised that he would circulate Henry's description to his constables and ask them to look out for the missing orderly, but he comforted Walter with the comment that in such cases most people turned up later of their own accord, looking more embarrassed than anything else. Given that Henry had experienced a shock, he thought that such behaviour was not unexpected. Walter was unhappy that nothing more was to be done at that stage, but accepted that since Henry was an adult and had been missing for less than two days, the matter was unlikely to be treated as an emergency. Fearing that Henry had met with an accident and was lying unconscious in a hospital bed, Walter then sent messages to every hospital in Paddington giving Henry's description and asking if an unidentified patient had been admitted. There was another family conference, and it was decided to put an advertisement in the *Penny Illustrated Paper*, which was duly arranged, although it was by then too late for an engraved portrait to go in the current week's edition. Walter also asked Reverend Day at St Stephen's to make an announcement during his Sunday sermon.

Walter and Jackie went out searching together, visiting any public houses where Henry might have called, not that he frequented such places, but it was possible that after the shock of witnessing Dr Mackenzie's death he might have felt in need of a restorative. They entered every shop along the way, stopped at market stalls, spoke to street traders, beggars and idle loiterers, showing them Henry's photograph, but returned home exhausted and none the wiser.

On the Friday morning Walter, without telling Alice the nature of his errand in case it distressed her, visited the mortuaries at the Kilburn and Paddington workhouses to ask if any unidentified bodies had been recently brought in, but the only one received which was still unnamed was at Kilburn and it was that of a young woman, probably an unfortunate, who had drowned herself in the Grand Junction Canal about two weeks previously.

At Kilburn police station, Walter learned that all constables had been alerted to look for Henry, but so far without result. Walter's next thought had been to interview the cabmen who drove along Ladbroke Grove Road, but due to the inclement weather on the night that Palmer had disappeared none could recall having seen him. Walter, seeing Alice's health decline with the pain of uncertainty, had then suggested employing a detective. Miss Doughty, he had heard, was clever and sympathetic, and did not demand fees beyond what a working man might afford. They had some money put aside for the wedding but agreed that they were willing to spend it on finding Henry.

That very morning Walter had been present at the funeral of Dr Mackenzie at All Souls, Kensal Green, and looked carefully about him during the brief but heartfelt ceremony. Henry was not there. Walter had been worried enough until that moment, but once he saw that Henry Palmer, a man of duty and sensitive emotions, had not attended Dr Mackenzie's funeral, he felt suddenly convinced that the young man was dead.

Frances felt a little guilty about taking the couple's wedding savings, but as she looked at Alice, who was making a great meal out of her little corner of cake, she thought that if Henry was not found soon, there might be no wedding, but a funeral. Walter gently took Alice's thin white hand and stroked it as if it was a piece of bone china that might break. He looked appealingly at Frances. 'Do you think you can help us?'

'I will make some preliminary enquiries,' said Frances, 'and if I feel there is nothing I can do, there will be no charge.'

'And you're to eat something,' growled Sarah, looming over Alice, 'because you're no good to your brother like that!'

Alice crammed a piece of cake into her mouth and burst into tears.

Once the clients had departed Frances gave careful thought to all the many possible reasons for Henry Palmer's disappearance. The two most important factors, she believed, were the character of the man, and the death of Dr Mackenzie. Everything that she had been told about Palmer suggested that he was most unlikely either to have turned to drink or gone insane. Even the possibility that the mortuary might close down following Dr Mackenzie's death, a matter that cannot in any case have been determined that same night, would not have been enough to provoke any unexpected behaviour. Palmer was a young man of proven ability who might easily have found another post on the recommendation of Doctors Bonner and Warrinder, and he had calmly and resolutely seen his family through far worse crises than this. It followed that he had been overtaken by some unforeseen catastrophe, which had occurred somewhere between Dr Mackenzie's home on Ladbroke Grove Road and his own in Golborne Road. If he had been taken ill, or met with an accident, and was lying insensible in a hospital or had lost his memory, or had died and was in a mortuary, the efforts of his family would surely by now have alerted an attendant to his identity. It was, thought Frances, far more likely that during his ten-minute walk under the concealing cloak of foggy darkness he had become a victim of foul play, which explained why those in the vicinity had seen, or professed to have seen, nothing. His body might in the course of time make itself known by foul odours emanating from a cellar or a drain. If Dr Mackenzie's death had had anything to do with Palmer's fate, it might only be that it had resulted in the young orderly having had the misfortune to be in a place where he would not otherwise have been at that time.

Frances, however, could not help wondering if Dr Mackenzie's death, even though due to natural causes, had been brought on by some external factor as yet unknown, something that might have resulted in Henry Palmer's disappearance. The last people who had seen Palmer alive were Dr Bonner and Mrs Georgeson. She composed notes to them saying that she would be calling for an interview, and ordered a cab.

CHAPTER TWO

ogic dictated that Frances should attempt to recreate Henry Palmer's last known journey, but the night was closing in and she did not feel bold enough to retrace his steps on foot in the dark and the fog, while a possible murderer roamed at large. That would have to wait until daylight, when she might at least, weather permitting, be able to look about her.

Before setting out on her first call, Frances asked Sarah to take a message to two friends of hers who were always happy, in return for a small consideration and sometimes gratis, to supply information about Bayswater trade, often of a nature that was not publicly known.

Charles Knight and Sebastian Taylor, usually known as 'Chas' and 'Barstie', were two enterprising and energetic individuals, men of business whose fortunes appeared to ebb and flow with the tides. Since the summer they had been enjoying a period of comparative calm and, for them, stability. Their nemesis, a loathsome young man carrying a sharp knife, who was known only as the 'Filleter' and often lurked about Paddington exuding a noxious air of menace, had not been seen for some weeks, and while they anxiously awaited the glad news that he was in a place where he could no longer trouble them, Chas and Barstie had decided to become citizens of Bayswater. They had accordingly taken accommodation in Westbourne Grove above the shop of Mr Beccles, an elderly watchmaker. Chas, bulging with optimism at this recent development, spoke airily of their 'apartments' and their 'offices', his words conjuring up a picture of vast suites of elegance and comfort, as if the apartment and the office was not in fact one and the same location and numbered more than a single small room, and was not at the top of two flights of damp, narrow stairs. The elevation of the premises above street level was, thought Frances wryly, what justified

Chas in claiming that he was going up in the world of commerce. They had recently established a company, The Bayswater Display and Advertising Co. Ltd, although whether that was actually the nature of its business Frances was unsure. Whatever it was they did, it seemed to involve long hours facing each other across a shared desk, a great deal of running up and down stairs, and occasional food fights.

'Mr Palmer's disappearance may have nothing at all to do with his occupation or any person at the Life House, but I must first satisfy myself of that before I dismiss the idea,' Frances told Sarah. 'If the gentlemen can tell me anything about the business, the directors or the employees, whatever it might be, that would be of the greatest assistance.'

※

Dr Mackenzie's lodgings were on the east side of Ladbroke Grove Road, just a little to the north of its junction with Telford Road. The houses in that location were not so tall or so grand as those in other parts of the long thoroughfare, and the builder had not thought it necessary to encrust them with pillars and porticoes, but they were respectable enough. As Frances stepped up to the door she saw the top of a housemaid's cap bobbing about in the basement area below. At the sound of the knocker, the maid turned her head up to look, her face a white circle, as pale as the cap, with watery grey eyes and a pinched nose. She said nothing, but made to go indoors at a pace that suggested that Frances might have to wait several minutes for admission. Moments later, however, the front door was opened by the landlady.

Mrs Georgeson was a capable-looking woman in her middle years. The hardened fingers that peeped from her mittens suggested a life spent in toil, but they were not roughened by recent work. Frances explained her errand while Mrs Georgeson studied her calling card as if it was a difficult acrostic. 'So he's not been found, then. You'd better come in.'

Frances stepped into the hallway finding it drab, and only tolerably clean; she felt sure that Sarah would have regarded the state of the cornices with something approaching indignation.

Little flaps of wallpaper that might once have been flesh pink but had died away to the colour of weak coffee, curled like dried leaves edged with brown. A single gas lamp turned to its lowest setting supplied just enough light to pass through the hall, but failed to conceal an enforced neglect which the land-lady might have hoped her potential tenants would not notice. Queen Victoria stared from the only portrait on the wall with an expression of stern disapproval.

'There are only gentlemen lodgers here,' said Mrs Georgeson, as she led Frances down the stairs at the rear of the house. 'That was the position when Mr Georgeson and I chose to supervise the premises and so it has remained. Respectable single gen-tlemen, preferably those in the professions, they are so much more reliable.' Mrs Georgeson, while having no ambitions to appear genteel, was determined to be accounted worthy, and revealed that her husband was engaged in work of the utmost importance to society. She was so evasive when Frances politely enquired as to the nature of Mr Georgeson's occupation that she could only conclude it had something to do with sewage.

Near the foot of the stairs they met the housemaid on her way up, a tall thin girl, with long untidy curls of light hair wrig-gling from an over-large cap. She looked like a plant that had grown in too little light and was searching for the sun. She observed them gloomily, turned without a word, and went down again. At the bottom of the stairs there was a small, dark parlour, and the maid passed through it and disappeared into the next room, where a loud metallic clatter announced that this was a kitchen where she was busy either scrubbing pans or knocking them together to give the impression that she was. There was a faint odour of overcooked egg.

Frances and the landlady sat at a small table, where a large brown teapot that looked as if it needed a good scouring stood next to some used cups. Mrs Georgeson frowned at them as if she felt something needed to be done about this situation, and glanced at the kitchen door.

'Please don't trouble yourself,' said Frances, quickly. 'I would like you to tell me all you know of Dr Mackenzie. How long did he live here? Did your other tenants know him well?'

Frances learned that Dr Mackenzie had occupied the upper-most apartment in the building for the last three years, and had been a quiet and largely solitary individual. A Mr Trainor, who travelled in medical sundries, had lived on the ground floor for ten years and was, if anything, even quieter than Mackenzie. Mrs Georgeson did not think either man had visited the other's apartments. The first floor had been empty at the time of Dr Mackenzie's death following the departure abroad of the previous tenant, although a new gentleman had since moved in. Mr and Mrs Georgeson occupied comfortable rooms in the extensive basement and Mary Ann, who was sixteen and had worked there for a year, slept on a folding bed in the pantry.

'Please describe the evening when Mr Palmer called to report Dr Mackenzie's death,' asked Frances. 'This is extremely important, since as far as I have been able to gather you were the last person to see him before he disappeared.'

Mrs Georgeson made a little grimace as if the fact alone brought her closer to tragedy. 'Of course I'll tell you all I can but it's little enough. And I have already said everything to Mr Crowe. Poor Dr Mackenzie had been so unwell, worn down and tired, and I said to him perhaps he ought not to go out as the weather was cold and foggy, and it might get on his chest and then you never know what might happen. But he insisted he had to go, and so I promised to wait up and see that he got a hot drink and perhaps a little sip of brandy when he came in. I was just starting to worry that he was late back when Mary Ann went to answer the door, and the next thing I knew she rushed down here in tears saying there was a man called to say Dr Mackenzie was dead. Of course I went up at once and found Mr Palmer in the hallway talking to Mr Trainor, who had come out of his room when he heard the commotion. I was told that Dr Mackenzie had suffered a fit and was now a customer of his own establishment.'

'Had you met Mr Palmer before that day?'

'No, never. None of us had.'

Frances was disappointed. Only someone who knew Palmer well could judge whether his mood and behaviour that night were characteristic of him. 'Can you describe how he appeared to you?'

'Well, he was upset of course, as you might expect, but not crying or anything like that. Shocked, I would say, but quiet and dealing with it like a man. He had a message to bring, a duty to do and he did it.' She nodded, approvingly. 'He told me there was to be a private viewing for the doctor's friends and relatives next morning at ten, and I would be very welcome to attend, so of course I went up to pay my respects. Dr Mackenzie was a good man, always thinking of others, never of himself. He was in a little room at the side, laid out very nice with flowers and candles. Poor gentleman,' said the landlady wistfully, 'he had looked so ill these last few months; I'll swear he appeared better once he was dead. Some of them do, you know, more at peace, all their troubles gone.'

'Did Mr Palmer look like someone who might go away and have too much to drink to steady his nerves, or a man whose mind might break down with grief?' asked Frances.

Mrs Georgeson considered this for a moment, and then shook her head. 'I would say not. He just sighed and said he would go off home to his bed, but he didn't think he would be able to sleep after what had happened. He said Dr Mackenzie had collapsed right into his arms and he would never forget it.'

'Did you see Mr Palmer out?'

'I did.'

'And did you see where he went – what direction he walked in?'

'Oh I couldn't say – it was that bad out I just saw him to the bottom of the steps and then shut the door. Mary Ann might know, as she was back and forth.'

'In that case, I had better speak to her.'

Mrs Georgeson called the servant from the kitchen, and Mary Ann emerged, peering about her as if short-sighted.

'This is Miss Doughty, the detective,' said Mrs Georgeson.

The transformation was immediate. The girl suddenly straightened from her miserable slouch, her mouth forming a dark circle of surprise. 'Oh, are you the lady in the stories?' she exclaimed.

'Stories?' said Frances. 'You mean in the newspapers?'

'No, I mean the halfpenny books. *The Lady Detective of Bayswater.* They've got pictures and everything.'

Frances gulped, having no idea that anyone had seen fit to illustrate her adventures and sell copies to impressionable young people. Her immediate instinct was to deny any connection, but then she realised that it was a situation she might turn to her advantage. 'I have not seen the stories you mention, but they may very well be about me,' she said.

Mary Ann beamed with excitement. 'Oh you are *very* brave, Miss!' she said, admiringly.

'Thank you,' said Frances, a little worried at what it was she was supposed to have done. 'Now, I would like you to sit down and tell me everything you can remember about Mr Palmer who called here to say that Dr Mackenzie had died.'

Mary Ann sat at the table, and stared at Frances as if she was a lady of very great moment.

'He was a nice-looking young man,' she said, 'very tidy and clean, with good manners; and sad. He said that Dr Mackenzie had fallen down all of a sudden, and he and the other doctor had done what they could to help him, but they were sure he was gone. I went to fetch Mrs Georgeson and then came back up the stairs because – to see if I was wanted for anything.'

Mary Ann's milky face went a little pink and Frances realised she had crept up to the hallway to get another look at Henry Palmer. 'But Mrs Georgeson said I should go back down to the kitchen, so I did. Has he still not been found, Miss?'

'No, I am afraid not. Did you see where Mr Palmer went after he left here?'

'Yes, I was in the area, and he came down the steps. He stopped for a while, like he was thinking about something, and then he turned and walked down the road.'

'Did he turn the corner and go down Telford Road?'

'No, I think he crossed over and went on walking. But it was very foggy and I didn't see him after that.'

Frances nodded. 'Thank you Mary Ann, you have been very helpful. I had better speak to Mr Trainor, now.'

'He's away on business,' said Mrs Georgeson. 'I expect him back on Thursday afternoon. I'll let him know you called. I'm sure he would be more than willing to tell you all he knows.'

'Then I will return to see him on Thursday. And now I would like to examine Dr Mackenzie's room. Has it been re-let?'

'Not as yet,' said Mrs Georgeson with an air of disappointment, 'but the room has been emptied, so there's nothing for you to see.'

'All the same,' said Frances, 'I will see it. Who disposed of the doctor's effects?'

'Dr Bonner. He and Dr Warrinder are the executors, but I think it's Dr Bonner who does all the work. Not that there was a great deal for him to take. Medical books, mainly. Business papers. He asked me to give the clothes to charity. Come with me.'

They ascended two flights of thinly carpeted stairs where Dr Mackenzie's apartments consisted of two small, comfortless rooms, a parlour and bedroom both with the simplest and plainest of furnishings. There was a sour, dusty smell as if the floor had been roughly swept but not assiduously cleaned.

'If you know of any single gentlemen looking for respectable lodgings …' said Mrs Georgeson, hopefully. 'They get a boiled egg and tea every morning.'

'I will be sure to mention that you have rooms available,' Frances promised. She had always assumed that medical men lived in some affluence, but it was clear that Dr Mackenzie had subsisted on a very small income. 'Did he have many visitors?' she asked.

'Some yes, his medical friends. No ladies – never any question of it. Dr Bonner called and Dr Warrinder, and young Dr Darscot.'

'Dr Darscot? I don't know that gentleman. Does he work at the Life House?'

'Oh, that I couldn't say. But he must have been a very great friend of Dr Mackenzie. He was very upset that night.'

Frances turned to her. 'That night?' she exclaimed. 'Do you mean the night Dr Mackenzie died? Dr Darscot was here?'

'Yes,' said Mrs Georgeson, unaware that she had said anything of interest. 'He came knocking at the door saying he wanted to speak to the doctor and it was very important and he wouldn't take "no" for an answer. I had to tell him; I said Dr Mackenzie has just died.'

'So Dr Darscot called quite late – after Mr Palmer had gone.'

'No more than five minutes after, I would say. When I told him the doctor was dead he went into quite a state, wouldn't hear of it, wouldn't believe it, said it couldn't be true, and demanded to go up to the rooms and see for himself. I told him, the body isn't there, it's at the Life House. Then he says he *still* wants to see in the rooms as the doctor had borrowed something from him and he wanted it back. I said I couldn't let him up there – that the only person I *would* let up there was Dr Mackenzie's executor, and once he had the papers to prove it was him he could do as he pleased. Then Mr Georgeson comes along and wants to know what the matter is and I told him. And he said the rooms were locked and would stay locked. And Dr Darscot looked very unhappy and ran out, calling for a cab.'

'Did he return?' asked Frances.

'No, I've not seen him since.'

'Do you have his address? I should like to speak to him.'

'No, but I expect Dr Bonner will know.'

'Very well, I shall be seeing him soon. And those were the only callers?'

'As far as I know, yes. Those nights when Dr Mackenzie wasn't at the Life House he was usually here working. He used to write medical papers and sometimes he gave talks to other doctors. And I think he had started to see patients again. Live ones, that is, only he didn't see them here. I don't know where he saw them. It was all work with him,' she said sighing. 'All work.'

'Did he get many letters?'

'Yes, from time to time.'

'Who wrote to him?' Mrs Georgeson bridled at the question and Frances paused, realising that in her eagerness to know the answer she had phrased the enquiry somewhat insultingly. 'Forgive me; of course you could not possibly have known that unless he told you. What I meant to say was did he ever tell you who wrote to him?'

Mrs Georgeson accepted the apology with a nod. 'He didn't say, but there were letters posted in London, and from Scotland, and from somewhere abroad.'

Frances had seen all that she wished, but asked Mrs Georgeson to write and advise her when Mr Trainor was available. She returned home to find visitors in the parlour; Chas toasting currant buns before the fire and passing them to Barstie, who was covering them liberally with strawberry jam spooned from a jar.

'Only the best, Miss Doughty,' said Chas with a smile and a wink, as Sarah brought tea and plates. He was looking comfortable and prosperous, and Frances hoped fervently that he was not about to make a declaration of affection. He had once hinted that her expertise in maintaining the account books of her father's business had excited his esteem, something he would not be able to acknowledge openly until he felt financially settled. While she wished him every success, she would be perfectly happy if he found another lady with which to share it. 'Now then, you wanted to know all about the late Dr Mackenzie and his associates. I'm sorry to say there isn't really a lot to tell.'

'A very peculiar place, the Life House,' said Barstie, thoughtfully. 'I shouldn't care for it myself.' Barstie, a slender individual lounging casually opposite his plumper friend, had, Frances knew, spent the last two years in the amorous pursuit of an heiress who had so far remained immune to his attentions, a situation which gave him a permanently mournful air.

'It's one business I can think of where the customers don't complain,' said Chas. 'If they're dead why they can't, and if they sit up again and take notice, well that's all to the good. And families will pay any amount for peace of mind and a decent disposal of the remains. Death is the one certainty in life. There's good money in death.'

Barstie sighed as if he could already see Chas making plans to open a new business.

'Dr Mackenzie was not a prosperous man,' said Frances. 'I have seen his lodgings and they were very modest.'

'He was a man of high principles,' said Chas, 'at least he always represented himself as one, and such men never prosper. He first promoted the idea of a Life House in 1862, although it was three years before he could open it. It was partly paid for with his own money, part came from Dr Bonner and the rest was collected by public subscription. He was paid the smallest salary he felt the business could afford, but it has not made a good profit yet, although it may well do in future. Funerals, on the other hand – you could name your price. We could start small, Barstie – lap dogs and kittens, pet monkeys and such like.' Barstie's despondency increased, but Chas breezed on.

'Dr Bonner, now he *is* financially comfortable, but it's not because of the Life House. Did well out of his medical practice, did even better by marrying a widow with property but no standing in society. Better still, she ignores him and spends all her time on ladies' committees. He amuses himself nowadays by seeing rich patients with troublesome ailments who pay for his discretion, and elderly persons with something in the funds who he can persuade to become customers of the Life House.' Sarah poured tea and handed him a cup, and he smiled and helped himself to a bun. 'You are very kind, Miss Smith.' Sarah did not look especially kind, but then she so rarely did.

'Dr Warrinder,' said Barstie, 'is not a man of wealth, but neither is he poor. He used to be a consultant at the Hospital for Diseases of the Throat and Chest in Golden Square. Then there was that unfortunate occurrence three years ago, when a lady died after an operation. Words were said and Dr Warrinder thought it best to retire – from tending to the living at any rate. He lives quietly and modestly now.'

'And Dr Darscot?' asked Frances. 'Does he work at the Life House?'

The two men glanced at each other with surprised expressions and shook their heads. 'No, the only men employed at the Life House are the three directors and the two orderlies. No one called Darscot.'

After they had left Frances examined a local directory, but that too was silent on the subject of Dr Darscot. That was not in itself suspicious; Mrs Georgeson had described him as a young man and he was probably a recent arrival in Bayswater. Whoever he was, he was a close associate of the late Dr Mackenzie and as such she would need to find and speak to him.

❧

Early the next morning as the mist began to lift Frances took
a cab up to the Life House, the place where Henry Palmer's
last-known journey had begun. As she crossed the bridge over
the Great Western Railway with Kensal New Town to her right
and the gasworks to her left, she recalled being told that not
so many years ago none of the houses and streets she had just
driven past, including the northern part of Ladbroke Grove
Road, had existed; all had been farmland and Portobello Lane
had wound its lazy way through the countryside towards the
cemetery. Then an enterprising gentleman had decided to build
a great estate, and the farms had been dismantled and the land
covered with houses. He had declared this to be progress, but
there was some disagreement as to whether this was really the
case. Frances had read in the newspapers of men in politics who
called themselves 'progressive', and she had sometimes heard
them denounced as dangerous fellows who only wanted to take
a man's property away and change everything for the worse, but
she could not help thinking that progress might also do good.
It was one of those difficult questions she needed to reserve for
the time when she would be permitted to vote. She was not,
she thought, so naïve as to imagine that men held the right
opinions on everything, even though this was something she
had often been told.

The cab passed some dingy yards crowded with broken carts
and wagons, like graveyards for abandoned vehicles, then crossed
the bridge that spanned the murky waters of the Grand Junction
Canal, a watercourse that some humorous person had once
dubbed 'the River Styx' since it bordered the General Cemetery
of All Souls Kensal Green. Frances saw to her left the roof of the
non-conformist chapel inside the perimeter wall, then the cab
turned right down Harrow Road and took her down Church
Lane, which lay opposite the church of St John the Evangelist.
The lane, which led down to the canal bank, was flanked on
its western side by cottages that had once formed part of old
Portobello Lane and predated the recent building in the area,
and on the other side by newer houses. The eastern side of the
lane had once consisted of plots of open land with gardens and
smallholdings. It was here that Dr Mackenzie, anxious to find

a location for the Life House near to the great cemetery, had been fortunate enough to secure a small parcel of land at a reasonable price. Tucked out of the way, and with the occupants of the rented cottages having little say in the matter, the Life House had been built, and so discreet was its operation that despite the fact that its purpose was generally known, its presence there had become accepted. This was due in part to the respect in which Dr Mackenzie was held in Bayswater, but mainly to his care in ensuring that the business did not create a public nuisance.

The Life House was a great deal smaller than Frances had imagined – a square, one-storey building with small windows just below the level of the roof to dissuade prying eyes. A single chimney wafted a coil of grey smoke into the greyer sky, but there were other brick protrusions, which Frances suspected were for the purpose of ventilation. The building presented a plain wall to the street, with no obvious entrance, but a path, which was just wide enough to admit six men bearing a coffin, wound about its corner. Frances followed the path and found a door on the eastern side of the building which faced away from the street, looking upon some walled yards and the back of a warehouse. It was a simple, but very solid-looking door with a heavy lock and neither bell nor knocker. A brass plate was inscribed PRIVATE – VISITORS PLEASE USE CHAPEL ENTRANCE with a little arrow pointing the way. The south side of the building faced the canal although separated from it by a railing and some stout trees, and here Frances found a smaller door with a knocker, and a brass plate inscribed CHAPEL.

It was possible she noticed, for anyone leaving the Life House and intending to walk south, to avoid going up Church Lane and along Harrow Road, and instead cut through a small passage between the houses on the west of the lane to reach Ladbroke Grove Road. Frances assumed this must have been the start of Henry Palmer's walk home and would also have been the easiest route for the coffins to take, just a short step to the east entrance of the cemetery.

Frances knocked at the chapel door and after a few moments it swung inwards a few inches, and she was faced by a bored-looking young man with tousled hair wearing a medical orderly's overall. The odour that crept from the doorway was a powerful suggestion of carbolic mixed with the flowery sweetness of scented candles.

'Do you have an appointment Miss?' asked the young man.

Frances presented her card. 'I do not,' she said, 'but I have been engaged by Mr Henry Palmer's sister to enquire into his disappearance. Are you Mr Hemsley?'

He stared at the card, 'Yes, I am, but visits are by appointment only, and there are no burials waiting in any case, so I oughtn't by rights to let you in.' Despite this he looked as though he might be persuaded without difficulty.

'I understand that Mr Palmer is a very good sort of person,' said Frances. 'Everyone is terribly worried about him and his poor sister is making herself quite ill. I am sure you would do anything in your power to help find him.'

'Well, Palmer is a good sort, there's no doubt about that.' He hesitated. 'I suppose there's no harm in letting you see the chapel. But not the wards, mind, I'd lose my place if I let you in there.'

He stepped back and opened the door fully. Frances entered and found herself in a small room, with plain coffin shells and lids and trestles propped against the walls. A crucifix and two candlesticks stood on a small table covered with a white lace-edged cloth, forming a kind of altar. She had quite hoped to glance inside the ward, if only out of curiosity, and had to admit that there was a challenge in gaining admission to places where she was not allowed, but there was a wheeled stretcher placed across an inner door which she was sure must connect the chapel with the ward, a guardian to dissuade prying eyes.

'What can you tell me about the night Dr Mackenzie died? I understand you arrived for duty at midnight?'

He scratched his head. 'That's right. I got here at the usual time, expecting to see Palmer just about to leave, but instead it was Dr Bonner who told me what had gone on. He said there was to be a viewing the next morning, and he and Palmer had already carried the doctor into the chapel, so we got him laid out properly with flowers and such, and then Dr Bonner went home, but he was back soon after seven o'clock. Then Dr and Mrs Warrinder arrived a little later; they'd been sent a telegram.'

'Who else came for the viewing?'

'Mrs Bonner, she never misses one, and then a middle-aged person, I think she was Dr Mackenzie's landlady, and Mr Fairbrother, he's a young surgeon come up to London to study, he's been assisting Dr Bonner, and there was a young man, only he hadn't come for the viewing at all, in fact he didn't even know Dr Mackenzie had died, he came to ask if Palmer was there. I think Palmer's sister is his sweetheart. That was the first we heard he'd not been home the night before.'

'What about Dr Darscot? I had heard he was a friend of Dr Mackenzie.'

Hemsley shook his head. 'No, I don't know a Dr Darscot, but there are any number of doctors who come to look around the wards, so he might have been one of those.'

'You were on duty here until midday, which would be the time that Mr Palmer would normally arrive. Did you wait here for him?'

'Yes, well we all hoped that he would come, we thought perhaps he had had something urgent to do that had kept him from home, and maybe he had sent a message and the message got lost, and he would be here as usual. You could rely on him like that. There had only ever been the one time when he hadn't come and that was when he was too ill to get out of bed, but he'd still made sure to send a note so that we knew and could get someone in.'

'But he never came back.'

'No, and there was no note or anything. I stayed on for a little longer, and saw the fire was properly tended and then Dr Warrinder came in, as they couldn't get anyone else in a hurry. The next day they got some medical students to take care of the place, and now there's a new man, Renfrew, he started a few days ago.'

Frances looked at the connecting door. Hemsley followed her look and gave a little knowing smile, but made no comment. 'I see that visitors for a viewing must knock at the chapel door, but how do the doctors and orderlies gain admission? Do you all have keys?'

'All the doctors have a set. I have one and so does Palmer.'

Frances wondered if someone might have waylaid Palmer to steal his keys, for what purpose she could not imagine, but it was a possible motive for an assault that could have ended in the missing man's injury or death.

'Has anyone ever tried to steal your keys?' she asked.

'No.'

'Or asked to borrow them?'

He looked uncomfortable. 'I've been asked by press-men to let them in to take a look around. One wanted to borrow my keys and I'm sure he meant to have copies made. Been offered good money, too. But I didn't take it.'

'So, if Palmer is missing then his keys are too?'

'Yes, Dr Bonner had to order the locks changed and new sets of keys made.'

Frances made a note of Hemsley's address; he was lodging with a family in St Charles Square, off Ladbroke Grove Road. He confirmed that he walked to and from the Life House along the main road, using the side alley that led to Church Lane and assumed that Palmer would have done the same, as it was the fastest way.

Frances left the Life House, following the path that Palmer must have taken. She was not afraid of walking, and recalled the long journeys she had undertaken on foot through rain and mud, when her father had been alive and grumbled at every small expense.

Reaching the upper end of Ladbroke Grove Road, she passed the walled perimeter of All Souls and the gates of the eastern entrance to the cemetery, then crossed the bridge which afforded her a fine view of the canal on either side, with its tugs and barges. The gasworks, she was obliged to admit, was not an attractive sight, although of undoubted utility, as was the bridge over the lines of the Great Western Railway. In all it took some ten minutes for her to reach Dr Mackenzie's lodgings, and there she stood for a few moments at the bottom of the steps, where Palmer had paused. Why had he done so? Was he thinking about something, or had he seen something or someone that had attracted his attention? Frances gazed about her but could see nothing of importance.

She turned left as Palmer had done and started down the road again, crossing Telford Road, and reaching the junction with Faraday Road. Had Palmer turned left here or had he gone on to Bonchurch Road? Either way he must have reached Portobello Road, walked a short distance and then taken a right turn into Golborne Road, with its rows of shops and lodging rooms above. All the routes would have been well lit, although the yellow lamps might have found it hard to penetrate the enveloping fog that had persisted on the night of Palmer's last known walk. Both Faraday and Bonchurch Roads were entirely residential, whereas Portobello and Golborne were busy commercial streets where even late at night one might have expected to find many people about. If Palmer had lost his way he might have stumbled into a basement area, yet had he done so he would have been found soon enough. A trapdoor above a cellar might have been left carelessly open, but Frances felt sure that Walter's enquiries had covered that possibility. He had been very thorough. All the houses looked well-kept and occupied, and the residents would have noticed something amiss.

Supposing, however, that Palmer had not gone straight to his home, but had had an errand to perform, one that would have taken him along a different route? Supposing he had been sent on this errand by Dr Mackenzie? Frances had been told repeatedly that in recent months Mackenzie had looked tired and ill. Might he have had a secret worry on his mind?

She arrived home and the walk in the crisp air had warmed her. A note had arrived from Dr Bonner saying that if Frances would call on him at 2 p.m. he would be very pleased to speak to her about the unfortunate disappearance of Mr Palmer.

Chapter Three

Dr Bonner's home was one of the handsome five-storey residences on Ladbroke Grove Road. There was fresh white paint, and polish, and a trim maid in a starched apron and a smart cap with stiff lace points. Somewhere Frances felt sure there was a large Mrs Bonner in a great deal of whalebone and a fashionable gown planning a busy afternoon of calls, over a silver tea service crusted with scrollwork, and a pile of sugared cakes, while a stern nursemaid ensured that the Bonner offspring were scrubbed pink and perfectly behaved.

Frances was shown up to the consulting rooms on the first floor, where she found a small, portly gentleman of about fifty with plump fingers and a ready smile. Dr Bonner wore his shiny pate without embarrassment but cultivated a long, sandy coloured ruff of hair at his nape and soft, well-trimmed side-whiskers. It gave him an air that combined abundant geniality with trustworthiness. Although Frances had approached him for an interview unconnected with her own state of health, his manner was so well established that he could not help but gaze upon her as if she was a new patient, who had come to him with some delicate female ailment and to whom gentle reassurance was essential.

Dr Bonner greeted her politely and gestured her to a comfortable easy chair of deep-buttoned brown leather, then sat facing her, not from across his desk, which was a great expanse of polished walnut, but from another such chair drawn up in front of a fireplace. Frances looked about her and saw shelves of medical books, glass cabinets of instruments, and anatomical pictures of great artistry and tasteful restraint. Her family doctor, Dr Collin, was a busy man with a large practice and his consulting room reflected that. Dr Bonner's room was how a museum of modern life might show how a doctor's room ought to appear, beautifully maintained, but quite unused. Frances thought that Dr Bonner was a man who did exactly as much work as he wished to do.

'It is a particular pleasure to make your acquaintance,' said Dr Bonner. 'An old friend of mine sent his granddaughters to the Bayswater Academy for the Education of Young Ladies and suffered much anxiety over that unfortunate matter. His gratitude that you were able to resolve it was very marked.'

Frances, who despite all that had occurred, entertained the greatest respect for the former headmistress of that establishment and continued to pay her visits, smiled at the compliment.

'I naturally entertain considerable confidence in your ability to discover the whereabouts of Mr Palmer,' he added, with a smile of the most penetrating sincerity.

'Do you believe,' asked Frances, 'that the disappearance of Mr Palmer and the death of Dr Mackenzie are connected in any way?'

He evinced a gentle surprise. 'Connected? No, I don't believe so.'

'And yet they did occur on the same day.'

'Hmmm.' Dr Bonner laced his fingers and appeared to be giving the matter some thought, although Frances sensed that he did it only to indulge a lady. 'I can see why you might think so. It has been suggested, principally by people who have never met Mr Palmer, that he was so upset by what he had witnessed that he suffered a brainstorm, as a result of which he laid violent hands upon himself or else met with a fatal accident. Myself, I cannot believe it. When Palmer left the Life House he was of course greatly sorrowed by what had occurred, but he was a sensible man, as must all men be who follow his line of work, and he had a task to perform, which I had every confidence he would carry out, and indeed he did, as I later discovered.'

'How would you describe him as an employee?'

Bonner smiled, as if seeing the man before him. 'Reliable, sensible, diligent, respectful. I can assure you that had we thought he was the sort of person who would lose his head and become alarmed as easily as people have been suggesting, we would not have engaged him in the capacity we did. A man who had dealt with his own tragedy – the accident that claimed his father – would be the last man to throw a fit at the loss of his employer.'

'Supposing,' said Frances, expanding on her new theory, 'that Dr Mackenzie had some worry on his mind. Might he have confided it to Mr Palmer? Perhaps Mr Palmer had an urgent errand to carry out for Dr Mackenzie that he had to keep secret?'

Bonner looked astonished.

'I am only guessing, of course,' said Frances.

'Oh,' said Bonner, after a long pause, 'I would say you are very wide of the mark. Dr Mackenzie regarded Palmer as an employee and not as an intimate friend who he could take into his confidence. If he had personal worries, I am sure he would have confided them in me. But he did not.'

'Apart from yourself, who were Dr Mackenzie's closest friends?'

'There is Dr Warrinder, of course, who assists in the management of the Life House.'

'Is that all?'

'As far as I am aware.'

'And he had never married?'

'No, he had not.' Bonner gave a little shake of the head and a sad smile. 'Oh, I can guess what you are thinking.' Frances doubted this very much, but let him go on. 'You are thinking that he was a dull fellow without sentiment, but that was not the case. There was a lady he admired, indeed loved, many years ago, a lady of beauty and accomplishment but with no fortune. Unhappily, her father prevailed upon her to marry a man of wealth, who treated her with great cruelty, and Dr Mackenzie swore he would have no other lady for his bride and would wait in the hope that she might one day be free.'

Frances was not entirely convinced by this story, but decided not to pursue it. 'Did he know a Dr Darscot?'

'Yes, but how well he knew him I cannot say.'

'Did he have a club, or belong to any societies?'

'No, I wish he had.' Bonner sighed despondently. 'Perhaps if he had indulged in some recreation he might not have placed himself under such a strain. But I am afraid all he ever thought of was work. Not only the Life House, but he spent his evenings writing medical pamphlets, he lectured occasionally, and in recent months he had also started to see some patients again.'

'Where were his consulting rooms?'

'He had none. I allowed him the use of mine as a favour.'

'I understand that you and Dr Warrinder are his executors.'

'Yes. The principal concern of his will was to safeguard the future of the Life House. He owned a half share in the business and I own the other half. Mackenzie's will divided his share equally between Dr Warrinder and myself, and his personal property was wholly assigned to the use of the Life House.'

'Was there much in the way of personal property?' asked Frances.

'Very little. When the report has been completed it will almost certainly show a value of less than £100. Considerably less, I would say.'

'But he was in receipt of a salary?'

'Yes, a modest one.'

'In addition to which he saw patients and wrote pamphlets and lectured, lived very frugally, was unmarried, followed no recreation and had no vices.'

Bonner twiddled his fingers. 'I see what you mean, but I saw all his papers and can assure you that he had very little to dispose of. I can only assume that he gave sums to charity of which I was unaware. That would be so like the man.'

'He had no family?'

'An elderly mother in Scotland, to whom he wrote occasionally. I suppose he might have sent her some money. And there was a brother, but I do not think they have been in communication since before he went to Germany. That was a great many years ago.'

'Germany?' asked Frances.

'Yes. Dr Mackenzie was born and educated in Edinburgh, but more than twenty years ago he went to study with some very eminent medical men in Germany. That was where he first became acquainted with the principle of "waiting mortuaries", as they are generally called. The idea impressed itself very greatly on his mind and he made it his special study. Realising that there was no such establishment in Great Britain, he determined to found one and returned to London for that purpose.'

'I was not aware that there were establishments in Germany similar to the Life House.'

'Oh yes,' said Bonner, appearing more comfortable now that he was in his own area of knowledge, 'the very first of them was in Germany – a physician called Hufeland opened one in 1792, naming it the Asylum for *Vitae Dubiae*, or doubtful life, although it was more commonly termed a *Leichenhaus*.'

'I speak no German – does that mean Life House?'

'I am not familiar with the language, however, I have been told that it simply means "mortuary". When Mackenzie first promoted his scheme here the press took up the word and mistranslated it as Life House. He at once saw that this was a name that inspired hope and so adopted it for his use.'

'Has his family been notified of his death?'

'I do not have his brother's address and did not find it in Dr Mackenzie's papers, but I did discover a notebook with his mother's address and sent her a telegram, then followed it with a letter giving all the circumstances. I have not received a reply.'

'You dealt with his personal effects?'

'I did, such as they were. Many of the books you see behind me are from his library. Their monetary value is minimal, I assure you.' Frances glanced at the bookshelves, and while she was no great judge of antiquarian books, was content to believe that the collection of well-thumbed medical volumes was unlikely to be a significant item in Dr Mackenzie's estate.

'And what in your opinion was the cause of his death?'

'Principally, I believe a seizure of the heart was no doubt the immediate cause, but he also suffered an affliction of the intestines which contributed to his debilitated condition. People thought he was a man with a great worry on his mind, and perhaps it might have seemed so, but in fact what they observed was the unhappiness of a man who was in constant discomfort with his bowels. I think the poor man must have suffered more than anyone – even those closest to him – realised. The advance of sepsis in the area was very rapid.'

Frances paused to write her notes and Bonner looked more cheerful, anticipating that this signaled the end of the interview.

'And now,' she said, facing him once more, 'I would like to

examine in detail the events which occurred at the Life House on the evening of Dr Mackenzie's death.'

'Ah – yes – but of course.' He settled back in his chair, making every effort to appear unconcerned.

'You were already there when he arrived?'

'Yes, I had come to do my regular rounds and check with Palmer that all was well, and advise him of any new patients or forthcoming interments.'

'Were you expecting Dr Mackenzie to call?'

'Not at that precise time, but it was his habit to call in often, so I was not surprised when he did.'

'Was there anything at all of an unusual nature that you can recall about that evening – an event, a comment made either by Dr Mackenzie or Mr Palmer, or something in the manner of either that struck you as noteworthy? Even the smallest observation would be of assistance.'

Dr Bonner looked sad, as if he was about to tell an anxious wife that her husband might not rally. 'I am sorry, I have given this a great deal of thought as you can imagine, but it really was an evening like any other.'

'What were you doing when Dr Mackenzie arrived?'

'I was in the ward, discussing one of the patients with Palmer. The gentleman had showed signs which we believed suggested he might be revived and I examined him, but concluded they were due to other processes.'

'What time was this?'

'It was about ten o'clock.'

'Please describe for me in as much detail as you can what happened next.'

Bonner passed a hand across his brow. 'Mackenzie arrived and we greeted each other, and he said he was just looking in for a few minutes. We discussed the patients and Palmer continued on his rounds. Palmer was examining a patient and Mackenzie went to look on, and then —' Bonner gave a little gasp that was almost a sob, 'it was really very sudden and without any warning at all, he suddenly clutched at his stomach and then his chest, and went very white. Palmer said something like "are you all right sir?", but the poor man was in too much pain to speak. I went to assist, but before I could reach him he had fallen against Palmer, who supported him and prevented him from falling to the ground. Moments later he collapsed entirely. Palmer and I got him onto a bed, then Palmer fetched my instruments and I examined him. We then carried out every restorative method at our disposal. You can imagine, Miss Doughty, that in an establishment such as the Life House the medicines and equipment are second to none and right to hand. If any man is about to suffer a critical seizure this would be the best place for him to do so, with the most favourable chance of recovery. I worked for the best part of an hour with Palmer assisting me, but to no avail. There was no respiration, no pulse, and none of our efforts could restore them. Of course the final, unequivocal signs of death had not appeared, but I was aware that my dear friend had become a patient in his own establishment. Both Palmer and I were very upset, of course, but Palmer remained calm and practical, and asked me what he might best do to help. I thought of sending a telegram to Dr Warrinder, but as it was late at night and I know he retires early, I could see nothing to be gained by rousing him from his bed. I decided to send for him early the next day.

'After some thought I decided to lay Dr Mackenzie in the chapel; that is the side room where we place patients in a plain coffin for relatives to view them if they require it, also we coffin bodies there prior to burial. In view of the respect in which Dr Mackenzie is held, I thought it would be appropriate to invite selected medical friends to view him the next day. I told Palmer to call at Dr Mackenzie's lodgings on his way home and let them know what had occurred, since I know his landlady Mrs Georgeson worries about him and would have been most anxious at his failure to return. There was only an hour left of Palmer's period of duty, so I told him that once he had delivered the message he might proceed home, and that I would attend to anything else required. In any case the other orderly, Mr Hemsley, would be arriving very soon. Palmer said he would do as I asked and he left. I am sorry to say I have not seen him since that moment.'

There was a brief pause and Frances realised that Bonner felt that he had said all he could.

'Who was the next person to arrive?'

'That would have been Dr Darscot,' said Bonner, readily. 'He had called to see Dr Mackenzie at his home and had been told the news by Mrs Georgeson. He came knocking at the chapel door in a very agitated state. He viewed the body and calmed down a little, and then he left.'

'Do you have his address?'

'I am afraid not.'

'It may be in Dr Mackenzie's papers. If you could look through them and let me know, I would be very grateful.'

'Of course – anything I can do to assist. But how can Darscot help find Palmer? If he knows anything surely he would have come forward by now?'

'Dr Darscot's visit to Mrs Georgeson was made only minutes after Mr Palmer left. He may have seen something but not realised its importance.'

'Ah, I see. Yes, of course.'

There was also the possibility, thought Frances, of Darscot knowing of some concern that Mackenzie had confided in Palmer and not in Bonner, but she decided that there was little to be gained by mentioning it. Dr Bonner, like so many medical men, thought he knew everything of importance apart from those things that no one knew.

'Could you describe Dr Darscot to me?'

'Oh – er – quite young, I suppose, about thirty. Respectably dressed. Nothing very remarkable about his appearance.'

Frances glanced at her notebook. 'As Dr Mackenzie's executor you must have examined his correspondence,' she said. 'I don't know if he kept copies of the letters he sent, I know many professional gentlemen do. And of course there will be the letters he received from medical friends, from his mother and his friends in Germany. You may prefer not to show these to me, of course, and I would understand that, but it is possible there might be some clue in the letters, an observation about Mr Palmer, perhaps.'

'Oh!' said Dr Bonner, startled.

'You *did* find letters amongst his effects?'

'No, I – I can't say that I did.'

'Would you not have expected to find them? Mrs Georgeson told me he regularly received letters.'

'You are quite right, of course,' said Bonner, dismayed. 'I confess that when examining his effects I only concerned myself with what I actually found, and I never stopped to consider what I ought to have found that was not there.'

'Did you carry out the work alone or with another?'

'Mrs Georgeson's maid assisted me. Perhaps she might know something.'

Frances, with the feeling that she would spend the investigation doing nothing but travel up and down the length of Ladbroke Grove Road, could only agree.

'What happened to Dr Mackenzie's keys?'

'You mean the keys to the Life House? They were in his pocket. I have them here.' Bonner opened a small drawer in his desk and took out a bunch of four keys on a brass ring. 'The keys to his residence were on here, too, but I returned them to Mrs Georgeson.' The largest key, he explained, was for the main entrance of the Life House. A smaller one was the chapel door key and there were two internal keys, one for the door that separated the chapel from the ward and one for the door that separated a front office room from the ward. Frances thought that only the main key was of a memorable design, and whether this was deliberate or had been supplied by a humorist she did not know, but the loop of the key, instead of being rounded, was oblong and reminded her of the outline of a coffin viewed from the side. It was engraved along its shank with the name of the locksmith.

'So there are only five sets of keys,' she said, 'one for each doctor and one for each orderly.'

'That is correct.'

'And prior to Mr Palmer's disappearance none have ever been missing?'

'We are very careful with them. Of course, I assume that Palmer, wherever he is, still has his. When he had been missing for three days we decided to take the precaution of changing the locks.'

'Are the new keys identical to these?'

'Very similar.'

'May I see them?'

He seemed surprised at this request, but pulled a bunch of keys from his pocket. Frances examined them, and saw that the loop of the new main door key was a little more rounded at the corners and less coffin-like than its predecessor. She handed them back.

'Might someone be interested in stealing a set of keys, a press-man perhaps? Might he even be prepared to try and rob Mr Palmer to obtain them?'

Bonner raised his eyebrows. 'That is possible, I suppose. Press-men have tried to get into the Life House — never with any success, and one can never know to what levels of criminality they will stoop.'

'And before you changed the locks, no one attempted to gain entry?'

'No, we were alert to the possible danger and were most vigilant that no unauthorised person should be able to enter the premises.'

'On that subject, Dr Bonner, I would like to arrange a visit to the Life House.'

He stared at her blankly. 'I am sorry, I do not understand you, Miss Doughty.'

'I am trying to trace Henry Palmer's movements on the night he disappeared. Clearly they started from the Life House. I wish to tour the premises.'

Bonner was sufficiently taken aback that it was a moment or two before he could form a reply. 'But *clearly* he was seen after he left. In any case, the Life House is private property and it is an inflexible rule that apart from the chapel room, only medical men may enter.'

'And medical women?' asked Frances pointedly. 'They do exist.'

He laughed. 'I have never been approached by any such. No, Miss Doughty, if you wish to enter the Life House you must first obtain a medical degree, and then, and *only* then will I consider your application.'

Frances returned to Mrs Georgeson's house to find that the land-lady was busy showing a gentleman the vacant apartments, while Mary Ann was making an ineffectual attempt at scrubbing the kitchen floor. It was not hard for Frances to persuade the house-maid to leave her work and sit down in the parlour to talk.

'I understand that you assisted Dr Bonner when he dealt with Dr Mackenzie's effects?' asked Frances.

The girl nodded. 'Yes, not that there was a lot of effects.'

'Do you recall seeing any letters about?'

'Letters?' Mary Ann thought for a moment, her gaze wandering about the room as if the letters might be found on the wall or the ceiling, but seeing none, she added, 'No.'

'But Dr Mackenzie did receive letters?'

'Oh yes. Not a great many, but some. All letters that come here get put on the table in the hall and the tenants help themselves.'

'Did you clean the doctor's room?'

'I clean all the rooms, when asked. He didn't ask very often.'

'And did you ever see letters lying about?'

She frowned and chewed her lower lip. 'There's that little desk in there. There used to be letters lying on it sometimes, and he said he didn't want it tidying or he'd never find anything, so I left it alone.'

'And there's a wastebasket. I suppose you emptied that when you cleaned.'

'Yes, all what was in there got burned up.'

'Were there letters in there?'

'Sometimes.'

'So – letters on his desk and letters in the basket. On the last day, the day he died, when Dr Mackenzie went out did he leave the room locked?'

She nodded. 'Yes. All the gentlemen have keys and lock their doors. Mrs Georgeson is very insistent on that.'

'Does anyone apart from Dr Mackenzie have a key?'

'Mrs Georgeson.'

'And did Dr Mackenzie's room stay locked until Dr Bonner came to deal with all his things?'

'Yes.'

'And you helped him?'

'Yes.'

'I want you to think carefully about what happened on that occasion. Try and imagine what was in the room. Were there any letters on the desk or letters in the wastebasket?'

Mary Ann thought so hard it made her eyes bulge, then she shook her head. 'No, none at all.' Frances was just digesting this information when the maid added, 'There was something else – or at least *not* something else. Oh I don't know how to say it – something that wasn't there. I was looking about and I just thought to myself, there's something that's gone that ought to be here only I can't quite think what it is. And do you know, I still can't think what it was.'

'Well if you remember, you must be sure to inform me. It could be very important.'

Mary Ann nodded eagerly. 'Will I be in one of the stories, Miss?'

Frances smiled encouragement. 'I can't promise that, but you never know.'

As Frances was on her way out she encountered Mrs Georgeson in the hallway bidding the prospective new tenant farewell. He was an odd, creeping little man with a forlorn looking hat. Frances felt sure that he would suit the house perfectly.

'You're back soon, Miss Doughty,' said Mrs Georgeson. 'Has Mr Palmer been found?'

'I regret not, but I am continuing to make enquiries. I am wondering if Dr Mackenzie had some concerns, maybe of a personal nature, that meant he asked Mr Palmer to go on an errand for him, and Mr Palmer needed to honour that request even after the doctor's death. I don't suppose you know of anything that might have been troubling Dr Mackenzie?'

Mrs Georgeson shook her head. 'I'm afraid I don't. He never confided anything in me, and I never ask my gentlemen personal questions.'

'Do you know what happened to Dr Mackenzie's letters? Only there were none found in his room. Did you go into his room after he died?'

'No, I left that to Dr Bonner. If there were no letters then Dr Mackenzie must have disposed of them himself. Speaking of letters, I don't know what to do with this one.' She took a letter from her pocket. 'It came this morning, from abroad. Funny stamp and strange writing. He's had them like this before.'

Frances looked at the envelope. 'It may be from one of Dr Mackenzie's medical friends in Germany. Why don't I take it to Dr Bonner? He'll know what to do with it.'

Mr Georgeson hesitated, then handed Frances the letter. 'I don't suppose it makes much odds now.'

Back home, Frances, in a dilemma, showed the letter to Sarah. 'It doesn't seem right to open another person's correspondence, even when that person is dead. I have no authority to do it; in fact the only persons who do are his executors. Perhaps I should take it to Dr Bonner and let him open it and then ask him to show it to me.'

'He might say no,' observed Sarah.

'Yes, he might, as he would be entitled to.'

'Well, *I* think you should open it and read it.'

Frances struggled with her conscience. 'That would be very dishonest.'

'Suppose there was something in it, something important that might save Mr Palmer's life? What then?'

The struggle weakened. 'Yes, that is a very good point. Perhaps, under the circumstances …'

'And then you can give it to Dr Bonner afterwards.'

'But, won't he notice it's been opened?'

Sarah gave a curious little smile and held out her hand for the letter. 'He'll be none the wiser.'

Frances was not sure what mysteries Sarah was about to perform and decided it might be best not to know. She gave her the letter.

Five minutes later the letter was back in Frances' hands and she found that the envelope had released its gum and the paper could be slid out and unfolded.

'Oh how stupid of me,' said Frances as she stared at the dark spiky handwriting. 'It's in German. I suppose I thought – but then if Dr Mackenzie lived there all those years – oh dear!'

As far as she was aware none of her acquaintances could speak German, and she felt unwilling to employ a stranger in case awkward questions were asked as to how she had come by, and indeed opened, a letter that was clearly addressed to another person. The prospect of purchasing a German dictionary and grammar and trying to translate it herself was neither appealing nor likely to ensure a quick or accurate answer.

'Mr Garton has travelled a lot,' said Sarah. 'He often says he has been to every place in the world worth seeing. He might know someone who could help.'

'And I hope I may rely on his discretion,' said Frances. She knew Cedric Garton well enough to do without the formality of a note and, since his apartments were only a minute's walk away on the same street, she decided to call and discover if he was at home.

While Frances always enjoyed the company of that man of refined and sometimes unusual tastes, she felt less pleasure at the thought of encountering his manservant, Joseph, who, while undoubtedly devoted to his master, always made Frances feel as if she was being examined for those qualities he might best desire in Cedric's intimate friends, and was always found badly wanting. To her surprise therefore, when Joseph saw her on the doorstep he looked almost pleased at her arrival, and admitted her to the house with some alacrity.

'Miss Doughty, you have come at a moment when I fear you are greatly needed. Mr Garton has met with a — well there has been a small — well, you must see for yourself. Your assistance would be most valued.'

Frances was shown into Cedric's delightfully appointed drawing room, and Joseph knocked on a side door, opened it cautiously and peered in.

'Sir - Miss Doughty is here to see you.'

'Oh —' said a muffled voice from within which was undoubtedly Cedric's. 'I am not sure whether I am in a fit state to be seen. It is all very unfortunate.'

'What is the matter?' Frances asked Joseph.

The manservant uttered a sigh. 'Mr Garton, as I am sure you know, is a devotee of the cultivation of the manly form to its greatest perfection, and to that end he recently became a student of Professor Pounder.'

'I am afraid I don't know that gentleman —' Frances paused, recalling an advertisement she had seen in the *Bayswater Chronicle*. 'Oh – the boxing instructor?'

'Not boxing, Miss Doughty, no,' said Joseph with a roll of the eyes, 'Mr Garton would not indulge in coarse pugilism. He has taken up the exercise of sparring – the noble art of self-defence for the gentleman amateur.'

Cedric appeared in the doorway, with an uncharacteristically rumpled shirt, open at the neck. For one awful moment Frances thought his face was covered in blood, but then she saw that he was clasping a large beefsteak to one eye.

'Sparring,' he declared. 'I had no idea the fellow was going to strike me!'

He strode in, half fell into a chair and leaned back, still clutching the steak. Joseph yelped in horror and ran to get a towel to protect the furnishings.

'Did you strike him back?' asked Frances.

'I most assuredly did! I was the terror of the establishment. There will not be a beefsteak to be had in the whole of Bayswater now.'

Frances had some experience in dealing with minor injuries from her years spent working in her father's chemist's shop on the Grove. The walking wounded were more likely to come there than go to the expense of a doctor, although her father, who had a horror of doing anything gratis, had always insisted she sell them something, usually a box of Holloway's Pills which claimed to be able to cure everything and therefore suited all eventualities. 'Well, perhaps you could let me see what the matter is; I may be able to help. I am not sure if steak is the best treatment.'

Cedric reluctantly peeled the steak away from his eye and Frances handed it to Joseph, who took it away and returned with a basin of water and a cloth. A few moments were enough to establish that the skin around Cedric's eye was unbroken and the eye itself was undamaged. The main injury was a swollen semi-circular contusion and a large bruise to Cedric's self-esteem.

'How does it look?' he murmured faintly.

'It is a beautiful colour and I think Joseph will be at some pains to find a necktie that will match the shade.'

'Oh, you are too cruel. May I have the steak back?'

'Only if it is cooked and on a plate. I shall ask Joseph to wet a towel in cold water and apply it to the eye – that will take the swelling down.'

After a few minutes Cedric, his confidence restored, felt able to survey the damage in a mirror, flicking a blond lock from his forehead with a gallant toss of the head. 'A battle wound,' he said. 'I am a hero of combat. Set upon by a gang of the very worst type of rough, all of whom I dealt with and sent on their way sustaining only this light blow, which I wear with pride as a mark of my victory.' He smiled. 'Thank you Miss Doughty, you are the ministering angel of the hour, a veritable Nightingale or Seacole. I am sorry to have greeted you with my dress in such disarray, it was most impolite. Please make yourself comfortable and I will return a new man. Joseph – a pot of tea and a beef-steak sandwich if you please!'

A few minutes later Cedric was freshly spruced and cologned, and a tray of comestibles had appeared. Joseph had sliced the steak as thin as paper and arranged it in little fried ribbons on pieces of toast with a pot of relish, although Frances preferred and took a plain biscuit with her tea. 'I confess,' she said, 'that my call today was not of a purely social nature, but in order to entreat your help. Do you happen to know a reliable and dis-creet person who would be able to translate something written in German? Or perhaps you speak the language yourself?'

Cedric nibbled toast and smiled kindly. 'Oh I wish I were worthy of such confidence! The brain is a delicate thing and should in my opinion be exercised as little as possible. I try not to think too much, it can spoil all the pleasure of life. Of course I speak Italian, as I lived there so long and was obliged to acquire it, and I have some French and fragments of Greek, oh and a little Turkish and Arabic, but I would not claim to be a student, these things seep into my poor head and will not go away.'

Frances, nodding regretfully, unfolded the letter and gazed at it. 'Such curious handwriting,' she said.

Cedric glanced at the envelope, and she could see that she had attracted his interest, for there was a little sparkle of mis-chief in his eyes. 'Hmm, a missive to the recently departed Dr Mackenzie. I will not ask how you came by it, as you might shock me with your reply. Well, let me see it, I might essay a guess.'

He took the letter and after a few moments said, 'The sender is a Dr Ervin Kastner of the *Leichenhaus* – a mortuary that is – in Hamburg. A close friend, as they appear to be on first name terms. It says —' There was a long pause, during which Frances refreshed herself with tea. 'Yes, I think I have it; it says,

> Dear Alastair,
> Regarding the disquieting matter mentioned in my earlier letter you will be pleased to know that against all expectations Friedrich's health is much improved and his doctors are confident that he will make a full recovery. Even so, I am aware that we cannot rest easy and as soon as he is well enough I will speak to him about the matter that concerns us.
> With all good wishes
> Ervin

Frances, who knew that Cedric was very much more talented than he liked to admit, had no doubt that this was an accurate translation, and asked him to repeat it while she carefully wrote the words in her notebook. Dr Kastner, she assumed, was an old associate from Mackenzie's time in Germany and it appeared that 'Friedrich' was a mutual friend whose health had been giving cause for anxiety, but there was clearly another difficulty connected with this, something Dr Kastner had not seen fit to put in writing, something that had led to considerable unease for them both. It now looked very probable that it was Mackenzie himself who had destroyed his earlier correspondence, which might have been of a sensitive or secret nature, and possible, too, that his worries about Friedrich had contributed to both his ill-health and his death. She wondered if Mackenzie's hidden concerns had been a factor in the disappearance of Henry Palmer.

CHAPTER FOUR

At the end of a long day Frances had a note of her own to compose, to Mr Max Gillan, the assiduous reporter of the *Bayswater Chronicle*, whose articles about her career had given her both an unwarranted notoriety and a satisfying number of clients. There was a discreet arrangement whereby Frances provided Mr Gillan with interesting stories and he gave her information that she might not otherwise have been able to obtain.

Frances' letter asked Mr Gillan to keep her informed of any interesting developments in the search for Henry Palmer, and she also told him of a rumour pervading Bayswater that Palmer had been given an important secret task to perform by Dr Mackenzie, which he had decided to honour even after his employer's death. She did not mention that the originator of the rumour was herself. The doctor, she added, was still deeply mourned by his medical friends Doctors Bonner, Warrinder and Darscot, and asked Mr Gillan if he had an address for the last-named gentleman.

A detective, Frances reflected, as she and Sarah sipped their evening cocoa, like the police force needed to have eyes and ears everywhere. She was very fortunate not only to have the advice of Mr Gillan and other friends, but the services of young Tom Smith, a relative of Sarah's who had once been the Doughtys' delivery boy and now worked for the new owner of the chemist's shop, the enterprising and energetic Mr Jacobs. That gentleman had recently disappointed the mothers of all the single girls in Bayswater by announcing his intention to marry a young lady of fortune in the spring. Both the shop and young Tom had prospered and he was already in the process of outgrowing his first uniform.

Tom also carried messages and ran errands for Chas and Barstie, and knew every street and byway in Bayswater. There was no one better to spot anything out of the ordinary; something moved or changed or missing. Sarah had been to see Tom, showing him Henry Palmer's portrait, and he had said he would set about the task. A fee was of course involved; in fact Frances was unable to recall Tom ever having carried out a commission without one. There were many very unusual words in his vocabulary, but 'gratis' was not one of them.

※

Frances had been intending to go up to Kilburn police station and speak to Inspector Gostelow, but the following morning that journey was rendered unnecessary by an early visit from Walter Crowe, who had just been there himself and found that nothing had yet been discovered. He declared that he would go there every day whatever the weather, until Henry was found. Frances could not help thinking of a time less than a year earlier when she had never set foot in a police station, neither had she anticipated that she would ever do so, and yet now it seemed that they were places where she was often to be found.

She had little comfort to offer Mr Crowe, but reported what she had learned, and put forward her theory that Dr Mackenzie had employed Palmer on some urgent task, the necessity for which even his death could not erase. Crowe said that if there was such a mission he knew nothing of it, but he would speak to Alice in case her brother had confided in her.

Alice, he told her sadly, was no better, but then she was also no worse, and he was grateful to Sarah for calling with little treats to tempt her appetite. Frances nodded and smiled, as if Sarah's efforts to get nourishing food into Alice were something she already knew about. Walter said that Alice's friend, Mabel Finch, also liked to call on her, but since Mabel had been sweet on Henry and there had been something approaching an understanding between them, it naturally followed that all the young women ever spoke of was the missing man, and he was not sure if this helped Alice or the reverse. Frances discovered that Mabel would be visiting Alice that evening and said that she would call and speak with her.

Busy as she was with the Palmer mystery, Frances knew that she was not so established in her profession that she could afford to ignore other clients. A note had arrived that morning from a lady who wished to discuss a question of a delicate nature concerning the arrangements at the Paddington Baths on Queen's Road. Frances was eager to see Dr Bonner and deliver Dr Kastner's letter, which had been neatly resealed in its envelope and Sarah, seeing that she was torn between the requirements of two clients, volunteered to interview the lady. She did not like to think that females who went for a refreshing bath were being interfered with and thought the complaint ought to be dealt with at once.

Dr Bonner was more than happy to see Frances again. It was with some anxiety that she watched him open the letter, but he seemed not to notice that he was not the first person to do so.

'Ah, as I suspected, the letter is in German,' he said. 'As I mentioned, Mackenzie lived there for many years and was fluent in the language. I don't speak it myself, I am afraid.'

'May I see it?' asked Frances, innocently.

'Do you speak German?' he asked with some surprise.

'No, but I thought I might be able to make out some names.'

'Well, I can see that the sender is Dr Ervin Kastner. He is the director of a waiting mortuary in Germany, very similar to the Life House. Mackenzie worked closely with him for many years and they were good friends.'

Frances peered at the letter and he hesitated, then handed it to her. 'What unusual handwriting! It is very hard to make anything out,' she said. 'Is that a name? Frederick or something very like it.'

'Friedrich is a German name, yes that may very well be it. Kastner may be referring to Friedrich Erlichmann.'

'Is he also a doctor?'

'No, but he writes and lectures on the subject of suspended animation. I have some of his pamphlets here. Dr Mackenzie translated them into English.'

Bonner rose and went to the bookcase, from which he extracted a slim publication from the shelf and handed it to Frances. She noticed for the first time that he walked with a slight limp. 'This is his first and best-known work,' said Bonner, easing himself back into his chair. 'It still sells well. Please do take it with my compliments.'

The title of the pamphlet was *A Recovery from the Disorder of Death*.

'Of course you are far too young to remember, but Mr Erlichmann was quite a celebrity a number of years ago and intimately associated with the foundation of the Life House here. He was a very young man, no more than twenty, when in 1862 he suffered a grave illness and was to all purposes apparently dead. Mackenzie was studying in Germany at the time and of course made a point of interviewing him. Erlichmann told him that he had actually been certified dead and placed in his coffin, and was on the point of being lowered into his grave when, fortunately for him, the signs of life appeared and he was revived just in time.

'When Mackenzie returned to England and was trying to establish the Life House he initially met with very little interest. The project is an expensive one as you can imagine, the land had to be purchased, and the house built to a very specific design. The Paddington vestry would not countenance the matter and Mackenzie exhausted all his savings, but it was not sufficient and his efforts at raising funds produced very little. I came in with him as a partner, but we were still short of what we needed when Mackenzie thought of bringing Erlichmann over to England to lecture about his experiences. You have never seen him but Friedrich Erlichmann is a man of excellent address and is, so many of the ladies have told me, considered to be extremely handsome. His command of English at the time was somewhat wanting, but Mackenzie was able to write his speeches for him. The lectures were very successful and Erlichmann became quite the lion of Bayswater; no elegant dinner was complete without him and the stories he told of his experiences both chilled the blood and opened the purses of our patrons. I understand – and this is only a rumour, of course – that he was summoned to a private audience with the Queen. Perhaps she hoped that Prince Albert might not be beyond recovery. If so, she was undoubtedly disappointed.'

'Do you think Mr Palmer might have gone to Germany?' asked Frances.

'Whatever for?' exclaimed Bonner.

'He might have gone in connection with some business of Dr Mackenzie's.'

Bonner looked doubtful. 'If Mackenzie had any business in Germany in recent years, I am unaware of it. He has friends there still and there may be some exchange of medical information, but that is all.'

Frances perused the opening lines of the pamphlet. 'Is death merely a disorder,' she asked, 'like the influenza; a condition from which one may recover with the correct treatment?'

Bonner smiled and nodded sagely. 'That is what Mr Erlichmann believes. You are aware of course of the work done for so many years by the Royal Humane Society on the recovery of those drowned?'

'I am,' replied Frances, 'but I had always imagined that those who recovered were not in actual fact dead but in a state of suspended animation, and therefore alive and wanting only warmth and other treatments to restore them. Does Mr Erlichmann claim that he was indeed dead?'

'He undoubtedly showed every sign of death recognised by medicine: the body cold, the eye flaccid, no sensibility to pain, and respiration and pulse both arrested. Every sign that is, except one. The one, to my mind, infallible sign of death – putrefaction of the tissues. But in so many countries those early signs are seen as certain proof, and so men and women are hurried to their graves still living.' Bonner leaned forward with an intense stare, like a storyteller who had reached the most dramatic part of his narrative. 'Imagine, Miss Doughty, the plight of young Erlichmann. Fully sensible of all that went on around him; unable to move, unable to speak, yet he could feel the hands of the attendants placing him in his grave clothes, feel himself being lowered into his coffin, hear the lamentation of his friends as they gazed upon his face. Imagine the horror of hearing one's own funeral dirge and seeing the approach of the coffin lid as it descends, sealing you from the world forever, knowing that you are about to be placed in your grave.'

'I cannot imagine such a thing,' said Frances. 'How was he able to make his plight known?'

'He believes that the violent emotions which he experienced had the effect of starting the heart and blood moving again. The coffin lid had actually been fastened down and he felt himself being lifted and carried to his grave when at last he found that he was able to move, and he knocked and knocked until his hands bled. His friends tore off the lid amidst great exclamation, and,' Bonner concluded triumphantly, 'found him rosy faced and warm.'

'A most fortunate escape,' said Frances.

'But just think how many others have not been so fortunate – how many living persons who might have been recovered but have actually been coffined and buried, and how frightful a fate befell them when the warmth of the earth restored them to life only to perish alone and confined in the terrible darkness, in a situation of the most appalling horror.'

'But surely,' said Frances thoughtfully, 'if a person is placed in a coffin while still alive and the coffin is then sealed they might not come to themselves at all, but perish in a very short while, and never be conscious of their plight?'

'Ah, I understand your thoughts, Miss Doughty. You are suggesting that the amount of life-giving air in a coffin is insufficient to support the human frame for very long, and this is true *if* the unhappy individual is fully awake. Indeed, if he struggles to escape and gasps a great deal he will suffocate in a very short while. But a person who has been inadvertently coffined in a state of suspended animation will not be in want of so much air and might live a great deal longer.'

'And once buried he or she would be unable to escape or alert others,' said Frances, 'and would die in the dark, alone, afraid and struggling for breath. How cruel!'

'There you have it!' said Bonner. 'That is why the Life House supplies the service it does. And for the greater comfort of our customers, those who wish it may have additional assurances. For those buried beneath the earth we can, for an extra fee, provide a breathing tube through which they may both suck air and call for help, and a bell so they may give the alarm. For those in vaults or catacombs there is a small air vent and a lever is placed by the hand, which may be operated by even the weakest individual, which will at once open an aperture for more air and sound a bell to alert the attention of an attendant. This, for reasons of hygiene, will only be the case for a short while, no more than two weeks. After that, we do accept the fact of death, and as is required by the cemetery, the inner shell is sealed in lead and placed inside a heavy coffin. One of the vaults in All Souls cemetery is reserved for the sole use of customers of the Life House.'

❧

'According to Dr Bonner,' Frances told Sarah, as they enjoyed a simple luncheon of bread and butter with boiled eggs, 'there is only one true way to be sure that a man is really dead.'

Sarah thought for a moment. 'Chop his head off?'

'That would certainly be effective, but imagine a case in which you might wish to preserve the man alive, but cannot. No, the one sure sign of death is putrefaction. Until that starts there may be some hope of recovery.'

'Well that's not right,' said Sarah. 'My uncle Albert had a leg that went rotten and they cut it off, and he has a wooden one now but no one tried to tell him *he* was dead.' She snorted. 'I should like to have seen them try!'

'You may have something there,' Frances admitted. 'Dr Bonner has lent me a book by a Reverend Whiter and *he* refused to believe that anyone was dead until the entire body was completely dissolved. He says that the more serious a disease the longer it takes to cure, and since people who have revived from death have often done so very quickly, this proves that death is only a slight disorder after all. Even the waiting mortuaries attract his criticism since many do no more than leave the bodies to decompose, so as to be sure that they are dead, and do nothing to try and re-animate them. I think Dr Mackenzie's principle, whereby his patients are regarded as living until proven dead, does address that concern. It seems, however, that the worst offender is the undertaker, who stops the mouth and nose and binds the body in linen, so if there is any chance of recovery he makes it quite impossible.'

'You're not to have *me* laid out with people poking and prodding,' said Sarah. 'Dead is dead and I'd rather be done and finished with it. And don't them who come back go mad? What good is that?' She paused. 'And I know what you're thinking, and you're not to think it. I've seen enough dead to know it, and your father was gone to his maker and no doubt about it.'

Frances didn't want to admit it, but her thoughts had been tending that way. Her father had died in the cold winter and his body laid out in his room with no flicker of reviving warmth. None had seemed necessary. Suppose she had lit a fire and rubbed his limbs, would he have come back to her? She would never know.

Sarah's interview with the new client that morning had revealed that ladies who used the private bathing pools and slipper baths in Queen's Road had been complaining to the manager that young men had been using the vantage points of nearby tall buildings to spy on them through the glass roof. Gentlemen who heard of the menace treated it as a joke and ladies who objected had been told it was all in their imagination. Sarah, who thought that ladies' imagination was a product of men's imagination, which became most apparent when men were faced with something they wished to ignore, said that she would deal with the nuisance.

The luncheon plates were being cleared away when Frances received a visit from Mr Gillan of the *Bayswater Chronicle* and was able to expand on her theory that Palmer's disappearance and Dr Mackenzie's death were in some way related. Gillan, who had some mysterious way of his own of extracting information from the police, which Frances suspected involved beer, reported that Palmer's absence was now being taken very seriously, and patrolling constables had made thorough searches, but found no clues.

'I have had a very interesting conversation with Dr Bonner, who told me about how the Life House was first established,' Frances told Mr Gillan. 'Apparently, it was partly due to an extraordinary young man called Friedrich Erlichmann, who had the most horrible experiences and came here to lecture about them.'

'Oh the public like a good tale of the ghastly and the grue-some,' said Gillan, 'even when they pretend they don't. That was a while back, I was a very young correspondent then, just starting to learn the business, but I do remember him. Did Dr Bonner mention the scandal?'

'The scandal?' Frances sighed and asked herself why people never told her the important things. 'No, curiously that was a detail he omitted. What happened? And please avoid delicacy, it wastes so much time.'

Gillan smiled. 'Oh all sorts of accusations being flung about, and openly, too.'

'About Mr Erlichmann?'

'Oh yes. Suggestions of fraud. And then, all of a sudden it stopped. Not because the public had moved onto some new sensation, not a bit of it. It just – stopped. I never did get to the bottom of that.' He looked thoughtful and Frances suspected he had scented a story. 'I won't have the time to look into it myself, I'm covering the Monmouth Club affair, but if you could come to the office one day I could get you in and you can have a look through the old copies of the *Chronicle*.'

'I shall go there immediately,' said Frances, and rose and went to get her coat.

Mr Gillan saw her expression and decided not to argue.

'I thought the Monmouth Club affair was settled?' enquired Frances. The Monmouth Club was the site of a recent scandal in Bayswater. It had claimed to be a respectable organisation where young gentlemen could enjoy wholesome amusements. The *Chronicle* had with some relish, denounced the club as a gambling hell, where betting and card playing and billiards went on all hours of the day and night, not excepting Sundays. The club had also not hesitated to supply its members with alcoholic beverages at times that completely disregarded the licensing laws. Several young men had got into debt and robbed their employers and were in prison as a consequence, and one had committed sui-cide. The manager of the club had taken grave exception to the exposure and tried to bring the force of the law down upon the *Chronicle*, but the affair had been absent from the newspapers for some little while, and Frances had thought the case abandoned.

'Settled? Not a bit of it,' said Gillan, shaking his head, but would not be drawn further.

They departed together and Sarah put on her fiercest bonnet and went out.

※

When Mr Gillan introduced Frances to his colleagues in the offices of the *Bayswater Chronicle*, she was surprised to find herself treated with some deference. She felt sure that in due course his lively mind would produce a highly decorated report of her visit for the amusement of the *Chronicle's* readers. There was a large storeroom with heavily bound volumes of the newspaper going back to its inception and Frances thought what a pleasure it would be on an idle day, if she was ever to have such a thing, to come here and read through the newspapers of yesteryear. It also amused her to imagine others coming to do the same and it struck her as strange that someone might one day, perhaps in a hundred years' time, read Mr Gillan's colourful accounts of her exploits and wonder what kind of person she had been.

The *Chronicle* was a weekly publication, which was fortunate, or she might have had many hundreds of editions to look at, and it was very much taken up by advertisements and national or foreign news. The most interesting part of the paper for Frances was page five, a treasure trove of local information: the often controversial incursions of Mr Whiteley's shopping empire into the life of Bayswater, the arguments in the Paddington vestry, reports of meetings and speeches, charitable organisations, public health, the antics of thieves, dreadful accidents, obituaries, police court news, and the many clubs, societies and entertainments to suit every taste and interest. It was possible, she reflected, for a person to live a full, interesting and profitable London life without ever going east of Paddington station.

Frances soon learned that in 1863 Friedrich Erlichmann had given lectures at many different locations in the capital, one of which was Westbourne Hall on the Grove, speaking movingly of his miraculous recovery from death. He had been introduced by Dr Bonner as the wonder of the age, and each lecture had been crowded, especially, it was said, by members of the fairer sex. Frances sometimes despaired of her sex, since they seemed so often to pay attention to a gentleman's looks and not to the sense, or otherwise, of what he was saying. She hoped that she would never be so shallow. The *Chronicle* reported the lecture given in Bayswater in some detail and here Frances learned little that was new, since the wording was essentially the same as had later been published in pamphlet form. Dr Mackenzie was briefly mentioned as having assisted as translator and interpreter. Erlichmann had been greatly applauded and was afterwards entertained to a grand dinner.

There had been, she found, only one small difficulty. All the lectures had passed off to universal acclaim except for the one at Westbourne Hall. As Erlichmann began to speak, a woman in the body of the hall had risen to her feet and loudly denounced him to be a fraud, although she offered no reason why she thought so. She was quickly but gently removed. Erlichmann had later been questioned by the *Chronicle* and said that the woman was of unsound mind, and had been pursuing him ever since he had arrived in London. He believed that she had been driven insane by the fear that her late husband, Arthur Biscoby, a Bayswater physician who had died a year previously, had been buried alive. This explanation was accepted and the objector was not heard from again.

Frances decided to look through the death notices and found the demise in October 1862 of Dr Arthur Biscoby, aged forty-three, who had left a wife, Maria, a son and two daughters. The eldest child was just seven. An inquest had been held, which supplied some useful information. Dr Biscoby had held a post in Germany at about the same time that Mackenzie was there, although there was no indication that the men had ever met or that Biscoby had shown any interest in waiting mortuaries. In 1861, Biscoby had returned to Bayswater to start a general practice, but unfortunately he had become addicted to strong drink and his mental capacity, moods and income had all gone into a sharp decline. After a bout of excessive drinking he had been found dead in bed, a victim of alcohol poisoning. Evidence was given that he was bankrupt and had been suffering from melancholia. There had been great sympathy for his destitute widow, and a kindly coroner's jury had declared the death to be an accident. Given the inquiry, which must have involved opening the body, no one but an insane person could have been under the illusion that Dr Biscoby had been buried alive.

The *Chronicle* office had copies of the Paddington postal directories and the one for 1862 included an entry for Dr Biscoby, but there had been none subsequently for his widow. Eighteen years later the unhappy Mrs Biscoby was, thought Frances, either in a workhouse or an asylum, or, more likely, dead. Despite the suggestion that her outburst had been the product of some mental distraction, it was possible that she had known something that might cast some light on the letters Dr Kastner had written to Mackenzie. It was a very long chance, but Frances decided to ask Sarah to go to Somerset House first thing the next morning and see if she could find out if and when Mrs Biscoby had died and if any of her children had married.

Sarah had been keeping a close watch on the area around the Paddington Baths, and reported on her return home that she had been rewarded by paying particular attention to the activities of young male shop workers who lodged nearby. They were, she discovered, beguiling the few minutes of their allotted luncheon time with a little Alpinism, finding windows and ledges from which they could obtain a frosted-glass view of female forms. She had, without drawing attention to herself, discovered an ideal place where she might wait to intercept their activities, and planned to return there the next day. Any young man descending from his eyrie would feel a firm hand on his collar and be able to view a rather less lissom and more muscular female form than he usually favoured, and very much closer than he might wish. Frances prudently suggested that Sarah might undertake that errand in the company of a policeman, but her eager assistant, who had undoubtedly been experiencing the pleasurable anticipation of seizing the miscreants, took some persuading. Frances explained that Sarah was to undertake a very important enquiry at Somerset House, and would be pressed for the time to do so if she was also obliged to drag wriggling malefactors to the police station. Once Frances had described the tale of Mr Erlichmann and Mrs Biscoby, however, Sarah, who enjoyed a good mystery, especially if it involved a vengeful female, was obliged to admit that it was interesting.

❊

Next morning Frances was busy interviewing several new clients, the most promising of whom was a gentleman of means who wanted her to discover the family connections of a prospective business partner, but in a very careful and discreet manner that would not alert the object of his interest. Frances had the strong impression that should she succeed in this delicate task, further valuable recommendations might follow and was anxious that this enquiry should be carried out promptly and successfully. She at once composed a letter to Chas and Barstie, who knew everyone of note in Bayswater involved in any endeavour that concerned money.

Her next visitor was banker's wife Mrs Pearson, a lady of considerable dignity who spent the first ten minutes of the interview explaining to Frances that consulting a private detective was something far beneath her usual mode of behaviour. She could scarcely imagine how a young woman, who she had been given to understand came from a respectable if impecunious family, could have thought to enter such an unsavoury profession; it was something she found profoundly shocking. There was a long silence during which Mrs Pearson, as if watching a sideshow entertainment, waited for Frances to provide evidence of her degraded status. Frances saw before her a stout woman of fifty-five dressed in the most recent fashion, resplendent with fur and lace, and a festoon of pearls and garnets about her throat. 'How may I help you?' she asked quietly.

The client explained that her maid, who went by the name of Ethel Green, was nowhere to be found and she feared for the girl's safety. The maid, who had been in the house some six months, was twenty-three, a girl with rather greater personal attraction than was entirely good for her, who had learned to dress well and copy the manners of her betters and so present herself almost as a lady. This attainment had gone far beyond the bounds of what was appropriate for her humble position and had put the girl in some danger. She thought that as a result the girl had been stolen away. The maid had last been seen going out smartly dressed on Sunday 12th September. Frances knew that ladies sometimes made gifts of discarded gowns to favoured servants and asked the lady if she had done so, as this would have afforded her a very good description of what the maid was wearing. The client said that she had not given any of her clothing to the maid, as it would not have suited her. She said nothing more on the subject but from her manner, Frances gained the impression that the maid was considerably more slender than her mistress. Mrs Pearson said that she had now employed a new maid, one that would not give herself such airs, but she wished to be assured of the safety of the missing girl.

Frances agreed to take the commission, but could not help wondering why a lady so proud as Mrs Pearson should feel such concern about a maid, one who was not a long serving and valued retainer but who had been with her for only a few months. There was, thought Frances, more to the matter than the lady was willing to say.

Mrs Pearson departed in her carriage and Frances was then obliged to spend an hour comforting a tearful Mrs Chiffley, while reporting a complete lack of success in locating her missing parrot.

Sarah had still not returned from her duties when it was time for Frances to call at Mrs Georgeson's lodging house, where she was pleased to find the ground floor tenant, Mr Trainor the surgical traveller, at home and willing to be interviewed.

Mr Trainor was a small man dressed in dark grey, which matched the colour of his hair and inexpertly trimmed whiskers. He smelled of gutta-percha and the burnt rubber scent of dead sap was the liveliest thing about him. He presented such a desiccated appearance, his body bent like a hollow shell from which all soft living matter had been scooped, that Frances suddenly thought with a shudder that were he three days cold and laid out in that grey suit in his coffin, he might not look very much different. He was, he explained, a salesman who had for some years enjoyed a position of some responsibility with a company that manufactured dental supplies. He lived alone, a situation that suited him perfectly and had, he assured Frances, a great many friends who came to see him or whom he visited in order to enjoy a game of chess, in which he admitted to some skill. He was, he said proudly, a founder member of the Bayswater Gentleman's Chess League. Frances received the impression that this was his only recreation, which he found more than sufficient for his amusement.

He offered Frances a seat by the fire, which produced more smoke than heat. There was a piece of bread and cheese set nearby ready to be toasted for his supper.

Trainor recalled very well the evening on which Henry Palmer had called to report Dr Mackenzie's death. 'I heard the doorbell of course, but I would never have thought to pry, it is not my habit to come out of my room to intrude on visitors, only I heard such loud exclamations in the hallway that I knew something was very amiss and – I freely confess it – I put my head out of the door to see what the matter was. There was a young fellow standing on the front step and Mary Ann was crying, but before I could say anything she turned around and ran to get Mrs Georgeson. I thought it would be wise not to leave the messenger alone at the door, so I came out into the hall and asked him what the trouble was. The young fellow said he was very sorry to be bringing bad news, but Dr Mackenzie had just fallen down in a fit and died. Of course I was very shocked to hear it, as Dr Mackenzie was by no means an old man, though he had been looking very unwell of late. I think he had something on his mind, as he always looked preoccupied as if a great weight was pressing on him.'

'Was there anything especially remarkable in Mr Palmer's manner,' asked Frances, 'beyond what one might expect of a man in those unfortunate circumstances?'

'No, nothing. He was upset, of course, but he seemed perfectly sane and collected. Mrs Georgeson came and he explained to her what had happened, and that Dr Bonner would be calling in due course to deal with Dr Mackenzie's effects. He said that if friends of Dr Mackenzie wished to go up to the Life House and pay their respects, Dr Bonner had taken it upon himself to ensure that his associate was decently laid out in the chapel there, and they would accept visitors from ten the next morning. Well, there was nothing I could do so I went back into my room.'

'Mr Palmer came into the hall, I believe?'

'Yes, it was a terrible foggy night and very cold, and Mrs Georgeson invited him in and closed the front door, but he only came in a short way.'

'He wasn't invited down to the parlour – or to look in Dr Mackenzie's room?'

'Not that I saw.'

'Did you see him leave?'

'No, he was still talking to Mrs Georgeson when I returned to my room. But I heard Mrs Georgeson bid him goodnight, and then the front door opened and closed again. That was just a minute or two later.'

'And I believe there was another visitor who came to see Dr Mackenzie that same night?'

'Ah yes,' said Trainor with some indignation, 'and what a commotion *he* made! Banging on the front door as if he would break it down. I thought it *very* impolite. And I could hear the conversation in the hallway quite clearly without any need to open my door. Mrs Georgeson told him Dr Mackenzie was dead and he absolutely refused to believe it. He seemed hysterical. I was about to go and offer Mrs Georgeson my assistance, but then her husband came and spoke to the man and sent him packing. The next thing I knew the fellow was in the street calling out. I looked out of the window to see what sort of type he was, but I was surprised to see him very respectably dressed. It turned out that he was shouting for a cab, and I was just wondering if he would have any luck in finding one when, as it so happened, one came past and he jumped into it and off he went.'

'What direction did he go in?'

'Up the road – north, towards Kensal Green.'

'Would you know him if you saw him again?'

'I doubt it very much. It was dark and he was muffled against the cold and the fog. I didn't see his face, although …' Trainor paused, thoughtfully. 'I couldn't swear to it, but now I think about it, he may have been a man I have seen here before, calling on Dr Mackenzie – one of his medical friends, I believe, but I am afraid I don't know his name. About thirty, well dressed. Very ordinary features.'

'And this visit on the night of Dr Mackenzie's death took place just a few minutes after Mr Palmer left?'

'Yes.'

'If he comes here again, would you let me know?' asked Frances, presenting her card. 'I would like to speak to him because he might have seen Mr Palmer in the street that evening and could give me some clue as to where he went.'

'Oh, I doubt that he would be of any help,' said Trainor. 'He was in a fast cab and Palmer was walking, so they would not have encountered each other.'

'How do you know he arrived by cab?'

'I don't know how he arrived. But he left by cab, I saw him.'

'It is his arrival that interests me. When this gentleman left he was going towards Kensal Green, but Palmer was travelling in the opposite direction, so I agree, they could not have met then, but if the man came up the road when he arrived he might have seen Palmer walking home.'

Trainor shook his head. 'No. Palmer walked north when he left here.'

'But Mr Palmer lives in Golborne Road,' said Frances, 'so he would have travelled south from here. Mary Ann saw him go that way.'

'As to where Mr Palmer lives or what Mary Ann saw, I have no information,' said Trainor, 'but I am sure that a minute after the noisy fellow drove off in a cab, I saw Palmer walking north.'

Puzzled, Frances rose, went over to the front window and peered out into the street. 'Show me where you were standing,' she said and Trainor obliged.

'I was looking out as the cab drew away,' said Trainor, 'and I suppose I fell to musing about the fog and how changeable the weather had been, first hot then cold and one hardly knew what to expect. And then I saw him, and I thought to myself, oh it's that young fellow from the Life House coming back again, I hope he has not brought more bad news. And then I thought, but supposing it is good news, that Dr Mackenzie is not dead after all but only thought to be dead – but then he walked past the house and did not come in.'

'And you are sure it was him?'

'Oh yes, well I spent a minute or two speaking with him face to face, and as you see there is a lamp immediately outside, and he wore no muffler, so even in the fog I could see his features.'

'Did he walk straight up the road or make a turning?'

'Straight, as far as I could see, but after a short way he was lost in the fog.'

'Have you told the police of this?'

'No, I was not here when they called, and I did not know until you told me just now that he lives in Golborne Road.'

'Then I had best go see them myself,' said Frances. 'There is a constable who patrols a point near St John's Church and he may have seen something.'

Frances hurried to Kilburn police station, which stood on the corner of Salisbury Road. She was not well acquainted with the inspector there but found him polite and willing to hear her, especially when she showed him her card. He promised to alert the attention of all his constables to the possibility that Henry Palmer had not, as supposed, walked south but north on the night of his disappearance, and assured Frances that careful searches would be made.

Frances hurried home and composed a note to Walter Crowe, who she knew would be out making his own enquiries almost as soon as he had read it.

*

While Frances considered what best to do next, she received an unexpected visit from Tom Smith. Tom was constantly on the alert for two things – food and business opportunities, so when he arrived at the apartments, Frances knew that it was not to pass the time of day. He was either foraging for cake or hoping to earn money, or quite possibly both. Tom took off his smart peaked cap with the chemist's shop emblem, made a brief and unsuccessful effort to smooth his hair down, and let his gaze flicker about the room, beaming with anticipation as he spied a covered dish and lifted off the domed top to inspect what lay within. Finding the contents to his liking he extracted a currant bun, split it, impaled half on a toasting fork and set to work.

'Any butter?' he enquired.

Frances went to get the butter.

'An' jam if you've got any! I bet you 'ave!'

Frances paused. 'Now then, Tom, how do you intend to earn your butter and jam, that's what I'd like to know,' she said.

'An' sixpence.' Tom stared at the bun and, dissatisfied with the progress of the toasting, munched the other half untoasted just to keep him from starvation while he waited. 'I've 'eard,' he said whilst licking crumbs from his lips, 'that you are looking for a Mr Darscot.'

'Well so I am, a *Dr* Darscot that is.'

'Oh, 'e's no more a doctor than what I am! But 'e's the man you want, an' I know because I sometimes carry notes for 'im. An' I know 'e's been to see that Dr Mackenzie, the one what pegged it the other day, so it 'as to be the same man or 'is bruvver what is the same thing really as either way you'll find 'im out.'

Frances fetched the jam. 'Describe this Mr Darscot.'

'About thirty, dresses like a real good 'un, pays well. Brown hair, nothing special about the phiz, I mean not 'andsome and not ugly neither.'

'And what does this Mr Darscot do for a living?'

Tom sniffed the toasted bun with an expression of sublime satisfaction and then applied himself to the process of buttering. 'Oh, now if I was to ask a customer a question like that my business would disappear faster 'n a rum-mizzler up Seven Dials.'

'Really?' said Frances, having no idea what such a creature might be, but appreciating that it must move very quickly about that notably unsavoury part of London.

'But if I 'ad to guess I would say Mr Darscot doesn't do anythin'. At least not work-wise. 'e is a gentleman what 'as a lot of money. 'e goes to 'is club and to the races and to the theatre and such like, and is no trouble at all to anyone. But 'e don't actually *work*, because 'e don't need to. Sounds like a good sort of thing to fall into.' He sighed and absentmindedly spooned jam into his mouth from the jar.

'Do you know where he lives? I should like to speak to him.'

'That I dunno, but I can take a message for you, to 'is club. It's the Piccadilly.'

'He has a club on Piccadilly?' said Frances in surprise. 'He must be very well-connected.'

'Naw – not *on* Piccadilly, they just call it that. It's on Porchester Road and it's for Bayswater gents what don't want the bother of going up to town, or can't run to the cost, or can't get into the big clubs with all the lords and dukes and such like, so they call it the Piccadilly 'cos it sounds good.'

'Well, that's not a long step for you, so I will compose a note and ask if the gentleman would care to call. I assume that it would not be possible for me to call on him at his club.'

'I never get past the 'all porter meself, and ladies of any type, if you know what I mean, not even the ones what are proper ladies, aren't to be let in, ever.'

Frances went to her desk and wrote a note, then handed it to Tom with his remuneration. 'If you could deliver it as soon as you can and bring me a reply.'

Tom gazed at the sixpence. 'That's two jobs. *An'* the cost of the information.'

'You'll get another when you come back with the message.'

'Right you are!' said Tom. 'You're a real peach, Miss Doughty.' He stuffed the last of the toasted bun in his mouth.

'Are you still working for Mr Knight and Mr Taylor?' asked Frances, who liked to know the extent of Tom's expanding business interests.

Tom wiped his lips. 'Oh yes, more'n ever! Mr Knight says I got promise!' he added proudly as he made to leave. ''e says that if I go on the way I am goin' then when I am older I shall be a big captain of industry, whatever that is, but 'e says I got to learn to speak English, which is a funny thing to say 'cos I thought that was what I *was* speaking.'

He dashed away and soon afterwards Sarah returned in triumphant mood. Two young men seen spying on lady bathers had been duly delivered to the police station, in a bedraggled and submissive state, although not without some difficulty. They had resisted being apprehended by the policeman Sarah had reluctantly brought along on her mission, and who had suffered a black eye in the conflict. They then unwisely resisted being apprehended by Sarah, only to discover that a burly young woman brought up with eight battling East End brothers was hardly likely to be discomfited by two adolescent shopwalkers. Fresh from her victory, Sarah had gone to Somerset House in search of Biscobys, either the widow Maria, or her three children. She had been unable to find birth records for the children, who might well have been born when the Biscobys were in Germany, and could not, therefore, discover their Christian names. A Peter Biscoby, possibly the son, had died in 1872 aged fifteen. She had been luckier with the marriage registers. A Maria Biscoby had married in Paddington in 1863, possibly a remarriage for the doctor's widow. Sarah had ordered the certificates for both events and would call to collect them the following week.

Her next mission was to commence enquiries about Mrs Pearson's missing maid Ethel, not from her employers, but from her fellow servants who were more likely to know her secrets.

❋

As Frances and Sarah breakfasted next morning they discussed the current position of all their enquiries. Gentlemen might have laughed at them and said that even supposing it was right for ladies to talk of business it was a foolish time and place to do so, but Frances always found that a refreshing pot of tea with an egg or a kipper helped her to order her thoughts, and who knew but that they might start a new fashion? Tom arrived bearing a small gilt-edged card with a note to say that Mr Darscot would be honoured to speak with Miss Doughty at ten o'clock.

Mr Darscot presented himself promptly at ten and what a neat, smart man he was; a little below medium height, active and trim, with the cheerful air of one who was the master of his own time and fate. His clothing showed a refined taste with just enough display to indicate wealth without descending to crude ostentation; a flower bud in his buttonhole, a small pin in his cravat, which might have been a diamond, and a light walking cane with a silver top.

He seemed anxious to ensure that his manners were fault-less, paying polite compliments about the charms of Bayswater, the elegance of its inhabitants, the delights of Westbourne Park Road in particular and the arrangement of Frances' apartments. He was not, he said, usually resident in the capital, preferring the air of the country, but found rooms at the Piccadilly Club convenient when in town to see friends or his solicitor.

As she listened to him, Frances felt quite like one of the chattering spinsters of Bayswater who never made the news, but absorbed it and passed it on across the teacups, with a satirical comment and a little embroidery to make it more interesting.

'I understand that you were acquainted with the late Dr Mackenzie?' she asked, after she had decided that ten minutes of polite nothings were quite sufficient.

Darscot's bright expression was clouded with just the right amount of sorrow. 'I was, and how shocked and sad I was to hear of his death, at such a young age.'

'I was told by his landlady, Mrs Georgeson, that you were at his lodgings that evening and created quite a disturbance.'

He nodded, ruefully. 'Yes, and I have been out of town ever since or I would have called upon the lady to apologise. It was unspeakably rude of me and I am deeply ashamed of my behaviour. I shall go and see her, and humble myself before both the lady and her good husband as soon as I have left here.'

'Perhaps, Mr Darscot, you could start at the beginning and tell me how you became acquainted with Dr Mackenzie?'

'Yes, of course. I have known him for about a year. There had been some talk at the club about the Life House, and some fellows thought it a good thing and others felt differently. Well, I could see the sense of it, and so I thought it might be something to invest in, maybe pay a small sum every month and then when the time came – well, hopefully that would not be for many years, but then I would enjoy – although that is not quite the right word – the benefits. So I went up and spoke to the man there – he was an orderly and he told me where I should go if I wanted to speak to Mackenzie, which I did.' Darscot toyed with the cane. 'This is where the story becomes – well, the thing is that Mackenzie confided in me that he was in desperate need of funds, not just the little tip I could send him each month, but a substantial amount. He asked me for a loan.'

'How much did he want?' asked Frances.

'£500.'

Frances was astonished. 'That is, as you say, a very substantial sum. Did he say why he needed it? And was it for his own personal use or for the Life House?'

'I was given to understand that it was for the business. Of course,' added Darscot sadly, 'I appreciate now, on giving it further thought, that might not have been true.'

'Did you lend it to him?'

'Yes, I did, and he promised that he would repay it in six months, but I am sorry to say that he did not. He asked for more time to pay, and as I was not especially pressed myself and respected the man, I agreed, but three months later he said he wanted more time again.' Darscot hesitated. 'The thing is – well, it's private business so I would appreciate your discretion – just recently I er – found myself in some temporary embarrassment over a slow-running horse and needing to find some funds very quickly. I don't believe in holding liquid cash in too large an amount, just a thousand or so for emergencies, I like my money to work for me.' He paused again and Frances believed he was trying to judge if she understood his meaning.

'I am familiar with the financial world,' she said. 'Please go on.'

'Well, not having the time, or indeed the desire, to sell shares or mortgage one of my properties, the best means I had of acquiring the money quickly was getting that loan repaid. So I asked Mackenzie for it again and he said he would pay me at the end of the week, but the days passed and the matter became more pressing and still he did not pay. I started to think he was intending never to pay. In fact I had the impression that he was deliberately avoiding me. So I was already somewhat agitated when I went up there and when Mrs Georgeson told me he had died I didn't believe her – I thought he had instructed her to say that to put me off, to give him time to run away. So I went up to the Life House in a cab and found that it was true; the man was dead. Of course I was very ashamed of myself, then. And as it so happened the very next day I had a windfall ...'

'A fast-running horse?' asked Frances.

'Oh yes, a real corker! So that was alright.'

'Mrs Georgeson thought you were a doctor,' Frances pointed out.

'I know, well I didn't want to explain I was calling on Mackenzie to collect on a loan. It was a delicate fiction.'

'May I ask if Dr Mackenzie ever mentioned his orderly Henry Palmer?'

'No, but there was more than one orderly wasn't there? I can't remember which one I spoke to when I went up there last year.'

'When you went to Dr Mackenzie's house that night, how did you travel?'

'By cab, it was a filthy night. My cabman had a horrid cough, wheezed like an old engine, and when I got down he drove off so I had to get another when I left.'

'Did you see anyone walking along the street, either when you drove up or when you left?'

'Not that I recall, I mean it was dark and foggy and even if there had been anyone I might not have seen them, or even recognised them if I had. This is about Palmer disappearing, isn't it? I read about it in the newspapers. Strange business. Have the police looked in the cellars? A lot of careless folk about – leave their trapdoors open all hours.'

'I believe they have done so.'

It was clear that Darscot could offer no useful information about Palmer, but now there were new questions to be answered; what financial hardships had induced Dr Mackenzie to borrow £500, and had Palmer been involved either in the transaction or the circumstances that had required the funds?

Frances also wondered if Doctors Bonner and Warrinder had learned of Mackenzie's financial difficulties either before or after his death, and decided between themselves that it had no connection with Palmer's disappearance and had made a compact to conceal it from her. She determined to tackle them on that point and be blunt about it. There was a time and a place for delicacy, but she felt that this was long past. Perhaps Mackenzie, desperate for money, had applied to dubious, even criminal sources for further loans and used Palmer as a messenger, and it was that errand which had led to the young orderly's fate.

CHAPTER FIVE

Once Darscot had departed, Frances sent a note to Dr Bonner saying that she would call on him that afternoon and wished to see him and Dr Warrinder together. She felt obliged to pace out Henry Palmer's new route north, though not with any real hope that she would learn a great deal, although as she travelled up the road, looking carefully about her, she reflected on the possible reasons for him going that way. Mary Ann had seen him stop to think and then turn to walk south in the direction of his home, and Frances had no reason to doubt this. But something had happened shortly afterwards, either he had met someone or seen something or it could even have been his own musings – an incident or just a thought had made him change his mind, and after a very short while he had turned and walked north again. Once again she wondered if Palmer had some mission to carry out for his employer. Supposing he had thought at first that this duty had been rendered unnecessary by Mackenzie's death, but then, after further reflection, decided that it still needed to be done.

Where had Palmer been going? There was the Life House itself, of course, but he had not been seen there again that night and there were several other possible places along the route: Dr Bonner's home; Dr Warrinder's home; Hemsley's lodgings and the canal. Then there was the Great Western Railway and Westbourne Park Station, which was not far distant, or the London and North Western Railway, and of course Kilburn police station, as well as many other possible places she did not as yet know about. For an instant, she had a vivid mental picture of the distraught man casting himself in front of a railway train and being mangled into tiny pieces, but that, she knew, would hardly have gone unnoticed even if the remains could not be identified. At the very least the artist for the *Illustrated Police*

News would have been there the very next morning to make a sketch. Frances also reflected deeply on the revelation that Dr Mackenzie had borrowed a large sum of money that he had then been unable to repay, and the interesting fact that he had borrowed it from a man he had just met and not his old friend. Was this because he did not want Dr Bonner to know the reasons for the loan? Had Mackenzie known, even as he borrowed the money, that he would never be able to repay it and did not, therefore, want to cheat a valued friend? He might well have had fewer qualms about reneging on a loan from a moneyed gadfly like Darscot. Clearly it was something about which he felt unable to approach a bank.

Frances was struck by another possibility – that Dr Mackenzie had not, as certified, died from an affliction of the heart, but had taken his own life, something his friends would naturally have gone to some trouble to conceal, both out of concern for his reputation but also to avoid any taint on the Life House.

For the meeting, which took place in Dr Bonner's study, Frances had decided that the two doctors should sit side by side, and that she should be facing them. It was not, as it transpired, necessary for her to ask for this since the gentlemen naturally arranged themselves as she wished. In the minds of the doctors, they would seem to be presenting a united position, two men of the world confronting one young woman. To Frances, it was her position that was the more powerful as she would be able to see any unspoken consultation that passed between them before they responded to her questions.

Dr Warrinder was a gentleman of about seventy with weak legs, a mild manner of address and a misty look in his eyes. Dr Bonner folded his arms across his rounded stomach and assumed his usual expression of self-satisfied content, something that Frances intended to puncture at the earliest opportunity.

'I have asked to meet with you, sirs, because I feel there may be matters which, for perfectly understandable motives, you have seen fit to conceal from me,' she began.

Dr Bonner's genial beam widened until it was almost a grimace, but Warrinder looked nervous and appeared to be inspecting the carpet for matters of urgent interest to him.

'I am sure,' said Dr Bonner, 'that you have been given every piece of information that could be of any interest regarding the disappearance of Mr Palmer.'

'You must allow,' replied Frances, 'that the only person who is qualified to judge whether a fact is of interest to me is I myself. Now then, it has come to my notice that during the last year Dr Mackenzie was experiencing severe financial anxiety, although the reasons for this are as yet unclear, and that he borrowed substantial funds from another party to meet his obligations. I would like to ask if he approached either of you gentlemen for a loan, or indeed if either of you knew the reasons for his difficulties.'

Bonner's happy smile faltered and then, under Frances' continuing gaze, vanished.

'If you are aware of anything affecting the good reputation of Dr Mackenzie, I can assure you I have no wish to broadcast it. I am no gossip, neither do I have any wish to do harm to the business of the Life House. My only concern is to discover Mr Palmer, hopefully safe and well. But if Dr Mackenzie was engaged in some unusual dealings he may have used Palmer as a courier, and that may have led to his disappearance.'

'He did not come to *me* for money,' declared Warrinder. He glanced anxiously at Bonner.

'Nor I,' said Bonner, unable to resist a brief warning flicker of the eyes towards Warrinder.

'But there is more to tell,' said Frances. 'I know it, and want only the detail.'

'Oh, this is too unfortunate!' exclaimed Warrinder. 'I really feel I can say nothing!'

'I have been faced with such silences before,' said Frances. 'They only serve to increase my suspicions and delay my eventual acquisition of the information I require. Dr Bonner, will you speak? I must remind you both that a man's life may be at stake.'

Bonner looked pained and after a long hesitation, glanced at Warrinder, who reluctantly nodded. 'Very well, but only if I have your promise that what I am to say will not go from this room.'

'You have my word,' Frances assured him.

Bonner took a deep breath. 'The financial affairs of the Life House have always been supervised by Dr Mackenzie, in consultation with Mr Hawks, the bookkeeper. Our bank account hardly ever holds a great deal of funds in any case. But about a year ago, I hosted a grand reception to which I invited the most eminent and wealthy men of Bayswater for the purpose of acquiring donations and new customers. It was a great success and a welcome amount of money flowed in.'

Frances thought that it was in all probability this event that had resulted in the discussion at the Piccadilly Club that had attracted Mr Darscot's attention.

'About two or three months later, I was considering the purchase of new beds for the Life House and improving the amenities in the chapel. I asked the bookkeeper for the balance held in the bank account and found, to my astonishment, that a sum had been extracted without my knowledge. No less than £500. Such an action requires the signature of two directors and when I mentioned it to Dr Warrinder he told me that Mackenzie had asked him to sign something, but he had been under the impression that the sum required was very considerably smaller.'

'£25, I think he said,' muttered Warrinder, miserably.

'I made discreet enquiries and established that the sum for which Warrinder had signed was actually £500, and that it had been extracted by Dr Mackenzie. I also found, however, that since taking the money, Mackenzie had been gradually replacing it. Only small sums at a time, but they were very regular contributions, and it was our belief that he had taken the money as a loan only, and was in the process of repaying it. We realised that whatever the reason for the money's disappearance it was a matter of such delicacy that Mackenzie had felt unable to raise the matter with us. We discussed it at some length and decided that we would keep a watch on the situation, but that as long as the money continued to flow back in, we would say nothing. We decided to treat it as a legitimate private transaction, and that was what we told Mr Hawks.'

'When Dr Mackenzie took the money, what was the actual balance in the accounts?' asked Frances.

'Oh, about £600 I believe. No more, certainly.'

'Do you think,' Frances asked, 'that the reason Dr Mackenzie took on so much additional work recently – the new patients, the pamphlets, the lectures – was for the purpose of repaying the money he took from the Life House?'

'I have no doubt of it,' said Bonner, 'and of course it shows the fundamental integrity of the man.'

'Do you think Mr Palmer knew about this situation?'

'I really do not know. I think it very unlikely.'

'And then …' said Warrinder with a sigh.

'And *then*?' exclaimed Frances.

Warrinder flinched and appeared to be blinking back tears. 'It was about a week before he died. Mackenzie came to me and asked me to sign another paper. He said he needed £20 for a plaque commemorating a valued patron of the Life House. I looked at the paper, but it was very hard to make out his writing. I said I was suffering terribly with pains in my finger joints and was unable to sign anything, and suggested he see Dr Bonner. He was – upset.'

'Only he did not come to me,' Bonner interjected. 'My eyes are sharper than Dr Warrinder's and he knew he could not dissemble with me.'

'He came back to me a few days later asking how my hand was,' said Warrinder, 'and I told him the same lie. What else could I do? If I had said anything he would have known that we suspected him. I spoke to Dr Bonner about it and he said he would find some way of approaching him and perhaps offer some help.'

'But before I could do anything the poor man was dead,' said Bonner.

'Well that is very interesting,' said Frances, thoughtfully. The private loan from Darscot and the extraction of funds from the Life House had occurred at approximately the same time. The two events had to be connected. Mackenzie, she surmised, must have needed £1,000 but the Life House account would only supply half that amount and he had had to go to Darscot for the rest. He undoubtedly did not dare take all the funds of the Life House in case other expenses caused cheques to be returned which would expose what he had done. His desperate attempt to draw more money from the Life House shortly before his death was, she felt sure, for the purpose of repaying Darscot's loan.

'Do either of you know why Dr Mackenzie needed the money he took?' she asked.

They looked at each other and she could see that neither had any clue as to the reason.

'Was he a gambler? A drinker? Did he belong to the Monmouth Club?'

'Not that I am aware,' said Bonner. 'I can't imagine where he would have had the time, not for that or any kind of vice.'

'Do you think,' asked Frances, 'that Dr Mackenzie's worries could have been connected in any way with that unfortunate business with Mr Erlichmann? I mean of course the incident in 1863 which you, Dr Bonner, failed to mention to me, but which of course I have since learned of. Why do you think Dr Mackenzie was receiving letters from Dr Kastner in Germany concerning Mr Erlichmann?'

'I really don't think that a brief disturbance that took place seventeen years ago can have anything to do with Dr Mackenzie's financial distress,' said Bonner, confidently. 'No, I think you may entirely rule out that line of enquiry.'

There was no doubt however, despite Dr Bonner's easy manner, that Dr Warrinder had found the question unsettling. 'Have you anything more to tell me, Dr Warrinder?' asked Frances.

'Oh no,' he said, 'nothing at all; really I have no more information – none.'

Before she returned home, Frances extracted a solemn promise from both men that they had told her all they knew and would not conceal anything from her in the future. She did not believe either of them.

It was, she felt, useless at this point to ask further questions of the two doctors. She needed more information which she could use to prise out what she was sure were bigger secrets. She wrote to Chas and Barstie, asking if they had heard of any financial issues in which Dr Mackenzie might have been involved, be it investments, gambling, loans made or received, or sending funds abroad.

Sarah's enquiries about Mrs Pearson's missing maid had revealed little. Being a ladies' maid the girl had thought herself rather above the other servants, which had not encouraged friendly conversation. She had attended to her duties diligently and there had been no male callers, neither had she ever mentioned a sweetheart. On half days and Sundays she did dress in a manner above her station, and some of the servants thought that she hoped to attract a husband in a better walk of life, but they had to admit that there was nothing flirtatious or indecent in her manners, and no suggestion that she had ever made eyes at young gentlemen. Mrs Pearson had been entirely satisfied with her services.

That evening Frances and Sarah both went to the little apartment on Golborne Road where they found Walter Crowe and Mabel Finch keeping Alice company, alternately holding her hand and fluttering anxiously about her. The young woman still looked frail and thin, but there were some dishes of food, broken pieces of pie and cake and buttered bread, which looked as though they had been sampled, and even a glass of milk. As soon as Alice spied Sarah, she picked up the glass with trembling fingers and took a sip. Alice had recently returned to her work in the shop, and although the long days spent on her feet and sometimes ascending steps to fetch down items from high shelves was telling on her strength, it did provide an occupation which was far better than moping at home, and also relieved her of financial anxieties. Everyone had been very kind to her, she said. Many of the ladies who called in asked her in the gentlest possible way if there was any news of her dear brother, and when she confessed there was none, expressed their sympathy and their unshakable confidence that he would soon be found. All had offered to pray for his safe return and several had suggested she employ that clever Miss Doughty, who could find out everything.

Frances did not feel very clever and she did not share the confidence of the ladies of Bayswater. Between herself, Walter Crowe and the Kilburn police every possible location in the area where Henry Palmer might have come to accidental grief or been the victim of a crime had been thoroughly searched. She wondered if he had left Bayswater – but where could he be? Scotland? Germany? Anything was possible.

Walter had a copy of the new edition of the *Penny Illustrated Paper*, which had, as he requested, printed an engraved copy of the portrait of Henry Palmer with an appeal for anyone who had seen him to come forward. Thus far he had received five communications, one of an indecent nature, which he refused to describe, the others suggesting that a man of vaguely similar appearance had been seen in places as diverse as Liverpool and the Isle of Wight. 'It is early days yet,' he said, hopefully. 'They will print it again next week if he is not found before then.'

Frances began to wonder if she had been wasting her time on strange fancies. She knew that she had them and sometimes they led her true, but it could be that this time she had gone astray. She was often thankful for the blunt, practical views of Sarah, which could bring her down to earth with a well-needed jolt. Had the death of Dr Mackenzie and Palmer's disappearance on the same day been a coincidence after all? Did Palmer have reasons to want to disappear that had nothing at all to do with his employer? Reasons so urgent that after carrying out his duty at the Life House he had run away as originally planned?

Although these questions had already been disposed of at their first meeting, Frances asked Alice if anything had occurred to her since then about her brother's state of mind. Had he been unhappy in his work? Had he been in debt? Had there been any quarrels? The answer to all these questions was in the negative.

Miss Finch, a pretty young woman who knew how to display her eyes and hair and rosy cheeks to their best advantage, was just as mystified as her friends. She had known Alice for a year, since they worked in the same emporium. Mabel hesitated to mention the precise nature of her occupation in front of Walter, but alluded in the most delicate way to ladies clothing of a variety which both supported and enhanced the female form. She and Henry Palmer had been on terms of a singularly pleasant friendship.

'I am sorry to ask questions which may be of a prying nature,' said Frances.

'Oh, please, do not worry yourself about that!' exclaimed Miss Finch. 'If anything I can say will help to find Henry – I mean Mr Palmer – I will help you in any way I can and I care nothing for my own feelings on any point.'

'Had you and Mr Palmer spoken of marriage?' asked Frances.

Mabel simpered in a way that Frances understood gentlemen found interesting. She often wanted to take girls that simpered and give them a good shaking, but then she was not a gentleman. 'Nothing of that kind has actually been said, I mean, nothing out loud, but sometimes, there is a look in a young man's eye that one can read. I think you understand me?' She simpered again and Frances hoped that Mabel could not read the look in *her* eye.

'Did you anticipate that the ocular appreciation shown by Mr Palmer would eventually be translated into words?'

Mabel smiled demurely. 'I thought it very probable that it would.'

'And if Mr Palmer had made you an offer of marriage, how would you have received it?'

Mabel smiled at Alice, who pressed her fingers encouragingly. 'I would have blushed a great deal and told him I must speak to my father, then I would have confided in Alice, made the dear man wait a week while I planned my trousseau, and said yes.'

'Do you think Mr Palmer anticipated that if he made an offer it would be accepted?'

'Oh, I really don't know,' said Mabel, coyly.

'No? What did his eyes tell you?'

If Mabel had been holding a fan she would have pressed it to her heart. 'I think he may have known the reply would be favourable.'

'What I am endeavouring to discover, Miss Finch,' said Frances patiently, 'is whether Mr Palmer might have been in a state of violent emotion; disappointment in love, or whatever it is that gentlemen feel at such times, and, if he had been, he might have felt the need to be alone with his thoughts. How does that strike you?'

'I can assure you, Miss Doughty,' Mabel whispered, 'that whatever the reason for poor Henry going away, it was not I who was the cause.'

Alice broke in. 'Henry did observe only recently that he thought Mabel had a very fine complexion,' she said.

Given the nature of Palmer's occupation, Frances thought that as compliments went this was not altogether an outstanding one. Nevertheless, it was clear to her that there had been a strong attraction between the two young people, and neither had anticipated anything other than a mutually happy outcome.

'Is there anything that any of you can recall Mr Palmer saying, not necessarily immediately before he disappeared, but at any time beforehand which suggested that he might have had some secret anxiety troubling him? Did he say anything about Dr Mackenzie or Dr Bonner or Dr Warrinder that you thought even slightly unusual? Had he been given a task to perform which was not part of his normal duties?'

They looked at each other. 'He said he thought Dr Warrinder's eyesight was getting worse,' said Alice, 'only the poor gentleman didn't like to admit it.'

'Did any of you ever meet Dr Mackenzie?' asked Frances.

Walter and Alice shook their heads, but Mabel said, 'I haven't exactly met the gentleman, but he did once give a lecture at Westbourne Hall. That was about three months ago and Henry – I mean Mr Palmer – was assisting him by selling pamphlets, and he suggested I go along and listen as he had a free ticket and then we might take a walk afterwards.'

'Was it a very interesting talk?'

'I can't say as I thought so.'

'How did Dr Mackenzie impress you?'

'He was a very sad-looking person. I think he must have been handsome when he was a young man. I was told he was under fifty, but he seemed a great deal older to me. And then only about a week before he died, I happened to pass him in the street and I knew him straight away though of course he didn't know me, but he was quite bent like an old man, very unwell and tired and his beard was quite grey. I was sorry to hear that he had died but I cannot say that I was very surprised.'

❧

The next morning Frances once again called at Mrs Georgeson's house in response this time to a note from Mary Ann, who had remembered what it was that was missing from Dr Mackenzie's room.

The maid was apologetic and spent some time twisting her pale head on its stalk, needing considerable reassurance that the delay in her memory was a matter of no moment at all, the main thing being that it had returned. Frances eventually gave her threepence, which seemed to help.

'Dr Mackenzie used to have this travelling bag,' said Mary Ann. 'Sometimes he gave lectures in places where he had to go by train and stay overnight, and then he used to put his requisites in it and take it with him. That was the thing that was missing.'

'Do you know if he took it with him when he went out that last night?'

'I don't know; I didn't see him go out. But Mrs Georgeson was expecting him back, so I suppose he wouldn't have taken it.'

'Dr Bonner didn't pick it up? He might have used it to pack up Dr Mackenzie's papers and books.'

'No. He put Dr Mackenzie's books and things in a box, and arranged for a carrier to take them. He didn't take anything away himself. But the bag used to be in the wardrobe at the bottom and I cleaned it out and I'm sure it wasn't there.'

'Can you describe it to me?'

'Oh it was an old thing, brown leather, very worn and scratched.'

'Did it have any initials on it? Would you know it if you saw it?'

'Not any initials, no, but the leather on the handle was split and he had bound it up with a bit of cord. So I would know it by that.'

Frances was puzzled. Had Mackenzie taken the bag from his home that night or had someone else removed it? If Mackenzie had taken it then it suggested that he had lied to Mrs Georgeson about his intention to return home and was instead intending to go away, perhaps to avoid his creditors. But the bag would then have been discovered at the Life House after his death, and no one had mentioned it.

Before she departed, Frances asked Mrs Georgeson if she knew whether Mackenzie had been carrying his bag when he left, but the landlady was unable to remember. As far as she was aware it was not in the house. She did, however, supply Frances with two missives that had recently arrived for Dr Mackenzie, one from Scotland, and the other she referred to as 'another of those foreign letters'. Frances at once recognised Dr Kastner's handwriting.

Frances hurried home, and Sarah was deputed to do what was required to extract the papers and then take the German letter to Cedric Garton for translation.

The letter from Scotland was, for reasons of bad handwriting, almost as indecipherable as the German one. It was addressed 'Dear Mackenzie,' and signed formally 'S. Stuart MD', and was written on the printed notepaper of the Aberdeen Hospital for Incurables, which Frances assumed was an establishment for the care of the elderly and dying. The first word, which she was unable to make out, was either Brook or Breck, or possibly even Brooker, and then it read 'did not arrive. Please advise.'

Frances made a careful note of the content, including as precise a copy as she could make of the word she was finding so hard to decipher, and resealed the letter.

While Sarah was on her errand Frances received a visit from Mr Gillan. Having promised not to disclose what she knew about Mackenzie's financial difficulties, she could say nothing about the matter, but Gillan could easily see that she was busy.

'Do you have further clues about Palmer? Do tell!'

'Well you may print that Mr Palmer, who was supposed to have been last seen walking south down Ladbroke Grove Road towards his home, was seen just a few minutes later walking in the opposite direction. Invite your readers to supply any information if they saw him that night. They will be detectives in their own easy chairs.'

Gillan smiled. 'I like that, and so will they.'

'And Mrs Pearson's personal maid is missing.'

'Mrs Pearson the banker's wife?'

'Yes.'

'Well, I can't say I'm surprised. The woman is a termagant. She has a new maid every quarter. I think she eats them.'

'Perhaps you might elaborate on that.'

He laughed. 'Only that she would try a saint, and her girls always run off, usually in tears. But how are you involved in this?'

'She has asked me to find the girl.'

'Now that *is* unusual. Why should she bother when there are more maids to be had?'

'She thinks the girl has been kidnapped. Or so she says.'

Gillan shook his head. 'I wish you every success with that one.'
Frances wondered why everything was so complicated.

🌺

Sarah returned with a sheet of paper on which Cedric's elegant
sweeping hand had rendered Dr Kastner's letter in English:

Dear Alastair
Following my last hopeful letter I am distressed to inform
you that Friedrich has suffered a relapse and the doctors hold
out very little hope for him. I have tried to speak to him
but he is beyond anything now, and even if he has changed
his mind he would be quite unable to say so or to give any
instructions to that effect. I have made every effort to discover the identity of the solicitor with whom the documents
were deposited but without success. And even if I was to find
the man, I have no power to restrain him from carrying out
his duty. If Friedrich was serious in his intentions the results
could be catastrophic, and you would suffer far more than I.
At this juncture I am at a loss to know what to do and would
welcome your advice.
Assuring you of my friendship always
Ervin

🌺

Frances sent a note to Dr Bonner saying she had more letters
for him to see, and was rewarded within the hour with an invitation to take tea. Sarah, meanwhile, determined to return to
the Pearsons' house.

When Frances arrived at Dr Bonner's front door, a bustling lady
with a vexed and ill-mannered expression pushed past her and
departed in a carriage. Frances was shown into the parlour, which
she found as elegant as many another person's drawing room, and
was introduced to Dr Bonner's assistant, Mr Fairbrother. That
gentleman was no more than twenty-two, tall, slender and neatly
dressed, and, thought Frances, well-named, as he was not only

exceedingly handsome but appeared to be quite unaffected by it. Needing no whiskers to conceal any weakness in his features, he was clean-shaven. While Frances admired a luxuriant moustache as much as the next woman, she could also appreciate faultless grooming, so much so that she began to find Mr Fairbrother's appearance curiously distracting. Not liking to be distracted from her errand, she took care to rest her eyes as much as possible on the less pleasing countenance of Dr Bonner.

The prim maid served tea and coffee and departed, her manner as starchy as her apron. Bonner said that he would have liked to introduce Frances to his dear wife, who was from home, having just departed on an urgent errand, but hoped that they might meet at a future date, as her command of the tea table was so much better than his own. His deep regret at Mrs Bonner's absence was tinged with a hint of relief.

Frances handed Bonner the German letter which he accepted as if unsure what to do with it, advising her that since he had written to Dr Kastner two days ago to inform him of Mackenzie's death, she would not be troubled with similar letters in future.

Mr Fairbrother smiled with great charm and said that he did not speak German, but if there was any service he could offer to assist in the matter he would be delighted and honoured to do so.

Bonner opened the Scottish letter and frowned as he read it.

'May I see?' asked Frances and did not wait for his assent, but peered at it like an inquisitive aunt. 'I see it is from a doctor in Scotland. It has always been of great surprise to me that in medical matters, where accuracy is so essential, the clarity of gentlemen's handwriting is often wanting. Why, the first word in this letter quite defeats me. Do you think it has any bearing on Mr Palmer?'

'I doubt it,' said Bonner. 'The word is a little hard to read but I suspect it may be "Books". It seems likely that Mackenzie sent Dr Stuart a parcel of books that he did not receive. I will write to him and discover what it was he requested and see that he has them.'

'I don't suppose either of you gentlemen, or Dr Warrinder or Mr Hemsley, has seen Dr Mackenzie's travelling bag?' Frances asked.

'Travelling bag?' said Bonner, '– oh, I know the item you mean – no, I don't recall seeing it.'

'You didn't find it when you looked through his effects after his death?'

'No, I'm afraid I didn't.'

'Was he perhaps carrying it on the night he died? Might he have brought it to the Life House and left it there?'

'I don't recall. I didn't see it.'

'But when he went away to give a lecture, and intended to stay overnight, if he called in at the Life House on his way there, he would have been carrying the bag on such occasions?'

'Yes, he would,' agreed Bonner. 'I will ask Dr Warrinder and Mr Hemsley, only they would have known it to be Dr Mackenzie's property and have handed it to me. Mr Fairbrother, you have not seen a travelling bag – leather, well-used?'

Mr Fairbrother regretted that he had not seen it.

'But surely,' said Bonner, 'Mackenzie would not have been carrying it that night as he had no intention of – oh I see what you mean. He might have been about to go away and not mentioned it to me. Oh dear! The foolish man! I am sure I could have helped him out of any difficulty if he had asked me.' The doctor shook his head. 'There could be a simpler explanation, I suppose. It was a very old bag, perhaps he threw it away.'

Frances thought for a few moments, then she presented Dr Bonner with her notebook and pencil. 'May I ask you to draw a ground plan of the Life House?'

He was surprised but complied, and as he did so Frances sipped her tea and smiled at Mr Fairbrother, who sipped coffee and smiled back. 'I read in the *Chronicle* ...' he began.

'Oh, the *Chronicle* spins a wonderful tale,' she replied.

'It says that you are the most celebrated detective in Bayswater.'

Frances found her cheeks becoming uncomfortably warm. 'I have been fortunate recently in solving some mysteries which have attracted a great deal of attention,' she said. 'But I have not courted notoriety, in fact I have sought to avoid it.'

'Oh, I am quite sure of that – I hear that you are greatly admired, not only for your skill, but for your discretion.'

'That is very flattering,' said Frances, with a quaver in her voice.

'Ahem!' interrupted Dr Bonner. 'I have completed the drawing.'

Frances took it from him, grateful for the interruption, and studied it carefully. 'Now this is the main entrance on the eastern side. And only the doctors and orderlies have the keys, and only they or medical visitors are permitted to enter that way?'

'That is correct.'

'I see that immediately on entering the main door, there is a small antechamber.'

'Yes, we call it the office. There is a desk where the orderly may sit to do his paperwork, a cabinet with surgical equipment and materials, and a place where coats and umbrellas and galoshes may be left.'

'Then an inner door leads from the office to the ward.'

'Yes, that again is locked and secure.'

'When Dr Mackenzie arrived on the night of his death, did he use the main entrance?'

'Yes, he did.'

'And you told me earlier that when he arrived you were in the ward with Mr Palmer?'

'I was.'

'So if Dr Mackenzie had been carrying his bag that night, would he have left it in the office, or would he have carried it into the ward with him?'

'Ah, I see what you mean. Yes, he would have left it in the office, and I would, therefore, have been unaware that he had it with him.'

'Now, there then followed the unhappy death of Dr Mackenzie. And you decided that as there was to be a viewing the next day, his body should be removed to the chapel. This may be reached two ways, it has its own side entrance for use by the public, and there is also a door connecting it with the ward. Is that connecting door kept locked?'

'Oh yes, always, and the same persons who have the keys to the main door are the only ones who have the key to it.'

'How was Dr Mackenzie's body carried to the chapel – did you and Mr Palmer use the connecting door?'

'Yes, we did. Palmer unlocked the door, brought out the wheeled stretcher, lifted the body onto it, and took him through. I was able to afford him only a little assistance. My old affliction, the gout, was especially troublesome that evening.'

'So once the body had been placed in a coffin, Palmer left to go to see Mrs Georgeson. Which door did he use?'

'He would have gone through the office as his coat was there and he had to sign the record book to show that his period of duty had ended. Oh I see – that is very perceptive Miss Doughty, and I had not thought of it – if Mackenzie had left his bag there, then Palmer would have seen it.'

'And if he *had* seen it, would he have known it belonged to Dr Mackenzie?'

'Oh, undoubtedly.'

'So he might have picked it up?'

'He might have done, but I would not have seen him do it as I was still in the chapel. But why would he do such a thing?'

'He might have thought that as he was going to see Mrs Georgeson he should take it to her. Of course, it ought to have been left for you as Dr Mackenzie's executor, but in the excitement of the moment Mr Palmer might not have considered that.'

Bonner nodded. 'That is possible.' Out of the corner of her eye Frances saw Mr Fairbrother, his coffee forgotten, the cup held suspended halfway to his lips, watching her with great attention.

'And then you were left alone in the Life House and some while later Mr Darscot arrived.'

'Yes. He said that he had come from seeing Mrs Georgeson, who had given him the sad news, and he wanted to see Dr Mackenzie's body. I told him there would be a viewing the next morning and if he could return at ten he would be very welcome, but he insisted and as he seemed very upset, I agreed.'

'And he both came and left by the chapel door, and never entered the ward or the office?'

'That is correct.'

'So,' said Frances, 'even if Mr Palmer had not taken the bag and it was still in the office, Mr Darscot could not have taken it; in fact, he would never have been in a position to see it was there.'

'Yes.'

'And the next person to arrive was Mr Hemsley? Through the main door?'

'Yes, only …' Bonner looked thoughtful.

'Only?'

'Really,' he said with a regretful shake of the head, 'this is so hard to remember, but I think that if Dr Mackenzie's bag had ever been in the office that night it was not there when Hemsley arrived. While I was waiting for him I felt rather – well, familiar as I am with the sight of death, it is different when it is an old friend and it happens so suddenly. I was upset and felt in need of a little stimulant, and there is a small bottle of brandy we keep in the office, for occasions when people feel faint. So I sat down at the desk and took a small quantity to steady my nerves. I recall seeing Dr Mackenzie's overcoat hanging up on the hook and thinking that I would never see him come through that door again. I am sure that if the bag had been there I would have seen it.'

Frances nodded. She could only conclude that either the bag had never been there or that Palmer had taken it, but neither Mrs Georgeson, nor Mary Ann, nor Mr Trainor had mentioned Palmer arriving at the house with a bag.

'Mr Fairbrother, you were not there at any time that evening?'

He put his cup down. 'No, I was attending a lecture.'

'Do you have keys to the Life House?'

'No, I go there in the company of Dr Bonner, who has keys.'

There was nothing more to be learned and Frances returned home and wrote a note to Inspector Gostelow at Kilburn police station, describing Dr Mackenzie's missing bag and saying that she thought Palmer might have been carrying it when he left the Life House. She also wrote to Walter Crowe with the information and Walter sent her a message very soon afterwards, saying that he would spend every minute scouring the area between the Life House and Mrs Georgeson's for the bag. Frances had very little hope that it would be found. The police had already searched very thoroughly for anything of note and found nothing, and a worn bag lost on the 21st of September was likely to have been found, emptied of anything of value, thrown onto a rubbish heap and taken away long ago.

Sarah had learned nothing more about Mrs Pearson's missing maid, and seeing that Frances was despondent about her lack of

progress tried to interest her in a slice of apple pie, without success. Frances took out her notebook again and studied it. 'What
do you think that word is?' she asked, pointing to her copy of
the illegible word in Dr Stuart's letter.

Sarah regarded it from several angles. 'Blowed if I know.'

'Dr Bonner thought it was "Books".'

Sarah stared at it again. 'No that's never "Books". Where's the
's' on the end?'

'Or just "book" I suppose.'

'If that's two 'o's in the middle, they're the funniest ones *I*
ever saw.'

'Whatever it was didn't arrive,' said Frances. 'A parcel of
some sort.'

'Or a person. That could be a name. Anyway, I don't see
why we're puzzling our heads over it. Why not write to this
Dr Stuart and ask him?'

'I will,' said Frances. She felt impatient for a reply and at first
considered sending a telegram, but on reflection decided that a
peremptory demand for information from a complete stranger
might not be received favourably and she would do better to
use a little more leisure in which she might both introduce and
explain herself. She took notepaper and ink and wrote a letter,
took it to the postbox and then ate a slice of apple pie.

CHAPTER SIX

t St Stephen's Church on Sunday morning the Reverend
Day once again appealed to the congregation for information about Henry Palmer. There was an atmosphere of
silent regret. All present would have done their utmost to help
if they could, but no one had seen the missing man and no one
apart from his sister believed him to still be alive. Dr Mackenzie's
bag was also described, with the suggestion that Palmer might
have been carrying it. Reverend Day said that he would be happy
to speak privately to any person willing to come forward, or ladies
might prefer to call on Miss Doughty. Once again there was no
stir in the congregation, no sign that anyone had guilty knowledge. After the service many people, strangers to Frances, came to
wish her success and commiserate with Walter, who told Frances
that the same announcements had been made in other churches
too, and someone, he was sure, must have seen something.

It was too cold and wet to take a walk after church, so that afternoon Frances and Sarah contented themselves with some reading.
The approved literature for the Sabbath was of a religious nature
and Frances often used that quiet time to think of her family, and
offer the kind of private prayers that she somehow felt were best
made when away from a crowd, but on that day she managed
to persuade herself that Friedrich Erlichmann's pamphlet, which
considered the nature of life and death, was acceptable material
on which to focus her thoughts. Sarah, who had located a booklet
describing cases of doubtful death in melodramatic detail, perused
it with interest and a complete lack of guilt.

❧

The enthusiastic journalism of Mr Gillan had ensured that it
was a matter of public knowledge throughout the whole of

Bayswater that Frances Doughty, the celebrated lady detective, was engaged in the search for the missing Henry Palmer. The result was the arrival of a flood of messages recommending actions that she had already pursued, theories which she had already thought of, suggestions as to where Palmer might be which emanated from the imaginative brain of correspondents who knew nothing of the man's character, offers to find him on the payment of a substantial sum of money, and recommendations for fortune tellers and mystics.

The information that Frances would take commissions to find missing persons had also excited a confidence that she was able to succeed, and she received several letters asking for her help and saw two new clients. The wife of a printer's assistant, who had not been seen for a week, had come to see Frances in a state of both emotional and financial distress. The woman was just twenty-nine years of age, had seven children and was soon to become a mother again. Her husband, who had, when sober, claimed to welcome the impending addition to his family, had, after a glass or two of beer, expressed the hope that either his wife or the child, or preferably both, would not survive the accouchement. The unfortunate woman sat in Frances' parlour and wept and Frances gazed at her hopelessly and wondered if she could ever find the man, and if she did, whether returning him to his family would be a good or a bad thing for them. Frances promised that she would do what she could and assigned the investigation to her eager assistant, who implied with a grim expression that the husband, once safe in the bosom of his family, would devote himself uncomplainingly to meeting his responsibilities.

A harassed mother next brought in a red-faced blubbering girl who said she had lost her puppy dog, Rosie, in Hyde Park, an animal that was apparently the most beautiful and affectionate puppy dog in the whole world. They seemed to expect that Frances would either spend all available hours running about Hyde Park in search of the dog, or produce it by some form of conjuring trick. Frances decided to ask Tom if he could look for it, half dreading that he would find it and then she would be expected to find every lost animal in Bayswater.

The only comforting event was the satisfactory conclusion of the enquiries on behalf of the gentleman of means into the *bona fides* of the applicant for a business partnership. Chas and Barstie had greeted the information Frances had provided with some hilarity, as the name was one of several aliases used by a rogue who was currently wanted for misappropriation of funds in more than one country. The personal description of the individual and his method of address confirmed the identification. They supplied a list of questions to be put to the applicant by Frances' client, together with the anticipated replies, which would entirely satisfy him of the attempted deception. They added, however, that the client was not himself without blemish and it was up to him, after discovering the applicant's true identity, whether he had him arrested, or entered into a profitable business agreement based on mutual understanding. Frances did not convey this last comment to the client, who was suitably grateful, and promised early and generous settlement of the account.

The next morning Frances received a visit from Walter Crowe, who was in a state of very great excitement. He was bearing a rank-smelling object wrapped in brown paper, and was breathless and perspiring. 'Miss Doughty, I think I have found it! Dr Mackenzie's bag! Of course, in all my previous searches I had not been looking for such an item – rather a – well, to be frank with you I had anticipated finding a body – but early this morning I was walking along the canal side near the gasworks and saw something floating and pulled it out, and here it is!'

Sarah took one look at the parcel and grimaced.

'Let us take it down to the basement,' said Frances, and Walter, who was cradling his find as if it was an adored infant, agreed and they hurried down the stairs and outside, where he laid it reverently on top of the ashbin. Frances was less excited than her visitor, largely because she half expected to see something that would not prove to be the missing bag, but as the paper was pulled back she saw a wet, crumpled object, scuffed and scratched brown leather, and a handle with its leather covering split and bound about with cord.

'Well Mr Crowe, you have done wonders,' said Frances, examining the bag. 'Have you opened it?'

He shook his head. 'No. Of course I wanted to, but I thought it would be best done before a witness.'

'I agree.' Frances' first impulse was to take the bag straight to Kilburn police station, but she was concerned that having handed it to the police she would be thanked politely and it would be taken away, and she would never see inside it. She opened the clasp, which to her surprise parted without any difficulty, and pulled the bag open. The contents proved to be very disappointing; a shirt and a change of underlinen, neither of which were new, and a gentleman's shaving requisites, a brush and razor of very inexpensive manufacture but apparently unused, and a pot of shaving soap, unopened. After a very thorough search, feeling all about the lining, hoping for a hidden pocket or compartment, Frances had to admit herself defeated. She asked Sarah to fetch a map and Crowe showed her exactly where he had found the bag.

'What do you think I ought to do?' he asked.

'I think that it should be taken to the police. Let them know where it was found and they will pursue their enquiries.'

Walter, who had hoped for some wonderful revelation, a startling clue that would lead him to the missing man, looked very despondent as he left.

'It seems to me,' said Frances, as she and Sarah washed the stench of the canal from their hands, 'that the items found in the bag show that Dr Mackenzie *was* intending to go away on the night he died, although it would only have been for a short while. Unless of course they are merely the things he always kept in that bag. For a longer absence he would have had to purchase more when he arrived.'

'But there was no money,' said Sarah.

'There might have been a pocket book with money in his coat. Or if there was money in the bag any thief could have taken it and then thrown the bag in the canal.' Frances brought out her map and studied it. 'It was found by the towpath alongside the gasworks. Hardly any distance from the Life House. If Palmer had taken it, there would easily have been time for him to throw it in on his way to Mrs Georgeson's. But why would he do such a thing? Maybe he was protecting Dr Mackenzie's reputation by taking something from the bag and hiding it.'

Sarah shook her head. 'Whoever put the bag there didn't do it the night Dr Mackenzie died. That bag has never been in the water a fortnight. It was a good stout bag once all right, but the leather is that thin and worn in places, it would have been more soaked than it was. A day or two at most I would say.'

Frances nodded. 'I hadn't thought of that. You're right.'

Frances later spoke to Inspector Gostelow about the bag, which Walter had duly delivered, and found that he had drawn the same conclusions as she about Mackenzie's intentions and the length of time the bag had been in the water. He had asked his constables to pay especial attention to the area where the bag had been found, but he didn't see that there was any more he could do. The bag and its contents, once dried out and restored to a more hygienic condition, would shortly be examined by Dr Bonner, as Dr Mackenzie's executor, and who might take it away with him if he liked. Perhaps, suggested Gostelow, he might have some observations.

Frances went home, troubled. There was something about the bag that did not fit with a comment made to her very recently and she could not determine what it was. She decided to occupy herself with other concerns as she often found that a special corner of her mind would address a problem without her being aware of it. That evening she and Sarah, wearing their purple sashes of membership, attended a meeting of the Bayswater Ladies Suffrage Society in Westbourne Hall, where Frances had been prevailed upon to make a short speech about her work as a detective, while Sarah was deputed to act as doorkeeper in case any disruptive elements sought admission. The ladies were told that petitions were being made to Parliament, and the meeting ended in a surge of tea-fuelled optimism that it was only a matter of months before the women of Britain secured the franchise.

When Frances awoke the next morning she had the answer. Mabel Finch had mentioned that Dr Mackenzie's beard had become grey. Why then had he been carrying all a gentleman needed for a shave?

As Frances and Sarah discussed the question of Dr Mackenzie's beard over breakfast a letter arrived from Aberdeen.

Dear Miss Doughty

I have never met Dr Mackenzie, only being acquainted with him due to some pamphlets he sent me about his work at the Life House. I was not expecting to receive a parcel of books from him. The letter to which you refer was written the day before I learned of his unfortunate death. He had recommended to me the services of an orderly, a Mr Breck, who he described as a useful, active and reliable person, and was due to appear here to take up his duties on Thursday 23rd September, but the man did not arrive and after waiting a week I wrote to Dr Mackenzie to discover what had occurred to delay him. I can advise you that as at today's date, Mr Breck has not appeared and I have heard no word from him or indeed anyone else in connection with the appointment.

Yours truly

S. Stuart, MD

So at least the mysterious word was now clear: 'Breck did not arrive.' But who was Breck? It was not uncommon for a young man who wanted advancement, even in the case of something as workaday as a position as hospital orderly, to seek out a respected man and ask him to write a letter recommending him. But it was remarkable that having gone to the trouble of asking for the recommendation and impressing Mackenzie sufficiently that the letter had been written, and the position secured, Breck had then failed to keep the appointment or offer any explanation.

It was possible that Mr Breck and his ambitions and failings had nothing at all to do with the case, but Frances was aware that coincidences were beginning to accumulate around the time of Dr Mackenzie's death in an unattractive muddle, and she did not like muddle.

Frances was not sure precisely how long it might take to journey from London to Aberdeen, which was a considerable distance, and could not, she thought, be easily done in one day.

She studied her railway timetables carefully. Since Breck had promised to be in Aberdeen on the Thursday she had to work backwards and determine when he had to leave London in order to reach his destination on that day. Would he have had to leave London before Dr Mackenzie's death?

The answer was that he did not; there were overnight mail trains from London on the Tuesday night, and fast trains early on Wednesday to both Edinburgh and Glasgow, from where he might have obtained another train, which would have reached Aberdeen in time to keep his appointment with Dr Stuart. So Breck could have been in London on the night Dr Mackenzie died, or even the following morning.

But did Breck even exist? Had Breck been a name assumed by Palmer as he hurried north for some purpose devised by Mackenzie? Had he set out as planned, and then met with an accident on the way, and was he now either an unidentified body or an unconscious man far from home, that no one would ever connect with the missing Palmer? Or was Breck another man entirely? Was he perhaps someone she had already met under another name? Hemsley? Fairbrother? She couldn't see either Bonner or Warrinder masquerading as a medical orderly; Warrinder would have found the task too strenuous and Bonner was too much the avuncular, yet superior, doctor to act convincingly in a subordinate role. Whoever Breck was, Mackenzie's death might have induced him to change his plans and not make his journey after all.

There was one other possibility – that Breck was actually Dr Mackenzie himself, adopting a new name, a new appearance, and applying for a post far from London and planning to flee north to escape his creditors, but dying before he could carry out his plan.

But, Frances asked herself, would a man of Mackenzie's character do such a thing? Would he run away and abandon the Life House, into which he had put so much of his time and dedication and money, simply over some personal financial difficulty, especially when he had understanding friends whose mercy he might have relied upon? And how was he planning to explain this sudden disappearance? The abrupt departure of a man in

Dr Mackenzie's position would have caused immediate comment and cast grave suspicions on the affairs of the Life House, which would then as a matter of public demand come under scrutiny. The resultant enquiry would reveal that a large sum of money had gone missing from the Life House bank account.

Frances concluded that if Dr Mackenzie had decided to disappear in order to evade his creditors, then he would have provided a reason that would not excite suspicion. For one distracted moment she wondered if the doctor had not actually died at all, but had only pretended to be dead. That would certainly have had the desired result, but then she knew that following his death the body had lain in the Life House for almost a week before burial. It had been seen by people who knew him, and he would have had to fool not only Palmer and Bonner but Hemsley, Fairbrother, Darscot, Warrinder, and all the other people who came to the viewing the following day. No man could hold his breath for long and it would not take a doctor of medicine to observe that the supposed corpse was alive. She could easily have seen through such an imposture herself. The trick would only work if all the diverse people concerned – from Dr Bonner to Mrs Georgeson – had somehow conspired to effect it, and that idea was quite ridiculous. Nevertheless, she felt she needed to discuss the question with both doctors and was busy composing a note when Sarah, who had been out on a number of errands, returned with the certificates from Somerset House, which were especially illuminating.

In 1863, Maria Biscoby, widow, aged forty-three had married Richard Warrinder, MD, widower. The death of her son, Peter Biscoby, had taken place at Dr Warrinder's home.

Frances' first reaction was to be very annoyed that this fact had been kept from her, but she reminded herself that she was in possession of a great deal of information which Doctors Warrinder and Bonner were unaware that she had, and there were some incidents in the past history of the Life House which they might not have wanted broadcast to the world. A visit to Dr Warrinder was, however, called for and she sent him a message announcing that she would soon call, making it plain that it was a matter of great importance and that she also wanted to speak to his wife. If she had not received a reply she would have gone to his house in any case, but a message came back agreeing to an interview.

The Warrinders lived on Ladbroke Grove Road in an establishment very similar to that of Mrs Georgeson but altogether better kept, if containing nothing that had been purchased new in over forty years. Frances was shown into the parlour where Dr Warrinder waited to see her alone and a great deal of fuss was made about fetching tea and offering her refreshments, but no mention at all was made concerning the absence of Mrs Warrinder. Dr Warrinder looked nervous as, thought Frances, he very well might.

'I am sorry to see that Mrs Warrinder is not here,' said Frances. 'It is essential that I speak with her and I believe I made that very clear in my letter.'

'Oh, I am very sorry, but my dear wife is – er …' he floundered.

'Detained elsewhere? Indisposed? Unwilling to speak to me? All three at once? Please be specific.'

He sighed. 'Oh dear!'

'Dr Warrinder, I think when I asked very particularly to have an interview with Mrs Warrinder you may well have suspected my reasons. Refusing such an interview will not make me depart unsatisfied. What sort of detective would I be if I were to be put off so easily? Rather it increases my suspicions that you have something to hide and doubles my determination to find it out. If it has nothing to do with the disappearance of Mr Palmer then I will not use the information. Now then, can you confirm that Mrs Warrinder is the former Maria Biscoby, widow of Dr Arthur Biscoby, and the very same lady who accused Friedrich Erlichmann of fraud?'

Warrinder nodded.

'Good, then we have some progress. I have been reading some very interesting literature of late. Dr Bonner was kind enough to give me a copy of Friedrich Erlichmann's *A Recovery From the Disorder of Death*, a Gothic romance worthy of Mr Poe. I have also been perusing the *Bayswater Chronicle*, in particular the editions that deal with the visit of Mr Erlichmann to Westbourne Hall in 1863 and your good lady's observations on his veracity.'

Dr Warrinder's hands trembled and he made no attempt to pick up his teacup. 'I can assure you, Miss Doughty, that my dear Maria is of a quite different opinion now. At the time of her unfortunate outburst she had been recently widowed and was, therefore, in a state of some distress. She was not, and never has been, insane, as was alleged.'

'In that case, Mr Erlichmann's comments upon her mental state were tasteless to say the least – if indeed they were his comments. Dr Mackenzie was acting as his translator at the time, was he not?'

'Ah, yes, he was.' Warrinder squirmed in discomfort. 'It was all – very – '

Frances waited. 'I am a busy woman, Dr Warrinder. I would be obliged if you would simply tell me what you have to say and then I will be spared the time and the trouble of finding it out, which I undoubtedly will do.'

He slumped sorrowfully in his chair. 'Maria was very upset at what was said and threatened to go to the law. She said that Erlichmann had slandered her and that the *Chronicle* had published a libel, and was afraid that if she was thought to be insane then her children might be removed from her care. Mackenzie didn't take it seriously at first, he said that the lady had no funds with which to go to the law, but then it transpired that the solicitor, Mr Manley, was a relative and he was very indignant about it and took the case for nothing. Maria refused to speak to Mackenzie and Bonner tried to placate her, but failed. So I saw her. I was a widower with three children of my own and in a comfortable position in life. Maria, an excellent woman in every way, had been left in a state of great destitution by her foolish husband, dependent on the charity of a cousin for the necessaries of life, unable to give her children the establishment and education that befitted the family of a medical man.'

'I do not doubt the very sincere esteem for Mrs Biscoby that led to your making her an offer of marriage,' said Frances, 'but may I take it that it was agreed that once you were married and the fortunes of her children secured, she would cease to criticize Mr Erlichmann and also take no action regarding the slander and libel?'

'I – er – believe that we may have discussed that.'

'I am glad that we are clear upon that point,' said Frances. 'And now, if you please, I wish to speak to Mrs Warrinder.'

'Oh, is that really necessary?' said Warrinder, apprehensively.

'It is. Please reassure her that I have no wish to reveal anything that might harm the reputation of either the Life House or its directors.'

Reluctantly, he rang for the maid and asked if Mrs Warrinder could be advised that Miss Doughty wished to speak with her. He took it upon himself to remain in the room, something for which Frances could hardly blame him.

Mrs Warrinder was a robust and handsome lady of sixty. She was dressed in a violet shade of semi-mourning with a discreet line of dark pearls at her throat, suggesting a loss that was distant either in relationship or in time. Frances, still in mourning for her father and brother, felt no great anticipation of the day when she might temper her sombre black with some other acceptable colour.

'My dear,' said Dr Warrinder, 'Miss Doughty gives us her word of honour that she will not say or write anything that will do harm either to us or the Life House.'

'My only interest is discovering what has happened to Mr Palmer,' said Frances.

'I will do all I can to assist you,' said Mrs Warrinder pleasantly. Such anxiety as existed in the Warrinder household appeared to rest entirely with her husband.

'It is my belief,' said Frances, 'that Mr Palmer may have been in Dr Mackenzie's confidence over some matters concerning either the Life House or his personal arrangements. He may have been instructed to carry out some task. Therefore, I need to know about anything that may have been causing Dr Mackenzie some concern or difficulty.'

Mrs Warrinder's eyes hardened very slightly and her lower lip stiffened. Mrs Warrinder had not forgiven Dr Mackenzie for the slander of 1863.

Frances tried to find a careful and delicate method of introducing the subject and failed.

'What can you tell me about Friedrich Erlichmann?'

The lady nodded slowly and a little smile graced her mouth. 'I assume, my dear,' she said to her husband, 'that I am to speak openly. This is on the understanding that what I am to say remains within these walls. Any attempt by Miss Doughty to reveal what I am about to tell will be met with the full force of the law.'

'I can promise you,' said Frances, 'that will not be necessary.'

'Very well. You know I suppose that my first husband, Arthur Biscoby, and I resided in Germany for some years, where he both taught and practiced surgery. Friedrich Erlichmann was a student of medicine, but he failed in his studies, largely due to idleness. He left the university and we thought we would hear no more of him, but then we found that he was attracting a great deal of attention to himself by telling the tale of how he had been brought back from the dead. We thought little of it at the time, as Arthur had no interest in such things, but then we discovered that a Dr Mackenzie had become interested in the story and believed it. Arthur went to see Mackenzie and warned him that Erlichmann was no more than a plausible rogue, that he had known him during the time when he was supposed to have died and nearly buried, and nothing of the sort had happened or he would have heard of it. Mackenzie refused to believe him, Arthur called him a fool and no more was said. Not long afterwards we returned to England where, sadly, Arthur passed away. I then heard that Mackenzie was raising funds to establish the Life House in Kensal Green, and that in order to do so he had employed Erlichmann to lecture and write pamphlets for him. Now, telling a tale to amuse one's friends is one thing, but telling lies to take the public's money away from them is, in my opinion, quite another. That was why I made my attempt at denouncing the man at his lecture. It is still my opinion that he is a fraud and a villain, but as my dear Richard has pointed out to me, there are many genuine cases of recovery from a state of doubtful death and it would be most unfortunate if the Life House was to suffer for the sake of one charlatan.'

'I understand,' said Frances. 'But of course, here in Bayswater the establishment of the Life House rested to a considerable extent on Mr Erlichmann's story and even if the public were advised of other cases, that fraud could well taint the entire venture.'

'Precisely,' said Mrs Warrinder. 'Personally I am happy that Richard's connection with it is very peripheral and that he has quite given up the practice of medicine, so that any collapse of the venture would not reflect on him. Dr Bonner would also not be deeply affected, but of course to Dr Mackenzie it was his whole life.'

'He would have been very anxious indeed if he had feared that Erlichmann might confess his guilt,' said Frances. 'Did he think there was any danger of that?'

'I think there has always been a danger of it,' said Mrs Warrinder. 'Erlichmann was a blabbermouth when in his cups. I have a dear friend from my days in Germany with whom I still correspond. She once informed me that Erlichmann had confessed that the story of his marvellous recovery was not as he had told it and that he felt some remorse about the whole affair. He claimed that he was led on by Mackenzie and the promise of wealth.'

'Oh, do not concern yourself, my dear,' said Warrinder, quickly. He turned to Frances. 'Erlichmann has not yet spoken after so many years and it is unlikely that he will do so now. He still makes a tidy income from his lectures and pamphlets, and is often wined and dined liberally on the strength of the story – no, no we have nothing to fear on that score. Nothing at all.' The fear in Warrinder's eyes was unmistakable. Frances realised that Dr Kastner's letters had been translated by Mrs Warrinder, the one person the partners could rely upon to keep the contents secret. The letters had mentioned documents deposited with a solicitor and Frances now saw why Dr Kastner had been so troubled. Erlichmann, struck by conscience in his declining days, must have left a confession of fraud in a sealed letter to be opened on the event of his death, catastrophic to the Life House's reputation and income. Reputation was a hard thing to measure, but money was not. If she had learned one thing from Chas and Barstie, it was that a mystery would often be solved by following the money.

'I understand that Dr Mackenzie left his interest in the Life House to yourself and Dr Bonner. Has it been valued?'

'Not yet, no.'

'And will you both continue to run the business?'

'Ah well, that is something Dr Bonner and I have discussed. It will be very hard, I fear, to continue without the dedication and energy of Dr Mackenzie. We have not yet decided what to do.'

Frances could see what the dilemma was, but said nothing. She thought about it all the way home. She saw now that, in addition to his earlier financial problems, the reasons for which she had yet to establish, Mackenzie had been facing the personal and financial disaster that would have resulted from Erlichmann's confession. A planned flight looked more and more probable.

Later that day, she found herself discussing her theories with Chas and Barstie.

'How much would you say the Life House is worth as a business?' she asked them.

'Hard to say,' said Chas, leaning back in Frances' easy chair and introducing his toes to the warmth of the fire. It was late and cocoa and biscuits had been provided as a soothing preparation for a night of dreamless sleep. 'It's not your normal kind of trade now is it? I don't quite have a picture in my mind of how it operates.'

'I would want to see the accounts,' declared Barstie. 'That and view all the assets. Do they have creditors? Almost certainly. What business doesn't? Do they have debtors? I expect they do. Do they have debtors who are cast-iron sure to pay? That might be another matter.'

'I would say,' said Frances, 'that given the nature of the trade, their customers are likely to be respectable people of means.'

'Well, that's no guarantee of liquid cash,' said Chas, 'far from it.'

'The biggest asset must be the Life House itself,' said Frances.

'No,' said Chas, 'the biggest asset is the land it sits on. I mean, who wants to buy a mortuary unless you're a mortician? That land when it was first purchased all those years ago was probably being used to grow cabbages and I expect Mackenzie got it for a song. Then, instead of building some nice cottages like a sensible man would, and renting them out, he builds a mortuary. Don't call it a Life House, we all know what goes in there.'

'Never saw one of the customers walk out,' said Barstie.

'And then what happens?' Chas continued. 'One minute the whole area is fields as far as the eye can see, next minute it's all houses. If Mackenzie didn't kick himself for missing an opportunity he was a fool.'

'So the land will be worth a great deal more than its purchase price?' asked Frances.

'Very much more,' said Chas, 'except the disadvantage to the man who is only interested in the land is that it's got a mortuary stuck on top of it.'

'If the business was simply broken up into assets,' said Barstie, 'any buyer would either have to convert the mortuary into something else, like a warehouse or a workshop, which most probably wouldn't be worth their while, or knock it down and build houses. All that trouble and expense would bring the price down.'

'What about the business as a going concern?' asked Frances. 'Would it find a buyer?'

'Now that's an interesting one,' said Barstie, 'because the new building around the cemetery has brought many potential customers into the area. I think if we were to see the accounts we might find that business is on the steady up and up. That being the case it might be quite valuable as it is, to the right person, if that person can be found.'

'It's finding the person that often doesn't come cheap,' said Chas. '*Is* it for sale?' he asked, with a sideways glance.

'Not at present,' said Frances. 'I just thought that with Dr Mackenzie's death, the current owners might think of it.'

'Now you have the inside view,' said Barstie, smiling, 'any little hints you feel free to pass on …'

'Of course,' said Frances, 'and if you should hear of anything …?'

'Our pleasure!'

Frances was troubled. For reasons that she was honour bound not to divulge, she knew that Bonner and Warrinder were aware that the business was in danger of imminent collapse, and if they put it up for sale as a going concern, it might be sold to a person quite unaware of the bombshell that was about to explode. She could not decide what she would do if that situation arose.

❧

Early the following day, Frances returned to Dr Bonner's house but was told that he was at the Life House, as was Mr Fairbrother. She decided that she might essay another visit and accordingly was soon knocking boldly on the door of the chapel. The door was answered by Mr Fairbrother who greeted her with some surprise but a very welcoming smile. Frances wondered if there was anything of significance in his eyes, but whatever the skill required to read such things it was one she clearly did not have.

'Miss Doughty – is this to be a professional call in connection with Mr Palmer, or are you here for a viewing?'

'I had not appreciated that there was a deceased person here to be viewed,' said Frances. 'It is a professional call.' He stepped aside and she entered.

There was one coffin laid out on a trestle and in it the body of a lady who had once been rather plump, but whose face was shrunken and fallen, grey and blotched. She was packed about with great swathes of fresh cut flowers, and there were candles burning on the little altar exuding a sickly scent, and a great deal of carbolic. Her jaw was bound in a white cloth, but not so tightly that she would be unable to speak supposing that there was any life remaining, which, as far as Frances could see, there was most decidedly not. As a result the jaw sagged open, revealing a dark cavern of a mouth from which a foetid odour was escaping.

'It is not very pleasant, I am afraid,' said Mr Fairbrother, 'and unlike the undertaker we are not permitted to occlude any place where the natural functions of life may be apparent, neither are we to paint the face to make it appear as in life, as that might confuse matters.'

'I think I knew this lady,' said Frances. 'She was the daughter of a milliner and had a very bad husband. How did she die?'

'She fell down in a fit. I was told she was in love with her footman and lost her wits. Or some say that she lost her wits and only then did she fall in love with her footman.'

Frances thought it had been a close run thing. 'I was wondering how well you knew Dr Mackenzie,' she said.

'I worked under his supervision a number of times. I have only been in London a month and during that time I have mainly been studying with Dr Bonner.'

'When did you last see Dr Mackenzie?'

'Alive, you mean? The day before he died. I was here with Dr Bonner and he called in. I must say, he looked very unwell but it was not my place to say anything. Even in the short time I knew him I saw a decline in his energy. About a week before he died he arrived here having left his keys on his desk at home and was too exhausted to go back for them. I offered to order him a cab but he wouldn't hear of it, so I sat him down and gave him some brandy.' He shook his head. 'Poor man. At least he took my advice and rested for two or three days before he returned.'

'I regret that I never met him. Can you describe him to me?'

'He was quite tall but walked with a slight stoop, of a moderate build, tending to thinness, and with grey hair and whiskers.'

'Do you know where I might see a portrait of him?'

'Yes, as it so happens there is one which Dr Bonner has had placed in a frame to be hung here in the chapel as a tribute. It is in the office now – I will fetch it.'

Frances rather hoped that he might pass through the ward on his way to the office, affording her a glimpse of the interior, but he merely smiled as if he knew what she was thinking. He rapped three times on the connecting door, but did not open it, and left through the side door. The wheeled stretcher was in its usual place, but Frances leaned across it and gently tried the handle of the connecting door. It was locked. Fairbrother returned a minute later with the portrait.

'They do not yet entrust you with keys?' asked Frances.

'No, I am not employed here permanently. I had to alert Dr Bonner to admit me by the main door just now. In any case, we never open the connecting door while there is a visitor in the chapel. Prying eyes, you know.'

Frances studied the picture. It was of a man facing the camera, his head set well on his shoulders, his gaze even, and his eyes clear and untroubled. There were a few wrinkles at the corners of his eyes but they were not unattractive, and she could imagine how he had smiled them into being. Mackenzie had a full luxuriant beard, moustache and side-whiskers. He looked very much like a man in his late forties, but she thought that he might appear younger if he was clean-shaven.

'I believe it was taken a year ago,' said Fairbrother. 'Dr Mackenzie had become thinner of late, but this is a good likeness.'

Frances felt sure that the shaving materials found in Mackenzie's bag were items of such cheap manufacture that they could hardly have been intended as a gift. They must, therefore, have been for the doctor's own use. It now seemed probable that on the evening of his death Mackenzie had been on his way to Aberdeen, intending to shave off his beard and moustache before he arrived as Mr Breck. There might have been money or a ticket in his bag, both of which could have been stolen, either by Palmer or, more probably, a thief who had attacked Palmer and taken the bag. Perhaps the thief had become alarmed at hearing the bag described in sermons all over Paddington and decided to dispose of it.

'And now, if I may, I would like to speak with Dr Bonner.'

'I have already mentioned that you are here – he said he would come and see you in a moment.' He smiled. Frances smiled back. She hoped it was not a simper.

Dr Bonner arrived before they ran out of conversation; he was walking with a pronounced limp and leaning on a stick. 'My old affliction,' he explained with a pained smile. 'It is of no moment. What can I do for you, Miss Doughty?'

'I have been speaking to the Kilburn police regarding Mr Crowe's discovery of Dr Mackenzie's travelling bag.'

'Yes, extraordinary thing, that. I can't imagine how it came to be where it was. I took a look at it, and it was undoubtedly his. You may come and see it if you like, before I dispose of it, but there is nothing of any interest in it I assure you.'

'My understanding is that it contained only such items as a gentleman might carry if he was going to be from home for a night, but there was one thing I was told which engaged my curiosity.'

'Oh?'

'Dr Mackenzie was carrying shaving materials, but as I can see from his picture it was not something he had employed for many years, if ever.'

Dr Bonner paused as if the thought had never occurred to him. 'Do you know, Miss Doughty, you are right. Of course, if I am away I carry my shaving things as a matter of course and so did not think when I saw them in Mackenzie's bag, but now that you mention it, it *is* very strange. A man might decide to shave his beard for many reasons, to look younger perhaps, or at the whim of a lady.' He nodded. 'Yes, maybe there was a lady in the case. He might have been going to see her. We shall never know now.'

'Have you been contacted by a lady about Dr Mackenzie?'

'No, I have not,' he admitted.

On her way home, Frances realised to her annoyance that she had missed a valuable opportunity. She had been so eager to confront Dr Bonner on the question of the shaving materials and display her cleverness to Mr Fairbrother that she had not thought it would be better to ask to see the contents of the bag before revealing that she already knew what they were. If Dr Bonner had been complicit in any plan of Mackenzie's he might have removed the suspicious items before showing the bag to her. Even if he had, and she had challenged him, he would almost certainly have found a way of talking himself out of the anomaly.

CHAPTER SEVEN

hen Frances returned home, a gentleman was waiting to see her, presenting a card that announced him as B.H. Carmichael, MD of Carlisle, and clutching a copy of the *Chronicle* open at an article about Henry Palmer in which Mr Gillan had announced the involvement of Frances in the search.

Dr Carmichael was a tall, impeccably dressed gentleman of about fifty, with auburn hair, a well-trimmed beard and small gold-rimmed spectacles. Like so many of the people who sought Frances' assistance, he had the reserved, anxious look of someone who was about to speak of things he would rather have spoken of to no one.

He looked worriedly at Sarah, who sat nearby with a stern face like a great immovable brick edifice.

'My trusted associate, Miss Smith,' Frances informed him.

He accepted the description without comment and unfolded his newspaper. 'I read this morning,' he said in a pleasing, light Scottish accent, 'that you are looking for Mr Henry Palmer, and I wanted to ask what progress you had made, and whether you believe his fate is connected in any way with that of Dr Mackenzie?'

'Before I reply to your enquiry,' said Frances, 'may I ask what your interest is? Are you acquainted with either Mr Palmer or Dr Mackenzie?'

'I have never to my knowledge met Mr Palmer,' he said, 'but as a young man in Edinburgh I studied medicine with Mackenzie and knew him well. We did not maintain a correspondence and neither did I take any note of his career after he departed for Germany, and I myself have also travelled extensively. I recently learned that Mackenzie has established a Life House here in London and was a man of some moment, held in respect by all.'

Carmichael was silent for a brief interval and appeared to be labouring under some emotion, and then he put his hand in his pocket and extracted a cameo brooch, which he opened. It contained a faded portrait of a pretty young woman and a curl of auburn hair. 'This is my sweet sister Madeleine,' he said. 'Her memory is very dear to me, and I will not have a word whispered against a lady who was when on earth no less a blessed angel than she assuredly is now. I must tell you, Miss Doughty, that Mackenzie behaved towards my beloved sister in a most scandalous and reprehensible way, and his actions hurried her into an early grave.'

'It is rare to hear anyone say a word against the honour of Dr Mackenzie,' said Frances, surprised.

'None of his associates in London know what kind of creature he was,' said Carmichael, 'and of course he severed all his ties in Edinburgh when he went abroad. There was nothing I could do. I had not one shred of proof against him, or I would have had him pilloried or hanged or even called him out, since I care nothing for myself in this matter. But without evidence, I was helpless.'

'Such is sometimes the case with immoral persons or malefactors,' said Frances. 'Most are very foolish and careless, and leave evidence that can easily be found and brings about retribution, only a very few are clever and can avoid blame. But Dr Mackenzie, assuming that your suspicions are correct, cannot now suffer for any harm he has done. Take comfort from the fact that he can never again cause such unhappiness. Also, since what he did was so long in the past – the actions perhaps of a thoughtless youth – it seems that he may have learned to repent them and tried to make amends by selflessly serving others. He may, if one takes his life as a whole, have done more good than harm.'

'But what is that to me?' said Carmichael. 'These people to whom Mackenzie has been a benefactor are not my kin, not even my friends; they are strangers to me. I can think only of my poor sister.'

'I am sorry that you continue to feel such pain,' said Frances, who naturally wished to learn what it was Mackenzie was supposed to have done, but knew that Carmichael was unlikely to tell her, at least on a first interview, 'but can you advise me what it is you wish me to do? You have, as you say, no evidence against Dr Mackenzie and what profit would it give you now even if you could damage his reputation? He is beyond all punishment and your sister's name would be defiled. You might also harm the Life House, which is managed by gentlemen with whom you have no quarrel.'

'I have abandoned any thought of Mackenzie, who has gone to his just punishment,' he reassured her. 'I admit that it angered me greatly when I learned that he was so well regarded and I wanted more than anything to drag him into the mud where he belonged. I thought that if I could only prove what I knew then I might be able to manage things in a way that showed my dear Madeleine to be the spotless victim that she was. But I was powerless.' There was another long silence. 'My older sister, Ellen, is the wife of a medical man who lives in Kensington, and she is the guardian of some treasured mementoes of Madeleine. These are not items of anything more than sentimental value, trinkets and some prettily bound books.

'Three weeks ago Ellen wrote to me in the most terrible distress. Her health has been declining in these last few years and she has often sought comfort in Madeleine's books. Her husband is frequently from home and she is cared for by a nurse. Unfortunately, she discovered one morning that the nurse had gone and so had a set of silver snuffboxes and Madeleine's books, including a journal. I can only imagine that the girl thought because of the bindings they were of some antiquity and therefore valuable. I hurried down to see Ellen at once. It was then that she confided in me that Madeleine had written in her journal of certain matters that were so hideous that she had never discussed them with me or anyone else. Her one concern was to keep the memory of our sister pure, but the thought that this dreadful material had found its way into the hands of criminals was so upsetting that she was almost too ill to speak.

'The snuffboxes were recovered from a nearby pawnshop, but there is no trace of the books or, most importantly, the journal. If only Ellen had told me of it before! If I had had the management of the journal I would have ensured that it was used with great care to secure an action against Dr Mackenzie while my sister's name remained without a stain, but a crude blackmailer would have no such concerns.'

'But surely now that Dr Mackenzie is dead a blackmailer can have no further use for it?' said Frances.

'I hope not. But I want to ensure that it is found and placed in my keeping. It was my sister's, something she has touched and where she has revealed her soul, and that alone makes it precious to me. And of course, I have no wish for another person to see it, a person who never knew Madeleine and will judge her harshly. I intend to lock it away safely and so preserve her character.'

'And you want me to find it?'

'Yes. I will go to any trouble, any expense!'

'You do appreciate, Dr Carmichael, that if I discover that a blackmailer has been plying his or her unpleasant business, I will have uncovered a crime. Do you expect me to say nothing about it?'

He stared at her. He was clearly so focused on his own dilemma that he had not considered other factors and, thought Frances, cared nothing for them. 'It is not a crime simply to possess a journal,' he said, 'only to use it for a wrongful purpose. It would be very hard to prove that the person who has it now is the thief, or that any attempt at blackmail has taken place, especially as the victim is now deceased. It would be best if the journal was simply found and passed to me, and no more said.'

'We may of course find that the journal has been destroyed, unless the blackmailer finds something else of value in it, such as the means of extracting money from another person.' Carmichael looked aside as if embarrassed. '*Is* there anything else in it?' pressed Frances. 'Is there something that perhaps has a bearing on another individual? Yourself perhaps?'

'I have committed no crime, my conscience is clear upon that point,' said Carmichael stiffly. 'I do not, as so many do, claim to have led a perfect life. Men are the morally weaker sex, and there may be things I have said and done which I cannot in all honesty be proud of, things which my dear sister, too pure to understand, may in her innocence have mentioned. I assume that I do not appal you and hope you will not judge me for my weaknesses. You are, it has been said, the very epitome of sympathy and discretion.'

'Do you know who might have the journal?' asked Frances.

Dr Carmichael looked faintly shocked. 'Oh Miss Doughty, I have no connection with persons of that sort.' It was apparent that he thought Frances did.

'Very well, I will make some enquiries. On what date did the theft occur?'

'It would have been on the 14th of September, but it was not discovered until the next morning. The maid had departed overnight.'

'Has the thieving nursemaid been apprehended?'

'The police are pursuing the case, but she has vanished like a spectre in the fog. We are sure that the name she gave was false.'

'And that name was …?' Frances enquired, pencil poised over her notebook.

'I am afraid I cannot recall it.'

'Then I had best interview your sister Ellen.'

'I am sorry to say that she lies dangerously ill, but she has already said all that she knows. I do not wish the family to be disturbed.'

'You leave me very few avenues of enquiry, nevertheless, the case interests me and I will see what I can do. Should you be approached by someone wanting to blackmail you or offering the journal for sale, you will of course let me know at once. I will require a full description and will then be able to arrange for an unobtrusive person to follow them.'

Frances glanced at Carmichael's card, which gave only his address in Carlisle. 'You may reach me through the Piccadilly Club on Porchester Road,' he said.

Frances had been making enquiries about the Piccadilly Club and learned that it was a place mainly frequented by foolish young men who had too much money and wished to be relieved of it, from which she supposed that a great deal of private wagering was conducted there. Carmichael did not, however, look like a betting man. 'When did you come to London?' she asked.

'I arrived on the 19th of September.'

'That was two days before Dr Mackenzie died. Did you make any attempt to contact him?'

'No, my hands were tied as the journal was missing. He was, I believe, unaware that I was even in London.'

'How long do you intend to remain?'

'For some little while. I am applying for some medical posts here and if I am successful I will make London my home.'

The financial arrangements having been settled, Carmichael was about to leave when he observed, 'I must confess when I heard that Dr Mackenzie was dead I did not believe it at first. I thought he might have fled and put another body in his place, to avoid being blackmailed over the journal.'

'Did you go to view the body?'

'I did not discover until later that there had been a formal viewing. But when I heard that he had died – the news was all over Bayswater the morning afterwards – I immediately applied to make a tour of the Life House and was able to do so with a group of other medical men on the following day. I thought it wise, however, not to reveal my interest. It was unpleasantly warm and the air was quite foetid. There were three corpses there, I recall; one very elderly female, at least a day past her proper burial date in my opinion; the other two were men in their middle years, but since I had not seen Mackenzie for some time I was unable to assure myself which of those he was, and it was not appropriate to ask.'

When Dr Carmichael had departed Sarah observed that she didn't like the look of him, but since Sarah did not like the look of any man, this was not unusual. 'Did you believe his story?' Frances asked her.

'Well,' said Sarah, 'I don't think he would ask you to find something that didn't exist, because there wouldn't be much of a reason to do that, but if he's telling you the truth about how his sister was too good to live, then I am an elephant in the zoo – which I am not.'

❧

Frances was used to the fact that clients would come to her and, for reasons of their own, deliberately conceal facts that would greatly assist her in the solution of their difficulties. Often, the conundrum to which they required a solution was not the one they stated, but something else again, something they had chosen not to impart to her. She would commence her enquiries based on what she had been told, but soon enough other facts would emerge which would take her back to the client and demand that she be told what had been hidden. Sometimes this would take several visits. Dr Carmichael was an ineffectual dissimulator, but she felt that she had for the moment extracted from him all that he was likely to tell her.

For some months Frances had been in the habit of retaining copies of the *Chronicle*, which other persons might have used to light fires, for the valuable information contained therein. She carefully studied all the newspapers that might have mentioned a theft of snuffboxes from a Kensington doctor, but found nothing. This was not conclusive since the crime might have been regarded as too trivial to mention, or indeed have never reached the notice of the press. She had no connections with the Kensington police, who were supposed to be pursuing the thief, but thought it very possible that Mr Gillan did, and composed a letter asking him if he knew anything about it. She was hampered by not knowing the name of the doctor, which Carmichael had been careful she should not know, but she could pursue that aspect if necessary. She had overcome larger obstacles.

More importantly there was the question of blackmail. If the journal existed, and Dr Carmichael's obvious anxiety strongly suggested that damaging material of some nature certainly did, then, despite Dr Mackenzie's death, it remained of value to a blackmailer. It was possible that Mackenzie had been approached shortly before his death, adding yet one more reason why he would want to flee London. As yet, Carmichael had not been approached by a blackmailer. Was the journal being held in some secret place, waiting for the moment when it could be used to most advantage? Or was it even now on the market, being passed from grubby hand to grubby hand?

Frances wished she might have been able to enter the Piccadilly Club and keep a watch on anyone approaching Carmichael. The only person she knew who was already a member was young Mr Darscot, Mackenzie's creditor, but he seemed an unsuitable person to engage as an agent, being without the necessary cool head. She smiled to herself as she imagined young Tom a little more grown up and in a smart suit, being dispatched to join the club and act as her eyes. While she waited for him to gain some height, someone else would have to be employed and she at once thought of Chas and Barstie, who would also be well attuned to anything with a scent of money.

Not so long ago they would not have been considered as members of the Piccadilly Club, having no fixed abode in Bayswater or possibly anywhere else, and no attire – at least none un-pawned – in which to make a suitable impression. The recent election and its business opportunities, while not actually making them rich, had elevated them and brought them new friends, and they would see the advantages to be gained by making the acquaintance of men of notable fortune and little sense.

The other issue she felt she needed to pursue was more sensitive. Had Dr Carmichael had a sister called Madeleine? Had this young woman of impossible virtue really expired in saintly odour many years ago? If she had, what was the nature of her death? Any questions she might ask on this subject might, however, alert someone like Mr Gillan to the fact that there was more than ordinary interest in the matter and risk exposing the very matters that Carmichael wanted kept private. The records at Somerset House would not assist her as they included only deaths in England and Wales, and not Scotland.

Frances' other cases were progressing more satisfactorily. The missing husband had been traced sleeping off the effects of overindulgence in beer in a cell at Paddington Green police station, from which Sarah claimed him. She had then carefully explained to him the responsibilities of parenthood, giving him to understand that were further explanations required she would be willing to provide them. He was then returned, in penitent mood, to his wife and offspring, of which there were now eight. Frances did not have the heart to charge for her services and authorised Sarah to provide a gift towards the layette, to be placed in the new mother's hands only.

Rosie, the puppy dog, was discovered on the following day by Tom, being teased by a gang of street urchins who demanded five shillings for their prize. Tom offered them a shilling and while they debated this disappointing fall in their expectations, he snatched up the dog and ran all the way to Frances' rooms. Rosie, unharmed but very dirty, was smartly removed by a stern-faced Sarah who washed the protesting animal thoroughly, tied a pink ribbon around its topknot and took it back to its delighted owner.

❋

This activity by Frances' assistants, for which she ensured they were well remunerated, gave her time to reconsider the position of Dr Mackenzie in some detail. A year ago he had taken £500 from the Life House by deception and borrowed another £500 from Mr Darscot. Frances now thought it probable that the sums were required to pay a blackmailer, who had threatened to expose Mackenzie's involvement in the Erlichmann fraud, or his unsavoury past in Edinburgh, or both, or even some other transgression of which she had no knowledge. Whatever the reason it was sufficiently sensitive that he had felt unable to ask his friends for help, even assuming that either could have conjured up £1,000. Mackenzie had worked himself to exhaustion in an effort to repay the Life House, but pursued by Darscot for his loan, had tried once again to dupe Warrinder into allowing him to extract funds from the business, and failed. He had then received Dr Kastner's letters regarding the immediate danger posed by Erlichmann's illness, and had also quite possibly been threatened by someone with Madeleine Carmichael's journal. Mackenzie had been facing not only financial disaster, but a catastrophic descent into ignominy and shame. Despite all this, he still felt impelled to protect the reputation of the Life House and would not wholly abandon it. He must have hoped that Erlichmann might rally, or that his letters would not amount to proof of wrongdoing, or that Kastner might be able to suppress them.

Frances had earlier rejected the idea that Dr Mackenzie had feigned death because of the impossibility of fooling all the observers, and the unlikelihood of so many disparate persons being engaged in a conspiracy, but on reflection she could see that there was another much simpler plan. Dr Mackenzie had had an accomplice. All it required was one trustworthy, efficient and loyal helper, and there were only two people qualified for that role – the missing Henry Palmer and Dr Bonner.

Frances went to see Bonner again and this she knew was going to be a difficult interview. It was never a pleasant thing to accuse a person, especially a man in Dr Bonner's position, of planning or even carrying out an underhand and possibly criminal action, but it was not the first time Frances had done such a thing and she reflected that it was unlikely to be the last.

CHAPTER EIGHT

There were, thought Frances, many stages of an investigation that went on for any length of time and they could be measured by the reactions of people she was obliged to interview on several occasions. In some cases initial suspicion and discomfort transformed after a time into hope and then gratitude. Those such as Dr Bonner, however, who anticipated that they would only need to speak to Frances once, were all generosity and good humour at their first meeting, helpful but serious at the second, surprised but polite at the third, irritated though still co-operative at the fourth, openly annoyed at the fifth and frightened at the sixth. This was the sixth time she had interviewed Dr Bonner.

Frances had no proof of what she was about to say and indeed was not sure if she believed half of it herself, rather she had determined to say something as controversial as possible in the hope that she might provoke some reaction and thereby arrive at the truth.

'Dr Bonner is busy,' said the starchy maid at the door.

'I doubt it,' said Frances. 'Please don't be offended, I know you are only saying what you have been instructed to say, but really it is pointless for him to dissemble. I intend to see him today and will not be deflected.'

'Dr Bonner is busy,' repeated the maid, tonelessly. 'I will say that you have called and he will make an appointment when he is ready to see you.'

'Tell him,' said Frances, 'that I know what he did.'

There was a palpable frozen silence.

After a few moments the maid, without a word or even a change in expression, turned on her heel and proceeded upstairs to Dr Bonner's consulting room. Frances waited and was rewarded a few minutes later by the return of the maid who, staring at some point to the right of Frances' face, told her she could go up.

Dr Bonner's normal manner was under some strain and he greeted Frances with forced politeness observing that their interview would, due to extreme pressure of important work, necessarily be brief. Frances looked about her and saw no evidence of any work, important or otherwise.

'I was mystified by the message you sent to me via my maid, which I feel must have become somewhat muddled in the repetition,' he said, sinking into his chair with a slight wince of pain and propping one foot on a cushion.

'That is possible,' said Frances, generously. 'What I would like you to tell me is where is Dr Mackenzie?'

Bonner's head jerked back in astonishment and after a bewildered moment, he gave a short laugh. 'Miss Doughty am I hearing you correctly? Dr Mackenzie is dead and in his coffin.'

'Is he?'

'I can assure you he is. Whyever would you think differently?'

Frances maintained her composure. 'It is my belief, indeed I am certain of it, that Dr Mackenzie intended to leave London and assume another identity, not only that, but he made arrangements to have people believe him to be dead. He cannot have achieved this alone.'

Bonner continued to treat her words with amusement. 'On that point at least we are agreed. It would be impossible to achieve alone.'

'Precisely.' Frances allowed a few moments to pass. 'How interesting. I mentioned that he had reasons to want to falsify his death, but you have failed to ask me what they might be. Is that because you already know?'

Dr Bonner opened his mouth to reply, but thought better of it, as if there was no response he thought he might safely make. He made an effort to maintain his mask of merriment but failed, and his expression slid into a frown.

'I think,' said Frances, 'that he came to you as a friend and a respected and knowledgeable man, and asked for your help. He needed to leave, but to protect the reputation of the Life House he had to make it appear that he was dead. I think you instructed Mr Palmer to assist in the deception. There was a masquerade at the viewing the next day, but thereafter the place where his body should have been was taken up by a wax model or stones or some such thing. Whatever was coffined and buried was not a body. Dr Mackenzie has gone away and Palmer may also have been sent away to ensure his silence.'

Bonner, serious now, shook his head. 'This is quite astounding, Miss Doughty. I suggest that you contact the undertakers, who will be able to confirm that they did indeed bury a body and not some waxen object or a heap of stones. I will provide you with the name and address of the firm, and a letter of introduction authorising them to tell you what you need to know.'

That was quite a challenge and he may have expected her to back down, but she simply nodded and said, 'Thank you, that is very kind. Of course, the assurances of the undertaker will only go to show that *a* body was buried – not *whose.*'

Bonner was momentarily speechless and then threw up his hands in a gesture of exasperation. 'Whose else would it be?'

'I can't say. Another of your customers? An unidentified body from a mortuary … or …' Frances hesitated as the worst possible thought came from the back of her mind where it had been lurking for some days. 'There is one man missing and unaccounted for – Mr Palmer.'

Bonner stared at her, aghast. 'I have seen and heard many things in my career, but the things that come from your imagination horrify me.'

'What horrifies me,' said Frances, 'is that so many of the terrible things I imagine I later find out to be true. Where is Dr Mackenzie's coffin interred?'

'It was deposited in the catacombs at All Souls, Kensal Green.'

'Excellent. That makes our task easier, as there is no digging to be done. We may go and view it, assuming that it is still there.'

'Of *course* it is still there!' exclaimed Bonner. 'Where else would it be? Do you think I spirit away coffins on my back in the middle of the night?'

'Has it been sealed in lead?'

Bonner paused. 'Not yet. Life House customers, providing certain hygienic requirements are met, are allowed to remain coffined without lead seals for two weeks in case signs of life appear. Dr Mackenzie's coffin will be sealed very soon.'

'Then there is no time to waste.'

It was some moments before Dr Bonner understood her meaning. 'Are you suggesting that we open Dr Mackenzie's coffin?'

'I am.'

'You will need an order from the Home Office,' he advised, smiling at her naivety.

'I see no difficulty over that,' Frances replied.

'Do you not?' Bonner chuckled.

She stared back at him confidently. 'None at all. I could have one in my hands in a matter of days.'

There was a long silence, during which Bonner's attempt at humouring her drained away.

'Miss Doughty,' he said wearily, 'you have my word as a man of honour that Dr Mackenzie did indeed die at the place and time notified, and is interred in the coffin that bears his name. Is that not enough for you?'

'I would be failing in my profession as detective if I was to accept as truth without question any fact that I was able to check for myself, even one attested to by a man of honour,' said Frances.

Bonner shifted in his chair, showing some unease, only a part of which may have been due to the discomfort in his foot. Frances watched him, but said nothing. He looked up at a framed portrait on the wall – a recently hung picture of Dr Mackenzie, a copy of the one that had been put on display at the Life House. 'Poor fellow!' he said shaking his head. 'Miss Doughty, I really wish you were right in all your strange fancies. I wish he *was* in some place where he could be content and useful and not lying in his coffin. But he died that night, died in my arms, and there was nothing I could do. A man not yet fifty and worn out with care and work.'

'What happened?' asked Frances.

'I have already told you what happened.'

She shook her head. 'I think there is more.'

There was a quiet space of time long enough to take two breaths and then he capitulated. 'If I was to tell you, would you promise not to make your peculiar allegations public? Do you know what damage that could do?'

'I make no promises. But I might be prepared to temper my actions based on what further information I receive.'

He took his handkerchief from his pocket, and wiped his palms and forehead, then carefully folded the fabric before putting it away. 'Very well. You recall that I told you of the lady in Germany who Mackenzie loved?'

'Yes, the one forced to marry a brute for money.'

'Indeed. The day before he died Mackenzie came to me and told me the sad tale. He said he had never ceased to love her and indeed she him. He assured me, however, and I believe him absolutely, that their acquaintance was wholly innocent, but such was their mutual affection that a crude mind might have put a certain interpretation on it. Any suggestion of scandal would of course have exposed the poor lady to the most dreadful ill-use from her foul husband and they had determined that much as it pained them, they must never see each other or communicate again. In the last few weeks, Mackenzie had received letters from friends in Germany, which showed that even this was not enough. The husband has been descending into madness and reached a kind of monomania on the subject. He actually believed that Mackenzie was living in Germany and visiting his wife. Mackenzie could think of only one way of protecting her – he must make this evil individual believe that he was dead. He asked me to help him.

'Yes, we did consider carrying out a deception, although we never discussed the detail. Palmer knew nothing of it, but we might have engaged his assistance at a later date. On the night of his death, Mackenzie came to the Life House and told me that he had decided to go through with it. He looked terribly tired and ill. He died, Miss Doughty, there was no pretence about it, he fell and died.'

'And you accuse *me* of telling fanciful tales,' declared Frances. 'Dr Mackenzie's story is identical to the plot of a sensational novel reviewed in the *Bayswater Chronicle* last month – *For the Love of a Ladye* by Augustus Mellifloe.'

'I do not read such things,' said Bonner, frowning.

'Obviously not, and I am sure that he knew it. He had good reasons to want to disappear, but they were not the noble and selfless motives he claimed and most assuredly nothing he wished you to be aware of. Now then, if you still maintain that he is dead I would like to view the coffin and if I see any reason to have it opened, then I will insist on it being done.'

'I have nothing to hide,' said Bonner, 'but I remain anxious that the reputation of the Life House is not impugned. Very well, I can see that you will not desist from this madness until you have your way. I will arrange for you to see the coffin as you request and you may bring all the witnesses you want, invite the press if you wish, so long as the excursion is represented in a proper light.'

Frances, taking Dr Bonner at his word about inviting the press, informed Mr Gillan that her eminent medical acquaintance was putting together a little party of interested persons to tour the catacombs at All Souls, and that he might make up one of their number, since it might provide an interesting and instructive item for the *Chronicle*. Dr Bonner was as good as his word and a visit was arranged for the next day.

CHAPTER NINE

r Bonner, who kept a smart little carriage, offered Frances and Sarah places for the journey, and there was also enough room for the svelte form of young Mr Fairbrother. Sarah looked at Mr Fairbrother with a furrowed brow as if to say that no man ought to appear as handsome as he did, and then stared very closely at Frances.

They proceeded up the Ladbroke Grove Road and then turned left into Harrow Road. The cemetery, thought Frances, was like a town in miniature and just as the needs of Bayswater had given rise to beautiful shopping promenades and market gardens to feed the demands of its inhabitants, so the needs of the cemetery had also to be fed, but in different ways. As they approached the fine, arched entrance it seemed that every business in the vicinity was in some way supplying the requirements not so much of the dead as the living who mourned them. Shops and yards bore signs declaring the businesses within to be that of stonemason and dealers in statuary, and from their doors came the continuous sounds of grinding and polishing; but only one kind of stone and marble was being fashioned. The goods on display were species of blank tombstones to serve as examples, taking the form of weeping women, angels, ivy-clad crosses, hourglasses and similar solemn testimonials. Other establishments were for the sale of fresh flowers and wreaths or *immortelles*, whose painted porcelain blooms were the perfect expression of the sadness of loss and a reminder that no living thing, however well preserved, can last forever. Most of the vehicles on the road were hearses and most of the men pausing for refreshment at inns were in undertakers' weeds.

On the way Dr Bonner regaled his companions with some of the history of All Souls, and its many beautiful acres and elegant monuments. While Frances was partial to contemplating statuary she reflected on the prevalent custom and taste for viewing the cemetery as a pastime or even an entertainment. On a fine afternoon, fashionably dressed ladies and gentlemen came to stroll and talk or sit and eat sweetmeats, much as one might visit a garden that was no more than just a garden. To Frances, however, the cemetery served only two purposes for the visitor, one was to visit the tombs of the dead to remember those friends and relations who had departed. The other was to consider the living, and especially to examine inside oneself, and think of how short a time there was to become the person one ought to be.

At the entrance to the cemetery they were joined by the other members of the party, Dr Warrinder, who had arrived in a hansom, looking unhappy, and Mr Gillan, beaming with anticipation and holding a notebook and pencil at the ready.

A cheerful looking red-faced gatekeeper presented them with an illustrated handbook which included a map of the cemetery and introduced them to their guide, a small, serious man dressed in funereal black whose usual role was to preside at interments. He was, as they were to discover, a tireless fount of all information regarding the history and customs of All Souls.

He began by informing the party that they were to take no note of recent reports that curious sounds had been heard in the catacombs as he was able to reassure them that these were solely due to the wind entering the gratings. He only mentioned this as he wished to ensure that the ladies were not alarmed. Sarah said that he need not worry on her account as she did not believe in ghosts and even if she did, she did not think that something that was made of nothing could do her any harm. Their guide smiled thinly, as if too polite to mention that even something that was made of something was unlikely to be able to harm Sarah.

On the way to the chapel they passed a greenhouse which, they were informed, had been established by the cemetery to supply a demand for fresh flowers that even the nearby nurseries were unable to meet. Frances wondered if that was really true and what the proprietors of nearby nurseries thought about the rival establishment.

As they walked along the path to the chapel, Frances was obliged to comment that there was a great deal of costly marble in the grounds, some of it in the portable form of urns and tablets, and wondered if there was any danger of robbery, but she was assured that a night-watchman who was accompanied by a dog and carried a gun, patrolled the grounds, and also took particular care to observe the entrances of the catacombs and mausoleums.

There were, explained their guide, three separate catacombs in the cemetery, one below the Dissenters' Chapel in the east and two below the central chapel, where services were conducted according to the Church of England. The catacomb that lay under the building's colonnade had long since been filled, but the one they were about to see extended under the whole chapel and still received deposits. The remains of many distinguished persons, including surgeons and physicians of note, were to be found there.

'Dr Mackenzie was impressed from his first visit to All Souls many years ago by the dignity and hygiene of its arrangements,' said Dr Bonner, 'and while a catacomb vault will cost more than a burial in the earth, it will hold many coffins and is no trouble to maintain.' He was walking a little more easily than the previous day, but still required the assistance of his stick.

'Did he have any funeral money put aside?' asked Frances.

'None, I'm afraid. Dr Warrinder and myself were obliged to meet the expense.'

The iron gates of the chapel were open and its interior, with an altar below a far window and a double row of dark wooden pews on either side, was like a church, but a church built only for one purpose. Here there would never be the joy of marriage or christening or the celebration of life, only burials and loss. Its centre was dominated by an extraordinary structure – a high oblong plinth, black and shiny as jet, a carved pillar at each corner, its sides dressed in velvet and on top, a deep platform with gilded surrounds. Frances was just wondering if it might be an unusual kind of coffin, when the guide explained that it was a catafalque for the conveyance of remains into the catacombs below, the method for which would become apparent shortly. The machinery operated on the hydraulic principle, which meant that it employed liquid operated by a pump.

Frances hoped that they might ride down to the catacombs on the great black plinth which would have been quite a novelty, but to her disappointment the guide, who had now lit a lantern, unlocked a side door and she found that she was expected to descend by a narrow, steep stone staircase whose builders had not anticipated that it would ever be used by ladies whose heavy skirts made progress very difficult, or by gentlemen with weak legs. The guide looked on anxiously as Dr Warrinder tottered down the steps and Mr Fairbrother offered Dr Bonner his arm for support.

Frances had not been quite sure what to expect, a large room like a dungeon, perhaps, and was astounded at the sight of something resembling a wine cellar that might have lain below a great castle or a money vault suitable for a bank. They were looking down a corridor easily wide enough to admit several people walking abreast and lit by gas lamps. The plain arched roof and walls were not the grim bare stone she had antici-pated; all were painted white. On either side were vaults for the deposit of coffins, each large enough to hold a dozen or more. She was told that the catacomb was arranged in six aisles and there were 216 vaults in all. The guide showed them the shining metal columns down which the catafalque was able to descend with smooth dignity, and the pump, with a great iron handle, which took two strong men to operate.

'It is very much lighter here than I expected,' observed Gillan. 'Why, I can see to write in my notebook.'

'Only the main corridor has gaslight,' said the guide, 'but on a fine cloudless day it can still be very bright.' He indicated glass globes let into the ceiling, each at the base of a circu-lar aperture. 'They collect the light and disperse it, and it is reflected back from the walls. On a day like today, however, we will need my lamp.'

He led the way and they walked along the corridor pass-ing by the vaults, each arranged and sealed according to the wishes of the owners, some with iron gates, and coffins lying on trestles within, some filled with stone shelves, some divided into individual compartments called *loculi*, intended for a single coffin, walled up or covered only by a sheet of glass. There was, they were told, space for five thousand bodies and it was as yet only half filled. The atmosphere was cool and dry, and there was little detectable smell, mainly dust and mould, the dry hint of dead flowers and old velvet. As they walked, the visitors' boots crunched on scattered fragments of stone on the flagged floor and waded through drifts of dead leaves that had blown in through ventilation gratings.

Other narrower unlit corridors led away from the main one and as they passed each junction, the gentle lamplight gave a hint at more shelves loaded with coffins, reaching further than it was possible to see, its glow passing over the shapes giving a slight and disconcerting movement to the shadows.

At last they stopped and the guide turned and faced them, saying, 'We are going down here to the vault owned by the Life House, which is at the very far end. From now on the lamp will be the only light.'

The group stood quietly looking about them and no one spoke, but just as the guide was turning to lead the way, there came, echoing and whispering, flowing down the aisles from the depths of the catacombs, a sound that was almost like a voice. It spoke no words that they could understand, but sighed sadly like a lost soul. Dr Warrinder gave a little gasp.

'Oh take no notice of that,' said the guide. 'The winds of the last few days have howled and cried like so many demons.'

There was a rustling like the sound of a newspaper being opened, and then a sudden piercing shriek that made them all jump. 'Yes,' said the guide, imperturbably, 'it does that from time to time. We're not sure why. This way.'

Frances reflected that in order to perform his duties the guide needed nerves of the finest steel, either that or no nerves at all.

'Are there many visitors to the Life House vault?' asked Gillan.

'Very few,' answered the guide, 'but of course the cemetery guards make regular patrols of the catacombs, and will walk down to the end and back as required. But it is very quiet here and if a bell was to sound there would be no mistaking it from any location. Personally, I have never heard a bell and neither has anyone else.'

'Which only shows that the medical men have done their duty diligently,' said Dr Bonner, meaningfully.

They proceeded down the aisle and from time to time the guide raised his lamp, to show what lay within the vaults on either side, its yellow light smoothing the brassy shine of nameplates while he spoke of persons of note, or coffins of unusual dimensions or with fine ornamentation, or some interesting story attached to the death. Further on they began to pass empty vaults, where the light passed over bare walls and stone shelves.

'As you may guess, the Life House coffins, not being triple sealed when initially deposited – as is usual – are kept in the furthest location from the others.'

'Is it safe to go there?' asked Gillan. 'Is there not a danger from breathing the bad air?'

'I can assure you,' said Bonner, puffing a little with the effort of the walk, 'that we take the very greatest care to ensure there is no unpleasantness. The process of decomposition of the dead and the decomposition of wounds that once followed surgery before the introduction of Professor Lister's antiseptic method are not very different, and we have a far better understanding of these things than was once the case. You will not experience the slightest discomfort or danger.'

Gillan did not look convinced.

'The bodies are packed in charcoal,' Bonner continued, 'and the coffin is of stouter construction than the usual single shell to avoid odours. There is an air tube but that also contains charcoal. A lever is placed by the hand of the deceased and a system of pulleys means that a light pressure is sufficient to open a wider aperture and also cause a bell to vibrate.'

Frances could detect a faint breath of wind on her cheek and heard a new sound, a gentle whispering which was, she assumed, caused by the movement of trees, the noise filtering down through the ventilation gratings. The 'voice' came again, and this time they were almost expecting it, so it was not so much of a shock. 'Hhhhhh …' it went, 'Hhhhhh …' with a rising, querulous pitch. No one commented. 'Hhhehhhh … hhhhehhh …' They walked on.

'Just a little way down here,' said the guide.

'Are there many coffins in the Life House vault?' Gillan asked.

'No, only four. The last one is Dr Mackenzie's from a week ago. The one before that was last January.'

'And Mackenzie's is still unsealed?'

'It's a stout single shell, sealed, but not yet in its final lead or outer coffins. Here we are.'

The Life House vault was barred and the door was padlocked. There were deep shelves against one wall, three of them bearing coffins and on a trestle in the centre the gloomy shape of the newest addition.

'Hhhhhh!' came a sudden shriek and everyone jumped back, because the sound seemed to be coming from within the vault.

'There's a ventilation shaft very nearby,' explained the guide. 'The sound can do all sorts of strange things – I'll swear it can go around corners, sometimes.'

He lifted the lamp and in its soft glimmer they saw a metal plate on the end of the coffin: Alastair Mackenzie, MD.

'Has anyone entered this vault since Dr Mackenzie's coffin was placed here?' asked Frances.

'No,' said the guide. 'We do inspect the deposited coffins, but as you see that can be done through the bars. We don't need to go inside. It has been locked ever since the coffin was placed there.'

'Who has the keys?'

'The owners and the cemetery guard.'

'But has anyone else apart from the cemetery officers been down here?'

'There have been a number of parties like yourselves, but all accompanied by a guide. Most are people come to inspect their own family vaults and they will not have been in this part of the catacombs.'

Frances saw that Mr Gillan was giving her a curious glance.

'Hhheeeeennnnnn,' said the voice from within.

Frances nodded. 'Can we not open the door? I should like to see inside.'

'Only with the owners' permission,' said the guide.

'I have no intention of allowing anyone apart from myself and Dr Warrinder to enter this vault,' said Bonner firmly.

'I cannot imagine why a young lady should wish to look inside,' said the guide. 'Now if you would all follow me, there is a vault which has a remarkably fine display of *immortelles*.'

Frances tried to think of some way she could persuade the guide to open the gates, but was obliged to admit defeat. Reluctantly she turned to go with the others.

'Hhhhennnnrryyyy!' sighed the wind.

She stopped. 'Oh please don't be alarmed, Miss,' said the guide, 'the wind can play the strangest tricks on the imagination.'

'It said "Henry",' said Frances.

'Do you think so, Miss? Well, it didn't sound like it to me.'

'Does it say that a great deal?' she demanded. He looked puzzled. 'Does it say the name Henry a great deal?'

The guide looked at Dr Bonner and even in the dim light Frances could see his pitying smile. 'I am afraid this can happen when a lady with a bit of an imagination comes down here – she can start to have all sorts of fancies. I suggest we escort her back upstairs.'

Frances hurried back to the vault. 'Open the door,' she said.

'I'm afraid I can't do that.'

'I *insist* you open it!'

'Miss Doughty, you are overwrought and we should leave at once,' said Dr Bonner.

'Hhhhennrryyy!'

'It sounds like "Henry" to me too and I've never been overwrought in my life,' declared Sarah.

'Lead the way,' said Bonner to the guide.

'I agree,' said Warrinder. 'The cold is affecting my rheumatism. Let us go.'

'Not until the door has been opened,' said Frances, resolutely.

'That is up to the owner of the vault,' said the guide. 'Are you the owner of the vault, Miss? I don't believe you are.'

Frances had to admit that she was not.

'Well then,' said the guide, 'that is the end of the tour and I do hope you have all found it interesting.'

'Oh my Lord!' exclaimed Gillan. He was peering through the bars into the vault. 'I can see something moving!'

'That's impossible!' said the guide.

'See for yourself.' He stepped back, and as the guide moved forward with the lamp Frances could see that Gillan's face was as white as a new corpse.

'There's nothing in there except coffins,' said the guide. 'How can anything be moving? Nothing can get through the bars.'

'Rats?' suggested Warrinder.

'There are no rats down here,' said the guide. 'Nor mice, nor anything alive other than ourselves.' He moved the lamp back and forth. 'No, it's a trick of the light.'

'Hhennryyy!' said the voice and gave a loud shriek, and then they all saw it, a dark shape, moving around on top of the coffin.

Warrinder gave a scream. 'Oh! It's Mackenzie! He's alive! He's alive! Quickly man, quickly, open the vault! I am part owner and I authorise it!'

The guide glanced at Bonner, who appeared to be struck dumb with terror.

'Do it!' shouted Warrinder. 'Do it at once! You may save a man's life!'

The guide shrugged and took a heavy bunch of keys from his belt.

Frances felt her heart thudding loudly as the key turned with a grinding noise that was echoed by a loud scream from inside the vault.

'Oh poor fellow!' exclaimed Warrinder, holding his hands to his face. 'Somebody save him!'

The door swung open and the guide ran in, followed closely by Frances, Sarah and Gillan. The shape moved and turned, and as the lamp was raised towards it Frances saw the reflection of eyes, small eyes, bright as glass beads. The lid of the coffin had risen to create a slit about an inch high and protruding from it was something like dark shriveled twigs, and then Frances realised what it was she was seeing – fingers, rotting fingers, a last desperate appeal for help, while sitting on top of the coffin, pecking at the fingers with an irritated look in its eyes, was Mrs Chiffley's parrot.

CHAPTER TEN

rances would always remember that moment, which was printed upon her mind like a photograph. Dr Warrinder, his hands raised, his features transfigured in joyous acclamation; the guide, his mouth fallen open in surprise; Mr Gillan, his eyes gleaming like an antiquarian who had found a treasure-laden tomb, rapidly sketching the scene in his notebook; young Mr Fairbrother, backing away in alarm; Sarah, as unflappable as a mountain; and Dr Bonner, his face contorted in anguish, the dim light casting his features into a mask of tragedy.

Their guide was the first to speak. 'Ladies, gentlemen, I earnestly request that we should all leave. I need to inform the cemetery authorities at once.'

'Oh, but what about Mackenzie?' exclaimed Warrinder. 'We must recover him immediately – we may still be able to restore him! Quickly, before it is too late!'

Bonner groaned and placed a hand on Warrinder's shoulder. 'Come along, my dear fellow. I can assure you there is nothing we can do for him.'

The guide made an attempt at politely ushering the ladies to the stairs, in the hope that the gentlemen would follow, but to his discomfiture, the ladies would not permit themselves to be ushered.

'I want that parrot,' said Sarah.

The guide stared at her.

'Well, it's no business being here.'

'And I might add,' said Frances, 'that allowing it to remain might result in the destruction of material that could be important in any future medical examination. Moreover, I know the identity of the owner and can restore it to her.'

The guide unwillingly acquiesced, but not before declaring to Mr Gillan's considerable disappointment that only he, as official guide, should be allowed to go any further into the compartment. There, not without eliciting squawks of protest, he extricated the bird and handed it to Sarah, then relocked the iron doors. He then shepherded the little party back to the stairs, and the cool and soothing gloom of the Anglican chapel. Mr Gillan did not remain with them long, but with the news hot in his pocket, bounded away at a most unfuneral pace in the direction of Harrow Road in search of a cab. Mrs Chiffley's parrot bore the indignity of being tucked firmly yet gently under Sarah's arm with mounting concern, as if fearing that it was about to be plucked for the pot. It repeatedly called upon 'Henry' for assistance, that being, Frances assumed, Mr Chiffley's Christian name.

Once the catacombs had been locked away from visitors, their guide abruptly left, and Frances, after instructing Sarah to bear the aggrieved parrot back to its owner and mention that an invoice for her fee would follow shortly, was left with the three medical men, all of whom were in varying stages of distress and confusion. Fairbrother approached the velvet-draped altar, where he bowed his head and appeared to be praying, Warrinder was walking unsteadily up and down, wringing his hands as if still convinced that there was some hope of restoring some life to the owner of the blackened fingers, while an exhausted Bonner, who seemed to have aged ten years, had sunk into a pew.

Frances approached Bonner and he shrank back from her, an encouraging sign, she thought. 'Perhaps,' she said, taking a place beside him, 'you have something to say to me.'

'Whatever would I say that I have not already said?' he exclaimed.

'The truth. The things you have previously omitted to mention.'

He bridled, but Frances had long ago lost any patience or respect for those who avoided telling her what she wanted to know by standing on their reputations, which often did not bear a close examination.

'This is hard enough for me to bear without your insinuations,' he protested.

'I must confess,' said Frances, 'that had I been asked before this morning what I thought might be found in Dr Mackenzie's coffin, I would have replied stones, or bricks, or lead – anything that might weigh the same as a corpse, anything, indeed, except a body, let alone that of Dr Mackenzie. It does now appear that there is indeed a corpse in the coffin, but I have yet to be convinced of its identity.'

'Oh this is absurd!' Bonner exclaimed in exasperation.

'Dr Mackenzie told you a story that would not reflect on his honour, to persuade you to help fabricate evidence of his death. Mr Palmer may have been involved in the deception, or if not, he was sent away on some errand. You and Mackenzie together then placed a body in the coffin. I am sure there are many unclaimed corpses lying in workhouse mortuaries to which a doctor might have had access without arousing suspicion, and it was just a matter of waiting until one came along that resembled Dr Mackenzie. People who are told they are viewing a body of a named person will see what they expect to see. Any differences will be put down to the relaxation of features after death. So – tell me Dr Bonner – where is he?'

At the altar, Mr Fairbrother had stopped praying and turned to stare at her with an expression of frank astonishment.

'Really, Miss Doughty,' said Bonner, 'it seems to me that you have mistaken your calling and ought to be writing works of popular fiction. Detective novels would suit you very well.'

'Do not attempt to distract me with insults. You were, on your own admission, present when the body was placed in the coffin, so you must know from whence it came and whose it was.'

Bonner gestured frantically with his fists, dropping his stick, which Frances had to pick up for him. It was a weighty object with a gnarled top and she thought that his gout must be troubling him more than he might like to admit. 'I do, of *course* I do; the body is that of Dr Mackenzie. I cannot account for the mechanism in the coffin having been operated, but I am sure that any examination will reveal that he died from a weak heart as certified by me, and at the time and date stated. I suspect that the mechanism in the coffin was at fault, or was operated by the gases of decomposition, which would account for what we saw.'

Despite her best efforts, Dr Bonner refused to move from that position, and Frances was obliged to comfort herself with the thought that a proper identification, post-mortem examination and inquest would soon follow. She could be patient. Nevertheless, with her suspicions very thoroughly aroused, she could not help being concerned that those most likely to be called upon to identify the exhumed body were Dr Bonner, and the dim-sighted and easily duped Dr Warrinder. There was, she reflected, no one who knew Mackenzie well enough to be asked to identify the body who was not also a trusted friend or employee and therefore potentially an accomplice. 'It is my intention,' said Frances, 'to reveal my suspicions to the police and insist that the identification of the remains is carried out by several persons.'

'Do as you please,' said Bonner, flapping his hand at her dismissively, 'you will only make yourself appear ridiculous.'

Fairbrother, shaking his head, turned from her as if afraid that she would question him next, but Frances thought that if she had any questions to ask him this would be better done when his mentor was not present.

Some worried-looking gentlemen came to take the body away and a few moments after they had descended into the catacombs, there was a gentle gurgling of liquid from the pump and the catafalque began to sink smoothly through the floor. The process took about fifteen minutes and then there was a wait for the coffin to be fetched before the watery whisper started again, and the black draped coffin began to be seen. While Frances was not afraid of a coffin as such, seeing one rise up out of the floor almost as if it was doing so under its own power was a trifle unnerving. When the catafalque was once more in place, Frances approached it before the cemetery officials could return and, to the astonishment of the three medical men, lifted the cloth to satisfy herself that the coffin was indeed that of Dr Mackenzie. She could do no more and it was soon borne away to a waiting hearse to be removed to Kilburn mortuary.

'I will of course attend the inquest,' said Frances. 'I especially look forward to the establishment of the deceased's identity.'

Dr Bonner, she thought, was giving an extraordinary display of innocence, but that should come easily to him. Was it not a part of his profession to soothe the sick with half-truths and offer the dying the comfort of lies? Perhaps he was relying on the passage of time obscuring the features of the deceased and his reputation as a medical man of eminence in the district securing the hoped-for result.

Frances had only a short distance to walk to Kilburn police station where, as she might have anticipated, the desk sergeant regarded her as a young lady who had perhaps taken too much in the way of drink, or was subject to attacks of hysteria, but he promised to make a note of her concerns about suitable persons being chosen to identify the remains. 'If you are in any doubts about me,' she told him, 'I suggest you have a word with Inspector Sharrock at Paddington Green, who will vouch for the fact that when I make a great deal of noise about something it is not without good cause!' Inspector Sharrock, while publicly holding Frances to be a meddler who ought to be out looking for a husband and not concerning herself with murders, had, she felt sure, been obliged to admit to himself if no one else that she had successfully concluded a number of knotty cases. She was advised that Dr Hardwicke, the coroner, would be hearing cases at Providence Hall, Paddington on Monday and that the proceedings would, in all probability, open then.

The one mystery that Frances felt sure she would never solve was how Mrs Chiffley's parrot had ever come to be in the catacombs, although she could essay a guess. The Chiffleys did not live very far from All Souls. In all probability the bird, after circling the grey houses of Kensal Green, had been attracted by the delightful shrubs and flowers of the cemetery and had flown down to disport itself amongst the gravestones. Perhaps it had subsisted on fragments of bread from the picnic baskets of visitors, and been captured by one of the cemetery officials who had then concealed it and scoured the newspapers for an advertisement offering a reward for its return. That reward was now hers, but it would, she was sure, be followed by anxious requests from the public to search for every missing songbird in Paddington.

❧

That Sunday after church Sarah wanted to entertain Tom to tea, partly, thought Frances, to introduce him to a more genteel manner of refreshing himself and fit him for the more prosperous future he had been promised, but also, she felt sure, to divert her from matters of business and quiet her mind. Tom duly arrived as smart and spruced as it was possible for him to be by his own efforts, which meant that Sarah had only to wash and polish and arrange him for about twenty minutes until she thought him fit to sit at the table. Tom revealed that he was now in business on his own account. He had organised a band of 'men' as he called them, although Frances felt sure that none of them was much more than twelve, and they would assemble in the doorway of Mr Beccles' shop on the Grove, which was commodious and rarely busy otherwise, to be assigned their tasks. Busy gentlemen in the Grove were starting to learn where Tom's little army could be found and he now had a thriving trade. They slept in a small attic room above the shop, which Mr Beccles said they could have for nothing if they made deliveries for him. Sarah gazed at the diminutive businessman with almost maternal pride, and flicked her napkin at him whenever he felt tempted to wipe crumbs from his mouth with a sleeve. She gave him a bag of buns before he left.

Unusually for the first day of an inquest, where little more than evidence of identification was to be expected, the little hall on Church Street was crowded, and there could be no doubt as to which case was arousing the public interest, since the only others to be heard were rather more commonplace deaths due to a drunken fall, hydrophobia, and want of nourishment.

Mr Gillan was there with the light of anticipation in his eyes and Frances did not have to enquire as to the reason why large crowds had shown such an early curiosity about the proceedings. Doctors Bonner and Warrinder and Mr Fairbrother were also in attendance, as were Mrs Georgeson, Dr Carmichael and Mr Darscot. Frances was surprised to see her own doctor, Dr Collin, there as well, and wondered what his involvement might be. She was unable to contain her impatience and with an alacrity that might well have seemed like forwardness, took a seat beside Mr Fairbrother. Dr Bonner, nearby, sat lost in thought.

'Have you seen the body?' she asked. 'What was your conclusion?'

'I have,' said Fairbrother, 'and I fear that you are due for a disappointment. It is without a shadow of a doubt that of Dr Mackenzie.'

'Oh!' said Frances, with some surprise. 'But can you be quite sure? You have not known him long.'

'Yes, I am quite sure. I have been in his company a number of times, sometimes for several hours together when on duty in the Life House. I should add that Dr Collin was an acquaintance of Dr Mackenzie and has confirmed the identification.'

Frances pondered this. 'Surely the features of the corpse were very much altered?'

'Not at all, he was perfectly recognisable.'

'Then the body cannot be that of Dr Mackenzie,' Frances stated firmly. 'If it was, after the lapse of time, some of which was spent in the warmth of the Life House, he would be greatly decomposed. Some other body, that of a man of similar appearance, was placed in the coffin before it was deposited in the catacombs.'

Fairbrother shook his head. 'My experience in these matters is necessarily limited, but I am given to understand that the rate of decomposition of bodies or different portions of the same body can vary to a considerable degree, often for no reason that medical science can explain. I think you are mistaken and I have no doubt that on the basis of the evidence given today the coroner will determine that the body *is* that of Dr Mackenzie. However, it is intended that a full post-mortem will be carried out by a Home Office man, with Dr Collin assisting and myself taking notes, and that should remove all suspicions, even yours.' He looked very pleased with himself. 'It will be a most valuable experience for me.'

The inquest proceedings were necessarily brief and Dr Hardwicke, the coroner, as Fairbrother had anticipated, accepted that the remains were those of Dr Mackenzie and ordered a detailed post-mortem. Frances had assumed that this was a normal requirement given the circumstances under which the corpse had been removed from the catacombs, but Hardwicke commented that his order followed from some unusual circumstances presenting themselves at the initial examination. Frances demanded to know what these were, but both Fairbrother and Bonner were frustratingly tight-lipped. The inquest was adjourned.

Walter Crowe, who was by some curious means of communication absorbing the same hollow-eyed appearance as his betrothed, came up and tipped his hat to Frances. 'This is an interesting development,' he said. 'What can it mean? Do you think it has any bearing on poor Henry's fate?'

'I wish I knew,' said Frances. 'I am still not at all convinced that the body is that of Dr Mackenzie, and I have a theory for which there is as yet no proof, but I will continue my enquiries.'

In a brief conversation with Dr Carmichael she reassured him that she had agents looking for the missing journal without informing him that they were also checking on the *bona fides* of Dr Carmichael. She was aware that he was a source of further useful information, if she could only discover a means of extracting it, and with a new strategy in mind, made an appointment to see him later that afternoon.

There was also the opportunity for a discussion with Mr Gillan, who informed Frances that his contacts knew nothing of any theft of snuffboxes from the house of a doctor in Kensington.

Frances returned home in a state of some despondency, her best hope being that a detailed examination of the body by an expert might cast some light on the mystery, albeit he would be starting from the possibly incorrect assumption that the dead man was Dr Mackenzie.

Her only comfort was the appearance of two more clients. The first was a young gentleman who wished to know if his sweetheart was entertaining his attentions only so that she might enjoy the valuable gifts with which he showered her. Frances had no experience of romance, but suggested to him that rather than engage a detective he should, instead of expensive gifts, shower his sweetheart with items of sentimental value only, such as notes and flower buds and judge her love by her appreciation of these tokens. Secretly Frances had some sympathy for a young lady with such a distrustful lover. She charged the gentleman a guinea for her advice and sent him on his way.

Her next client was a woman who believed her neighbour was stealing her washing, but had never been able to catch her in the act. Her face bore marks of an earlier discussion with the neighbour on that subject. Frances took the commission, although she knew it would not be well paid and decided to send Tom or one of his 'men' to watch the washing lines, and see what transpired.

There was no progress in discovering Mrs Pearson's missing maid, indeed Frances thought she was unlikely to make any until the client told her the real reason for her concern. Nevertheless, she felt confident that the case would be solved in time, with some patient wearing away of the lady's natural reticence, and possibly a sharp reminder to shock her into an admission. If she could find a missing parrot a lady's maid ought not to present any difficulty, but then on that principle, neither should Henry Palmer.

She received a note from Chas and Barstie to say that they had been accepted as members of the Piccadilly Club, and would keep an eye on the activities of Dr Carmichael.

That gentleman duly presented himself after luncheon and was anxious to know what progress Frances had made in her enquiries. Frances faced him across the parlour table, her notebook and pencil at her fingertips, and favoured him with a gentle smile intended both to place him at his ease and make him lower his guard. 'I am gathering information both personally and through my many agents,' she said. 'I am presently making arrangements to go to Edinburgh to pursue my enquiries further.'

'Edinburgh?' Dr Carmichael exclaimed. 'I am afraid I don't understand. The journal and the blackmailers are, in all probability, in London. If any approach is made to me it will be done here. Why should you go to Edinburgh?'

Frances' smile expressed levels of patience and geniality it had never before achieved. Even Sarah looked faintly troubled. 'As you yourself have explained to me, the circumstances described in the journal and which could well have led to the blackmail of Dr Mackenzie occurred in Edinburgh. I will need to acquaint myself thoroughly with them, and look into family connections and friends who could be of importance. There may also be matters that affect you. I mean to leave no stone unturned, Dr Carmichael, you may be assured of that.'

Dr Carmichael did not appear comforted by Frances' proposed expedition to Edinburgh or her reassurance of thoroughness. His expression showed unease rather than anything else. 'But – that would be a matter of some expense.'

'It would of course, but you have already said that you would be willing to pay anything to have the difficulty resolved.'

'I had not anticipated ...' He struggled to express himself, but abandoned the attempt.

'The other question is the thief of the journal. This, as you have said, has most probably already been sold, however, the maid may well be a known character in the underworld, one who has several aliases and a whole host of disreputable associates, one of whom may be our quarry. I know you don't wish me to trouble your sister, Ellen, but if you could speak to her and obtain an exact description of the maid, and the name she was using, I would be very much obliged to you. Also, I will want to discuss the matter with the Kensington police who are pursuing the theft and may be willing to advise me of their progress. I have not been able to establish the full details of the crime and I therefore require the name of the police officer who has charge of the matter. Do you know the name and address of the pawnshop in which the snuffboxes were discovered? I will need to speak to the owner.' She took up her pencil and prepared to write.

'I am afraid I don't ...'

'No matter, I can soon discover it,' said Frances, cheerfully.

Dr Carmichael abruptly rose from his chair. 'Miss Doughty, I ...'

'Yes?'

He wavered, then sat down again. 'I cannot finance a visit to Edinburgh. Also, I do not wish you to involve the police. The maid, so I understand, was a very commonplace looking person and with a name she might have shared with a thousand such.'

Frances put down her pencil. 'Do you wish me to proceed at all?'

'I – yes – I need the journal back.'

'You make it very hard for me. Well, if I am not to go to Edinburgh perhaps you can furnish me with some information.'

'I will do what I can,' he said unwillingly, which was exactly the result Frances had been hoping for.

'On what date did your sister Madeleine pass away?'

He looked startled. 'I don't see how that can be of any consequence.'

'It may not be, but I like to know as much as I can about any person concerned in the matter under enquiry.'

'If you must, I suppose,' he grumbled. 'It was in the summer of 1859. June 16th or 17th – I remember it was just a few days after her birthday – she was twenty-one.'

'And the cause of her death?'

Carmichael hesitated. 'It is very painful for me to speak of this. She was in a severely weakened condition and died of blood poisoning. A stronger woman might have rallied, but Madeleine was always very delicate.'

'Pardon me for asking this very impertinent question, but — '

He held up his hand to stay her. 'I think I can guess what it is you are about to ask. My sister's memory is sacred and pure to me. Let it remain so.'

'And yet her state of health has an important bearing on the blackmail of Dr Mackenzie.'

'That is true, although what may actually have been the case, or what a young woman of her limited understanding in such things might have feared, or been led to believe, may be quite different.'

'You have not seen this journal, but your sister Ellen has done so. Did she tell you what it said?'

'No, only that it showed Mackenzie to have told many lies, lies that revealed he had treated Madeleine cruelly.'

'In what way?'

Carmichael, his face a picture of loathing, appeared to be steeling himself to divulge unpleasant matters. 'He led her to believe that he had a pure and noble affection for her. Mackenzie's brother, David, had already revealed to me that he entertained the sincerest esteem for my sister, but as he was then enjoying only the salary of a humble clerk, he had decided to refrain from addressing her on the subject until he was further advanced in his career and in a position to marry. Madeleine, although she respected David Mackenzie, did not love him; indeed she could not do so, he has a coldness about him that she found uncongenial. Mackenzie knew full well what his brother's intentions were, but he was an unscrupulous rogue able to masquerade as a man of wit and charm, and exercise great persuasiveness. He was easily able to engage Madeleine's girlish affections, but he then grew suddenly inattentive. I believe that he had transferred his addresses to a lady of fortune. All this I suspected, but could not prove. He denied that he had had any more than the briefest acquaintance with my sister, and that no words other than the usual courtesies had been exchanged. If she had pined away for his love then he professed to be quite unaware of her feelings. Her journal, however, tells another tale, exposes his lies, shows him to be the cruel and heartless adventurer that he really was.'

Whether or not he spoke the truth Frances could not say, but his emotion as he recalled events of more than twenty years ago was undeniable.

'The brother – David – he and Dr Mackenzie were thereafter on bad terms?' Frances asked.

'Yes, the cause is obvious.'

'What is his current profession?'

'He is still at the Procurator Fiscal's office, but in a position of greater responsibility.'

'But soon afterwards Dr Mackenzie left Scotland for Germany. Why was that?'

'Not everyone believed his protestations of innocence,' said Carmichael, with a subdued note of triumph. 'His reputation suffered and he was unable to obtain advancement. He saw an escape abroad as a means of making a new beginning. He knew that waiting mortuaries were of interest only to the wealthy.'

'What surprises me,' said Frances, 'is that the character of the man you describe in Edinburgh is quite different from the character of the man who lived in Bayswater. How do you account for that?'

'Much time has passed. Who can tell what experiences he has had which might have changed him? Or perhaps he had not changed. No – I think he had not. There may yet be secret crimes and vices to be uncovered.'

CHAPTER ELEVEN

When Carmichael had gone, Frances turned her mind once more to the disappearance of Henry Palmer and did what she always did when a problem seemed to have arrived at an impasse; she supplied herself with a really large pot of tea and went back to the beginning. Henry Palmer had last been seen just after 11 p.m. on Tuesday the 21st of September, walking north up Ladbroke Grove Road, his intended destination and purpose unknown. Because he had disappeared on the same night that Dr Mackenzie had died – or was supposed to have died – Frances had assumed that the two events were linked. She had found out a great deal about Dr Mackenzie's activities and no doubt would discover more, but none of this had solved the mystery of Henry Palmer. She had been looking at Palmer's disappearance as an isolated incident, but supposing it was not? Suppose, she thought, Palmer had been sent on an errand by Dr Mackenzie or was walking north for some reason of his own, and had become the victim of a crime? Might there be a gang who had chosen Kensal Green and Ladbroke Grove for their robberies? That would mean that there had been other events of a criminal or suspicious nature in the area, which at first glance appeared to have no connection with Palmer. Frances brought out all her most recent newspapers and over toast and tea, she and Sarah pored over them.

'What we are looking for is anything of an out-of-the-way nature that took place either before or after Mr Palmer's disappearance, and in the same area. Let us look three months before and all dates since. It might not even be a crime, or at least it might not look like one. Was there a curious accident, perhaps, or something that went missing and was advertised as lost? The only difficulty is of course that it might have been such a small affair that it was never in the newspapers, or even reported to the police, so we need to think about gossip and rumours, too.'

'Or someone dead who was supposed to have died natural but was really murdered,' said Sarah. 'Hmph!' She prodded a death notice with a fat finger. '*She* went young. I'll bet he has a new wife *and* a baby this time next year.' Frances reflected sadly that the death of a married woman of childbearing age was not as unusual an event as it ought to be, and that if conjugal happiness was never to be hers, which seemed very probable, then she might count herself fortunate. She wondered if she would feel herself to be as fortunate in this respect at forty as she did now at twenty.

Several hours of earnest endeavour concluded in a small result: the ascent of a balloon at Kensal Green on the 4th of September, and two persons drowned in the canal, a boy who got out of his depth while bathing on the 2nd of September and the body of an unfortunate woman taken from the water on the 22nd.

'I wonder if the female body was ever identified,' said Frances, since there were two young women she would very much like to trace – Mrs Pearson's missing maidservant, Ethel, and the nursemaid who had stolen Madeleine Carmichael's journal.

When the woman's body was found it was believed that she had been in the water for at least two weeks, but Frances thought that such an estimate could be stretched by several days either way. Mrs Pearson's maid had last been seen ten days before the discovery of the body, and the thief eight days. The body could be that of either of the missing women. There was a brief mention in the newspaper of the inquest, which had taken place at Kilburn mortuary. The post-mortem examination had been carried out by Dr Bonner assisted by Mr Fairbrother, and the conclusion was that the unknown woman had drowned. 'Supposing,' said Frances, 'this was not, as has been concluded, the death of a despairing unfortunate, but either a suicide due to remorse for some terrible thing she had done, or, what is almost as bad, a murder. She could have had criminal associates who decided to kill her for secrets she held; perhaps they were able to render her unconscious by a method that left no trace, or else left a trace that was attributed to an accidental cause, and then threw her in the canal.'

'You'll have to get her dug up,' said Sarah, matter of factly

'I may need to at that, but before I do I will speak to Dr Bonner about it – or perhaps Mr Fairbrother.'

There was a long silence and then Sarah gave her newspaper a good shake.

'You do not care for Mr Fairbrother?' asked Frances.

'I didn't say so.'

'And yet I have that impression. How has he offended you?'

'He hasn't,' said Sarah. 'Not yet. But he might do, so I keep on my guard.' She gave a firm nod.

❧

The next morning, Frances, having learned all that she could from the newspapers about the unclaimed body in the canal, which was little enough, set out for Dr Bonner's house. When she had first entered into the detective business, which she had done as a matter of personal and urgent necessity, she had begun with no idea as to how persons in that profession went about their daily tasks. It had seemed to her to be the height of rudeness to call upon someone she wished to question without first submitting a letter of introduction and a card requesting an interview at their convenience. How she had envied Inspector Sharrock of Paddington Green, who, with not the slightest pretence at observing any of the proprieties, was often so bold as to demand entry to people's homes by the front door without a moment's notice of his intentions. How she had shuddered at the idea that she might do so herself and yet she had done it, and not only that, she had, to her shame, enjoyed it. Now that she was better known in Bayswater – largely because of Mr Gillan, who never allowed humble truths to inconvenience him in his search for a tale to entertain readers of the *Chronicle* – it often sufficed to present her card at the door and then walk in for all the world as if she had been invited. She was a detective and people expected her to be impolite. It was not, she thought regretfully, a good outcome to her endeavours, but she had to earn her bread and this was the opportunity that had presented itself.

Dr Bonner's starchy maid was even crisper than usual. She held herself stiffly erect as if any movement of her wrists against the knife-like edges of her cuffs might have unfortunate consequences. 'Do you have an appointment, Miss?' she asked, knowing full well that Frances did not.

'Dr Bonner has made it clear to me that in view of the unusual circumstances, he will not hinder me in my investigations,' replied Frances. The maid looked at Frances as if she was attempting to sell her bad meat.

'He is too busy to see visitors.'

'The consequences of the recent inquest on Dr Mackenzie, I suppose,' said Frances. 'In that case, it is more than ever imperative that I see him at once. It is a matter of life or death, but chiefly I think, of death.'

'You may wait in the parlour,' said the maid reluctantly, 'I will tell him that you are here.'

'Thank you,' said Frances, 'I will wait for ten minutes and then if he has not appeared, I will go up to his consulting room. You needn't trouble yourself, I know the way.'

As she entered the hallway, sensing the maid's glance of displeasure settle on the back of her neck like an angry wasp, she was surprised to see Mr Darscot coming down the stairs.

'Good afternoon Mr Darscot, I hope you are well?' she enquired, wondering what business the young man had there.

'Oh, I could be better, Miss Doughty,' he said, shaking his head with a mournful expression that was almost comic. 'I am such a poor fellow with my nerves and this business with Mackenzie coming out of his grave has quite unsettled me. Dr Bonner has been kind enough to prescribe a remedy, which I hope will be a complete cure. I assume – indeed I very much hope – that you are here in your professional capacity and not as a patient?'

'That is the case,' Frances reassured him.

'I expect you know that all of Bayswater is abuzz with the news that you have been called in on the case of the missing man – we expect good tidings very soon! And if there should be anything I can do to assist you, please do not hesitate to ask, as long as it doesn't involve any actual – well, danger.'

'I shall bear your kind offer in mind,' said Frances, 'and please do not concern yourself about danger; my assistant, Miss Smith, takes care of all matters of that nature.'

When Mr Darscot had departed, Frances settled herself in the parlour with a glance at the mantel clock, but was obliged to wait only a few minutes before the door opened to admit Mr Fairbrother.

'I am afraid Dr Bonner had quite forgotten any arrangement he may have made to see you and is in any case too exhausted by events to submit to any questioning,' he said. 'His foot, which as you know is afflicted with gout, is troubling him sorely. He cannot see you today. I hope that will not be an inconvenience.'

'Not at all,' said Frances. 'Had it been essential to speak with him immediately I would have intruded upon his presence whatever excuse he supplied. I will question you in his place.'

'Ah,' said Fairbrother, and Frances gathered from his manner that he had been deputed by Bonner to see her to the door and not submit to questioning himself.

'If Dr Bonner thinks I am deflected so easily he has not been reading the *Bayswater Chronicle*,' said Frances. 'My adventures are a regular feature in its columns and I can assure you that it does not publish the whole story.'

Reluctantly, Fairbrother closed the door behind him and sat down. 'Shall I ring for some refreshments?'

'No, let us to business at once. I just saw Mr Darscot here, can you advise me of the reason for his visit?'

'Oh, that is quite impossible – firstly because he received a private consultation with Dr Bonner, and even had I been present, which I was not, the confidences of the patient are always honoured. And I am afraid I cannot assist you regarding the examination of Dr Mackenzie's remains. The Home Office has sent for Professor Stevenson of Guy's Hospital and he is a very busy man and has not yet commenced his work. Even if he had, I would be obliged to remain silent until evidence is given at the inquest.'

'Professor Stevenson is an expert on poisons,' recalled Frances.

'Oh yes, one of the most respected men in the country.'

'Then I await his findings with especial interest. But I have not come here to ask about Dr Mackenzie, I am here on another matter with which you were directly concerned.'

'Oh?'

Frances handed him her copy of the *Bayswater Chronicle* and pointed to the short item about the inquest on the unknown woman. 'I don't understand,' said Fairbrother when he had glanced at the piece, 'I remember it of course, but what possible bearing can it have on Dr Mackenzie or Mr Palmer?'

'Perhaps none,' Frances admitted, declining to mention that she was clutching at a very slender straw, 'but there is a theory that I am pursuing which requires me to know more about this case. Since it has been reported on and concluded I assume that you are free to discuss it.'

'I – yes – I will help you of course – but might I ask —'

'My reasons? No. Am I correct in assuming that the identity of the woman has never been established?'

'That is correct, yes.'

'Can you describe her? Her age, her height, any distinguishing features?'

'As to her age, that can be hard to establish with any precision where there is significant decomposition and the person is poorly nourished. She was a fully developed adult; that much is certain, but not very aged. We thought between twenty and twenty-five. She was about five feet four inches in height, no injuries or birthmarks. She had borne at least one child. I believe she may have suffered with her teeth as her incisors were growing crookedly and impacting the gum, which must have caused her some pain. But it is most unlikely that she was a class of person who would have consulted a dentist.'

'What was her state of health prior to her death? Poorly nourished, you say?'

'Yes, decidedly so. The stomach was empty and she had not eaten solid food in quite some time.'

'But she did not die of starvation?'

'No, the state of the lungs demonstrated that the cause of death was drowning. We formed the hypothesis that she had become destitute and took a desperate course of action.'

'How was she dressed?'

There was an awkward pause. 'She – was not fully clothed.'

'I beg your pardon? What was she wearing?'

'Undergarments only, no shoes.'

France stared at him. 'That is very extraordinary. Surely if she had been wandering the street in that state someone would have noticed.'

'Dr Bonner, who has more experience than I, informed me that he has seen many cases of suicide by drowning where the individual removes their outer clothing before entering the water.

We thought that the woman in question had done so, leaving her gown and shoes on the canal bank, where they were stolen.'

'I see. No jewellery of any kind, I assume.'

'No, but there were signs that she had once worn a wedding band and earrings. Pawned, I imagine.'

'And the garments she was wearing were of a poor kind?'

'As a matter of fact, they were not.'

'No?'

'Well, I am no – er – expert on such things of course,' Fairbrother said with some embarrassment, 'and I was obliged to accept the advice of Dr Bonner – who – ah – being a married gentleman —'

'I understand. What *can* you tell me of the garments?'

'They were of good quality and undamaged.'

'Then they had a monetary value,' said Frances. 'The lady might have been able to pawn them, change them for some ragged ones. Instead of which she chose to jump to her death wearing clothes that might have fed her for some little time.'

'It does seem so, yes.' Fairbrother shifted in his seat and looked as though he would have very much welcomed some liquid refreshment at that moment. 'We did talk about it, I recall, and I think the conclusion was that she had once been a very – er —' he drummed his fingers on his knees, 'sought after – er – person who might once have enjoyed valuable gifts, but she had fallen on hard times due to ill health and saw no point in extending her unhappy life.'

Frances thought that the medical gentlemen had been too hasty in concluding that the deceased was an immoral woman, but that, she had observed, always seemed to be the first thought of gentlemen in any walk of life. The dead woman might equally well have been a maidservant who had been given her mistress's cast-off clothing, or stolen some coveted garments.

'Was any attempt made to identify her through these clothes? You might have taken them to Whiteley's or any other Westbourne Grove drapers.'

'We might, I suppose, but we did not.'

'Why not?'

He seemed puzzled. 'I am not sure. I never thought to do so.'

'Were they retained against the possibility that someone might come forward and identify her?'

'No, she was buried in them.'

'In a pauper's grave, I assume?'

'Yes. A common grave in All Souls.'

Frances consulted the *Chronicle* again. 'According to this report, the body was displayed before burial in a nearby stable and persons invited to view it for identification.'

'Yes, but only briefly as we thought it might be a hazard to the public health. Quite a number of persons whose relatives were missing came to see it and there were one or two names suggested, as is so often the way in these cases, but no one felt certain enough of the identity to claim the body and pay for the funeral.'

'Do you have a record of the names?'

'No. Dr Bonner asked me to pass them on to the police, which I did.'

'In a case such as this, even if they had identified the woman it might not have been reported in the newspapers,' Frances said. 'I must go back to Kilburn police station and enquire there.'

Fairbrother appeared to be about to make an observation.

'What is it you have to say, Mr Fairbrother?'

'It is only – have you considered, Miss Doughty, that your undertaking is quite an unsuitable one for your age and sex? I have heard that there are lady detectives, but their enquiries are on matters more suited to their sensibilities. The behaviour of female servants, for example. Surely it is not appropriate for you to be examining into such horrid deaths as many men would find themselves unable to contemplate.'

'And yet women are employed to lay out bodies,' she reminded him.

'But they are a quite different class of women, not delicate ladies,' he protested.

'Are we not all the same creatures?'

'Well, I – I think —'

'Then think again, Mr Fairbrother.' Frances rose. 'And now I must go and speak to Inspector Gostelow. If you recall anything about the death of the unhappy woman found in the canal which you have not yet mentioned, please let me know at once.'

Frances was a little disgruntled with Mr Fairbrother, but as she walked up to Kilburn she reflected that he was very young both in age and experience, and had the tendency to adopt without question the attitudes of those he saw as wiser than himself. He was eager to learn at the feet of men such as Dr Bonner, who she felt sure could have found a host of reasons why women should not become detectives, or be permitted to exercise the vote or undertake medical training. Mr Fairbrother was not yet his own man, and might never become so without proper encouragement, but he was not, she thought, a lost cause.

🌟

Inspector Gostelow was a quiet man and a thoughtful one. He struck Frances as someone who had seen a lot of life and was undisturbed by any form of behaviour however unusual, including the aspirations of a young woman to be a detective. Frances explained that she had been engaged by a client to find a missing maidservant and was wondering if the body found in the canal might provide an answer. He listened carefully and respectfully, and gave her statement proper consideration.

'The report of the medical men suggested that the body had been in the water for at least two weeks, so we are looking for someone who went missing between the 1st and 8th of September,' he said. 'Of course, we have to allow for the fact that the doctors' opinion may not be accurate – I would always allow a day or even a week either side. I myself have seen bodies taken from cold water that I would have imagined to be two weeks dead and later discovered it was more like two months.'

'The maidservant was last seen on September the 12th. She was called Ethel Green.'

'Then I would say that it is possible it might be her, but the body was never identified and has already been buried.'

'I understand it was displayed and several people came forward to suggest names.'

'They did, but no one suggested she might be a maidservant or mentioned anyone called Ethel, and our enquiries came to nothing. One woman was convinced it was her sister, who was a washerwoman, but she turned up drunk three days later. Another one had hysterics and said it was a lady who'd died and been buried and had come up out of her grave. But even if the corpse *had* got up and walked into the canal without anyone noticing, it was too recent a death. And there was a very low fellow who gave a false name, and cried and said it was his wife, but I think that was for the benefit of his new ladylove. To be plain, Miss Doughty, and from what I have heard of you I believe you are a young lady who prefers plain speaking to a display of false delicacy: the state of the body was such that I would feel very little confidence in any identification. The only distinguishing feature was the teeth, which had grown crooked, and amongst certain sections of the population that is not an unusual thing to find.'

'I was told that her clothes were of more than ordinary quality.'

'That is true. But there were no marks to distinguish them from any others widely sold in Bayswater.'

Frances was disappointed that she had not learned more, but was pleased that Gostelow had treated her with respect.

After a brief and carelessly assembled luncheon, Frances paid a visit to Mrs Pearson to report on her endeavours to date. In particular she wanted to establish if the missing maid had had crooked teeth, a feature that had not previously been mentioned. Mrs Pearson was extremely surprised and somewhat offended to be asked if she or any other member of the household had thought to view the body taken from the canal. No one, she said firmly, had been to view the corpse. When Frances asked about the maid's underclothing the lady reacted so violently that she thought she would be dismissed from the case, but once Mrs Pearson's purple face had returned to its usual red, she informed Frances indignantly that no one could provide any information on that subject. Ethel, she thought, had not had crooked teeth and had never complained of toothache, but then she did not examine the mouths of her maids and thought that if the girl had had this defect she might have been able to conceal it.

Mr Pearson returned from business at that moment and Frances asked if he had any observations on the question of Ethel's teeth. Mrs Pearson directed an angry stare at her, from which she understood, if she had not already deduced this, that any mention of the maid's underclothing in Mr Pearson's presence would be an insupportable insult. Mr Pearson, a small, meek-looking man with rounded spectacles, said that he took no notice of his wife's maids. Frances thought it was possible that the crooked teeth might be a feature that would be more obvious in a body that had undergone some decomposition, easier to conceal in life, especially if the woman had been sensitive about them.

As Frances neared her home she saw someone leaning against the gatepost, a man – long, thin and clad in black like an overgrown greasy spider. To her dismay she recognised an individual she had hoped she had seen the last of some months ago. She didn't know his real name, but because of the nasty sharp filleting knife he carried and presumably a propensity to use this implement on people he disapproved of, he was generally called 'the Filleter'. Frances had first encountered him when he was pursuing Chas and Barstie, on a matter they had refused ever to discuss. They were mortally afraid of him and would leave Bayswater at a moment's notice if they thought he was around. Frances was not afraid of the Filleter, but she found his company uncongenial, mainly because he was filthy about his person and smelt as if he had bathed in a rubbish pile.

She made only a slight hesitation in her step, which she hoped he would not notice, then squared her shoulders and walked resolutely on. He looked up at her as she approached and smiled, revealing a row of discoloured teeth. He was polishing his knife on an unpleasant looking piece of rag, but slid both away in a pocket as she drew near. He tipped his hat. 'Well now, if it isn't the famous detective,' he said in a soft voice that was so much worse than a harsh one for hinting at danger. 'You'd better watch yourself, Miss Doughty, you'd better be careful. It doesn't do for ladies to be poking and prying where they might get hurt. There's villains out there, villains much worse than me.'

Frances thought that there could not be many who were worse than the man before her, but decided not to mention it. Her sentiment, however, must have been apparent in her look. 'Have you come to ask my assistance or are you simply here to utter threats?' she asked coldly.

'Oh, neither, I was just here to pass on a message to your two friends.'

'If you want me to tell you where they are, I cannot help you.'

He grinned again. 'No need. They leave a trail wherever they go and I've already tracked them to their new place in Westbourne Grove. Quite a nice little business they have there. But they decline an interview. So just tell them from me, that I've got no quarrel with them now. They don't have to run, not on my account.'

'I am sure they will be very pleased to hear it,' said Frances. 'They are doing their best to make a respectable living and want nothing to do with you.'

He laughed. 'Respectable? I don't think so. And they'll fall into my hands again soon enough. But they're little fish and I've got more important things to attend to, so they can swim away for now.'

'What is your name?' Frances suddenly demanded.

He seemed taken aback. 'What is that to you?'

'I think someone ought to know. Today I have been trying to find the identity of a poor woman taken dead from the canal. I find it sad that she has lived and died and been put into a pauper's grave with no one to mourn or remember her. Perhaps one day you may suffer a similar fate.'

He nodded. 'That may be.' There was no trace of regret in his voice.

Frances climbed the steps to her door, but when she looked around he had gone.

Frances wrote a note to Dr Carmichael saying that she had been looking into the possibility of the body in the canal being that of the missing thief of his sister's journal, and asking if the maidservant had had crooked teeth.

She was able to pass on the Filleter's message later that day when Chas and Barstie called to dine. They were disturbed to hear that their old enemy was back in Bayswater and relieved, albeit with some reservations, that he had promised not to trouble them in future. 'I sincerely hope and trust that he did not offer you any insult?' said Chas, frowning.

'I do not think he means me harm,' said Frances. 'And whatever his business may be, I intend to stay well away from it. But now – to other matters. I trust you are becoming the leading lights of the Piccadilly Club?'

They glanced at each other. 'It is a very curious place,' said Chas, 'and there is no doubt that large sums of money change hands there privately. Cards and billiards and such, and considerable speculation on the horses. We also detected that there are men of business who seem to have no permanent office, but conduct all their affairs at the club. And there are things which I will not speak of to a young lady.'

'Are there no respectable persons there?'

'The club is a useful place where gentlemen who are staying in Bayswater may reside for a short time, and they often come and go with no idea that they are picking their way through a nest of snakes,' said Barstie.

'I am sorry to have sent you there,' said Frances.

'Oh, do not be concerned on our account!' exclaimed Chas. 'We are men of the world and we understand a great deal that the foolish and inexperienced do not.'

'What is your opinion of Dr Carmichael?' asked Frances. 'Does he have any unsavoury associates?'

'He seems to have no associates of any kind,' replied Barstie, 'which is strange in itself. He resists any attempt to open a conversation however trivial the subject.'

'Ask him the time of day and he will almost leap into the air with alarm, and then scurry away to his room,' agreed Chas. 'He does not gamble; if he drinks he does so alone and if there is a woman he favours I am unaware of her.'

'A man with no obvious vices is a man with a great many secrets,' said Barstie, darkly.

'Does he go out or does he keep to his room?' asked Frances.

'Something of both. It would be instructive to know where he goes,' said Chas. 'That man has business in hand, but he keeps it very close.'

'Have you made the acquaintance of Mr Darscot?'

'It is very hard not to,' said Barstie. 'He is a warbling fly who is every man's friend and brother, who will drink and gamble and chatter like a schoolgirl, and never allow a thought to cross his mind.'

'And yet he has, or claims to have, many valuable connections which a clever man might take advantage of,' said Chas. He rubbed his hands together. 'He may repay study yet.'

CHAPTER TWELVE

The inquest on Dr Mackenzie was to resume on the Friday morning, largely because it was a date convenient for Professor Stevenson. Frances had never seen the professor and was eager to do so as he was a celebrity in the world of medicine and a man to be admired. Anticipating that she would be rivalled for a place at the hearing by that portion of the population of Bayswater that had no business to attend to or could afford to leave it unattended, she determined to be at Providence Hall a full hour before the start of the hearing in order to be assured of a seat. This proved to be a wise decision. Her other investigations were safely in the hands of her assistants. Tom had already settled the matter of the missing washing, which proved to be the work of a gang of thieves none of whom was older than eight, and having left the client and her neighbour declaring eternal friendship and crying over a glass of beer, Tom had been deputed to keep an eye on the Pearson household. Sarah was being interviewed by Mr Whiteley, owner of the row of handsome shops on the Grove, who was busy constructing further properties in Queen's Road to enhance his empire. He was looking for a sensible woman to spy on rival establishments. Frances, who had no difficulty with Sarah undertaking any task in the pursuit of malefactors, was concerned that this was a somewhat degrading use of her services, but Sarah assured her that all the best shops employed spies and it had become quite a respectable calling.

Even as early as half past nine the little court was crowded with interested parties. The two main rival solicitors of Bayswater, Mr Rawsthorne and Mr Marsden, were there, both exuding professional politeness and private jealousy. Mr Gillan represented the *Chronicle*, but other pressmen had come from far and wide, and there were many who would be reporting back to Fleet Street, or even sending foreign cables. Dr Bonner was not present having sent Mr Fairbrother in his place, who informed Frances that his mentor was too unwell to make an appearance. Dr Carmichael was huddled in a corner, speaking to no one, and abruptly hid behind his morning paper when a new figure appeared. This gentleman was tall and spare with a grim expression, and bore a striking resemblance to the portrait of Dr Mackenzie. Frances, thinking it very probable that he was Mackenzie's brother, determined to secure an interview with him. She was able to approach near enough to hand him her card. He looked both surprised and insulted at her presumption. 'You are Mr David Mackenzie, I assume?' she said.

'Yes, Madam, I am,' he said severely, 'and we have not been introduced.' He stared at her card.

'I am a private detective engaged in the search for a missing man, Henry Palmer, who is an employee of your brother.'

'I know nothing of this Mr Palmer and have no need of a detective,' he said. He held the card out as if to return it, but she pretended not to notice the gesture.

'I was not offering my services in that capacity, but made use of my card to serve as my introduction. I am already acquainted with Dr Carmichael —' Frances glanced around, and saw that the man had vanished, 'who appears to have departed before the proceedings have even commenced. How curious.'

'Carmichael, here? That contemptible scoundrel!' exclaimed Mackenzie.

'Oh?'

His already hard gaze hardened further. 'If you have any pretensions at respectability, although given your profession I must doubt it very much, you will have nothing whatsoever to do with him.'

'I have only just made his acquaintance and would value your advice in that respect,' said Frances politely. 'If you would be kind enough to call on me when the proceedings have closed, I would like to interview you.'

He was a little disarmed by her courtesy, but not enough to thaw his antagonism. 'I am not sure, Madam, that I wish to be seen entering whatever apartments you may inhabit, or have any dealings with you in a public place.'

He made a curt nod of dismissal and began to turn away from her, but she moved quickly so that they still faced each other, and he recoiled in surprise and disdain. 'Very well, we may arrange to meet at the offices of Mr Rawsthorne, who is not only my solicitor but an old friend of my family.'

The name made him pause. 'Rawsthorne, you say? Hmm. He is the man I have employed to watch these proceedings.' There was a brief silence. 'Very well, if he can vouch for you I will consider it.' He turned and walked away, but Frances knew she had done enough.

By the time the inquest was due to begin, not only was every available seat in the little hall taken, but there were eager observers standing at the back, a seething knot of hopefuls in the foyer, and a disappointed crowd lurking outside.

'If we may commence,' said Hardwicke. 'This is the resumed inquest on the body of Dr Alastair Mackenzie, which was removed from the catacombs of All Souls Kensal Green on the 9th of October. I understand that allegations have been made suggesting that the body in the coffin was not a body at all, or if it was, it was not that of Dr Mackenzie. I wish to emphasise that I am entirely satisfied that this was indeed the body of Dr Mackenzie. I have here the death certificate signed by Dr Bonner on the 22nd of September. I have been given to understand that he is too unwell to attend; nevertheless, we can proceed without him. Dr Bonner has already given evidence that he had for some time been treating Dr Mackenzie for a weak heart and had advised him against overwork, as he had feared that the strain would be too much for him. This advice Dr Mackenzie ignored and when he collapsed in the presence of Dr Bonner there was so little doubt as to the cause that a certificate was signed without further enquiry showing that death was due to cardiac syncope. Dr Mackenzie's body was laid out at his own premises, the Life House, for a period of four days, after which Dr Bonner saw what he believed were sufficient signs of decomposition – due to a septic condition of the intestines – to be certain that the deceased was indeed dead. The body was coffined on Sunday the 26th of September, the funeral taking place on the following day. Following this, at the instigation of

Miss Frances Doughty –' there was a buzz of whispers in the courtroom and heads turned in Frances' direction ' – a visit was made to the catacombs at All Souls, where it was discovered that some motion of the body had taken place after the coffin was deposited. I ordered a full post-mortem examination to take place and I now call Dr Collin to give evidence of his findings.'

Dr Collin had always attended Frances' family and was a prime exponent of the genial manner, something that had become a little strained in Frances' dealings with him ever since the time she had suggested that he had made a mistake, especially as she was later proved to be correct. The circumstance had not been mentioned since, indeed any discussion of the subject had been very carefully avoided, but Frances was sure that he had never forgiven her. He stepped up to the coroner's table.

'I carried out the post-mortem examination of Dr Mackenzie on Wednesday the 13th of October under the supervision of Professor Stevenson, and with the assistance of Mr Fairbrother, who took notes. In doing so I was obliged to take into account the stated date of death of the doctor and the unusual conditions under which the body had been kept before it was deposited in the catacombs. I looked in particular for any signs that the mechanism in the coffin, which had been activated, might have been influenced by natural means such as the gases of decomposition causing motion of the corpse within the coffin. I was assisted in this by an engineer, who thoroughly tested the apparatus and who is present to give evidence here today.

'The contents of the stomach suggested to me that Dr Mackenzie's last meal had been taken on the night of the 21st of September and that he had been in a fasting state for some time thereafter. There were marked signs of decomposition as one might expect, however, they were not of the extent that I would have expected in the corpse of a man who had died some three weeks ago and been exposed to a warm atmosphere for almost a week before burial. Moreover, I did not detect the advanced sepsis of the intestines described by Dr Bonner. It is my opinion that as of the 13th of October the man had been dead for ten or maybe twelve days at most.'

A whisper travelled around the court, but was soon stilled as Hardwicke leaned forward to speak. 'Dr Collin, let me have this quite clearly from you. It is your belief, based upon your many years in medical practice, that Dr Mackenzie died at some date between the 1st and 3rd of October?'

Dr Collin was impassive. 'Yes.'

'But you are aware, of course, that the body was deposited in the catacombs at All Souls on the 27th of September?'

'So I understand.'

'Are you telling this court that Dr Mackenzie, the director of the Life House, the purpose of which is to avoid any possibility of premature burial, was himself buried alive?'

'Yes, I am.'

The courtroom, every occupant of which had been listening anxiously and quietly so as not to miss a single word, erupted in a torrent of exclamations. Newsmen scribbled rapidly and tore pages out of their notebooks, then ran to the door and handed the fragments of paper to messengers waiting outside. A cry went up in the foyer as the news poured forth to be followed by loud yells from the street. The sensational revelation, thought Frances, would be in America faster than one could imagine it possible. Hardwicke called for silence and the coroner's officers did their best to restore order, but it was some little time before the tumult died down.

'Any repeat of this disgraceful conduct and I will have the room cleared,' said Hardwicke sternly. 'Now then, Dr Collin, please continue. Did you form any conclusion as to the cause of death?'

'I did. Dr Mackenzie died of a collapse of the heart brought on by fright. It is my theory that he was placed in the coffin while in a state of suspended animation during which the signs of life were greatly reduced. The peculiar construction of the Life House coffin meant that he had a sufficiency of air for a man in that condition. He subsequently came back to a state of consciousness and was able to operate the mechanism with his hand, but he may well have been unable to call out for assistance. There was a bell in the coffin, but the charcoal packing around the body had moved, probably as a result of his struggles, and prevented its operation. There were abundant signs in the interior of the coffin that he had fought to escape, and there was damage to his hands and knees from his efforts in that respect.'

A groan of distress flowed around the little court, but Hardwicke did not suppress it and it passed. 'Were there any indications as to what had brought on the condition of suspended animation?'

'I observed the mark of an injection in the doctor's left arm and sought further advice on the matter.'

'Thank you, Dr Collin. If you would step down now, I would like to hear from Professor Stevenson.'

The presence of that renowned gentleman in such a tiny court was a matter of considerable excitement and all heads craned to look. The individual who stepped forward was tall and vigorous looking with a fine dark beard. He was, thought Frances, in the very prime of a man's life, about two and forty, when his strength and intelligence were at their peak. Everything about his manner and bearing invited confidence in his opinion.

'I am Dr Thomas Stevenson, Professor of Medical Jurisprudence at Guys Hospital, and adviser to the Home Office. I observed the post-mortem examination of Dr Alastair Mackenzie and removed samples, which I then subjected to a number of tests. My conclusion was that Dr Mackenzie had received an injection of *morphia*, although whether he administered it to himself or it was given by another individual it is impossible to say. The injection was made in the left arm and I have been told that the deceased was right handed. There were no indications on the body that he had been subjected to any forcible restraint, so it is very possible that even if he did not inject himself, it was received voluntarily. The amount of *morphia* in his system would, I believe, have been sufficient in normal cases where the individual was robust and in good health to produce unconsciousness and slow the action of the heart. It would not in such cases have been fatal or even have led to any lasting ill-health. Dr Mackenzie, however, was not a robust man and it is my opinion that the dose of *morphia* in his case could well have resulted in a state of very deep unconsciousness which might to outward appearances have given the impression of death.'

'In your opinion, was the injection the cause of death?' asked Hardwicke.

'Not directly. I believe that had Dr Mackenzie not been placed in a coffin but carefully tended, he might very well have awoken from his stupor.'

There was another rumble of chatter about the little court.

The next witness was a young man who appeared to be in a state of some excitement. He brought a little model with which he demonstrated the beautiful working of the interior mechanism of the coffin, and showed how it was constructed and operated with such glowing and voluble enthusiasm that Dr Hardwicke had to urge him to stop. The main result of his evidence was that the position of the lever admitted only one mode of employment, with the fingers, and he had never known any device to be operated in any other way or indeed at all. The court was left with the profound hope that the reason the mechanism had never before been operated was that the occupant of the coffin had been dead.

This completed the evidence, which, thought Frances, left the jurors in something of a quandary. There was little doubt as to the cause of Mackenzie's death, but it was necessary to determine the contribution made by the injection, whether or not a crime had been committed, and how much they ought to condemn the negligence of Dr Bonner.

Dr Hardwicke cut through the difficulty by addressing the jurymen, who gave great attention to his every word. 'Gentlemen,' he said, 'I am sure you appreciate that you have a very difficult task to perform. The revelation that shortly prior to his death Dr Mackenzie received an injection of morphine, even if it was not a fatal one, must give rise to considerable concern about the circumstances that led to his being placed in his coffin, which was then deposited in the catacombs while he was still alive. You may feel, as I do, that the absence from this court of Dr Bonner, the only person present at the collapse of Dr Mackenzie, apart from the unfortunately still missing Mr Palmer, is much to be regretted and renders it impossible for you to reach a verdict at this time. Dr Bonner may well be able to supply this court with valuable information about the tragic events and I must express my concern that his sudden indisposition has coincided with today's hearing.' The jurymen, sensing that they were about to be temporarily relieved of responsibility, nodded with some alacrity. 'It is my intention, therefore, to adjourn the proceedings in the hope that in one week's time Dr Bonner will be sufficiently restored to health to attend. Perhaps, if we are fortunate, Mr Palmer may have reappeared by then.'

As the proceedings closed, the pressmen made a unified dash for the door. David Mackenzie and Mr Rawsthorne rose from their seats and stood to one side, talking very quietly and earnestly. Frances sought out Mr Fairbrother, who was looking pale with shock. 'Please, I would rather not say anything just now —' he said and hurried out onto the street in search of a cab. Frances quickly followed him and when he saw this he increased his pace to a run, trotting down Church Street and waving wildly at passing hansoms, which were either occupied or being rapidly taken by pressmen struggling for precedence. As he looked about him seeking some avenue of escape, Frances gathered her skirts and ran after him. Astonished and dismayed to see that she was in pursuit, Fairbrother dashed out of Church Street and began to run up the better populated Edgware Road. In any formal race he would undoubtedly have outpaced her, but he had seriously underestimated the energy of a tall young woman unafraid of long walks, and her single-minded determination and willingness to fling herself pell-mell down a public street in a good cause. When he was finally able to hail a cab, the brief pause as he stepped in gave her enough time to catch him up and leap breathlessly inside. 'Miss Doughty!' he exclaimed in astonishment as she crushed in beside him.

There was the sting of sweat on her brow and it was a curious feeling, almost a good one. The two of them, red-faced and panting, stared at each other, he in alarm and she in triumph. 'Dr Bonner is not ill at all,' she gasped. 'Either that or he is suffering from nothing more deadly than remorse. And you have been deputed to tell him the verdict so that he may act accordingly. What is he about to do? Run away? Disappear like Mr Palmer? Make a pretence of being dead to avoid the consequences of his own actions? I doubt that the public or the police would countenance *that* happening a second time amongst the directors of the same business.'

'Oh this is too terrible!' exclaimed Fairbrother. 'I know that Dr Bonner is a good man and never meant to do any harm. And he has a great deal to worry him at the moment. He has had a letter this morning from Mr Marsden saying that a Mr Darscot has made a claim on Dr Mackenzie's estate for a debt of £500 and has a signed agreement to prove the matter, and there is nothing with which to pay! And now this! It could be the ruination of the Life House!'

'What has Dr Bonner told you about the night that Dr Mackenzie was supposed to have died?'

'Only what everyone knows!'

'Omitting, I assume, the little detail of the injection? Or did he mention that?'

Fairbrother ran the back of his hand across his brow and there was a darkly haunted expression circling his eyes. Frances felt sure that the recent revelations had come as a shock. 'No, he did not. Of course, Dr Mackenzie might very well have injected himself without Dr Bonner noticing.'

'And what happened to the needle and the phial? Where are they? Dr Mackenzie could not have injected himself at home and then walked to the Life House. He would have collapsed before he arrived there. Surely those items would have been on his person, or nearby, or in his bag? Has Dr Bonner concealed them? Because if he knew what had happened he must bear some of the responsibility for Dr Mackenzie's death. Did he lie about the sepsis to encourage a quicker burial in case the injection was discovered, and so inadvertently hurry his friend into the catacombs while still alive?'

Fairbrother shook his head in despair. 'I know that he will have an explanation.'

'Good, I very much look forward to hearing it.'

He uttered a groan. 'Dr Bonner *is* unwell. He really is! You must believe me! Please don't try and question him today! Could you not wait until he is better?'

'I will speak to him today and will not be talked or cajoled out of it. Please do not try.'

'No,' he said miserably, 'I can see that would be useless.'

'Has he employed a solicitor?'

'Yes – Mr Rawsthorne.'

'Who is not so fleet of foot as we and will no doubt be coming in a later cab.'

'You don't intend to question Dr Bonner without his legal man beside him?' said Fairbrother, alarmed.

'If at all possible,' said Frances.

'Then I will be there as witness!'

'As you please.'

'Strictly I could deny you entry to the house, if I wished,' he said, querulously.

'And how do you propose to do that?'

'I –' he avoided her gaze. 'I am not sure.'

'Then you had better let me in.'

By the time they arrived, there was no question of Frances not gaining immediate entry to Dr Bonner's house, where she found that gentleman sitting alone in his study. There was a bandage on his foot and his stick within easy reach. 'Forgive me if I do not rise,' he said dolefully. 'The gout is always at its worst when I am agitated.' Fairbrother scurried about pouring a glass of water from a carafe to which, at a slight signal from his mentor, he added a small measure of brandy.

'I will not explore your reasons for not being present at the inquest today,' said Frances, 'I have a feeling that your replies will be neither interesting nor useful. There was no verdict today; the hearing was adjourned for a week to enable you to attend. It was felt that it could not be concluded without your evidence.'

'I feared that,' said Bonner. 'I had hoped to be able to spend some time out of London, taking the sea air, but I suppose if I did so my absence might be misinterpreted.'

'The needle mark has been found,' said Frances. 'The matter injected has been identified as morphine.'

Bonner was silent and Fairbrother stared at him. 'The revelation does not surprise you,' he asked, shocked.

Bonner shook his head. 'No. I understand how it must look for me, but I had hoped to preserve Mackenzie's reputation. He does not deserve the name of suicide. I knew that he wanted to go away and allow the world to believe that he was dead. He told me he would inject himself with a sedative to help him simulate the appearance of death, but I am afraid he underestimated the effect of the drug on his weak heart.'

'The injection was not the cause of death,' said Frances.

'No?' said Bonner. 'But it can scarcely have been anything else.' Suddenly, his mouth trembled and tears started in his eyes. 'Oh, dear God! No! No!'

Fairbrother came to stand by Bonner's side. 'Miss Doughty,' he said, 'I think it would be best if I spoke to Dr Bonner privately. Grant him that, at least.'

The doorbell sounded and Frances, anticipating the arrival of Mr Rawsthorne, decided to depart.

❧

Frances spent the rest of her day fending off the attentions of persons who wished her to discover the whereabouts of pet kittens, monkeys, canaries and even white mice. One gentleman, however, a Mr Horton, was so persistent, claiming that he was actually in some grave personal danger, that she agreed to see him. He was plainly dressed and looked like a man who took as much care of himself as he thought necessary, but which was still not enough. His collar was worn, as were his cuffs, and he had paid too little attention to his hair, which was overlong and none too clean, but his appearance showed many signs of an attempt to appear respectable and he had not entirely failed. She thought him perhaps of the class of junior clerk or salesman, although unlikely currently to be in employment.

'Miss Doughty,' he began, 'I am in urgent need of help and I understand that it is to you that I must apply to be sure of success. You may be able to save my life!'

'I do not undertake dangerous missions,' said Frances, 'however, I will listen to what you say and advise if I can.'

'Oh, but you *must* help me! I have been to other persons in the neighbourhood and they all proved themselves quite unable. Then I chanced to hear of the affair of the parrot and I knew I must come to you!'

'Does this involve an animal of some kind?' asked Frances, apprehensively.

'It does indeed. The creature in question is an alligator.'

'You have mislaid an alligator?' she exclaimed. 'Alive or stuffed?'

'Oh very much alive, and I have not mislaid it at all, no, no, I very much wish I could, but the horrible beast will keep pursuing me and I cannot escape it.'

Frances took a moment or two to consider this. 'It pursues you?'

'Yes!' His hands were shaking and he used a soiled cuff to mop his forehead.

'Where, exactly?'

'Oh, everywhere!' he said very earnestly.

'In the street?'

'Yes, and when I am at home it lodges in my chimney and makes terrible roaring sounds. But I must reassure you that the fox has been dealt with. Yes,' he said with a satisfied smile, 'I have dealt with him myself, so you need not trouble yourself about the fox.'

'Mr Horton,' said Frances, after a little thought, 'I am not an expert in these matters, but I do believe the alligator to be an aquatic animal. And one moreover which is seldom to be found in Bayswater, where it might attract some attention.'

'I know,' he said, nodding. 'I understand the difficulty, for it does need to keep its skin wet, but it is a clever beast and basks in the Serpentine on a daily basis. It is there even now!'

Frances was briefly tempted to try and reason with Mr Horton, but realised that the unfortunate man was a stranger to reason.

'I really do not think I am equipped to catch an alligator,' she said.

'But if you could just speak to it and tell it to depart, I am sure it would do your bidding!' he pleaded.

Such a commission, thought Frances, might be one of the easiest ones she had ever attempted, since she felt sure that if the gentleman could imagine this obstinate reptile into existence than he might be persuaded to imagine it gone, but she did not wish to take unfair advantage of a fragile mind and in any case, the payment might prove to be as insubstantial as the alligator.

Politely but firmly she informed Mr Horton that she was unable to deal with his request and he departed, in a state of great disappointment.

Her last client gone, Frances and Sarah settled to enjoy a quiet evening when she received a note asking her to meet David Mackenzie at the office of Mr Rawsthorne promptly at ten o'clock the next morning.

CHAPTER THIRTEEN

Mr Rawsthorne had acted for the Doughty family ever since Frances could remember and had been a sympathetic support at the time of both her brother's and her father's death. How she wished that her normally parsimonious parent had been prudent enough to entrust his investments to the good care of Mr Rawsthorne and not chase after the fanciful dream that had led to his ultimate ruin. Had he been wiser she would even now be studying to qualify as a pharmacist, with the business flourishing in the safe hands of a good manager, instead of which she had been obliged to sell her inheritance to meet an unexpected mountain of debt. Unable even to obtain an apprenticeship after the association of the Doughty name with a number of sensational murders, she had been faced with a choice of depending on the charitable good nature of her uncle, or embarking on a risky career as a detective. Some months after taking that adventurous step, she felt herself growing towards financial independence but still balancing on the fine margin that lay between success and failure, the outcome far from certain.

Even Mr Rawsthorne was not immune to financial reverses since he had lost funds as a result of the recent crash of the Bayswater bank, an event which, while it would undoubtedly have occurred whatever Frances had done or said, had happened at the time it did because of her enquiries. The last few months might have been good to him, with the excitement attendant on the General Election, but he could not have been unaware that the loss of some important clients had been directly attributable to Frances. Nevertheless, he greeted her with his accustomed good humour, which was more than could be said for his clerk, Mr Wheelock, a grinning, ink-smeared scarecrow with hair like a bundle of brazen bedsprings dipping over his eyes. Frances, who hoped that she would never be so shallow as to judge solely on appearance, found Wheelock's manner insulting and could not reconcile Mr Rawsthorne's employment of him with his own solid reputation and pleasant nature. She had never broached the subject with Rawsthorne, but was obliged to assume that the clerk had some talent in the field of arithmetic, or an ability to keep important matters confidential that was out of the common way.

David Mackenzie, who had presumably been thoroughly briefed by Mr Rawsthorne as to Frances' good name, no longer looked at her as if she was an irredeemably immoral woman, only as someone who might, with very little encouragement, become one. After briefly rising from his chair to greet her, he sat primly, every muscle in his frame tightly tensed, alive with a sense of his virtue, which needed a constant and vigilant defence. Mr Rawsthorne, ignoring the discomfort in the office, sat at his ease behind his desk.

'Well now, Miss Doughty, say whatever it is you have to say,' said Mackenzie.

'I am hoping to find Henry Palmer, your brother's assistant, who went missing on the same night that he – well as it now appears, collapsed and was thought to be dead. The fact that the two events occurred on the same night cannot be ignored and so I have been trying to learn as much as I can about your brother, who may well have sent Mr Palmer away on some errand. I understand that you were not on cordial terms?'

'We were not,' Mackenzie replied curtly. 'We had not spoken in over twenty years.'

'Can you advise me of the reason for this?'

His mouth twitched in disgust. 'It is not a nice subject, Miss Doughty.'

'I hardly expected it would be anything trivial.'

'You may speak freely to the young lady,' said Rawsthorne. 'She has a strong constitution.'

'Hmm, well that is as may be,' said Mackenzie dubiously. 'If it was just the case of my brother's memory I would have no compunction about speaking my mind, but another's reputation is at stake, a fine and very beautiful lady, beautiful not only in her person but in her mind, her very soul.'

'You speak of Madeleine Carmichael.'

'I do. Twenty-two years ago she was the ornament of Edinburgh society and I was a junior clerk, working every hour I could to be something better. I knew I did not deserve the lady, but determined to apply myself so that one day I would be able to address her in terms of matrimony.'

'She knew of this?'

'She cannot have failed to be aware of my profound and honourable esteem.'

'And your brother? He knew of it too?'

He looked pained. 'Oh yes, he knew, but it made no difference to him. He also admired Miss Carmichael and set out to woo her for himself.'

'With what result?'

Mackenzie struggled with his memories. 'I cannot prove it, Miss Doughty, no one can, but I am convinced that he – prevailed – won her love, persuaded the innocent girl that to succumb to his crude desires was no sin – and to be blunt – ruined her.'

Frances nodded. 'Was there any result of this connection?'

'If you mean did she bear a child, she did not. Worse than that, far, far worse.'

'You mean her condition was a direct cause of her death?'

'*Alastair* caused her death!' he exclaimed with a little wail of distress. 'My own brother killed the finest woman who ever breathed!'

Frances was about to speak, but Mackenzie raised his hand for silence and took a few moments to regain his accustomed composure. 'Oh please do not ask me for proof, he was very clever and although we suspected him and tried every means at our disposal to bring the crime home to him, it was impossible. She died of septicaemia in the most terrible agony that nothing could relieve, following what can only be described as the work of a butcher. The case went before the Procurator Fiscal, but while the cause of death was never in any doubt the identity of the culprit was. Alastair gave evidence that he had never had any criminal connection with Miss Carmichael, and indeed that she had only visited him once, shortly before she died, telling him of her shameful plight and asking him for advice. He claimed that he had told her that her best course was to confess all to her father and throw herself upon his mercy. The court believed him. Some weeks later I learned that a lady who matched Miss Carmichael's description had visited him many times in his lodgings. I think, and Carmichael also thought, that my brother lied in court, and not only had he ruined a dear sweet girl, but in trying to escape the consequences of his infamy he brought about her death. Many people in Edinburgh thought the same and the feeling against him was such that eventually he decided to leave the city. A post came up in Germany about then and he left. I have not seen him since, nor have I wished to.'

'Dr Carmichael recently learned of some evidence that came to light which he thought might have enabled him to have your brother brought to justice,' said Frances.

'Oh? What evidence was this?'

'I believe it is in the form of a journal which his sister found amongst Miss Carmichael's papers. Unfortunately it was stolen, possibly by a blackmailer, before Carmichael himself saw it.'

Mackenzie looked puzzled. 'His sister? I am afraid I do not understand you.'

'His older sister. Her first name is Ellen, I believe.'

Mackenzie shook his head. 'Impossible. Carmichael only ever had one sister. Are you sure you are not mistaken?'

Frances consulted her notebook. 'I wrote it down as he spoke. Ellen, married to a doctor, living in Kensington —' she paused. 'Yes, he was very evasive about that – no surname, no address, and the lady is said to be too ill to be troubled. So ill that it seems she does not exist. Well, I have been lied to before.'

'So Carmichael had no proof. Well, it's all one, now.'

Frances wondered why, if the journal did not exist, Carmichael was so eager to have it returned, unless of course he had employed her for quite another purpose. 'You expressed a very unflattering opinion of Dr Carmichael,' she said. 'What can you tell me of him?'

'Only that he too was obliged to leave Edinburgh under a cloud a few years after my brother. He has spent a great many years languishing in some out of the way practices, most recently in Carlisle, although he does come to London from time to time to sample its more vicious entertainments.'

'I think I understand your meaning,' said Frances. 'Why did he leave Edinburgh?'

'He was accused by a lady patient of committing a criminal assault upon her person while she was under the influence of chloroform which he had administered for a minor operation. The lady had been confused, as patients often are following a period of unconsciousness, and it was not until she reached her home that she confessed to her husband that she thought something untoward had taken place. Carmichael was tried, but he told the court that chloroform has an unusual effect upon the memory and can provoke quite scandalous dreams and imaginings, especially in females. He was acquitted.'

'Do you think that was the right verdict?'

'All I can say is that I have been told privately that there were incidents involving other ladies who were too ashamed to make a complaint. And —' he paused. 'There are some things, Miss Doughty, that cannot be spoken aloud, even before men, let alone a young unmarried woman.'

Frances proffered him her notebook open at a clean page, together with a pencil. He stared at her, both surprised and affronted. 'Really, I —'

'If you write it down, it is set in stone, but only say it and it will disappear as if it was never spoken and then you and Mr Rawsthorne may, if you wish, pretend that it was never said.'

'It is too hideous and disgusting,' he protested. 'That any man would —' he compressed his lips in a tight line of distaste. 'Very well. I know for a fact that the lady who brought the case against him bore a very close resemblance to Miss Carmichael. I have also been told as regards the other ladies that there were strong points of similarity. There. That is Dr Carmichael's story and you may make of it what you wish. I do not say that his love for his sister was ever expressed in ways other than those of the very deepest brotherly affection and respect. That terrible crime I do not lay at his door. But his mind was, and is, unclean and drives him to do loathsome things. I have no doubt that he spends a great deal of his time visiting females of the lowest character, and that amongst persons of that class his tastes are well known.'

'Is there anything more you wish to tell me?'

'Oh, Miss Doughty, I wished to tell you none of it! But that is all I have to say. I will remain in London until the inquest is concluded, but I will return to Edinburgh immediately thereafter. My brother's remains have already been deposited where they were before and that is the end of my interest. Indeed, I am only here at the behest of my mother, who became very agitated when the dreadful story appeared in the newspapers.'

'Did you view your brother's body?' Frances asked.

'I did.'

'And you have no doubt that it was indeed his remains?'

'I have heard that you have made some strange allegations, for what purposes I cannot imagine. I recognised him by an old scar; it was on his temple, just hidden by his hair. I remember it well. It was I who gave it to him. There – enough!'

Frances took her leave and reluctantly felt that she must now accept that the body in the catacombs was that of Dr Mackenzie. As to Carmichael, whatever foolishness he was practising she wanted none of it. She determined to confront him at the earliest opportunity and say that she could no longer continue with the case as she had been asked to chase a chimaera. If his sister Ellen did not exist then it was very probable that the whole story was a lie from start to finish. There was no journal, no snuffboxes, no theft, and no light-fingered maidservant. Which meant that there was now only one candidate for the body in the canal, Mrs Pearson's missing maid Ethel.

There was a note waiting for her from Chas and Barstie, which left her still less inclined to continue with Dr Carmichael as a client. They had set an agent to follow him and found that while during the daytime he visited hospitals and attended medical lectures, he spent his evenings with a woman of doubtful reputation. Frances knew that she ought to be angry with Dr Carmichael for approaching her under false pretences, but this was ameliorated by the fact that she had always regarded him with suspicion. She was a little curious to know what he had hoped to achieve by engaging her services, but mainly anxious to be rid of him. She would have liked to face him down in the Piccadilly Club and felt annoyed at the sheer number of places that would not admit her on grounds of her sex. Frances recalled, not without some embarrassment, her masquerade as a young man in her late brother's suit of clothes, claiming to be a newspaper correspondent, in which guise she had first accosted Cedric Garton. It had been a dangerous thing to do and she would never want to do it again, but all the same there was a little voice at the back of her mind that would keep on reminding her how free she had felt without heavy skirts and petticoats weighing her down. She composed a note to Dr Carmichael asking him to come and see her at his earliest convenience.

Sarah returned from her first day as Mr Whiteley's spy. She had been disappointed to discover that although the task had appeared at the outset to involve a great deal of shopping, something to which she was not averse, Mr Whiteley was unwilling to supply the required funds for her to do this, saying only that she was to look, make a note of the quality of the goods and their price, and report back to him, but not buy. If they were items she might want, then she must pay for them herself, but she must buy at Whiteleys and nowhere else. Frances felt that they had uncovered the secret of Mr Whiteley's wealth, and wondered how far one might take prudence with money until it became parsimony and then meanness. Sarah was not, therefore, in the best of moods when Mr Horton reappeared in a state of agitation bordering on tears, insisting that Frances capture the alligator at once.

Sarah summed him up with a glance and informed him that she had seen the offending animal in the handbag department of Whiteleys, caught it, and killed it by snapping its neck. The brusque gesture of her fists left him in no doubt that she was thoroughly accustomed to dispatching unwanted livestock in this manner, and he blanched in terror and ran away without offering payment.

'You won't see *him* again!' said Sarah.

❋

Dr Carmichael arrived to see Frances on the Monday morning with a cautiously hopeful expression and slid into a seat in the little parlour. 'Have you discovered anything of interest?' he asked.

Frances faced him across the table and looked at him calmly.

'Yes, I discovered that you do not have a sister called Ellen.'

'Oh,' he said, crestfallen, and fidgeted with his fingers. 'I suppose,' he said at last, 'that it was foolish of me to imagine that I might be able to deceive you. I expect you have been talking to that cold fish David Mackenzie.'

'Never mind who I have been talking to – do you admit lying to me?'

'It was not exactly a lie,' he said grudgingly, 'it was – a necessary invention.'

'And the whole story you told me about how the documents had been found was also a necessary invention?'

He looked unhappy. Frances looked unsympathetic. 'I am afraid so,' he admitted.

'Very well.' Frances placed an envelope on the table. He picked it up and looked at her questioningly. 'My account,' she said. 'For the work I have done to date. Please examine it and finalise matters in due course.'

'What do you mean?' he exclaimed.

'I mean I cannot act for you.'

'Oh but – what about the journal – I must have it!'

Frances' undeniable contempt for the slippery and perverted creature before her was tempered by astonishment at his effrontery. 'Dr Carmichael, are you really telling me that this journal actually exists, because I am far from convinced that it does. I will not waste my time chasing after ghosts when I can act for clients who are able to tell me the truth.'

'It does exist,' he assured her, 'but I was obliged for reasons I cannot divulge to – well – be less than candid about the circumstances of its loss.'

'I would prefer it if my account was settled in cash before the end of the month,' said Frances.

He put the envelope back on the table. 'I will be honest with you, Miss Doughty.'

'That would be refreshing, but I am afraid it is a little late to start now. You need not trouble yourself to say more. Miss Smith will conduct you to the door.'

Sarah folded her arms and gave him a hard look, so that he might be in no doubt as to how this might be achieved.

He glanced nervously at Sarah, but he made no move to go and instead pushed the envelope closer to Frances. When Frances did not pick it up he pushed it closer. Still Frances ignored it. 'I do not, as you say, have a sister called Ellen,' he said. 'I found the journal myself when looking at some of my sister's things.'

Sarah rose to her feet.

'If you don't mind, this is all very distressing for me,' he said, 'and I am feeling a little faint. Might I trouble you for a drink of water?'

'Please, help yourself,' she said, indicating the carafe, and he seized upon it eagerly and poured a drink. 'I can scarcely credit that this journal, assuming it to exist, was not found until recently,' she observed.

He gulped at the water. 'I know how this must seem. I did examine Madeleine's letters and diaries shortly after her death, and have them in a safe place, but she also left some garments, which I have treasured, untouched. About a year ago – I don't know why – I looked at them and found the journal folded in amongst them. Possibly so that it should remain hidden. The journal revealed that poor Madeleine had visited Mackenzie often and that she feared she was in a delicate state of health. I realised that I had the evidence I needed that would finally result in Mackenzie paying for his terrible treatment of my dear sister.'

'I see,' said Frances, seeing that the appearance of an incriminating document and Dr Mackenzie's sudden need for £1,000 might not be unconnected. 'So you came to London to confront him with this journal and demand money from him?'

'No – no not at all! That would have been a secret revenge, but what I wanted was a public exposure. I decided to hand the journal to the police. It so happened that I had to come to London in any case as I was applying for a medical position here, and so I brought it with me.' He sipped at the water again. 'I also brought with me a letter, one that Madeleine had written to me when I was away at my studies, so that the police could compare the writing and be sure that it was hers. But before I could approach the police both the letter and the journal were stolen under circumstances I do not wish to describe. They were in a pocketbook which also contained some banknotes.'

'You may be obliged to describe this event in future,' observed Frances.

'I know, but I prefer not to at present. I was concerned, Miss Doughty, because there were some notes in my sister's journal which expressed her unhappiness at certain behaviours of mine. Nothing that broke the law, you understand, but matters that reflected poorly on my honour, things that I was most anxious should not be made public as it would be detrimental to my medical career. I waited with considerable trepidation to be contacted by a blackmailer, but that did not happen. Eventually, after being unsuccessful in my application for the position, I was obliged to return to my practice in Carlisle. I assumed that whoever stole the pocketbook was only interested in the banknotes and had thrown away the other items thinking them to be valueless. Recently I returned to London, once again hopeful of obtaining a position here. I was walking along Porchester Road when a messenger boy ran up to me and asked me if I was Dr Carmichael. I said I was and he gave me what I thought was a note and then ran away.' Carmichael put the glass down, wiped his hands carefully on a clean handkerchief, then took a small leather case with a brass clasp from his pocket and opened it, extracting a folded sheet of paper. 'This is what he gave me. It is one of my sister's letters – the very one that was stolen this time last year together with the journal.'

'May I see it?' asked Frances.

Hesitantly, he handed it over, and Frances gently unfolded the sheet. It was a very brief note, advising the recipient that their mother was almost fully recovered from a bad cold, and expressing the hope that his studies were progressing well and that he would be able to return home soon. The date, in 1857, the signature and the sentiments showed it unequivocally to be a letter from Madeleine Carmichael to her brother. 'Why do you think this was returned to you?' she asked.

'As proof that the journal was in someone's possession. As you see, the contents of the letter are quite innocuous,' he said, recovering the paper and putting it away reverentially, 'but of course the journal is not. Even though Mackenzie is beyond the reach of a blackmailer, I am vulnerable, and all the more so for having hopes of gaining a new and prestigious post.'

'Have you been approached by someone demanding money for the journal's return?'

'Not yet.'

'And what do you expect me to do?'

'Why, recover it, of course!'

'But you offer me no clue as to who might have it or where it might be found.'

'No, but I thought —'

'Yes?'

'I thought that in the profession of detective one often meets persons who are known for their criminal activities. I had hoped that you would easily be able to discover who is harbouring material of this nature.'

There was a long silence. Frances pushed the envelope back across the table. 'I really do not think I can help you.'

'But I must have the journal!' he exclaimed, with such a burst of emotion that Frances could not doubt that it existed and that his predicament was acute.

'Is it certain from its contents that you are the person named?'

'I am afraid so.'

'Was the letter handed to you without an envelope?'

'It was.'

'Can you describe the messenger boy?'

'No, by the time I realised what the paper was he had run away. But there are a number of them who seem always to be about Porchester Road. The boy may even know where the journal is being held. He may be a confederate of the criminal.'

'I see,' said Frances thoughtfully.

Carmichael took a wallet from his pocket and placed a banknote on the table. Had it been a Scottish banknote she might have shown him the door at once, but she saw that it was a good English one.

'Very well,' she said reluctantly, 'I will make some enquiries. In the meantime, you must be alert and tell me if you see the boy again. If anyone does approach you for money for the return of the journal you must agree to their demands, make an appointment to meet them and then inform me at once.'

'I don't want the police involved!' he said quickly.

'That is understood. I take it that all you want is the journal and you will not press charges against the thief.'

'Exactly so.'

Frances picked up the money and the envelope. 'You must be truthful in future or I can do nothing for you.'

With a nod Carmichael departed, and Frances and Sarah looked at one another. 'He is undoubtedly afraid,' said Frances, 'but for myself I am not convinced that he was not the person who blackmailed Dr Mackenzie. He is unaware, of course, that I know of Mackenzie's need for money and that it coincides with his first visit to London. The journal has probably been stolen by a criminal associate. I think he knows who has it, but not where it is.'

'What will you do?'

'I will ask Tom to make enquiries amongst the messenger boys who work around Porchester Road. Mr Knight and Mr Taylor will continue to keep watch on Dr Carmichael. It is possible that my discovery of his lies may rattle him into doing something incautious.'

CHAPTER FOURTEEN

rances despatched a note to Tom, and then spent a little time tidying her papers, an activity that always seemed to produce order in her mind and which she found very calming. She had just completed a simple luncheon when she received an unexpected visitor, a very serious looking Inspector Sharrock of Paddington Green police station. Sharrock, a stocky man with a face that looked as though it had been rubbed red with a nutmeg grater, often evinced a stern, almost fatherly concern at Frances' activities. He called on her from time to time, under the guise of supervising her and checking that she had not been murdered or worse, but also hoping to learn if there was anything of note she had discovered about some of the hidden crimes of Bayswater. This time there was no preamble.

'It might interest you to know,' said Sharrock, 'that I have come here at the very special request of a Mr Horton, who wishes me to place Miss Smith under immediate arrest for murder.'

Frances glanced at Sarah with some concern since the possibility of Sarah committing an act of violence was not a remote one. Sarah, who was doing some mending, continued her work without so much as a pause. 'Might I ask who the supposed victim is and when this event is said to have occurred?' asked Frances.

'You may. It happened last Christmas, and the victim is an alligator which Mr Horton assures me was a very particular friend of his. He says he witnessed the crime with his own eyes and it has caused him very great distress, and he will testify to it in a court of law if required. He also claims that Miss Smith has freely admitted, and indeed gloried in the fact that she strangled the unfortunate creature with her bare hands. Do you deny this, Miss Smith?'

'I will refrain from mocking a gentleman who I believe is more deserving of sympathy than censure,' said Frances, 'but I think it has not escaped your notice that Mr Horton is not exactly in his right mind.'

'Just so,' said Sharrock. 'It will be necessary to inform his friends and relatives, when we can find anyone to take responsibility for him, that he is the subject of delusions and they should have him properly looked after. I assume that the alligator incident is a fable?'

'Ah, not precisely,' said Frances and was obliged to mention the strategy for ridding herself of Mr Horton's presence. 'I have no doubt, however, that the animal in question does not exist.'

'I hope Mr Horton did not make any payment to you for this service?'

'The remuneration was as substantial as the animal,' said Frances. 'How he acquired that particular obsession I cannot say.'

Sharrock, who had clearly had no intention of arresting Sarah, threw himself into a chair. 'No chance of a cup of tea, I suppose?' The tea duly appeared and Sharrock gulped it almost boiling hot, without a wink of pain. 'I have spoken to Mr Horton and he has the type of mind which will seize on any incident and make it into a story. It seems that a lady whose parrot was missing has been telling all her friends about your success in finding the creature and he believed you might have similar powers over other animals. I have been told by members of the Piccadilly Club, where he is sometimes to be seen, that he once owned a leather travelling bag which somewhat resembled alligator hide, which he mislaid, and to him the item and the animal have become one and the same, and it has been haunting him. He seems to have a similar delusion about a fox. He has also accused Professor Pounder of assaulting him, and indeed he does have a recent abrasion on his face, but Horton is not a member of the professor's academy and none of the students have ever seen him there.'

'Perhaps he read about Professor Pounder in the *Chronicle*,' suggested Frances. 'It is interesting that Mr Horton does not create his ideas from nothing. He is a puzzle, but I do not intend to try and solve him.'

'Miss Smith is not the only person he has accused of murder,' said Sharrock. 'I am afraid in his unhappy brain all of Bayswater is peopled with individuals who wish to do him harm.'

Sarah grunted as if to imply that not all of these threats were improbable.

'But to other matters. I have been told that you are trying to discover the whereabouts of Mr Palmer and have been spreading a variety of rumours.'

'I am baiting a line,' said Frances.

He put his cup aside, wiped his mouth with the palm of his hand, and stood up. 'Well, you watch out for yourself, it's deep waters for a young woman. I would hate to see any of my daughters in this kind of work. It isn't right.'

'You would not condone females in the police force?'

'The very idea!' he said with a laugh, although with a glance at Sarah which suggested that if women were ever to be admitted, she would be one of the first.

The Inspector had scarcely departed when Frances received a rare visit from her landlady, Mrs Embleton, who did not as a rule intrude into the apartments of any of her tenants. Frances had a great deal of respect for Mrs Embleton, who ran the lodgings in a beautifully efficient way and was always a calm presence to whom any small difficulty could be addressed. That afternoon there was a hint of unease in the landlady's manner, which did not bode well for what she was about to say and she was holding a recent copy of the *Bayswater Chronicle*.

'Miss Doughty, I am sorry to approach you in this manner, but I feel I need to broach a difficult subject. It has been my observation that you receive a great many visitors, some of whom are persons of the male sex. The individual who has just departed is, so I have been given to understand, a policeman. His manners, if I might say so, left a very great deal to be desired. Not that I am suggesting even the slightest wrongdoing on your part and I assume that you do not receive these visitors while alone.' She gave a polite nod of acknowledgement to Sarah. Frances did, while Sarah was on her own errands and enquiries, occasionally receive visitors, even male persons, alone, but had taken the view that if she wished to succeed in her new profession, there were risks she must take and niceties she must abandon.

'I can assure you of the propriety of my behaviour at all times,' said Frances.

'Oh, I do not doubt it, and indeed any person of whom I did entertain doubts would not be within these walls. That is for the safety and peace of mind of all my ladies.'

Mrs Embleton, although she was as entitled as anyone in the room to be seated as she pleased, nevertheless remained standing out of respect for the independence of her tenant. Frances offered her a seat and refreshments, but she took advantage only of the former.

'Now, I am not one of those women who enjoy or even believe gossip,' said Mrs Embleton, 'and it has always been my view that stories printed in the newspapers are more in the way of entertainment for the idle rather than information for the educated, but it has been mentioned to me several times that you are – engaged in the occupation of private detective.'

Frances' heart sank. She had in the last few months grown accustomed to her new home and had even, albeit with a slight sense of guilt, come to enjoy its comforts, which were rather greater than those of the drab rooms above the chemist's shop on Westbourne Grove that had been her home from birth. The apartments were so warm and comfortable that she had hardly dared to hope they might be hers for always, and now it seemed that her landlady was about to ask her to leave.

'You are quite right, Mrs Embleton,' she said. 'And I can assure you that it is always my intention to act only for the most respectable persons. Some of the leading residents of Bayswater would be glad to advise you of my discretion and honesty and their satisfaction with my endeavours.' Not all of them, she reflected, since her enquiries had consigned some leading residents to gaol, not to mention an appointment with the hangman.

'Do not mistake me, I have no objection to your being engaged in that profession providing it is practiced with discretion and decorum,' Mrs Embleton reassured her. 'I myself was once obliged to engage a detective over a matter of some purloined jewellery and it struck me on that occasion that a respectable lady might bring something more delicate and seemly to what might otherwise, as conducted by a man, be a somewhat disagreeable proceeding. However, I must ask if you advertise this house as the one from which your business is conducted?'

'I have a card,' said Frances, 'but that only supplies my name and address, and I am selective about who receives it and I have not found it necessary to take out advertisements in the newspapers. Should I ever do so, I would supply a box number and not an address. So far all my custom has been obtained by word of mouth from satisfied customers.'

Mrs Embleton pondered this.

'Do you wish to terminate our agreement?' asked Frances. 'I regret I do not yet have the resources to rent a private office at which I might receive clients. If you object to my business then I must seek other accommodation.'

'It is not my objection, but the disquiet of the other ladies,' said Mrs Embleton. 'Mrs Allaby, on the ground floor, has been told some alarming stories by her maid, who has unfortunately been indulging in a very unsavoury variety of literature, one which purports to describe your adventures. She is afraid of being murdered in her bed by villains who come here to see you.'

'I am sorry to hear that the lady has been alarmed,' said Frances, 'and I was aware that some individual, whose identity I am unaware of, has been making up stories about a person who has some slight resemblance to me, but I do not see how I can bear any responsibility for that.'

'I have been shown a halfpenny story paper that illustrates this very house.'

'Oh dear!'

'And Miss Parmiter on the second floor, who is the quietest soul in the world and thinks of nothing but her charity work, has been accosted in the street by a person who asked her to solve a murder. She was very upset as you can imagine.'

'As would I be,' said Frances. 'I have never been asked outright to solve a murder and would not take such a commission.'

'Miss Doughty, you have never given me personally the slightest cause for regret that I accepted you as a tenant, and I would be loath to ask you to leave for reasons which are, I agree, no fault of yours, but I do have my other tenants to think of and they have been here many years without a breath of scandal. I must ask you to discover who is publishing these stories and make them stop.'

'They're very popular,' said Sarah.

'So, I understand, is all cheap literature,' said Mrs Embleton. She extracted a small booklet from the folds of her newspaper and handed it to Frances, who realised that her landlady had concealed the publication in the *Chronicle* in case she was seen carrying it. It was, she saw, published by the Bayswater Library of Romance. Entitled *The Daring of Miss Dauntless*, by W. Grove – undoubtedly a pseudonym – it was number eight in the series entitled *The Lady Detective of Bayswater*. There was only one illustration on the front cover. The caption was 'A Mysterious Stranger Arrives,' and it showed a muffled figure mounting the front steps of what looked strikingly like her apartment house down to the shape of the doorknocker and the house number.

'I do not think there will be any difficulty in making my wishes known to the author,' said Frances, noting that the item was printed locally, 'and I will persuade him or her, with a letter from my solicitor if required, to turn their attention to other subjects. The content, I observe, is rather flattering, perhaps overly so.'

'I have not read it,' said Mrs Embleton, in a tone that implied that she did not wish to.

There was a knock at the door of the apartment and the maid peeped in, clutching a card. 'If you don't mind, Miss, it's a young gentleman, very respectable, who says he wants your help, and he hopes he is not intruding, a Mr Fairbrother.'

Mrs Embleton's eyebrows rose a fraction of an inch.

'Mr Fairbrother is a student of medicine who is studying with Dr Bonner of the Life House,' said Frances. 'If that is all, Mrs Embleton, I would like to admit him as this will be a professional consultation.'

Mrs Embleton glanced at Sarah, who showed no sign of moving from her chair, and departed, leaving the little book behind her, which Frances swiftly pocketed. Moments later, Mr Fairbrother came hurrying up the stairs.

She saw at once that he was in a state of some anxiety and the polite formalities were dashed through in unusual haste.

'Is Dr Bonner well?' asked Frances. 'It would be very unfortunate if he was indisposed and unable to attend the resumed inquest.'

'Dr Bonner has gone to Brighton for a few days, where he hopes the sea air will do him good, but he will be back in London next week. I have been busy pursuing my studies in the meantime, since he has very kindly allowed me to consult his extensive medical library.'

There were a few moments of uncomfortable silence. 'Was there any particular subject that was commanding your attention?' asked Frances. Fairbrother had that sickly look about the eyes that spoke of a sleepless night and he seemed all set to have another. He was very pale, and there were unmistakable signs that his hand had trembled during his morning shave.

'Yes. I am sorry to say there was, and now I really do not know what to do!' He wrung his hands, distractedly.

'Is this a medical matter?' asked Frances, puzzled at why he should have come to her if it was.

'It is only partly medical – that is the origin of my dilemma. Oh, how I wish – ' he uttered a groan of despair, ' – how I wish these thoughts had not come into my head, but now that they are, there is nothing I can do about them, and I am tormented with doubt!'

Sarah raised her head to glance at the clock on the mantelshelf, then grunted and took up her knitting.

'Please calm yourself, Mr Fairbrother,' said Frances, 'and tell me everything.'

He nodded. 'As you know, Miss Doughty, I have been in London attending lectures and taking further instruction from Dr Bonner in preparation for what I hope will be my final studies towards gaining my MD. He has very generously allowed me to lodge in his home and also to assist him in many ways that have added greatly to my medical knowledge. I am most grateful to him for all his kindness to me.'

Fairbrother, Frances realised, had at last seen that his mentor was not entirely to be trusted. She said nothing. Although she could guess some of what was about to follow, she would not place the matter in doubt by putting words in his mouth. To fully understand it himself, he needed to say it for himself.

'No man of course may be right about every matter all the time,' he went on. 'Even the very cleverest will make an honest mistake. The best of men, the most trustworthy, are those who make the fewest mistakes and then have the courage to admit it when they do. I had always believed Dr Bonner to be of their number. But now – I am sorry to say it – I am not so certain of him as I was.'

There was a wasteland of near silence. Sarah was winding on wool and the click of her needles had ceased, leaving only the whisper of yarn as it flowed across her fingers.

'You do not question me, Miss Doughty?' said Fairbrother, as if hopeful of some reprieve.

'No,' said Frances, 'that will come later.'

He sighed regretfully. 'As you know, earlier this month Dr Bonner performed a post-mortem examination at Kilburn mortuary on a young woman whose body had been recovered from the canal, and I assisted him. My duties were simply to observe and take notes. Of course, as the examination progressed many matters of interest arose and I questioned Dr Bonner in order to add to my knowledge. I had never previously attended an examination of the body of a drowned person, neither had I seen a corpse which had been long immersed in water, although I had done a little reading on the question and I knew, therefore, that a body which has lain in water will –' he stopped. 'If the subject distresses you, Miss Doughty, then perhaps I ought not —'

'Please go on and be as comprehensive as possible,' said Frances.

'Very well. A body that has lain in water will present a very different appearance from one that has lain in air, or in the earth. To begin with the process of putrefaction will occur far more slowly, and it may be very difficult for the examiner to arrive at a date of death which could have occurred days or even weeks before, if the body has been kept very cold. A body may be brought out of the water after being a month or two submerged and be perfectly identifiable. Once the body is brought out into the air, changes will occur very quickly, such as a bloating and darkening of the features. It so happened that Dr Bonner was taking me on a tour of Kilburn mortuary at the time the body was brought in and I had the opportunity to view it very soon after it was taken from the water, and observe the changes which would result from its exposure to air. I was surprised to observe firstly that the body was rather more decomposed than I might have expected from one that had been immersed in water, and that there were no rapid changes. I mentioned this to Dr Bonner, and he assured me that he had seen many drowned bodies and because the conditions of the water varied so much, so did the post-mortem appearances, which could be very confusing. He thought it probable that the body had lain there for at least two weeks, perhaps more, trapped possibly by some obstruction and had only recently come to the surface.

'I accepted his judgement, but I was obliged to mention that while the body was pliant and all rigidity had passed off, showing that death had taken place certainly at least a week earlier, there was very little sign of soaking and wrinkling of the skin, and none at all of loosening of the hair. That seemed to me to indicate that the body had not lain in the water for very long. Dr Bonner reassured me that the degree of such changes was variable and quite in keeping with his opinion.

'We were both satisfied that this was not a violent death as there was no sign of any struggle. I was very surprised to find lividity – that is the staining due to blood ceasing to circulate and accumulating instead by gravity – on the back of the body and not the front, as I had always imagined that bodies in water adopted a prone position but Dr Bonner advised me, and I have since found that to be the case, that females may float face upwards. All the same, there was something about the pattern of the marks of lividity that troubled me, although I did not press it at the time.

'We then proceeded to open the body.' Fairbrother drew a deep breath, and glanced at both Frances and Sarah to see if there were signs that either woman might faint, and, seeing none, continued. 'There was no water in the stomach, which surprised me, as I would have expected to find some in a drowned person, but Dr Bonner informed me that there are cases of rapid drowning in which that symptom is not present. The lungs undoubtedly showed all the symptoms of death by drowning and there was no difficulty in assigning that as the cause.'

Fairbrother rubbed the heels of his hands into his eyes, then looked up at Frances with an expression of great unhappiness.

'I have never before questioned any of the things Dr Bonner has said to me, but after the incidents at the Life House and your enquiries, my mind turned again to the post-mortem and it came to me just how many points of difficulty there were and how at each turn Dr Bonner was able to convince me, through his experience and the respect I held for him, that his view was correct.

'In the last day or two, therefore, I have consulted his library and my further reading leads me to suppose that Dr Bonner has been in error over a number of things. Putrefaction in water, I have discovered, takes place in a different order to that in air. Discolouration of the skin commences in the face and neck and then passes down the body. If a corpse is exposed to air, then the first putrefactive discolouration appears in the region of the abdomen, and spreads from there to the upper and lower body. Miss Doughty – the body of the drowned woman showed that pattern, as if she had decomposed lying in air and not water.

'And then there was the pattern of the lividity. The body would not have floated to the surface until made lighter by the gases of putrefaction, but even if it had been trapped underwater in a supine position and then floated up, the pattern of the lividity would have been different. The staining will not appear in those portions of the body that have been in contact with a firm surface where the blood vessels are compressed. If a body has lain in water the pattern will differ considerably from that in a body that has, for example, been laid out on a bed or the ground. I wondered about this at the time, and even made a sketch in my notes of the pattern.'

'So let me understand this,' said Frances. 'The final conclusion of the post-mortem was that the woman had died from sudden drowning probably several weeks before, and that the body had lain trapped underwater before rising to the surface a short time before it was found?'

'It was, but we could not determine whether she was a suicide or if the death was accidental. It was certainly not a case of murder.'

Frances gazed at the unhappy young man before her, older than her by perhaps two years, yet despite all that he had seen in the purely medical sense, less knowledgeable of the world and also quite unused to solving the kind of dilemma with which he had suddenly been faced. Her only advice was for him to do what she herself did, clear away all the thoughts that confused him and start again.

'So, although you were able to form opinions of your own at the examination, Dr Bonner was able to overcome your conclusions with convincing arguments. Arguments that seem less convincing now that you have had time to reflect.'

'That is the case.'

'Very well. What I would like you to do is try to put out of your mind everything that Dr Bonner told you. Think only of your own observations and the facts that you have accumulated through your reading. Now imagine that *you* are the senior man conducting the post-mortem examination of that body and that I am your student, and let me know what your conclusions are. Please take your time. Sarah, I believe Mr Fairbrother might benefit from some refreshment. Will you take tea?'

'Oh no, I really cannot abide tea. A cup of coffee would be greatly appreciated.'

Sarah was unable to conceal a smirk as she rose and went down to the kitchen.

When they were settled comfortably with the coffee pot and some biscuits, Fairbrother, who was a little less distracted than earlier, spoke. 'Based on what I observed, I think that the body was that of a young woman who had drowned quite suddenly, but had been extracted from the water soon afterwards and had then lain on her back on a firm surface in the air, for a week at the very least, and had then been placed in the water where she had been for no more than two days.'

'So she might have drowned in the canal and been pulled out and left lying in some spot on the bankside, and then put back in the water later on?'

'Yes, that is very possible. There are many inconspicuous places where a body might be hidden for a while. Or she might have been taken from the water and thought to be living and cared for in someone's home until it became certain that she had died, and then replaced in the water. For the avoidance of funeral expenses perhaps.'

'Or to conceal the fact of her death. And the probable date of her death?'

He thought about this for a full minute. 'When I saw the body it was the 23rd of September. She had not been in the water long, perhaps a day or two, no more, given the wrinkling of the skin from saturation. The cold of the water would have arrested decomposition, which was already somewhat advanced. It is my opinion that she had been dead for at least a week, perhaps a little more when she was placed in the water. So the date of death was anywhere from the 12th of September to the 15th.'

'And not the estimate of more than two weeks before as suggested by Dr Bonner?'

'I am afraid not. Of course, I could be quite wrong, I accept that.'

'There are,' said Frances, 'two places which are very close to the canal where bodies may lie for days undisturbed. I speak of course of Kilburn Mortuary and the Life House. Presumably a missing body would be noticed at once?'

'Oh yes, and very careful records are kept of bodies received and removed for burial. No young woman who had drowned was brought into the Life House. Also the body of an unknown person would never be brought there, the Life House is for paying customers only, they would go to Kilburn, or if found nearer to Bayswater, Paddington workhouse.'

Frances nodded. Mrs Pearson's maid had last been seen on the 12th of September, and could well have stolen fashionable undergarments from her mistress, or even been given them by an admirer. But she had not, as far as Frances knew, been in a starving condition as observed in the unknown corpse. Had the girl been mistreated by her employer and run away, and the other servants were too frightened to admit it? Had the girl been involved in some disreputable or even criminal activity that had resulted in her being stripped and starved to weaken her, and then thrown into the canal? But why had she been pulled out and left lying somewhere and then thrown back in?

'I am not at all convinced that there was no crime involved in the girl's death,' said Frances. 'There certainly was in respect of the disposal of the body. If she did throw herself in the water then she is beyond any human blame, but the person who placed a corpse in the canal has broken the law. Have you considered going to the police?'

'Not until you mentioned it, no,' said Fairbrother, slumping under the weight of fresh misery. 'Must I?'

'I understand your difficulty. You are effectively accusing your respected mentor of negligence which has resulted in the concealment of a crime.'

'Oh, this is quite horrible!' exclaimed Fairbrother. 'I am wishing now that I had never spoken out. But it troubled me so! What can I do? If I were to accuse Dr Bonner I am sure he would be able to explain everything to the satisfaction of the authorities, as he did to me, and the only sufferer would then be myself. I would appear to be not only foolish, but worse than that – disloyal. I am sorry if I seem selfish, but I hope I have a promising future in medicine and who would employ me if they thought I might spy upon them and then report them to the police?'

'But to do nothing would not relieve your mind,' said Frances. 'What I suggest you do is approach another medical man and, without saying anything about your very specific concerns, explain that you have some pressing questions to which you cannot receive the benefit of Dr Bonner's experience as he is indisposed.'

'I suppose I could do so. But who would I approach?'

'What about Dr Warrinder? He is already known to you so it would seem perfectly natural for you to ask his advice. He is a man of very considerable experience, and I think a kindly person who would not judge you too harshly.'

Fairbrother looked more hopeful. 'Yes, I think I will. Thank you for that good advice.'

'But I will want to attend the meeting with you,' added Frances. 'The matters you have raised suggest that a crime has been committed. I am even now investigating the disappearance of a maidservant who was last seen alive at about the time that you believe the young woman in the canal died. Perhaps the unknown body is hers. So you must make an early appointment to see Dr Warrinder explaining that I will also be there as I wish to extend my knowledge of drowned persons because of a case I am pursuing. Send me a note in due course of the time of the meeting and I will be there.'

CHAPTER FIFTEEN

D r Warrinder was agreeable to receiving both Frances and
Mr Fairbrother at his home at 10 o'clock on Tuesday
morning. Frances had in the meantime been bending her
thoughts to the author of the booklet about Miss Dauntless, the
lady detective of Bayswater. This extraordinary lady, a creature
who clearly knew no fear, thought nothing of scaling the walls
of houses and clambering about on rooftops to listen down the
chimneys of suspects, leaping onto the top of a hansom cab and
whipping up the horses in pursuit of some luckless criminal, and
even facing down a gang of thieves with a gun. Frances sincerely
hoped that she would never be called upon to do any of these
dreadful things. There was nothing in the story that suggested the
culprit knew any more about her than could be gleaned from
the newspapers, apart from the fact that the author clearly knew
her address. She had already started to suspect Mr Gillan of the
Chronicle, who might well have started the enterprise to add to
his meagre income. She had wondered, too, about Miss Gilbert
and Miss John, leaders of the Bayswater Women's Suffrage Society,
who had altogether inflated ideas of her capabilities and were constantly telling people about her achievements, but the booklet had
not been produced by their usual publisher and was not on sale at
their meetings. She decided to write a polite letter addressed to the
author, W. Grove, care of the director of the Bayswater Library of
Romance, asking him or her to desist from identifying her with
Miss Dauntless, as it was creating some personal embarrassment.
She asked Tom to take it to the print works and tell them to pass it
on the next time a representative of that company called.

Tom had a surprise for her. Using his own initiative on the
question of Mrs Pearson's missing maid, he had surmised that
Mr Pearson might know a great deal more about the business
than he had claimed to know, which was nothing at all. Tom had,

therefore, followed Mr Pearson and found that he was a frequent visitor at a small but tastefully appointed apartment in Maida Vale, where the missing maid, who was beginning to show a more rounded appearance than had previously been apparent, was comfortably situated. Mrs Pearson's especial interest in the whereabouts of the maid immediately became clear. This left Frances with two difficulties. The first was what she ought to tell Mrs Pearson. That lady had become a client on telling her that she was anxious for the maid's safety, but she had clearly wanted another kind of information altogether and had not seen fit to ask for it. It was appropriate, therefore, for Frances to advise Mrs Pearson only of the information she had asked for and a letter was carefully composed saying that the maid was safe and well, and the lady need have no further anxiety on that score. She also advised that the maid would not be returning to her service but had found another situation. There she ended the matter, resolving that if Mrs Pearson wanted to know any more, then she could return and say so.

The second question was somewhat more vexing. Frances had felt hopeful that she had identified the unknown woman in the canal as Mrs Pearson's missing maid, but was now at a loss to think who she might have been. She had a list of missing women provided by the Kilburn police station, which covered not only the immediate area but all of Paddington, but none of them seemed to fit the description. Her theory that the body was in any way connected with Henry Palmer's disappearance was looking like a very remote possibility, nevertheless, it was the only line of enquiry that remained.

It was with this in mind that Frances appeared at the door of Dr Warrinder's house at the appointed time, only moments before Mr Fairbrother arrived. They were shown to the warm parlour where the maid brought refreshments, although none of those present appeared to want them.

'I am very flattered, Mr Fairbrother, that you have asked to consult me on a medical matter,' said Dr Warrinder. 'I might say that Dr Bonner has spoken most highly of you; your diligence and eagerness to acquire knowledge. That bodes very well for your future career. I am sorry that I have not made your better acquaintance sooner.'

'I am delighted to have your good opinion,' said Fairbrother, not without a tremor of foreboding in his voice.

'I am less certain of Miss Doughty's reasons for attendance at our consultation. Young lady, I fear that we may speak of matters that may disconcert you, or at the very least you may find them hard to understand.'

'Do not trouble yourself on my account,' said Frances, with a gentle smile. 'You may conduct the consultation exactly as if I was not present.'

'Ah – very well,' said Warrinder, bemused but not unwilling. 'Then perhaps we may begin. I understand, Mr Fairbrother, that you have some queries about appearances of a body after drowning, as you recently assisted Dr Bonner in such a case. I do happen to have in my library a very useful monograph on the subject, also one or two other items which I would like you to accept with my compliments.'

'Oh that is far too kind!'

'Not at all, not at all, my eyes do not permit me to read for long nowadays and the print can be so very small, it is most unfortunate. You, I am sure, will have no such difficulty. Now then, I know I put them on one side for you especially …' He rose from his chair and began to look about the room. 'Oh dear, I hope Mary has not tidied them away, or I shall have to go and fetch them again.' They waited as he looked about the room, which was cluttered with small tables and the kind of knick-knacks that people accumulate over half a lifetime, and spend the rest of that lifetime having them polished.

'Are they the items on the table beside the bust of Hippocrates?' asked Frances.

Dr Warrinder was so startled by her question that he turned abruptly and knocked over another small table, which was draped in a purple-fringed velvet cloth and bore a small collection of framed photographs. 'Oh dear!' he exclaimed, staring about him.

'Allow me to assist you,' said Fairbrother, jumping to his feet. 'Please be seated and I will attend to everything.' He took Warrinder by the elbow and guided him back to his chair, then knelt on the carpet by the fallen pictures. 'Have no fear sir, the carpet has prevented any damage, and all is well.' He began to replace the pictures on the table. 'Of course, I do not know how they were arranged before but I am sure your maid will advise me. There.' The smile suddenly vanished from his face.

'What is the matter?' asked Frances.

'Oh dear, I do so hope nothing is broken!' exclaimed Warrinder.

Fairbrother had picked up one of the pictures and was staring at it as if confronted with some ghastly apparition. Frances went over to look. The subject of the picture was a pale, slender young woman with a sweet smile curving her lips. There was a black velvet bow tied to the scrollwork of the ornate frame.

'Who is this a portrait of?' asked Frances.

Warrinder come over to peer at it. 'That is the late Mrs Templeman. She is my wife's great niece. Recently passed away, I am sorry to say.'

'How recently?' asked Fairbrother, like a man who had lost his voice and had had to re-learn the power of speech.

'Oh, I am not sure I know the exact date, but not long ago.'

'Was it before or after the night when Dr Mackenzie collapsed?' asked Frances.

Dr Warrinder frowned. 'I – er – before. Very shortly before. Two or three days. It was a Sunday, I do remember that.'

'That would make it the 19th of September,' said Frances.

'The 19th?' exclaimed Fairbrother and gave a great sigh of relief. 'I had thought, just for a moment – but it had been pressing on my mind … I must have been imagining it … and yet …'

'Did you think,' asked Frances, 'that Mrs Templeman resembles the woman who was taken from the canal?'

'Yes, I did, only it could not possibly be her, because the date of death is far too recent to account for the decomposition. Also, if Mrs Templeman had drowned, I am sure I would have heard of it.' He turned to Dr Warrinder. 'Mrs Templeman did not drown, did she?'

'Drown? What a curious idea!' exclaimed Warrinder. 'She was a very delicate young woman and expired in her bed after a lengthy illness. There was, I assure you, no opportunity for her to drown.'

'I was obviously mistaken,' said Fairbrother. He put the picture down, but it continued to fascinate him. He found the books and returned to his seat.

'May I?' said Frances, holding out her hands for the books, and with an expression of surprise he handed them over.

There was a paper on the subject of examination of bodies of the drowned and two more general volumes, one on the conduct of post-mortem examinations and another on diseases of the chest. The two gentlemen smiled indulgently as Frances opened the books, as they might have done if a child had tried to read a treatise far beyond its understanding, and she realised that neither of them was aware that she had from an early age been used to perusing the medical volumes in her father's small collection.

As the gentlemen's discussion turned to the subject of post-mortem lividity, Frances discovered what it was she had been looking for.

'Dr Warrinder?' she asked. 'Forgive my interrupting you, but can you advise me if Mrs Templeman suffered from a disease of the lungs?'

'Er – yes, in her final weeks she was very afflicted with pneumonia.'

'And this causes an accumulation of fluid in the lungs?'

'It does, but I can't see what —'

Fairbrother gasped. 'Of course, I should have realised!'

'What is all this about?' asked Warrinder.

'Perhaps nothing at all,' said Frances, 'but if you could answer some questions about Mrs Templeman it would be of very great assistance.'

'It would set my mind at rest on a matter of concern,' pleaded Fairbrother.

Dr Warrinder looked surprised. 'Oh, well, if you wish it.'

'Did Mrs Templeman have a family?' asked Frances.

'There was a child born, but it did not live.'

'And did she ever suffer with her teeth?'

Warrinder stared at Frances. 'How could you possibly have known that?'

'Did Dr Bonner know that she suffered with her teeth?'

'Bonner? No – I don't think he was ever acquainted with her.'

'Who was her medical attendant?'

'Dr Collin, in the main, although when he was not available Dr Mackenzie did sometimes call to see her.'

'Can you describe Mrs Templeman's teeth?' asked Fairbrother anxiously.

Warrinder's surprise had transmuted into astonishment. 'I really do not see why —'

'Oh, please, I beg of you!' exclaimed Fairbrother. 'And I very much regret it but I cannot say; I cannot explain why I need to know.'

'How extraordinary!' said Warrinder. 'Very well, I can tell you that the poor woman's incisors grew very crooked and she was most ashamed of them. Maria begged her to see a dentist, especially as it seemed that the teeth were pressing on the gum and giving her a great deal of pain, and she did go and he wanted to take them out, but she wouldn't agree to it, she didn't want a horrid gap in her mouth.'

'And you are quite *quite* sure that she died on the 19th of September?' asked Fairbrother.

'Yes, I am.'

'And when was she buried?'

'Oh – it would have been the next week – yes, it was the Monday of the following week.'

'Monday the 27th?' said Frances.

'Yes, I do recall that because it was the day of Mackenzie's funeral, also.'

'And was the body at her home during the interval?'

'Only until the following day. We had a private viewing for the family on the morning after her death and she was taken to the Life House that same afternoon.'

Frances and Fairbrother looked at each other. 'Then that accounts for the faster decomposition,' said Frances.

'Whatever do you mean?' exclaimed Warrinder. 'What is all this about?'

Fairbrother rose from his seat. 'Dr Warrinder – I hardly know what to say.'

'I think,' said Frances, 'that for the moment you had better say nothing.'

❀

Later, in a nearby café over a cup of coffee and a pot of tea that neither of them felt much like drinking, they discussed what was to be done. 'I am ruined,' said Fairbrother.

'That is nothing to the odium that will pour upon Dr Bonner's head,' Frances observed. 'At least if the body in the canal *does* turn out to be that of Mrs Templeman we know that she was not the victim of a crime. But Dr Bonner must have been at the Life House during the period when Mrs Templeman's body was held there, which was from the 20th to the 26th of September, and I can't believe he never examined her once during that time, so how come he didn't recognise the body taken from the canal?'

'Perhaps this is all a mistake?' said Fairbrother hopefully.

'Did *you* examine Mrs Templeman?'

'No, I don't recall her at all. But then I spent most of that week assisting at post-mortem examinations at Paddington workhouse. I was at the Life House for the viewing of Dr Mackenzie, but not for several days thereafter.'

Frances suddenly recalled something. It may have meant nothing especially since the witness was so thoroughly unreliable, but all the same it could furnish a clue. She looked through her notebook for what Dr Carmichael had told her of his visit to the Life House.

'I spoke recently to a medical gentleman who toured the Life House wards on the 23rd of September when Mrs Templeman should have been there, and he told me that there was only one female patient, who was very elderly,' said Frances. 'Can you account for that?'

Fairbrother looked mystified. 'I cannot.'

'Is there a record kept of the times when orderlies or doctors are on duty in the Life House?'

'Yes, the orderlies sign a record book when they arrive and again when they depart. The doctors also make a note when they have done a round of examination, and of course the admission of patients and burials are also recorded. It is very meticulous.'

'Good. I will need to see the entries for the days between the 19th and the 27th of September. I suggest we proceed to the Life House at once.'

'I can only admit you to the chapel,' said Fairbrother, 'but I will bring the record book which is held in the office.'

'Might I see the office?'

He shook his head. 'Oh no, visitors may only enter the chapel, nowhere else. I am in enough difficulty already without transgressing again. Dr Warrinder is bound to speak to Dr Bonner about our interview when he returns, and I dread to think what he might say and do.'

'You may place all the blame on me,' said Frances. 'I questioned you with great violence and fearsomeness, and dragged the information out of you and then took the whole matter forward myself.'

It was a moment or two before he saw the import of what she had just said. 'When you say "took the matter forward", to what are you alluding?'

'Well, we must have the body exhumed, mustn't we? Until we have proof that the body in the canal was actually that of Mrs Templeman we can make no further progress.'

'But – the distress that this will cause – to Dr Bonner, and Dr Warrinder!'

'Dr Bonner has been lying to me repeatedly since our first meeting and you will forgive me if I feel no guilt at any distress he may feel. As to Dr Warrinder, do you think he will want to leave a relative's body in a common grave? If Mrs Templeman was *your* relative, what would you do?'

Fairbrother had no answer and unwillingly accepted that Frances would proceed to do what she felt necessary, whatever he might say about it.

They took a cab up to the Life House, where Fairbrother, after knocking on the chapel door, spoke to Hemsley, who fetched the record book and returned to the wards. Only then was Frances admitted. The little chapel was much as she had seen it before although there were no burials waiting. 'I don't suppose,' said Frances, 'that under the exceptional circumstances, I might be permitted just to look inside the office and the wards?'

Fairbrother turned pale. 'Please, I beg you, do not attempt it!'

'But you are the senior medical man here. You have the authority to admit me.'

'Mr Hemsley would inform the partners.'

'You could instruct him not to.'

'If you were to be taken ill, I would be blamed.'

'If I am willing to brave a visit to the wards then I believe you should be brave enough to admit me. The circumstances are very unusual.'

He wavered, but at last he shook his head. 'No! I dare not!'

'Then I will apply to Dr Bonner again on his return,' said Frances. It seemed somewhat inappropriate but needs must, and she took the heavy volume to the little altar and rested it there.

Nothing of any moment appeared to have occurred on Sunday the 19th of September. The orderlies had been medical students who, said Fairbrother, regularly took the Sunday periods of duty. Dr Mackenzie had visited during the afternoon.

Henry Palmer had reported for duty at midday on the 20th of September and made detailed notes of his work. He had made hourly surveys of the patients, cleaned the wards, tidied the flowers, and tended the fire. The admission of Mrs Templeman was recorded at 4 p.m. and Palmer had seen to everything necessary. He had been alone in the Life House until 7 p.m. when Dr Mackenzie had called and examined the patients, including Mrs Templeman, staying there for an hour. Neither Bonner nor Warrinder had been there that day, and Palmer left at midnight, being replaced by Mr Hemsley.

There had been no visitors until the following morning, the 21st of September, when Dr Warrinder attended between the hours of 9 and 10 a.m. and examined the patients. Even with his poor eyesight, thought Frances, he can hardly have failed to recognise his wife's niece. Palmer had then signed in at midday, for what would prove to be his last period of duty. Dr Bonner had arrived at 9.30 p.m. and Dr Mackenzie had called half an hour later. Palmer's signature, which was a little shakier than his usual neat handwriting, showed that he had departed at 11 p.m.

In the crucial hour before Palmer had left, Frances knew, events had occurred that the record book would not show. Mackenzie had suffered his collapse, there had been attempts by Bonner and Palmer to revive him, and his body had been consigned to the chapel. Palmer had arrived at

Mrs Georgeson's at about 11.10 p.m., but had then turned north again about five minutes later. At about 11.30 p.m. or thereabouts, Mr Darscot had arrived at the Life House by cab and viewed Dr Mackenzie's body, and then departed a few minutes later. There was no record of this, but Fairbrother said that visitors to the chapel were not recorded; there was merely an appointment book.

Following Darscot's departure, Bonner had been alone until Hemsley arrived and signed in at midnight. No visitors had been admitted to the wards at any time during this period. Hourly examinations of the patients had been carried out as usual by Hemsley. There was no record in the book to suggest that Palmer had ever returned.

Although Bonner had been alone in the Life House before the arrival of Hemsley, he had been in a state of some distress at the sudden death of his friend. Frances thought that he would easily be able to persuade a court that he had not examined Mrs Templeman at all, and that his failure to recognise her in Kilburn mortuary was, in the circumstances, unsurprising. The record book showed that Bonner had departed at 1 a.m. and returned at 8 a.m. the next morning, the 22nd of September. The names of the attendees at the viewing of Dr Mackenzie's body were not recorded. Hemsley had left at midday and Dr Warrinder had stayed on until a temporary orderly could be found.

'You did not go into the ward that day?' Frances asked Fairbrother.

'No.'

'Where did you go after the viewing?'

'I assisted Dr Bonner at Paddington mortuary.'

Frances reflected that it was very possible for someone on duty alone in the Life House to allow in an unauthorised visitor and not record the fact. Bonner had only been unaccompanied briefly, but both Palmer and Hemsley had been alone there for substantial periods of time. So when had Mrs Templeman's body been removed?

'Since there was a family viewing of Mrs Templeman's body at her home on the morning of the 20th, I assume that there was not one here?' she asked.

'I believe not,' said Fairbrother.

'But Dr Mackenzie, who had attended her in life, examined her body only a few hours after it was admitted here, and we must assume that he recognised her then. Dr Warrinder would have seen her the following morning when he made his ward round, and even with his poor eyesight he must have known his wife's relative. So if the body in the pauper's grave is indeed Mrs Templeman, what happened to her after Dr Warrinder's round?' Frances studied the book again. 'You were next in the ward on the 25th of September assisting Dr Bonner while he tried to find a replacement for Mr Palmer.'

'Yes.'

'And did you and Dr Bonner examine Mrs Templeman's body?'

Fairbrother frowned. 'I don't recall it. In fact, I rather think it was not there.'

'But she was not buried until two days later.' Frances peered at a note in what she felt sure was Hemsley's muddled hand. 'Ah,' she said at last, 'I think this says that Mrs Templeman's body was taken to Kilburn mortuary on the morning of the 24th of September. Why was that done?'

'I think I can guess. In cases where decomposition occurs very quickly and there is no doubt that the person is deceased, but the family has not yet completed arrangements for burial, bodies may be placed in a conventional mortuary where they are kept in cold conditions so as not to constitute a danger to health.'

'I'd better speak to Mr Hemsley again, and since I cannot go to him, you had best bring him to me.'

Fairbrother recognised the unspoken word 'now' at the end of that sentence and hurried away, returning a minute later with Hemsley, who looked as though he might have been awoken from a doze.

'Mr Hemsley, do you recall a patient here by the name of Mrs Templeman?' asked Frances. She showed him the admission entry for the 20th of September.

'Not specially, that's Palmer's writing. Has he been found?'

'Not yet, no. I see that Mrs Templeman's body was removed to Kilburn mortuary on the 24th of September. Can you advise me of the reason for that?'

'I can't say. I just get orders to move them or sometimes the undertaker's men call with an authority to take the bodies.'

'I was informed by someone who toured the Life House that Mrs Templeman was not on the ward on the 23rd of September. Where was she?'

He scratched his head and looked at the book again. 'In the chapel, I expect. She couldn't have been anywhere else.'

'But there was no family viewing here for Mrs Templeman. Why would she be in the chapel?'

'Well, sometimes, if the patients get a bit – well, you know – we don't want them in the ward and we take them off somewhere a bit colder. Now I come to think about it, when they took her away she wasn't on the ward, she was coffined in the chapel. Yes, that was it, I remember now! She was so bad she had to be coffined almost at once, and then she had to be taken away early.'

'Was she already coffined in the chapel when you came on duty on the night of Dr Mackenzie's collapse?'

He frowned. 'I expect so. I don't rightly remember.'

'Did *you* transfer Mrs Templeman to the chapel?'

He shook his head. 'I don't think I did. It must have been Palmer.'

'Would he have recorded that?'

'We have to record when a patient comes in and when they go out, but not moving from the ward to the chapel. So – no, if he did it wouldn't be in the book unless he chose to.'

'Isn't that the kind of thing that a man like Mr Palmer, with his attention to detail, would have recorded?'

Hemsley looked surprised. 'Er – yes, I suppose it would be.'

'Do you recall a young woman's body being in the chapel?'

'There was a coffin in there ready for burial, but I couldn't say whose it was.'

Frances felt she had learned all she could from Hemsley, who returned to his duties.

'It is clear that I was mistaken,' said Fairbrother. 'The body in the canal cannot have been that of Mrs Templeman, who was admitted here on the 20th of September and removed four days later. While I was assisting Dr Bonner at Kilburn on the 23rd, the lady's body was coffined here.'

'When you attended the viewing for Dr Mackenzie,' said Frances, 'was Mrs Templeman here then? In the chapel?'

'There was another coffin here, yes.'

'Open or sealed?'

He paused.

'Sealed, then.' Frances concluded. 'Did you look inside it?'

'No.'

'Exactly. For all we know her body was already in the canal and is even now in a pauper's grave. The only question is, who put it there and why?'

'But this is all conjecture! Can we not agree to proceed no further?'

'You know I cannot,' said Frances. 'I will have the body taken up.'

'That could take many weeks,' said Fairbrother. 'You would need to obtain an order from a magistrate and then he will approach the Home Office. And there is no guarantee of success.'

'I think,' said Frances, 'I may know a way to help things progress a little faster.'

Fairbrother, who had hoped to dissuade her, was disappointed.

❧

Back home Frances sat at her writing desk, selected her very best quality notepaper and her finest pen, and began a letter: 'Dear Mr Gladstone …'

CHAPTER SIXTEEN

D r Bonner returned from his sojourn in Brighton a duller and a lighter man, having consumed almost nothing except mineral water and a little fish for some days. Frances went to see him and found him hardly able to walk for the pain of his gouty foot, relying heavily on his stick and the assistance of Mr Fairbrother.

Frances extracted from him the fact that he had not previously been acquainted with Mrs Templeman. He said that when he had arrived at the Life House on the evening of the 21st of September, Palmer had informed him that the lady's body was very decomposed and he thought it should be removed to the chapel.

'Of course I trusted the man's judgement, and said he might do so. I did try to assist him, but my foot was very sore and painful, and he said I should rest and he would attend to everything.'

'So it was Palmer alone who took her body into the chapel?'

'Yes.'

'And sealed the coffin?'

'Yes.'

'And where were you when he did this?'

'I was in the office.'

'No note was made of the movement of the body to the chapel. Would Palmer not usually do that?'

'Yes, unless – I may have offered to do so myself, but clearly I did not. I – may have had a little brandy for the pain,' he admitted.

Frances was faced with the possibility that it was Palmer who, unseen by Bonner, had placed Mrs Templeman's body in the canal, replacing it in the coffin with – what? Another body? Something else, such as stolen goods, which he wanted to conceal? Had the purpose of consigning the body to the canal not been so much the disposal of the corpse but the use of the coffin for another purpose? If so, had Palmer acted on his own initiative, or, as seemed more probable, at the direction of another?

'Is Mrs Templeman buried or deposited in the catacombs?' asked Frances.

'Neither. There is a family mausoleum.'

'Then it is above ground, with a key held by the family?'

'Yes.'

Frances looked at Mr Fairbrother, who was looking almost as ill as Bonner. 'One body at a time,' she said.

❧

As Frances had expected, a very dignified Mrs Pearson called to see her, asking for the address of her erstwhile maid so that she could call upon her personally and see for herself that the girl was well. Frances said that the maid's address was a private matter, but she would undertake to send the maid a letter asking her to write to Mrs Pearson and give her the reassurance she required. If there was any other matter apart from the girl's safety and state of health that concerned her, she would be pleased to commence a new investigation. Mrs Pearson clamped her mouth shut and with a suspicious gleam in her eye, departed. Frances had no doubt that Mr Pearson would shortly experience a painful interview with his wife.

A delivery brought Frances a pleasant surprise, tasteful bouquets of fresh flowers not only for herself, but for her landlady and the other tenants of the house, accompanied by sincerely apologetic letters. The writer was the proprietor of the Bayswater Library of Romance, who expressed regret that the ladies had been distressed in any way by the publication of the adventures of Miss Dauntless. The object of the stories had been to reassure the public that crime did not pay and that the sins of evildoers would be found out due to the actions of courageous ladies such as the heroine. To avoid any inconvenience, future stories would make it very clear to readers that Miss Dauntless lived in quite another part of Bayswater.

To Frances' relief, Mrs Embleton, who appreciated pretty flowers and a polite apology, pronounced herself satisfied.

The next visitor was less welcome. Inspector Sharrock, who was not quite sure whether to appear fierce, concerned, or aloof, and succeeded in being uncomfortably none of the three.

'So, how is business for Miss Dauntless?' he asked.

'Miss Dauntless no longer resides in this part of Bayswater,' said Frances. 'I didn't know you were a reader.'

'My wife likes 'em. She says it takes her mind off things. What things she needs taking her mind off of I couldn't say. Now then, I want you to tell me if you have chanced to set eyes on Mr Horton since we last discussed him and if so, what he said, and whether or not it made any sense.'

'I have not seen him since then,' said Frances. 'Has he run away?'

'No, worse than that, the man's dead.'

'Oh, I am sorry to hear it.' Frances pictured the unhappy gentlemen making away with himself by a variety of different methods, and then rebuked herself for having such unpleasant things in her imagination. 'I assume since you are here that the circumstances of his death are in some way unresolved?'

'Dr Collin is cutting him up even as we speak. There was a strong smell of alcohol about him and he was found tumbled into an area on Gloucester Terrace. So it may have been an accident, but I'm not so sure. He has bruises on him that are several days old, the result perhaps of a previous assault.'

'Can you think of any reason why someone should have murdered him?'

'Perhaps he annoyed someone. He certainly annoyed *me*!' Sharrock stomped away with a scowl.

Chas and Barstie arrived to report on the activities of Dr Carmichael, which had provided no further clues, but they had also heard the circulating rumours about Mr Horton's demise.

'Not right in the noddle, I am sorry to say,' said Chas, tapping the side of his head.

'Did you know him?'

'Not as such, only he came to the Piccadilly Club sometimes, and a few days ago he made a great commotion and had to be shown the door. Pilled I don't doubt.'

'I beg your pardon?'

'Blackballed. Not to be let in again.'

'Inspector Sharrock told me he had suffered some bruising. Perhaps that was as a result of his being ejected from the club?'

Chas and Barstie looked at each other.

Frances folded her arms and gave them a firm stare. 'Now then gentlemen, I think you know something.'

'Oh, I would hesitate to say anything that might create difficulties for someone who I believe to be a person of admirable character,' said Barstie.

'Not to mention a useful source of business,' added Chas.

'Mr Horton's bruises were not suffered as a result of any criminal action, we can assure you of that,' said Barstie. 'It was more a matter of gentlemanly recreation.'

Frances recalled something. 'I believe that Mr Horton had accused Professor Pounder of assaulting him, but there was no evidence he had ever been to the academy.'

Chas and Barstie looked at each other again.

'Is Professor Pounder a member of the Piccadilly Club?' she asked.

'Not precisely,' said Barstie, 'but he is known to the gentlemen there and is sometimes a guest.'

'Are you saying that he has been involved in fighting there?'

'The Professor would never indulge in fistic matters outside of the ring,' said Chas.

Frances bethought herself of some of the things that had been happening at the Monmouth Club, the manager of which was about to take the *Chronicle* to court for libel.

'Has Professor Pounder been running an illegal boxing and gambling club in the Piccadilly?' she asked.

'Oh no, no, nothing of the sort!' exclaimed Chas, quickly.

'Not at all!' said Barstie.

'Well then, what *is* he doing?'

'He gives free demonstrations of self-defence,' said Barstie. 'All quite legal and above board. No prize fights. He wouldn't think of it.'

'When you say free demonstrations, that would suggest he engages in some form of combat with other persons?'

There was a pause and Barstie decided to stir the fire, while Chas looked around hopefully for tea. None appeared.

'He might do,' said Chas, at last.

'I wouldn't say he doesn't,' said Barstie.

'Does he fight only other pugilists? Or members of the club?' asked Frances.

'It's not *really* combat,' said Barstie, 'not as one might understand it, not as the police might want to interpret it. No, nothing of the sort.'

'Did the late Mr Horton, by any chance, have such a non-combative encounter with Professor Pounder?'

'It was more of a friendly challenge,' said Chas, 'the kind of thing that jovial fellows might do to entertain themselves.'

'Nothing wrong in that,' said Barstie. 'All amateur, all legal.'

'Well, I am very pleased to hear it,' said Frances, 'and since it is legal and friendly there should be no difficulty about your describing it to me.' She waited.

'It's called the one minute challenge,' said Chas, at last. 'Pounder is the finest exponent of the noble art of self-defence up to and including the Marquess of Queensberry, and it is his pleasure to offer to engage in sparring with any man for one minute. And if that man can land a blow on him in that minute he wins a guinea. It's a harmless enough amusement.'

'I see,' said Frances, 'and I imagine that the members of the Piccadilly Club assemble to watch these one minute exhibitions?'

'Oh yes, very edifying. Very entertaining.'

'And make wagers on the outcome, perhaps?'

Barstie shrugged. 'If a gentleman wishes to make a private wager for his own amusement, who can stop him?'

'So,' said Frances, 'Mr Horton took Professor Pounder up on his challenge and learned to regret it.'

'He did indeed!' said Chas. 'In no small way. And it could have been much worse for him, but the Professor was very kind to him, and chose not to hurt him too much. He took more damage tripping over his own feet than anything the Professor laid on him.'

'As a result of which,' said Frances, 'he went about telling anyone who would listen that Professor Pounder assaulted him and then next thing we know he is found violently dead.'

Chas and Barstie had the good grace to look concerned. 'I would be willing to bet my life that the Professor was not involved in that,' said Chas. 'He is the very devil in the roped ring, but out of it he is a better gentleman than many who were born to it.'

'Well,' said Frances, 'I suppose that Mr Horton's demise is none of my business, unless it had some connection to Mr Palmer's disappearance, which I doubt. But if you should hear anything of interest, do let me know.'

At the final day of the inquest on Dr Mackenzie, Dr Bonner appeared, his debilitated condition eliciting little gasps of sympathy from the assembled crowds. He seemed to have aged about twenty years in the last two weeks, and those who were used to seeing his spry, plump frame and genial smile were shocked to see how shrunken he had become. He tottered to his place on a stout stick, helped by Mr Fairbrother, without whose slender but firm arm it seemed he would have fallen. Dr Hardwicke gazed at Bonner with more than usual interest, as if assessing how much of the witness's condition was due to actual illness or a performance worthy of the best theatres, designed to avoid the consequences of his ineptitude. Dr Hardwicke's expression showed that he was inclining to the latter opinion.

'I wish to question only one witness,' said Hardwicke, 'Dr Bonner.'

A whisper of anticipation swept around the little court like a swirl of fallen leaves before it settled into a dry heap of silence. Bonner took his time approaching the coroner's table and was permitted to take a seat nearby.

'Dr Bonner, how long have you known Dr Mackenzie?'

'About eighteen years. We met when I attended a lecture he gave on the subject of —' he paused, 'cases of doubtful death.' A sound like a barely concealed groan gathered about the court.

'And you have been his business partner, personal friend and, I understand, his physician for that period of time?'

'Yes, I have.'

'Could you tell the court about Dr Mackenzie's state of health in the last weeks of his life?'

'Certainly. He had been under a great deal of strain, working long hours and sometimes forgetting to take proper nourishment. I frequently advised him to take better care of himself, but that was advice he chose to ignore. I sounded his chest and was of the opinion that there was a weakness in his heart. I prescribed stimulants, but whether or not he took them, I don't know. He was a very private individual.'

'Before the evening of the 21st of September this year, had you any notion that he might be considering taking an unusual course of action?'

'On the previous day he mentioned to me that he had some personal worries and was considering leaving London, but I did not believe he would actually do so.'

'Can you tell the court what happened that evening?'

'Yes, I arrived at the Life House in the usual way and was in conversation with my assistant, Palmer —' he paused again and glanced at Frances as did many of those present. 'I am very sorry to say that we still have no news of him. But a short while later Mackenzie arrived and he seemed very agitated. He took me to one side and said that he needed to leave London that very night. He told me a story about how this action was necessitated by his having to protect the reputation of a lady. At the time, I believed him, but I am now of the opinion that he was not telling the truth.'

There was the scratching sound of busy pencils.

'What do you believe to be the real reason?' asked Hardwicke.

'Nothing so honourable as he represented, I am afraid. He wished to avoid his creditors.'

A mutter of surprise flowed about the courtroom and Hardwicke called for silence.

'I have no knowledge of how he incurred these debts and can only assume he made some unwise investments,' Bonner went on. 'If I had known it at the time I would not have condoned his leaving and I think he realised that, which was why he tried to deceive me. Even so, I tried to dissuade him. I pointed out that if he was to suddenly go away people might think it had something to do with the Life House and not his personal situation. He said that he intended to fool the world into thinking that he was dead, and would inject himself with a drug that would help in the dissimulation. I advised him against doing so in the strongest possible terms, but he would not listen. He was in a very distraught state and I went to get a glass of brandy for him – we keep some on the premises for medicinal purposes – but as I turned my back he must have injected himself and before I could do anything, he fell. Palmer assisted him onto a bed and we tried for some little time to revive him, but it was impossible. I thought that his heart had collapsed under the strain. I myself was, as you may well imagine, in a state of some considerable distress. Palmer took the body into the chapel out of respect and I sent him to report the sad circumstances to Mackenzie's landlady. The body gave every appearance of death. A few days later, I believed I had seen signs of advanced putrefaction, but of course, I may have been mistaken …' Dr Bonner pressed a handkerchief to his eyes. 'I can only offer the court my sincerest apologies,' he said, his voice breaking with emotion, 'and state further that it is my intention to retire immediately from medical practice, and once I am recovered from my present debility – if God grant that I should recover – I will devote all my energy and my fortune alike to works of charity.'

Dr Hardwicke looked at him with eyes like those of a very ancient mollusk and then turned his gaze towards the jurymen. 'Gentlemen, you have already heard the medical evidence and might I remind you that it has been stated here that the cause of Dr Mackenzie's death was a failure of the action of the heart due to fright, and that his death took place after he had been deposited in the catacombs. Professor Stevenson has given his expert opinion that the injection of morphine did not in itself cause the death of Dr Mackenzie, but produced a condition that caused him to be – unfortunately – buried alive. I wish at this point to express my disgust for certain illustrated publications, which have treated this unhappy situation with levity. You, of course, may have your own opinions as to the culpability of Dr Bonner in this matter and whether any further enquiries are necessary. If you wish to retire, you may do so.'

There was a lengthy whispered conversation between the jurymen and a great deal of nodding after which the foreman stood up. 'We have reached a verdict. We find that Dr Mackenzie died of heart failure due to fright, brought on by the very unusual circumstances. We have considered recommending that charges of negligence should be brought against Dr Bonner, although we do not believe his actions to be of a criminal nature. In view, however, of his state of health and intention to retire, we do not think any further proceedings would be of value. We would like to add, however, that the entire operation of the Life House has been ill-conceived and ill-administered. We suggest that any current occupants should be decently buried and the business closed down.' The foreman sat down amidst murmurs of approval from the watching crowds. Mr Fairbrother escorted a relieved looking Bonner from the building although Frances thought that as they headed to a cab, the senior man's footsteps were a little more agile than they had been indoors.

'So, that is the end of the Life House,' said Mr Gillan, as he handed in his copy to a runner. 'Did you know that it was all a fraud in any case? Some letters have just been published in Germany from Friedrich Erlichmann, who died last week and left a statement saying that his whole story was a lie from start to finish. Now, if I could only find that Mrs Biscoby who denounced him all those years ago I would be a happy man. What a story that would make!' Mr Gillan, who was preparing to attend the Old Bailey next day when he expected the *Chronicle* to trounce its accuser over the Monmouth affair, was in especially good spirits.

'You appreciate a good story, I know,' said Frances.

'Oh yes!' He winked. 'The exploits of Miss Dauntless!'

'Written by yourself, I suppose?'

'Oh, I wish that was true!' He laughed, tipped his hat and walked away.

The next issue of the *Chronicle* reported at great length on the scandal that had resulted from Friedrich Erlichmann's legacy. The waiting mortuaries in Germany and Austria had not suffered too greatly since none of them had been established on the basis of Erlichmann's claims. All had highly respected medical directors who were able to defend their establishments, and put before the public many instances of doubtful death exposed. The Kensal Green Life House, however, had no such support. The *Chronicle* described with some relish how coffins were being removed for detailed examination of the contents and then burial, after which the doors of the establishment were to be shut and sealed forever. Dr Mackenzie's dream had survived him by a matter of weeks.

❦

A few days later, early in the morning before it was light, a small group of men including Mr Fairbrother and Mr Lauderdale, the dental surgeon who had attended Mrs Templeman, proceeded to All Souls Cemetery Kensal Green, where, by special dispensation, they were admitted at a side entrance by an official. Some of the men had medical bags and one bore a camera, but several carried spades. It was a grim little procession, made all the worse by a fine mist that seemed to settle on everything almost like a film of oil or glue that could never be entirely removed. The official led the way with a lantern, moving effortlessly through the avenues of graves, some of them with carved figures contorted with grief that loomed out at them like spirits, and so assured was he that he seemed to glide as he walked, so that all the men began to feel uncomfortably as if they were following a ghost they knew not where, and a sense of dread began to settle over them. So said Mr Fairbrother to Frances as he described the scene to her later on, but she thought he might have been reading too much Wilkie Collins.

The official identified the location of the common grave recently covered with earth where the body of the woman found in the canal had been interred, and some workmen came and erected wooden screens with a canvas cover to keep out the seeping wet. The ground was boggy and soft and could hardly have been any wetter than it was, but that was all to the good as the spades dug in easily and deep, and clumps of mud were soon being piled to either side like malodorous soil heaps. As time passed the men became aware that outside their close shelter the sun had begun to rise and the hint of warmth only made the air within more oppressive. Despite the liberal sprinkling of stinging disinfectants on the black gummy earth, which was already contaminated with the liquids of putrefaction, the stench, even before the first frail coffin was reached, became overpowering, and several of the gentlemen were obliged to hold cologne-soaked handkerchiefs to their faces.

'Pauper burial,' said the official, who seemed to be immune to the smell. 'Cheap coffin, like matchwood. No lead, of course. That's why we keep these well away from the others.'

Soon, a spade struck wood, and space around the coffin was cleared, and men descended into the grave and put ropes in place to haul it up.

'How can you be sure this is the one?' asked Lauderdale.

'This is the one,' said the official. 'It's the last one in the grave – I was here when they put it in.'

The coffin, which was sodden and dripping black fluids, was hauled up and placed across two wooden blocks, then a crow-bar was inserted about the edge of the lid, which gave up the seating of its nails without a great deal of force being required.

The face, of course, was gone. Whatever resemblance it might have had to anything other than a grinning doll fashioned to attract demons had long since disappeared. But, thought Fairbrother, she had not so long ago been young, and clinging to life, and even beautiful. The thin form had shrunk, so even the stained frills and folds of her grave clothes were loose upon her.

'Well?' said the official.

'I am sure,' said Fairbrother, 'that this is the body of the woman I examined at Kilburn mortuary on the 23rd of September.' He leaned forward as far as he dared. 'There is embroidery on the collar of her chemise,' he said. 'If you could remove the collar, and have it washed and made presentable then maybe someone might recognise it.'

Mr Lauderdale, who had a stronger stomach than most, examined the teeth of the corpse, then stepped back while a photograph was taken. He nodded. 'I told the lady, I'd never seen such twisted teeth before on a person of quality. That's

Mrs Templeman. I've no doubt at all about that.'

'In that case,' said the assistant coroner, 'I suggest her family will not want her returned to this grave. The body must be placed in a dry shell and removed to Kilburn mortuary to await re-interment. I do not think,' he added, 'that the Home Office will drag its feet in opening the mausoleum in which Mrs Templeman was thought to have rested.'

Mr Fairbrother, shivering still, even many hours later and despite consuming several cups of scalding hot coffee, regaled Frances with his account of the events, saying that he expected a Home Office order to be issued almost at once and dreaded what might happen once the newspapers heard of it, which he expected would be within the hour, if they had not already done so. The coroner had taken charge of the embroidered collar, which had been washed and saturated in a liquid almost as foul as that in which it had been soaked, and it had been taken to Mrs Templeman's mother, who had seen it and promptly fainted. There was, said Fairbrother miserably, nothing in the world with greater power to convince — not a coroner's decision, not a dentist's knowledge — than a mother's instantaneous unconsciousness. It surpassed the most erudite determination of a bewigged judge and the opinions of a whole panel of doctors.

'When will the mausoleum be opened?' asked Frances.

'Within the week. A knife to trim the ivy and we will have the answer.'

CHAPTER SEVENTEEN

lthough she was not concerned with the death of Mr Horton, Frances studied the newspapers to see if there were any developments and saw that Professor Pounder – which was not, it seemed, that gentleman's real name, the truth being somewhat more commonplace – had been arrested and charged with killing Mr Horton. Horton, it was reported, had taken up Pounder's challenge of a one-minute bout which was generously offered to all members of the Piccadilly Club and had approached the combat with a greater expectation of success than was actually warranted, given that Mr Horton weighed about nine stones and the Professor, a former Queensberry Cup winner and in the peak of condition, more than thirteen. Mr Horton had lost rather badly, though not as badly as he might have done if the Professor had chosen to use all his skill and strength. The betting from the assembled gentlemen had not been so much as who would win, but how abominably Horton would lose. Horton had been bruised, angry and humiliated, and as a result had been telling people in his distracted way that he had been assaulted.

Pounder, interviewed by the police, had admitted that Horton had come up to him in the street very drunk one night and tried to pick a fight, which he had refused, and he had fended off the man's attacks, but denied having pushed him, saying that Horton had been alive but inebriated when he departed.

'It's just too bad!' said Cedric, when he arrived to tell Frances all about the fate of his instructor. 'Pounder is the quietest, most gentle fellow in the world when he is not thumping other pugilists. All these types are – they are perfect brutes when they put on the gloves, and Pounder was the best brute of all, his muscles are second to none and everyone who sees him admires them.'

'It seems to me that there is no real proof against him, only conjecture,' said Frances. 'Mr Horton was a man who made enemies easily, although I am sure he did not mean to; I believe he was not quite aware of what he was saying much of the time and how it might be received. There was no malice in him, and now I think back on it, I should have had more compassion for the man.'

'You must find out the real murderer, then,' said Cedric.

'Oh, I think that is not a commission I am equipped to take.'

'Nonsense, Miss Dauntless is afraid of nothing! She will rise to any occasion, dare any danger, fight any foe!'

'Miss Dauntless may, but I will not.' Frances paused. 'Did *you* write those stories?'

Cedric affected great indignation. 'You have seen them – do you think they are an exemplar of my literary style?'

'No – probably not, although I am sure you could turn your hand to anything if you chose.'

'If I was ever to write,' said Cedric, with a toss of the head, 'and I am far too addicted to idle pleasure to think of doing something so arduous and unprofitable, but *if* I did, I would lie on a couch and allow the most delicious poems to drop from my pen, adorning the vellum like costly jewels.'

'I can see that *Miss Dauntless Saves the Day* is unlikely to be one of your works,' observed Frances.

'But I do mean it about poor Pounder,' said Cedric, earnestly. 'Can't you help? The police think they have their man and I suppose I can see why, I would arrest him myself if I was a policeman and didn't know his character. You said Horton was a man who made enemies. A dozen fellows might have killed him.'

'True, but he was also so wild in his allegations that people took no note of them. How could he be a danger to anyone?'

'Perhaps someone did take note. Perhaps the matter was a serious one.' He heaved a sigh. 'Pounder has no family, at least none that will acknowledge him. I have been to see him in his cell and arranged a legal man for him, and he tells me he knows nothing of Horton and cannot tell me who might have wanted to murder him.'

'Are the police sure it is murder?'

'I am afraid so. There are marks on his body that show he fought against being tipped over the railing. But Horton was very inebriated and not a great weight. It did not take a man of Pounder's development to do it.'

'Did Horton have any family?'

'None that anyone can discover.'

'So the only people he might have spoken to apart from, I assume, the police or strangers he accosted in the street were fellow members of the Piccadilly Club.'

'It seems so, and he was a member only for a short while, before his behaviour led to his being ejected.'

'Well, I shall make enquiries amongst the members, on the Professor's behalf.'

'You are a wonder, Miss Doughty, I know he will be most grateful.'

Frances was able to meet with Chas and Barstie later that day. She had suggested that she might visit them in their suite of offices, but they had declined on the grounds that they were having extensive decorations done, and came to see her instead.

They knew of Pounder's arrest, which was all the talk of the club, and, like Cedric, did not believe he was a murderer. 'If I was ever to engage in a fight,' said Chas, 'that is the man I would want standing beside me, but it would be a fair, honest fight, and not some underhand affair.'

'Gentlemen, what I want you to do is speak to everyone you know who might have known Mr Horton and find out what other stories he might have told. What are Mr Horton's connections? His friends, his enemies, his family; which may of course all turn out to be the same thing. There might have been something in his ravings after all.'

'Horton spoke openly in the member's saloon bar many times,' said Barstie. 'Anyone might have overheard him, friend or not. He was especially outraged about Pounder, although I do recall a mention of an alligator that had been murdered. Or was it a fox? He seemed to have got the two mixed up in his head. He said the Piccadilly Club was full of scoundrels, cheats, frauds and murderers and he could prove it. I don't believe anyone took much notice.'

'I think,' said Frances, 'that someone did. Someone became afraid that Horton's ravings might strike a chord and be taken seriously. Is there any other dubious business being conducted at the club?'

They paused.

'Is there any business being conducted at the club which is *not* dubious?'

'Well, you know how it is, when gentlemen assemble, all the talk is of making money,' said Barstie.

'So I am given to understand,' said Frances.

'It is a fertile field. There are deals done and profits made without a gentleman stirring from his easy chair or even allowing his cigar to go out.'

'All the talk now is about the Life House and what a fine prospect it is,' said Chas. 'Prime building land, and after what has happened, in all probability to be had dirt cheap. I know there are several members taking an interest.'

'Doctors Bonner and Warrinder are not members?'

'Oh no, it is a young man's club,' said Barstie.

'Young and wealthy and reckless,' said Chas, happily.

'Was Mr Horton the only member to make allegations against Professor Pounder?'

'As far as I am aware. Most of the younger men took his challenge. No one succeeded and most received a bruise or two, but that was all part of the amusement, and all took it in good part except Horton, who was the only man who didn't like losing.'

'I have one more question to ask you,' said Frances, showing them a copy of one of Miss Dauntless's adventures.

'Do you read those?' asked Barstie. 'They are very good!'

'What I want to know is are you gentlemen the publishers?'

Chas was examining the booklet. 'Cheap paper, but then if you want to reach the masses at a halfpenny a copy that is the only way.'

'Profit in numbers,' said Barstie. 'We should look into it.' They both nodded. It was either a convincing act or they had nothing to do with the publication.

❧

There were two other members of the Piccadilly Club who might have had something to say about Mr Horton and Frances determined to speak to both of them.

Mr Darscot arrived cheerful and fresh-looking, with a dewy buttonhole, a new ruby pin and his smart little cane, although there was facial evidence that he ruefully admitted showed he had come off worst after his minute with Professor Pounder. 'He's the very deuce of a chap,' said Darscot, 'though as courteous as they come before and after. He might have been harder, but I think he took pity on me.'

'How well did you know the unfortunate Mr Horton?'

'Oh, no more than all the members did, which was not at all well. Poor fellow, he was most disliked. His bout with Pounder was treated as a joke, and the joke was all on Horton, because he imagined he might win and then got very cut up when he didn't. The difference between Horton and the rest of us was that we did it to amuse ourselves, and he thought it a serious matter. All the same, I was sorry when he was blackballed – he wasn't a bad sort of fellow, if a little soft in the head. Does he have any family?'

'I know of none, I am afraid.'

'Only, if he has no one to make any arrangements for him, I suppose I could get my man to do it. I'll have to find out when the funeral is, pop along, pay my respects.'

'I know that Horton made a number of allegations against Professor Pounder after the bout, but that Pounder was not the only man to be accused by him. Did you hear of any others?'

'Not by name, no. He was always very vague. Something about an alligator … ? But I did have the impression he had been badly stung by some financial deal he had conducted while in the club. Really he was very foolish to have done that. I would not dream of making an investment especially as regards shares or property without at least employing a reliable man to do all the hard work for me. I must admit, I had lent poor Horton some cash – not a great deal, £50 or so, he said he needed it to tide him over. I don't suppose I shall see it again, but I do have his IOU and if he turns out to be worth anything I should like to know. These mad fellows sometimes have estates they have quite forgotten about.'

'Did he ever threaten to go to the police about being swindled?'

'Oh yes. Nearly every day. But he was only a member for a few weeks and then he was shown the door. After that he used to walk up and down outside the club muttering to himself. I think the club owners were thinking of having him removed by the police. Very sad, but there was no harm in him.'

'So any member might have met up with him outside? It's not a long way from the club premises to where he was found dead.'

'Yes, and Pounder was at the club that night. But then most of us were.'

❧

Frances' next interview was with Dr Carmichael, who confirmed that he had not as yet been approached by anyone about the missing journal. He seemed uncomfortable when questioned about the Piccadilly Club, saying that as far as he had been aware it was merely a place where good lodgings could be had. He had since found that the members were not as respectable as he had been led to believe and was seeking new accommodation. He had never fought with or spoken to Professor Pounder and had not to his knowledge had much in the way of conversation with any member of the club. He could recall some talk about a troublesome member who had been asked to leave, and then made to leave, and had sometimes seen a man walking up and down outside the club, who occasionally approached members as they went in or out. The fellow had looked distracted, and shaken his fist and uttered threats, but everyone had ignored him.

❧

As Mr Fairbrother had predicted, the revelation that the body in the pauper's grave was that of Mrs Templeman had excited some curiosity about who, or possibly what, was in that lady's coffin, and the cemetery was more than usually busy with sightseers who clustered around the Templeman mausoleum hoping to see something gruesome. The removal of Mrs Templeman's coffin was to take place at night after the cemetery gates had been shut to visitors, and while Frances was not permitted to view the arrangements, Mr Fairbrother was. Frances awaited his next visit with some impatience. It occurred to her that due to the nature of her enquiries she had been spending more time in his company than she ever had with any young bachelor, and it had been a not unpleasant experience. He was intelligent and ambitious, with good prospects, and, she was forced to admit, very handsome, although that was not something she thought ought to sway her in any man's favour. Surely a kind man with a good mind might by bad fortune also be very ugly, and she ought not to think less of him for that. Mr Fairbrother's only fault – and what man did not have faults – was that he had a very shallow understanding of what a clever woman might achieve, but that, Frances thought, could be mended in time. As soon as the idea crossed her mind she tried to dismiss it. She had only to gaze in her mirror to see that she would never be courted by a handsome man.

Frances returned home to find that she had a new client, a Miss Horton. The lady was neatly and respectably dressed, but every thread of her clothing spoke of poverty and making the best of meagre means. Her red fingers and sturdy forearms suggested a lifetime spent as a washerwoman. She was about forty and had the unhappy air of someone who was enduring a long expected tragedy with acceptance, sadness and a pang of relief.

'How may I help you?' asked Frances, having established that the lady was indeed the sister of the recently deceased Mr Horton.

'I have just travelled down from Manchester to see to my poor brother's affairs. I read in the newspapers last Friday that he had been killed, but I couldn't come to London till yesterday, as my mother is very ill. A friend of his, a Mr Darscot, has kindly offered to help with the arrangements, but I have been unable to discover where poor Herbert was living. I had a letter from him about six months ago, asking if I could send him some money, and I did send a few shillings, but when I went to the place, it was a lodging house on the Balls Pond Road, and the landlord told me Herbert had left three weeks ago leaving unpaid rent. He had heard Herbert talking about the Piccadilly Club, though he never believed that he was really a member, but I went there, and the secretary came and spoke to me. He was very kind and said that Herbert had been a member, but only for about a month and left without paying his dues, and when he joined he gave a false address.'

'I am sure that someone will read of the inquest in the newspapers and come forward,' said Frances.

'I am afraid he was in the habit of taking lodgings under a fanciful name,' said Miss Horton, regretfully. 'It was just his way. Would you be able to find his rooms? I can't afford to pay you very much but with Mr Darscot's assistance ...'

'I think you ought to know that Mr Darscot may not be as disinterested as you suppose. He has told me that he lent a sum of money to your brother and he may be hoping to recover it.'

She smiled. 'Oh, he has been quite open about that. I told him that I very much doubted that Herbert had fifty pence let alone £50, and he said he suspected as much and it didn't matter.'

'Of course you will want to be able to find any little mementoes of your brother he might have left.' Frances thought that since Horton was not likely to have had money to travel by cab, he had probably taken rooms not too far from the Piccadilly Club. The messenger boys who made that part of Bayswater their domain might well have noticed him. 'I think I may be able to help,' she said.

❦

Had Frances been asked to predict the outcome of the examination of Mrs Templeman's coffin she would have said that she hoped to find stolen goods, but she knew and Fairbrother knew what they were both dreading. She had tried not to think about it, but the idea would keep coming back like an angry spirit that obstinately refused to stay dead. When Fairbrother came to see her, his face told her everything before he even spoke.

'It is very bad news, I am afraid. There is a body in Mrs Templeman's coffin, and it is, without a shadow of a doubt, that of Henry Palmer. Fully clothed and with his keys still in his pocket. The police have been notified and will be informing the family. It will be a terrible shock to them.'

Frances thought of Mabel Finch and her simpering love, and Palmer's honest and reliable nature, and his shy affection. How she had wanted them to be united and happy as far as any couple could be in life. She did not want Palmer to be a mouldering corpse in a coffin with his future stolen from him. She thought of Alice and Walter, and wondered how they would fare.

'His poor sister, she was quite ill with worry,' said Frances. 'And there was a young lady he was interested in who returned his esteem. Such a tragedy for them both. I am sorry that I was not able to help more, but it seems that when I was first consulted he had already been dead for some time.'

'But you did help them, Miss Doughty. You found him, and I think without you he would never have been found. They will be able to say their farewells and it will be a great comfort to them. At least —' he paused. 'There is, I am afraid, another possible source of pain for those who knew him.'

'You are referring to the cause of death?'

'I will be assisting Dr Collin at the examination tomorrow and cannot of course express any official opinion before then.'

'But an unofficial opinion?'

He smiled, ruefully. 'I knew you would press me most directly to say what I think.'

'And will continue to do so if necessary.'

'Very well, but it is always possible I could be mistaken. I believe Palmer was attacked with a weapon of some kind, a cudgel, perhaps, or even a hammer; it was hard to tell, but it will become clearer later. He was struck several times on the back of the head. His skull was broken.'

'Murder, then,' said Frances.

'I fear so.'

'Which explains the reason for the substitution. It was done in order to conceal a body that had clearly met with a violent death, while disposing of one where death had occurred through natural causes. But where can the crime have taken place? There would be blood splashes, would there not?'

'There would indeed, but it was a very foggy night and there was a misty rain that would have quickly washed away any traces.'

'What if he was killed indoors? We don't know where he went after leaving Mrs Georgeson's. Several people concerned in the business of the Life House live close by – but the simplest solution is that he went back to the Life House, to help Dr Bonner, from a sense of duty. Any other location would mean the murderer had to transport the body through the street, not an easy thing to arrange, even in the fog. Could he have been killed there? And who changed over the bodies? And when?'

'There is no note in the record book of him returning to the Life House and he was very meticulous about signing it,' Fairbrother objected. 'The walls of the wards are whitewashed and would easily show any traces of blood. Hemsley cleaned regularly and has said nothing about any bloodstains.'

'But suppose that Palmer did go back, who would have been there when he arrived? Dr Mackenzie, but he had already injected himself and was unconscious, and in any case he had been taken into the chapel. Then there was Mr Darscot – he was travelling by cab and would have got there before Palmer, who was on foot, and Dr Bonner let him into the chapel. But Palmer had the keys and would have let himself in at the main door, and he would quite possibly have been on the wards, alone while the others were all in the chapel. Could someone have entered and killed Palmer without the men in the chapel hearing anything?'

'I must doubt that,' said Fairbrother. 'The wall between the chapel and the wards is not very thick.'

'But the outer walls, I suspect, are thicker.'

'They are, very much so. I assume you agree that Dr Bonner cannot have been involved. He is very lame and quite incapable of carrying bodies around.'

'The road around the Life House is very secluded,' said Frances. 'Mr Palmer may have been killed just outside the building by someone who followed him and then struck him down, used his keys to enter, and carried the body indoors. That would explain why he didn't sign the book, and why there were no blood splashes inside and why the men in the chapel heard nothing.'

Fairbrother nodded. 'And of course the murderer would have had his cudgel in his pocket and taken it away with him.'

'But who put the body in Mrs Templeman's coffin? And why throw Mrs Templeman into the canal at all, when the two bodies might have been fitted into the same coffin and buried together?'

'That would be indecent!' exclaimed Fairbrother.

'More indecent than murder?' Frances turned to Sarah, who was looking at them with an expression of extreme scepticism. 'Do you have a comment, Sarah?'

Sarah's fingers didn't pause in her knitting. 'What I want to know is, if nothing of Mr Palmer's was stolen, why did anyone want to kill him?'

Neither Frances nor Fairbrother could answer that.

CHAPTER EIGHTEEN

As expected, the opening of the inquest on Henry Palmer's death the next morning was a brief formality in which evidence was taken of identification and the proceedings were adjourned to await the results of the post-mortem examination.

That morning's newspapers brought an interesting announcement. The Life House would formally close its doors in four days' time, when the last body was removed for burial. The property had been sold to an investor and once the business ceased, the building would be torn down and the land used to construct dwellings.

Frances realised that if she wanted to look inside the Life House she had very little time in which to achieve it. Dr Bonner had left London, and Dr Warrinder and Mr Fairbrother would not permit any infringement of the rules. She thought about trying to talk her way in when the new orderly, Renfrew, the only man who had not met her, was in charge, but entry was allowed only by application to a director, and entrants must be medically qualified or be medical students.

There was only one way she might achieve her object, she must persuade a doctor to take her into the building and vouch for her, and the only man she could reasonably ask to do this was Dr Carmichael. She would have to avoid any objections that might be raised to her sex by doing something she had promised herself she would never do again. Frances composed two letters, which were duly delivered, and then she and Sarah went shopping.

That afternoon, Frances, accompanied by Sarah who, with her features determinedly devoid of all emotion, was clutching a large parcel, called on Cedric and explained what she had been unable to put in writing.

'Let me understand this,' said Cedric, making little effort to conceal his amusement. 'You wish me to instruct you in the art of appearing masculine.' Joseph tilted an eyebrow in their direction. 'I have told you the story, have I not, Joseph, of my first meeting with Miss Doughty, or should I say Mr Frank Williamson, as she seemed to me then.'

'Many times,' Joseph murmured.

'It was not something I did willingly and I do not do it willingly now,' said Frances firmly. 'I know it is a grave risk, but I am driven by necessity. I am aware that if I am to do it, I should do it the best way I can, which is why I have asked your advice. I suspect that at my first attempt I was a very feminine boy.'

'Oh, you were, you were,' said Cedric nostalgically, 'but really I can't imagine why you feel you need lessons in being the man. You have obviously been practicing it since, and you already have the art.'

'I don't understand.'

'But I espied Mr Williamson only the other day and I thought he cut a very masculine figure. I decided not to hail you as I thought you might be about some secret task, but you were very convincing.'

Frances stared at him. 'You are mistaken. I have never, since the time we first met, donned gentlemen's clothing.'

'Oh? But I was quite sure it was you! The features, the walk, it was so like. If it was not you it must have been a relation.'

Frances was suddenly dry-mouthed and spoke with an effort. 'And – what was this man doing when you saw him?'

'Boarding a train at Paddington station.'

'To what destination?'

'I couldn't say. My dear Miss Doughty, you look quite unwell. Please be seated and Joseph will bring you a glass of sherry.'

Frances told him then – not all that there was to tell, as there were some things she could hardly bear to speak of. She said that she had not long ago discovered that her mother, whom she had supposed to be long dead, was quite possibly still alive, and that she had a younger brother, Cornelius Doughty, whom she had never met.

'Of course, I would like to know my family, but I am so afraid that they might not wish to know me that I have as yet made no attempt to discover where they are living. You will think me a coward, now.'

'Not a bit of it!' said Cedric. 'You are the bravest lady I know and how I wish I had hailed the young man I saw, or taken more notice of his train. But I promise you that if I see him again, I will not make that mistake. Now then, I see a little colour return to your cheeks, so let us talk about what you require me to do. Does that parcel contain the suit you wore previously?'

'No, that belonged to my late brother, Frederick, and was, I realise now, an indifferent fit. I have purchased a new suit of clothing that I believe will be better and Sarah can undertake to make any necessary adjustments.'

'I see, and – er – now this is a delicate question so you must forgive me – do you wish to have the garment altered so as to conceal your sex, or would you prefer it to be of a masculine nature but of a feminine cut?'

'Why would a woman want to dress as a man, but appear to be female?' said Frances in surprise.

'Indeed,' said Cedric solemnly. 'I am sorry to have mentioned it, how foolish of me.'

'I wish to masquerade as a man for professional reasons and must, therefore, appear to be a man. I would like you to instruct me on my gait and carriage.'

'Of course. Well, if you could retire to my dressing room and transform yourself we will set about it.'

Cedric's dressing room was a small marvel, with rows of tastefully cut suits, snowy shirts, brightly polished shoes, jars of scented pomade to sleek their owner's unruly blond locks, crystal spray bottles of cologne and trays of discreet masculine jewellery. 'I do not think,' said Frances, as Sarah helped her dress, 'that however hard I was to try I could ever be such an elegant gentleman as Mr Garton.'

'You look good enough to me,' said Sarah.

'He is quite the old-fashioned dandy!'

'Oh?' said Sarah. 'I didn't know they had a name for it.'

'Still, since I am to represent a medical student, a certain economy of attire would seem to be appropriate.'

Eventually, after forcing her long hair into a hat, Frances emerged, and stood before Cedric. 'Well,' she said. 'Now you must advise me on what else I need to do.'

He gazed at her for a while, an unreadable expression in his eyes. 'Very little,' he said at last.

'But does she look like a man?' demanded Sarah.

'A youth,' said Cedric. 'A handsome youth with all the promise of young manhood before him. Well, let us proceed.'

Although Frances' limbs were decently enough covered she felt uncomfortable. The fact that the shape of her legs could be seen, and the absence of the accustomed weight and bulk of skirts and petticoats suggested to her that she was proposing to step out in a public street clad in little more than her underlinen. Her previous masquerade had been made out of a sense of desperation, but this was more cold-blooded, more planned, and her buried concerns were re-emerging. Cedric asked her to walk about the room and at first she tried to strut in what she hoped was a manly fashion, but he quickly instructed her to stop and asked her instead to take her natural walk so that he could correct it. Frances found it hard not to think of how she was moving, but as she walked, began to feel once again that delightful sense of freedom she had experienced when she had worn her brother's suit. How easy it would be, thus clad, to run down the street! How she might be able to jump and climb and ride a bicycle, and a thousand things she might never even have thought of! She could do things that even Miss Dauntless would not contemplate.

It was an hour before Cedric had instilled in her the ability to walk, sit down, stand up, and put things into her pockets and take them out again, as if she had been a boy from birth.

'It is fortunate that you do not have a high voice, or, as so many girls do, have been accustomed to speaking like small children in order to attract the protection of men. Your voice will do well enough if you are careful.'

'I am very grateful for your assistance,' said Frances, 'and I know I can count on you to keep this secret.'

'Tempting as it would be to tell all my friends about this afternoon, which would greatly add to my notoriety – if that were possible – I can assure you that you may count on my silence.'

Although the resumed inquest on the death of Henry Palmer was not due for a few days, Frances felt sure that Mr Fairbrother would tell her what she wanted to know about the post-mortem examination if she demanded it with enough confidence, revealing the conclusions before he had the opportunity of wondering whether or not he should.

When she questioned him, however, she found that there was no need for either forcefulness or subtle persuasion; he recognised with a wry smile that it would be simpler for him to comply. Frances learned that there was no doubt at all in Dr Collin's mind that Henry Palmer had died after being struck on the head three times with a heavy object, perhaps some sort of carpentry tool. Only one weapon had been used. The first blow had probably been struck while Palmer was in a standing position and would have been enough to make him dizzy, but would not have been fatal. In all probability he would have fallen. He had been on all fours or lying down when a second blow had been struck and certainly prone, his face pressed to the ground when the third and fatal blow fell. The skull was not so much crushed as punctured, as if the weapon had a heavy end like a hammer. Fairbrother confirmed that there was no object in the Life House that might answer that description.

Frances was also able to elicit from Mr Fairbrother that he was attending a course of lectures and would not be at the Life House in the next few days, but that Hemsley and Renfrew had matters in hand, and Dr Warrinder would also call. This was a great relief, since the idea that she might encounter Mr Fairbrother during her excursion to the Life House in male attire appalled her. As long as her visit occurred during Mr Renfrew's period of duty she would be safe as she did not think Dr Warrinder, even if he did arrive, would recognise her if she kept her distance and took care not to face him directly. She asked Fairbrother if he knew the identity of the new owner, but he did not. The sale was very nearly complete and it was anticipated that the keys would be handed over shortly.

❦

The next morning, Frances, as Mr Frank Williamson, medical student, awaited Dr Carmichael. That gentleman, who had been told what to expect, must have convinced himself that Frances had not been serious when she had described her intentions or thought that, on sober reflection, she would abandon the idea. It was with some sense of shock that he saw her in male attire. 'Have you thought of going on the stage?' he said at last.

'Is that the only destination for a woman who dresses as a man?'

'That and prison, I would have thought. I am really not sure that this should be attempted.'

'If it is a question of your reputation, I believe I am the least of your dangers,' said Frances.

'What have you been told?' he demanded.

'It involves chloroform,' said Frances. 'Do I need to say more?'

He looked angry, but made no denials. 'No, you do not. Well, let us get this done quickly. If you are found out I can always say that I was deceived. Your masquerade is sufficiently convincing, no doubt from considerable practice. I am only thankful that your companion will not be accompanying us dressed as a soldier!'

They travelled up by cab, and on the way Frances explained that she was looking for the location of the death of Henry Palmer. 'I cannot anticipate the verdict of the coroner's jury,' she said, 'but it is possible that he may have been the victim of foul play. I have heard rumours that he was struck several times on the head by something resembling a hammer. I suspect that he was killed very close to the Life House.'

'Surely there will be nothing to see after all this time?' said Carmichael.

'I fear you may be right, but at least I should look.'

Before they approached the door of the Life House chapel, Frances searched carefully for any sign of a struggle, but there was nothing in the lane that led south to the canal, or any of the little ways around the building or the path that led to the front door. Even if Palmer had been killed there, the passage of time had erased any traces. Carmichael knocked at the chapel door and they were met by Renfrew, a small man who resembled a nocturnal rodent, down to the dark glittering eyes, pale whiskers and pink nose. He said little, but studied the appointment book in his hands and, noting that Dr Carmichael and Mr Williamson were expected, examined the doctor's card, and nodded approval. They were told to go to the front door and wait, and a few moments later he ushered them in. The office area was mainly occupied by a small desk and a coat stand, and there were shelves of leather-bound books; medical volumes, ledgers and record books. A glass-fronted cabinet held a few restorative items: brandy, a carafe of water, and some smelling salts. So meagre were the contents, so inadequate to deal with the kind of emergencies the Life House might have faced, that Frances felt sure that this was intended not for the use of the patients but visitors.

'That is only a very small part of what we have here,' said Renfrew quickly, seeing her expression. 'On the ward we have an extensive supply of apparatus and materials for the treatment of cases of doubtful death. I am sure you would like to examine them.'

Carmichael said that he would be very interested to do so and Frances nodded her enthusiastic assent, then Renfrew unlocked the door that led to the wards.

Carmichael glanced at Frances with some concern, afraid that at any moment the brandy, water and smelling salts would have to be pressed into action, but she had seen and smelled death before, and death, moreover, without the benefit of carbolic. The odour of putrefaction, whatever one did, could never be disguised. It was oddly sweet, but in a way that caught at the back of the throat and however much one resisted, it was like a sickly caress that impelled nausea. Overlying it was the sour stench of disinfectant that stung the nostrils and, thought Frances, helped matters more by providing an unpleasant distraction than anything else.

There was a curtain acting as a partition across the main ward and four beds on either side, but there were only two patients, one male and one female, segregated in the anticipation that a revival might occur. Frances saw that the 'beds' were little more than mortuary slabs, although dressed with sheets and blankets.

The corpses, for she could not think of them as anything else, were clothed and arranged like living patients, and though the heads were supported on pillows there was a tendency for them to drop back and mouths to sag open in a manner that could only suggest that life was extinct. Around each body was a mass of foliage and flowers, tubs and pots of growing shrubs, plants that climbed and straggled, their tendrils tumbling over the side of the beds and dipping to the floor. Each corpse revealed one naked foot, and tied to the big toe was a long cord leading to a bell that hung from the wall behind, another cord also being connected to a finger.

Renfrew proudly threw back the double doors of a tall cupboard, revealing blankets and towels, sponges, lint, galvanic apparatus, massage devices, hypodermic syringes, ammonia, naphthalene, ether and camphor, linseed meal and linen cloths for making poultices, cantharides blisters, cupping and scarification devices, stethoscopes, equipment for tapping fluid from body cavities, bottles of fragrant oils, suppositories, pessaries, and everything that a surgeon might need for performing a tracheotomy.

Frances looked over the contents of the cupboard, restraining herself from making any observations as she was a little nervous of speaking, but trying to look deeply interested, even impressed. Renfrew hovered beside them, then after a while, seeing that they did not need his assistance, sidled away and commenced his inspection of the male corpse, though Frances thought that testing for pulse and breath on an object with sunken eyes and already showing the darkening stains of putrefaction about the lips, was optimistic.

'I see no signs that anything occurred here,' she said softly to Carmichael, 'but it is not as light as I would wish because of the small windows. There is a lamp in the cupboard. We need to use it.'

Carmichael asked Renfrew to get the lamp. He looked surprised but left his duties, delved into the cupboard and extracted and lit the lamp. 'Is there anything I can assist you with?' he asked.

'We will tour the premises and make any enquiries later,' said Carmichael. Renfrew nodded and went back to his work.

'Suppose Palmer was killed here?' said Frances. 'What would I look for?'

'Hmm, well I was once called to a scene where a thief had cheated his confederate and as a result of the falling out, had been attacked with a jemmy. The first blow led to a crushing indentation in the skull, but in the room where it occurred there were no bloodstains. The skin was broken and blood had come to the surface, but it had not splashed on the walls. The victim then staggered into another room where he collapsed and his erstwhile friend completed the business. There was blood only in the second room. It was very much thrown about the place by the weapon.'

'So,' said Frances, 'the first blow simply starts the bleeding, but then the others scatter the blood.' She began to walk slowly around the ward, holding the lantern up to better see the floor and the walls, and the beds. Renfrew looked puzzled, but shrugged and went on with his work. Frances had gone around the perimeter lifting the lantern high then lowering it to scan every surface, before she saw what she had been looking for. It was in the crevice where the doorjamb met the wall by the exit to the office; something small and dark that resembled a clot of blood. She held the lamp close. 'What do you think?' she asked Carmichael.

Renfrew abandoned his work and came over to speak to them. 'May I assist you, gentlemen?'

'That will not be necessary,' said Carmichael, 'please do not let us interrupt you.'

'I was wondering what had attracted your attention,' said Renfrew with a suspicious glance, and started peering closely at the wall. At that moment, there was a faint tinkling of a bell. Renfrew jumped as if he had been stung and hurried away.

Carmichael turned and stared at Frances, who was standing behind him, smiling. Together they examined the dark brown gobbet. 'It does look like blood; the colour and consistency and degree of drying are right,' said Carmichael. 'Whether or not it is human it is impossible to know.'

'The fact that the spot is by the door that leads to the office suggests that Palmer was either entering or leaving the ward when it happened. But there were three blows. This blood must have come from either the second or the third. If this is Palmer's blood, then he died on this very spot.'

'You may well be right, but a single drop – that makes it very hard to prove anything.'

'There should have been more.'

'Oh yes, a great deal more.'

'Then the wall and floor have been washed. It is only because of the dark shadows in this crevice that this was missed.' She thought further. 'Dr Carmichael, I would like you to go and inspect the chapel.'

'Certainly. Any more instructions?' he added with more than a hint of sarcasm, which Frances chose to ignore.

'Yes, take Renfrew with you and engage him in conversation while you are there.'

Carmichael rolled his eyes, but complied. Renfrew had completed his tests of the male corpse and was staring at Frances as if he suspected her of having pulled a cord while his back was turned, in which suspicion he was entirely correct. When Carmichael asked to see the chapel, Renfrew paused, and seeing that Frances did not intend to accompany them, issued a curt instruction for her to touch nothing. He and Carmichael left by the connecting door, while Frances continued to stare at the spot of blood, trying to imagine what had occurred. An assailant with a hammer or a cudgel, bringing it down on the man's head, creating a depression in the skull, crushing tissues, the wound pooling into a well of blood. The cudgel rising and coming down again, and this time striking the crushed and bloody flesh; drops of blood flying out, spattering the wall, the floor and the assailant. The cudgel, its ugly head now sticky with a mess of blood and flesh rising again for the third blow … Frances followed its path upwards with her eyes, raising the lantern again, but higher this time, not looking at the wall, but the painted ceiling of the room and there she saw them, thin streaks and droplets of blood, like lines of stitching running across the paintwork, high above her head, where the weapon had thrown it off and where whoever had cleaned the walls had failed to look.

Through the thin walls of the partition Frances could clearly hear Carmichael in conversation with Renfrew. She took a coin from her pocket, a penny piece, and dropped it on the floor. When it had finished bouncing and rolling she picked it up again. When Carmichael and Renfrew returned she said, 'I hope I didn't alarm you – a penny fell from my pocket.'

'Oh, so that was what it was,' said Carmichael, 'I thought another one had woken up.'

Renfrew grunted, but went to tend the flowers.

'Look up at the ceiling,' said Frances. 'It's hard to see without the lantern light, but there is more blood there. Is that what you would expect to see?'

He nodded. 'Oh yes. There was murder done here all right.'

'Dr Carmichael,' she said, 'I am going to take a cab home and return to my proper attire without delay, but I want you to remain here and send Mr Renfrew with an urgent message to the police.'

Frances was now certain that both Dr Bonner and Mr Darscot had a great deal of explaining to do.

CHAPTER NINETEEN

ater that day, Frances had a slightly difficult interview with Inspector Gostelow of the Kilburn police.

'I am finding it hard to understand how you came to be in the Life House at all,' he said. 'Surely that is not a place for ladies.'

'It is not,' said Frances, 'which is why I have been snooping around it for some days, hoping to be able to enter while no one was looking. I knew I would not be allowed to visit, yet I felt sure there was something to see.'

'So how *did* you manage to get in?'

'It was when the orderly admitted Dr Carmichael and the student. The young man was careless in closing the door and I was able to slip in unnoticed, and saw – well, what I saw. Then I asked the student to send a message to you at once.'

Gostelow frowned. 'Well, that's a pretty tale and no mistake! I've spoken to Mr Renfrew the orderly and he says the young gentleman had quite a feminine voice.'

'Really?' said Frances.

Gostelow shook his head. 'I don't know what you've been up to, Miss, but if I was your father I would be very worried indeed. Still, we'll let it go for now, because it does seem that you have found something of interest.'

The door of his office opened and a constable peered in. Frances saw, to her surprise, the edge of a paper poking from his pocket, and recognised it at once as a copy of *Miss Dauntless and the Diamond Thief*. 'We've got Mr Darscot, sir, shall I bring him in?'

'Yes, and don't let me find you carrying reading matter about with you again!'

'Sorry sir.' He took the booklet out of his pocket, and Gostelow snatched it from him and put it in his desk drawer. 'Now go and get him. Miss Daunt – I mean Miss Doughty – you can go now.'

'If you don't mind, Inspector, I would like to stay,' said Frances.

'Certainly not! This is a police matter!'

'I have been investigating Mr Palmer's disappearance for some time and not only did I discover his body, but also the location where he was murdered,' Frances reminded him. 'Those are police matters, I believe. I may have some useful observations.'

He shook his head. 'Inspector Sharrock warned me about you,' he said.

'About my habit of solving crimes?'

'Yes, a most regrettable habit for a young lady. Still, I suppose we ignore it at our peril. Very well, you can stay as long as you sit tight and say nothing. Do you promise?'

'I will do my best,' she reassured him.

Darscot was brought in looking as fresh and dapper as ever, but with a wary look in his eye. He was taken aback to see Frances. 'Why, Miss Doughty – have they got you here too?'

She declined to comment.

Darscot was ushered to a seat facing Gostelow across his desk and despite the unusual circumstances, did his best to retain his air of assurance.

'Mr Darscot, we are enquiring into the death of Henry Palmer, which we now believe took place on the same night as the unfortunate occurrence concerning Dr Mackenzie.'

'Oh, I read all about Mr Palmer in the newspapers and as you know, I did go up to the Life House that night. I saw Dr Bonner and viewed Dr Mackenzie's body, but Palmer was not there.'

'Can you go over again the events that occurred when you went there?'

'Well, there is hardly anything to tell. I went because I wanted to see for myself that Mackenzie had indeed passed away, since he owed me a large sum of money, and found that he had – or at least it seemed so at the time.'

'You entered the chapel?'

'Yes.'

'Not the main ward?'

'Oh no, well there was no reason for me to go there, even if I was allowed in – it's only doctors there isn't it?'

'The thing is, Mr Darscot, we now know that apart from Dr Mackenzie, who was alive but unconscious at the time, the only other persons in the Life House that evening were Dr Bonner, Mr Palmer and yourself. And we now believe that after reporting to Dr Mackenzie's landlady, Mr Palmer, despite being told he might go home, instead returned to the Life House, no doubt from a sense of duty. We are also convinced that he died there. Both you and he were seen headed up to the Life House at about the same time, you by cab and he on foot. He probably arrived only a few minutes after you did.'

'Well,' said Darscot, 'I wish I could help you, but I cannot. I was admitted to the chapel by Dr Bonner, I viewed the body of Dr Mackenzie, and then I left. I did not see Palmer. He must have arrived afterwards.'

'How long were you there?'

'Not many minutes.'

'You departed by the chapel door?'

'Yes.'

'What about Dr Bonner? Where did he go?'

'I couldn't say; he was in the chapel when I left.'

Gostelow nodded. If, Frances reflected, Palmer had arrived shortly afterwards, then the only living persons in the Life House when he entered were Dr Mackenzie, who was unconscious, and Dr Bonner. But she did not know for certain exactly when Palmer had arrived, or even if he had arrived alone. The only thing that was certain was that by the following morning Palmer was dead, and his body had been switched with that of Mrs Templeman, whose corpse had been slipped into the canal, and most traces of blood splashing had been removed. She very much doubted that Bonner, afflicted as he was with the gout, could have done all that by himself, and certainly not in the brief period he was apparently alone in the Life House before Hemsley arrived. The only other man who had undoubtedly been on the ward that night was Hemsley. Had he helped his employer conceal a murder?

Gostelow glanced at Frances. 'Er – Miss Doughty, you have been looking into the Palmer case on behalf of his relatives. I – ah – wonder if you have any observations at this point?'

'I would like to ask Mr Darscot – when you were in the chapel, did you hear the sound of anyone in the ward? A person moving about, perhaps? A key turning? A bell? A knock on the door?'

'No, nothing at all.'

'You didn't see Mr Palmer that night?'

'Well, no, and I am not sure I would have recognised him if I did. I really would help you if I could.' Darscot was lounging in his seat, all smiles, playing with the little cane, the picture of affable innocence.

'And now I understand you are taking legal action against Dr Mackenzie's estate for the loan of £500,' said Frances, who suspected that the young man was more hard-headed about money than he liked to appear.

'Yes, well I am very sorry for what has happened, but a loan is a loan, you know.'

'May I see the agreement?'

Darscot laughed and made a great play of delving into his pockets and patting his coat, creating a rustling of paper and a chinking of coins and keys. 'Of course, I don't carry it about my person, it is with my legal man.'

'Perhaps, Mr Darscot,' said Frances, on a sudden thought, 'you might like to turn out your pockets?'

He glanced at the Inspector. 'Am I being accused of anything?'

'Not yet,' said Gostelow. 'Please do as the young lady asks.'

Darscot looked surprised, but obliged. The items he laid on the desk were a pocket book containing some banknotes, a memorandum book, a pencil, some visiting cards in a silver case, a bundle of tailor's bills, some coins and five keys on a ring. One key was small, but the other four were rather heavier.

Gostelow examined the pocket and memorandum books, but Frances picked up the bunch of keys.

'What are these the keys to?' she asked.

'The small one is for my rooms at the Piccadilly Club,' said Darscot, 'and the others are the keys to some of my properties in the country.'

'I think not,' said Frances. 'This is a set of keys to the Life House. Please don't deny it, it is too easily tested. So on the night of Palmer's death you could have let yourself into the Life

House at the front door using these keys, and could have been on the ward when he was killed. Which means you have been lying to Inspector Gostelow.'

'What do you say to that, sir?' asked Gostelow. 'Maybe you are the man who killed Mr Palmer.'

Darscot paled. 'No! I haven't killed anyone! All right, I admit that those are Life House keys. They're Mackenzie's. He let me have them as security for the loan.'

'He would never have done that,' said Frances. 'And in any case, these are not Dr Mackenzie's original keys, but a set that have been recently cut. It is the same locksmith but a slightly different design. A week before Dr Mackenzie died he arrived at the Life House very distressed, without his keys, saying he had left them at his lodgings. And then he didn't return for several days. You stole his keys, didn't you? And had them copied.'

'I borrowed them,' said Darscot. 'And I gave them back, so it wasn't stealing.'

'Why did you have copies made?'

'The man owed me money and I wasn't going to have him hide away from me.'

'I think,' said Frances, 'the Inspector would like to hear the truth about what happened on the night of Palmer's death.'

'You are looking at a very serious charge, sir,' said Gostelow. 'I would advise it.'

Darscot looked from one to the other, and sighed. 'I am really very sorry that I have said nothing before, but I have been worried out of my wits. I have done nothing wrong, or at least if there was any wrongdoing it was forced upon me. Inspector, if I was to tell you all, would you agree that I would not suffer any penalties?'

'That depends on what you have to say,' said Gostelow. He called in the constable. 'Mr Darscot is about to make a statement. Write down what he says.'

'To be truthful,' said Darscot, 'it is something of a relief to be able to tell you this. It has weighed upon my mind most terribly. Well, the thing is, as you know I went up to the Life House by cab to see if Dr Mackenzie was really dead or just trying to avoid paying his debts. And I had the keys and let myself in. You can imagine how I felt when I walked in and there were

Dr Mackenzie and Dr Bonner standing in the middle of the room, arguing.'

'Excuse me,' said Gostelow. 'But this would have taken place *after* Mr Palmer had reported that Dr Mackenzie was dead?'

'Yes, precisely! So I knew then that it was all a trick. I said straight out that Dr Mackenzie had some scheme to avoid paying me and Dr Bonner was very shocked. It seems that Mackenzie had told Bonner some fancy tale that he wanted to disappear because of an entanglement with a woman – I don't know the details, but it was all lies in any case. Bonner had agreed to help him because he thought it was a matter of honour. When I said it was to escape paying his debts, Bonner was very upset. He said he didn't want to help him any more. He said Mackenzie had got him to agree to something under false pretences, something that could damage his standing if it was found out. He asked how much the debt was and I told him £500. He wanted to know what Mackenzie had wanted the money for, but Mackenzie wouldn't tell him. I had no idea myself why he wanted it. Bonner asked Mackenzie why he couldn't have come to him if he was in money trouble, but Mackenzie wouldn't say. Whatever the reason, it was obvious that it was something very unsavoury. Then Bonner said something about money missing from the Life House bank account – I didn't know anything about that, of course, but Mackenzie was very upset and in tears, and admitted that he had taken it but was putting it back. Then Mackenzie said that if he wasn't so much of a coward he would kill himself, and if Bonner wouldn't help him he would have to run away.

'Bonner said he couldn't do that, he had already sent Palmer with a message that Mackenzie was dead, and he would have to go on with the plan, but Mackenzie said he couldn't face doing it and just wanted to go away. He was in quite a state by now, and Bonner looked very worried and we both tried to calm him down, but we couldn't. There was a syringe nearby; I don't know who had prepared it because it was lying there when I came in. Mackenzie already had one sleeve rolled up as if he had been preparing himself for an injection, and Bonner picked up the syringe and injected him. He said, "I don't know what you have been up to, but you needn't think you can run off." Mackenzie looked alarmed and then he suddenly collapsed. Whether from the injection or fright I don't know. So we got him onto one of the tables and Bonner took his pulse and found that – well, he thought the man was dead. And I remember saying to him, "Dr Bonner, you've just murdered Dr Mackenzie!"'

'And then we heard a noise behind us, and we looked around and saw Palmer – how long he had been there we didn't know, but he looked very shocked at what he had seen.

'Bonner went up to him and tried to placate him, saying that it wasn't what it looked like and he needed him to keep quiet, but Palmer wouldn't listen, he said he was going to the police. And he made to go out, but when he turned around Dr Bonner hit him on the back of the head with his walking stick. I think Dr Bonner was very upset, because when Palmer fell down, he hit him again, at least twice more. Of course, we saw that he was dead and when Bonner realised what he had done, he said he was ruined, but then he said that I had to help him, or he would blame it all on me. How it could be my fault I really don't know, it's not as if I even know how to give an injection, but Bonner said he was well thought of in Bayswater and had a lot of friends in high places, and if it came to it people would believe him and not me. So I was afraid, then, and said I would help him, but it was only because he threatened me. Of course, I had to do most of the work, but that was only because Dr Bonner was lame. Bonner said we had to hide the body, but we couldn't put it in the canal because it would be obvious that Palmer had been murdered, and then the police would look into it and ask questions. So I said why not get it buried, and he agreed. Dr Bonner washed the blood off the wall, and I took Palmer into the little side room where they have the coffins and put him in one. I had to get Dr Mackenzie into a coffin as well, it's a good thing they had that stretcher on wheels.'

'Why did you put Mrs Templeman's body in the canal?' asked Frances.

'I'd just done what Bonner told me to do,' said Darscot, 'and then all of a sudden he said I had to put another body in the coffin with Palmer, as otherwise there would be one body too many and they always keep records of how many there are. But I didn't know about that and I'd already fastened the lid down, so Bonner said I had to take it up again, and just at that moment we heard the outer door open. It was the other orderly. We only had a moment or two to think what to do, and then I said I'd take the lady's body and put it in the canal, and Bonner said to do that.'

'Did you steal Dr Mackenzie's travelling bag?' asked Frances.

'Yes. It wasn't really stealing was it, the man owed me money, and in any case I thought he was dead. I hoped there might be something of value in it, but there wasn't. Then when you started asking about Mackenzie, and the bag was being talked about all over Bayswater, I thought I'd better get rid of it, so I threw it in the canal.'

Gostelow looked at Darscot as he might have looked at a piece of refuse that he had just scraped off the sole of his boot. He glanced at Darscot's card. 'John Darscot, I am placing you under arrest for the offences of theft and acting as an accessory to murder.'

'Oh but —'

'Constable, place him in the cells.'

'My solicitor will hear of this!'

'No doubt, and he may even obtain bail, but in the meantime I want you where I can question you further when I have heard what Dr Bonner has to say.'

Darscot was removed.

When Frances left the police station she found Dr Carmichael pacing up and down outside, with a wild look in his eyes. 'I went to your home and they said you were here. What has happened?'

'Mr Darscot has been arrested, and the police will be questioning Dr Bonner.'

Carmichael uttered a great gasp of relief. 'Oh, you don't know what a great weight that is off my mind!'

'You are correct,' said Frances sternly, 'I don't, so you had better tell me.'

'The thing is, I discovered that Darscot was — how shall I say it — a close associate of the person who I suspect had stolen my sister's journal. I thought it very possible that it had come into his hands, but I dared not confront him directly. I managed by a ruse to enter his rooms at the Piccadilly and searched them, but found nothing. Even if he had had it once, he might have sold it on, but my concern was that he had hidden it and was simply biding his time, and any expression of anxiety on my part would show my weakness and he would take advantage of that. I have every hope of an excellent new post in London and dare do nothing that would jeopardise that. I dared not even mention my suspicions of Darscot to you in case you inadvertently alerted him. I suppose I thought you would have agents who would be able to keep watch and make their own enquiries.'

'I do,' said Frances, 'but without all the necessary facts my hands were tied.' A thought crossed her mind. 'That tale you told me about your sister's letter being given to you in the street. Was that the truth? Or another lie?'

He bowed his head. 'I am ashamed to say that was not true. I told you that so as to divert attention from Darscot.'

'Really, Dr Carmichael,' said Frances in disgust, 'I can scarcely act for you if you repeatedly tell me lies. You should be ashamed of yourself! I have been making enquiries of every person who frequents Porchester Road for this messenger boy, who you now say is an invention. Come by this afternoon and pay off your account, and we will have done.'

She turned to walk away, but he ran after her. 'But we have made so much progress in the case!' he exclaimed. 'The police will be looking into Darscot's affairs, and he is safely under lock and key, but you must try and find if he has any secret hiding places or unsavoury associates. Now is the best time to find those documents!'

Frances recalled Darscot's apparently selfless offers to help Miss Horton with her late brother's affairs, but 'selfless' was not, she thought, an adjective that could apply to Mr Darscot. Perhaps his desire to discover the late Mr Horton's lodgings had a sinister motive, although it seemed most unlikely that Darscot had entrusted anything of value to a man with such an unhappy brain. She paused. 'Very well, but you must still pay your account up to date including all my expenses, *and* a further advance. Do that, and I will continue to trouble myself with this foolish story as if it was the truth.' She walked away.

Back at her lodgings, Frances wrote to Chas and Barstie asking them if they could discover anything of interest about Darscot, especially his business affairs. She also sent a note to Tom who arrived before long, and asked him to redouble his efforts to discover where Mr Horton lived, employing as many other boys as he saw fit, and also if he knew of any other address for Darscot apart from the Piccadilly. 'Oh, 'e's a fly gent an' no mistake.' said Tom, 'ad me runnin' notes for 'im all over the place. Paid well, mind, so I kept the old clapper shut. I'm no buzz-man! Got any sardines?'

'All the sardines you can eat if you can find out where he lives when he is not at the Piccadilly Club. Mr Darscot has just been arrested, although I suspect he can afford a legal man who will have him freed on bail before too long. If there is anything to learn we must do it quickly.'

'I'll run off now, then,' said Tom, stuffing a sausage into a bread roll and pushing the resultant light repast into his pocket.

✿

Next morning, Mr Rawsthorne called on Frances accompanied by the unpleasant Mr Wheelock. Sarah brought refreshments and settled herself in a chair to observe the proceedings. Both the men were aware that Sarah, once the Doughty family's maid of all work, had been transformed into a lady's companion and assistant detective, but neither felt entirely comfortable with the new situation and both chose to ignore her, as if she had been a solid but unexceptional chest of drawers, a thing with neither eyes nor ears. Sarah was used to her invisibility and seemed not to mind, while Frances saw it as an advantage as her visitors might be more forthcoming.

'I have come,' said Rawsthorne, 'to speak to you on behalf of my client, Dr Bonner, who is currently in police custody. I believe you know something of the circumstances.'

'More than most, I'd say,' sneered Wheelock.

'Dr Bonner was sojourning in Brighton for the sake of his health, when most upsettingly he received a visit from the police, who not only questioned him about the death of

Mr Palmer, but took him into custody. He is now residing in a cell at Kilburn police station in a state of some mental and physical distress. I understand that you were instrumental in finding the body of Mr Palmer and the location of his demise. And, though I find this hard to credit, you somehow managed to be present when the Kilburn police questioned my client's accuser, Mr Darscot.'

'That is the case,' said Frances.

'Regular Miss Dauntless and no mistake!' said Wheelock. Sarah scowled at him.

'Did *you* write those stories?' Frances demanded.

'Oh, yes, I'm better'n Charles Dickens, me!' said Wheelock. Frances thought not.

'I must say, your endeavours never cease to amaze me,' said Rawsthorne. 'How I wish your dear father could be here now, to see you so celebrated.'

'You are too kind,' said Frances, reflecting that had her father been alive her exploits would probably have induced a fatal case of apoplexy.

'It is very possible that should Dr Bonner ever come to trial – and I am doing my utmost to ensure that that never happens – you may be called as witness for his defence. I have interviewed Dr Bonner, but he is adamant that he has done nothing wrong. He admits that he agreed to assist his friend, but for entirely honourable reasons. The plan was for Dr Mackenzie to pretend a collapse and then for Dr Bonner to convince Mr Palmer that the doctor was dead. Once Palmer had left, Mackenzie gave himself the injection to aid in the deception, but then Palmer returned unexpectedly. Mr Darscot witnessed what was happening and tried to extort money for his silence, but when Palmer said he would go to the police, Mr Darscot struck him with his cane and killed him.'

'Have you examined Mr Darscot's walking cane?' asked Frances.

'The police have it now.'

'And do they think it is capable of breaking a man's skull?'

'That is the one difficulty,' said Mr Rawsthorne. 'Young Darscot's walking cane is of the light decorative variety favoured by fashionable young men. Not only is it incapable of inflicting the wounds found on the deceased, it is quite the wrong shape. Dr Bonner's stick, however, is a far more sturdy object. There are no bloodstains on it, but the police are assuming it has been well cleaned. But Dr Bonner is adamant that he did not strike Palmer with anything.'

'I have interviewed Dr Bonner on a number of occasions,' said Frances, 'and like so many medical men, he is able to dissemble with great ease. I do believe, however, that Dr Mackenzie deceived him as to the true reason for his wanting to leave London. If I were you, I would place a watch on Mr Darscot and ensure that if he is bailed, he does not try to escape.'

'There's any number of good detectives about Bayswater who would do that,' said Wheelock. 'I shall see about employing one.'

Later that day, Frances attended the Marylebone magistrates' court to see Mr Darscot, assisted by his solicitor, the sour and surly Mr Marsden, granted bail on all charges. As he was hurried away in a cab, she sent Tom to follow on with instructions to place a watch on wherever he went and then report back.

As she left the court, Frances was approached by Mr Gillan.

'Well done, Miss Doughty, even for getting that slippery fellow this far. I take it you are aware of his true identity?'

'I am not,' said Frances. 'I had no idea he had another one.'

'He has several and this is not the first time I have seen him in such a situation, although the last time he was calling himself Dalton, and he was operating in East Marylebone with a series of petty thefts and swindles. He got six months on that occasion.'

'Do the police know this is the same man?' demanded Frances.

'Not yet, but they will do when I have spoken to them in about two minutes from now. An interesting customer, his specialty is being the sociable helpful type, and getting to know unsuspecting people. Next moment he is their new bosom friend, playing on their weaknesses and borrowing money they won't see again.'

'What about blackmail?' asked Frances.

'He's never yet been caught out in that, but it suits his style.'

'And moneylending?'

'Oh, I can't see him up to that. He spends money on styling himself up to look the gentleman, but after that it's all hand to mouth with him.'

'He told me that he had lent £500 to Dr Mackenzie about a year ago,' said Frances.

To her discomfiture, Gillan laughed. 'I doubt he has ever had such a sum in his hands, especially not a year ago when he must just have come out of prison. And even if he had, he wouldn't have lent it to someone else. No, with that fellow the money all goes in one direction. Now if you'll excuse me, I am about to have a word in someone's ear.'

CHAPTER TWENTY

On the way home Frances was deep in thought. If Gillan was correct then Darscot had never, as he claimed, lent Mackenzie £500. What if she removed the £500 loaned by Darscot to Mackenzie entirely from the story, as if it had never existed or even been needed in the first place. What followed? She suddenly realised that this made the situation very much simpler. Now there were not two lots of £500 but one, and instead of Mackenzie needing £1,000 to settle his debts, he only needed £500, the money he took from the Life House and had tried to pay back.

But if Darscot had not loaned Mackenzie £500, why was he insisting that he had? Again the answer was that there was only the one sum of £500. Darscot had blackmailed Mackenzie and demanded £500 from him, and Mackenzie had had to steal the money from the Life House accounts. The fact that Mackenzie had tried unsuccessfully to take money a second time, suggested that Darscot had renewed his demands. It wasn't a loan repayment that Darscot had been after at all, but blackmail money. No wonder he had been angry when he thought his quarry was pretending to be dead to avoid paying him.

But what was the subject of the blackmail? There were the Erlichmann revelations, but Frances didn't see how Darscot could have known about them, and in any case, the original blackmail had taken place a year ago before the danger had become known. The only other possible subject that Frances knew about was the scandal concerning Madeleine Carmichael. But even if the journal had fallen into Darscot's hands, how would he have been able to make the connection between Dr Mackenzie and something written twenty years ago concerning events in Edinburgh? Given what Frances had been told about the lady it seemed most unlikely that her journal would be in any way explicit about her sufferings, and Mackenzie, even if mentioned, was not an uncommon surname in Scotland.

❀

Tom reported that Darscot had returned to his rooms at the Piccadilly Club and had not strayed out since. His only visitors had been the club manager and his solicitor, Mr Marsden. Dr Carmichael had moved out into some nearby lodgings, which he had taken for a week.

Chas and Barstie arrived with more news, and a little embarrassed that they had not previously known anything about the devious Mr Darscot, or Dalton, or whatever other name he used.

'This is his longest sojourn in Bayswater,' said Chas, 'and very probably his last, even if he can wriggle out of this latest escapade. Have no fear, if he is acquitted we will have our eyes on him in future!'

'But it seems he is about to turn legitimate,' said Barstie, 'or what counts as legitimate in his circles. Mr Darscot is the new owner of the Life House.'

'But how can that be? He has no funds,' exclaimed Frances. 'I know he has made a claim on the estate, but that is far from settled and in my opinion, never will be.'

'A small payment on account has been made and the papers will be completed very soon,' said Chas. 'And when I find out how he has managed it, I will want to try it for myself.'

'Then you should have the opportunity of finding out,' said Frances. 'I would like you to call on him. Find out as much as you can about his interests; also if he has a journal which once belonged to a Madeleine Carmichael. If he does, he might be willing to sell it.'

❀

Chas and Barstie had no difficulty in obtaining an interview with Mr Darscot, the details of which they reported to Frances the following day.

They had found Darscot sitting alone in his room at the Piccadilly Club with a bottle of brandy. He was quiet, but neither drunk nor despondent.

'What can I do for you gentlemen?'

'This is in the nature of a business call,' said Chas. 'We have heard that you have been experiencing a little difficulty and were wondering if there was any service we might perform for you.'

Darscot looked wary, but waved them both to some chairs and offered brandy, which they declined.

'It is true that I have been accused of a number of misdemeanours,' he said casually, 'but as you see, I am a free man, and my solicitor has advised me, although at exorbitant cost, that he will be able to clear me of any suspicion.'

'You are not intending to leave Bayswater?' asked Barstie.

'No, it is best if I remain here. A sudden departure would not help my reputation, and in any case, all my business interests are here, and I am very comfortable. The manager has been to see me in some anxiety on that point; he seemed to imagine that I was about to pack my bags and leave. I have mollified him with assurances that I intend to remain, and what weighed with him far more, I paid my rent up to date. He is now satisfied.'

'I have heard that you have recently purchased an interest in a business hereabouts,' said Chas.

'Your spies are most efficient.'

'Thank you.'

'But, it will be some days before the papers are completed, indeed if they ever are, as this latest difficulty may cause a delay and it could be some weeks before I can turn my new property to any useful account.' He poured himself another brandy. 'I have to confess that securing an interest in the Life House has temporarily exhausted all my means. If you really wish to perform a service for me, then you could lend me £100.'

Chas affected to consider the matter. 'That is a useful sum and while we are not prepared to lend it to you, we might offer to make a purchase.'

'That is very kind,' said Darscot, in some surprise, 'but I am not aware that I have anything that might be worth that sum to you. I am not yet in a position to sell an interest in the Life House, although we might come to some arrangement over that, but it would not come to fruition for some time and I am in need of the funds rather sooner.'

'Do you not own any other properties?' asked Barstie.

'There are rumours that I do and I am sure I don't know where such ideas come from, but I regret that I do not.'

'Papers, then,' said Chas. 'I have heard that you may be the possessor of valuable documents.'

'Am I?' Darscot took a substantial swig from his brandy glass. 'I wish I were.'

'Let me be more specific,' said Chas in a firmer tone. 'A Dr Carmichael, who has until recently been lodging at the Piccadilly Club, claims that you have something which belongs to him and which he is most anxious to recover.'

Darscot gave a snort of amusement. 'Then you have been misled. I can assure you, gentlemen, I have nothing belonging to Dr Carmichael. If I did, I would be most happy for him to have it. Obviously, I would appreciate a small consideration for my trouble.'

'Then if the item is not in your possession, it may be in the possession of an associate of yours,' Barstie suggested.

'I do not have any associates. And if this item even exists, I know nothing of it.'

Chas and Barstie looked at each other. 'Perhaps I might jog your memory,' said Barstie. 'The item, according to Dr Carmichael, takes the form of a journal composed by his late sister. He believes that it was stolen from him by a friend of yours, which is how it came into your possession. The journal, understandably, has very considerable sentimental value.'

Darscot began to laugh heartily. 'Oh, I know what all this is about now! I recall a conversation with Carmichael, but that was a year ago when he made his first visit to London. The gentleman is an unwise talker in his cups and he became very maudlin about this saintly sister of his – who in my opinion was no better than she should have been – and how she had been mistreated by Dr Mackenzie who, it seems, was her lover. He was angry that a man he regarded as a monstrous scoundrel was now a respected person in Bayswater and he wished there was some proof of this so that he could denounce him.'

'But surely the journal was the proof,' said Barstie.

Darscot laughed again. 'Oh, he would have *liked* there to have been a journal, but there was none.'

'Dr Carmichael believes there is and he is very anxious to find it.'

Darscot leaned back in his chair, his good humour unabated. 'If you have had any dealings with him at all, you will know that the man is a fool. It was a joke, that was all, but he must have taken it seriously. After a few whiskies he said how sorry he was there were no papers to prove his suspicions and how he wished he could conjure them into existence. So I said that as it was a good cause, bringing a scoundrel to justice, he might consider doing just that.'

'You mean forging what he needed?' said Chas.

'Yes – well as I have said, it was just a joke. He had a letter of his sister's that he always carried about with him, so a clever forger could have copied the hand, and of course he knew details of the family and events, which he could have imparted to make the content convincing. Maybe he *did* approach someone, but it wasn't me. I have no skills in that area and do not know anyone who does.' He waggled the brandy bottle at them again, but they shook their heads. 'So gentlemen, I wish I could oblige you, as I would find £100 a very useful sum of money to have in my possession at the moment, but if that is what you require, I am unable to help.' He paused. 'You don't know a Mr Horton, do you? Used to be a member here before he was asked to leave, and then died in a drunken fall. I promised his sister I would help her look after his affairs, but she has been unable to discover where he lodged.'

❧

'I do not have that information,' said Chas to Frances later as he described the meeting to her, 'but even if I did I would be most reluctant to part with it, or indeed anything else to *that* fellow.'

'Do you believe he was telling the truth about the journal?' she asked.

'It all comes down to money,' said Chas, 'as indeed, in this materialistic world we live in, everything always does. Suppose Darscot to be lying and the journal does exist. If Carmichael succeeds in obtaining the appointment he has been hoping for, then in the long term the journal might be worth a great deal more to Darscot than £100, however, it is very clear that in his current position he is in immediate need of funds. It is my belief that if he had had the papers to hand he would have parted with them.'

'Of course, I am in no difficulty at all in determining which of Mr Darscot and Dr Carmichael have been lying,' said Frances.

'Oh?'

'The answer is very simple,' she said. 'It is both of them.'

When Chas and Barstie had gone, Frances asked Sarah to make a fresh pot of tea, and sat down to consider all the facts. She then sent a message to Dr Carmichael.

That gentleman, who had just learned that his application for the London post had been unsuccessful, arrived that afternoon looking despondent and revealed that he would be leaving for Carlisle in a few days. 'I am very unhappy that the journal has not been found,' he said.

'I believe,' said Frances, 'that there is nothing to be found.'

'Whatever do you mean?'

'I mean that it never existed. Either as an original in your possession or as a forgery made for you.'

'But —'

'Yes?'

He hesitated. The word 'forgery' was causing him some little concern. 'But you thought it might have been used to blackmail Mackenzie.'

'I believe that Mr Darscot blackmailed Mackenzie with *something*. There were four things in his favour. The first was Mackenzie's own guilty conscience, which made him susceptible. The second was Mackenzie's poor state of health, which may have impaired his judgement. The third was Darscot's detailed knowledge of the people and events in Edinburgh connected with your sister's death. The fourth was your sister's letter which, while innocuous in itself, was undoubtedly in her handwriting and which may well have convinced Mackenzie that further material existed. Of course, the latter two Darscot could only have obtained from you. Mr Darscot, who always tries to side-step any suggestion of involvement in wrongdoing, has said that he only mentioned the idea of forging the papers you needed to incriminate Mackenzie as a joke and that you had somehow deluded yourself into thinking that he had done so. I don't believe him. I think the two of you conspired to forge the papers so that you could bring Mackenzie to justice. No doubt he extracted money from you for this service. But in reality he did not trouble himself to find a forger, which might have proved an expensive and risky business. Mr Darscot strikes me as a man who will always take the easiest way. Instead, armed with the letter that you had loaned him supposedly for the forger to practise his art, and also with a wealth of intimate information, he approached Dr Mackenzie and found that he could easily be milked of funds.

'The reason that you have not been telling me the truth is that you did not wish to reveal that you had conspired to commit a felony. You were very anxious to recover the journal, which you imagined had been forged on your behalf, because it was evidence of your criminality. But there may well have been another reason. If Darscot could convince you that he was or could secure the services of a master forger, then perhaps he had also convinced you that he had created other material to your detriment.'

'You really don't expect me to confess to a crime, do you?' asked Carmichael.

'The crime is one of conspiracy which is impossible to prove since the forgery was never carried out, and Darscot has already stated before two witnesses that the conversation was a joke. I think you are safe from prosecution,' said Frances.

Carmichael considered her words. 'You promise you will not tell this to the police?'

'I think there would be very little point and I am satisfied that your motive was not blackmail, but bringing a criminal to justice.'

'Then why do you need me to tell you more?'

Frances considered this. 'That is a very good question. Perhaps I am anticipating the entertaining possibility that you might at long last be telling me the truth.'

He sighed. 'Very well. I admit that I did talk all too freely to Darscot about poor Madeleine and how aggrieved I was that the monster who had destroyed her was a respected man. Not only did he defile her, after promising marriage, but he then performed an operation to remove the evidence of his terrible sin, an operation from which she subsequently died in the most appalling agony. Who would not want to see such a creature in prison for his crime? Darscot did offer to help me, and he said that he had manufactured a journal and taken it to the police, who were making enquiries, but they had advised him that as the events took place in Scotland many years ago, it could take some months to achieve a result.'

'Ah, a clever move on his part to extend the course of affairs as far as possible.'

'Yes – I suppose I see that now. I had to go back to Carlisle and I heard nothing more, but then when I saw that there was another post in London I might apply for, I came back and met up with Darscot again, and he said the police were still making their enquiries. I was afraid to go to the police, as I didn't want to be associated with a forgery.

'Well, after Mackenzie died – or at least, was supposed to have died – I asked Darscot if it was possible to get the journal back, but he said that he didn't think Mackenzie was dead at all, that he had only pretended to be dead so he could run away. He said the police were more certain than ever that Mackenzie was a villain and they were searching for him so they could arrest him. Well that was good news, of course, but still nothing happened.

'I couldn't approach anyone at the Life House as I thought they might have colluded with Mackenzie in his escape, but I was getting impatient and Darscot suggested that as the police had taken so long I might employ an enquiry agent to find Mackenzie. He said he could act as an intermediary to protect my reputation.'

'For a price, of course,' said Frances.

'He would take nothing for his own assistance, but of course, I would have to pay for the agent's work.' Carmichael uttered a groan. 'I suppose the agent was no more real than the forger. What a fool I was! But I was just considering this

when I received a warning from a member of the Piccadilly
Club who had seen me talking to Darscot. He said that Darscot
was a swindler and I should not give him any money. So I told
Darscot I had decided not to employ an agent and wanted to
forget the whole affair, and asked him for the journal. Darscot
told me he didn't have it as the police had taken it to Scotland,
where they were looking for Mackenzie. I asked him for the
name of the police officer who was in charge of the search for
Mackenzie and Darscot said it was a man whose name he had
not been given as he was working in secret.

'By now I hardly knew what to believe. I said I thought he was
lying and he told me that if I reported him he had forged some
papers, which he was keeping in a safe place, and if I accused him
of anything he could have me sent to prison. I didn't know who I
could trust and then someone mentioned your name.'

Carmichael left and Frances wondered why, when she should
have nothing to do with such a creature, she continued to be
swayed into helping him. The answer, she thought, was in her
own curiosity, her need to find out the truth.

❦

'Well,' said Tom with a big grin on his face, when he called on
her soon afterwards, 'you 'ave been busy 'an no mistake! If you
get any more people put in prison there won't be no folk left in
Bayswater to be your customers, they'll all be in pokey.' He had
managed to scrounge a heel of cheese from somewhere and was
making short work of it with a bit of raw onion.

'I think I have a little way to go before that result,' said Frances,
'and a good many of my clients are honest folk, although not,
sadly, as many as I would wish. You, on the other hand, young
man, have been carrying out all sorts of errands for the dreadful
Mr Darscot. What do you have to say about that?'

Tom grinned. 'Well you can't blame the postman for what's
in the letter, what it'd be against the law for 'im to look into. So
I'm in the clear. And the coppers pay a good whack for information so I've been paid twice for the same job, which is good
work, says I.'

'So Mr Darscot will be in even more trouble, now?'

'Up to 'is neck. The coppers just come to the Piccadilly an' took 'im away again, and 'e weren't 'appy. Not one little bit!' He finished the cheese. 'Now then, guess what I've got 'ere!' He handed Frances an onion-scented scrap of paper.

'An address,' said Frances, 'in Redan Place. Not Mr Horton's?'

'Mr Victor Albert, as he liked to call 'imself, only yes, it's Mr 'orton, and the lodgin's ain't been let yet an' the landlord says 'e will give over the key to anyone what can pay the back rent.'

'Splendid,' said Frances. 'I will fetch Miss Horton and go there at once.'

❋

The landlord was a sullen, shabbily dressed person, whose manners brightened on the production of the requisite amount of coin. He seemed to be under the impression that Frances, Sarah and Miss Horton were potential tenants, and even showed them where the essential offices were, a lopsided wooden hut at the back of a dingy rubbish-strewn yard. They declined to inspect it. Mr Horton's lodgings consisted of a single room at the top of two flights of stairs that smelt of rotting food and worse. The room was notable for a lack of any attempt to make it comfortable. The bedstead was rusty and Frances dared not touch the mattress. There was a wardrobe with one door missing that contained a very few items of clothing, a water jug, a cracked basin grey with the dirty dregs of soap scum, and the most basic of toiletries. Miss Horton looked on everything, and tears started in her eyes and rolled down her cheeks. 'I had not known he had come to this,' she said. 'We have little enough at home, but I could have brought him there and made him comfortable. I wonder what he ever had to eat.'

'Miss Horton,' said Frances. 'Would you be so good as to look at the contents of this room, in particular any personal items, and let me know if there is anything here that did not belong to your brother?'

'Why, he was not a thief, Miss Doughty!'

'I am sure he was not, but he may have been given something by another person for safekeeping.'

'I see, well of course I will take a look – not that there is a great deal here. These few poor clothes are his – I recall the hairbrush as it belonged to our late father. The police gave me his pocketbook and a few coins that he was carrying, but there was nothing there that could not have been his.' Miss Horton made the search as requested, and found only some family photographs and letters and several pawn tickets, but concluded that there was nothing in the room that was not her brother's property.

Sarah was silent all this time, but at last she gave a grunt and rolled up her sleeves. In seconds the bed had been stripped of its ragged sheets and its hard pillow, and the mattress turned. Finally she took hold of the bedstead and pulled it away from the wall. It creaked horribly and Frances, who had feared that something alive and unpleasant might run out from the dark recesses that had been undisturbed for so long, was relieved that nothing that crawled or scampered was revealed. They saw a stained chamber-pot and one other item, something long, narrow and wrapped in newspaper, which Sarah retrieved and laid on the bed. Frances and Miss Horton peered at it as the papers were pulled back.

'I think *this* did not belong to your brother,' said Frances.

'I have never seen it before,' said Miss Horton. 'Is this the thing he was looking after for a friend?'

'In a manner of speaking, yes,' said Frances, picking it up. 'That is interesting. It is very much heavier than it appears to be.'

'Solid metal right through the middle I don't doubt,' said Sarah.

It was a gentleman's walking cane, with a fox's head device, and the silver top was crusted in blood.

CHAPTER TWENTY-ONE

'I think,' said Frances, when the incriminating object had been handed to the police, 'that Mr Darscot will find it very hard now to deny that he murdered Henry Palmer. Quite apart from the statement made by Dr Bonner, I believe the police will easily discover witnesses who have seen Mr Darscot with the stick, and of course his efforts to find Mr Horton's lodgings now look very suspicious. There is also the fact that the silver fox's head may prove to fit the wounds on Mr Palmer's skull exactly. I believe that young man will shortly be making an appointment that he would much rather not keep.'

'But what was Mr Horton doing with the stick?' asked Sarah. 'And do you think Mr Darscot killed him?'

'As to the latter, I am not sure. Horton, as we know, had a habit of becoming obsessed with artefacts that reminded him of animals, some of which he saw as friendly but more often as a threat. I think he formed an obsession with the fox's head stick and stole it from Darscot shortly after the murder of Mr Palmer, not realising that it was a murder weapon. Darscot was, of course, very anxious to get it back. It is possible that the two men fought and that Horton's death was an accident. It would certainly not have been in Mr Darscot's interests to murder Horton before he had found his stick.'

❧

The next morning the case against Darscot was heard at Marylebone magistrates' court and he was committed for trial on the charge of murdering Henry Palmer. Alice Palmer and Walter Crowe were in attendance, and while the young woman still looked deathly pale, the resolution of the mystery and the care of her future husband, friends and family would, thought

Frances, restore her health in time. Miss Finch was very solici-
tous of her dear friend, although she was enduring her grief
with the support of a most attentive young man whom she
favoured with her simpering smiles. Dr Bonner also appeared,
a pitiable looking creature, claiming that Darscot had blackmailed him into transferring his interest in the Life House, but
the fickle opinion of society had turned against him in the last
few days. No one objected when he was committed to take his
trial on a charge of murdering Dr Mackenzie and acting as an
accessory to the murder of Henry Palmer. Neither prisoner was
charged with the murder of Herbert Horton.

Mr Fairbrother, while deeply grieved at the fate of his
mentor, was thankful that the terrible business was almost at
an end, especially since the magistrate had explicitly stated that
his involvement was only as a pupil of Dr Bonner, and that he
had acted under the senior man's direction. Indeed, he had been
praised for the clever observation that the body in the canal and
Mrs Templeman were one and the same.

'Will you be seeking another tutor in London?' asked Frances.

'No, my sojourn here is at an end in any case. I am anxious
to study for my MD and have found a position in Edinburgh,
which I will be taking up almost immediately.'

'Ah,' said Frances, 'then it seems unlikely that our paths will
cross again.'

'Oh, one never knows,' he said, blithely. 'But it has been quite
extraordinary to meet you, Miss Doughty. I must confess, I had
my doubts about ladies studying to be doctors, but if they are all
like you, they may well come to be ornaments to the profession
– in certain limited spheres of work, of course.'

Frances did not trouble herself to ask what he might consider those limits to be. On her way home she reflected that it
was unlikely that anyone would ever know exactly what had
transpired on the night of Henry Palmer's death, but she felt it
very probable that Bonner had injected Mackenzie when he
had suggested abandoning the plan and running away. Palmer
must have witnessed what he perceived to be the murder of
Dr Mackenzie and had been struck down by Darscot to stop
him going to the police.

Tom came to see her, towing a boy of about his own age who needed some persuasion to accompany him. The boy was dressed in an odd assortment of clothing, none of which had been made for someone of his size, some of it too short in the body and some overly long. His face was a shade of mottled brown, which spoke either of some unknown illness, or being burnt by the sun, or, as was more probable, a long-standing unfamiliarity with soap and water. Sarah scowled at him, pushing up her sleeves as if about to test that conundrum.

'This is Ratty!' said Tom proudly. ''e's my best man.'

'Good afternoon, Ratty,' said Frances. 'Do you have any information for me?'

Ratty explored his ear with a dirty fingernail.

'He dint want to go ter the coppers, but I said 'e oughter,' said Tom.

'Don' like coppers,' growled Ratty.

'Then you can tell me whatever you have to say,' said Frances kindly.

'Go on!' said Tom, giving Ratty a shove.

Ratty wriggled uncomfortably in his clothes and capitulated, revealing a curious tendency to add extra syllables to any word he felt unsure of, as if by making it long enough he was sure to get all the necessary parts in. 'It's about that there Mr 'orton. The one what was shoved into the area an' bashed 'is 'ead in. I saw 'im, dint I? Outside the Piccadillilly Club, walkin' up 'n down th' Portichester Road, and cursin' and swearin' 'n then this woman comes up an' they 'as a few words what I dint catch, but I thought she were a doxy, 'cos they goes off arm-in-arm as friendly as anythin', 'n then not long after that, the Pounder, what does all the pugilistics, 'e comes out and 'e walks off on 'is own, but goin' the other way.'

'Can you say when this happened?' asked Frances, hopefully.

'I don' know the day, not like the day of the week or anythin', or any of the numbers, like,' said Ratty.

Frances sighed. Horton had been a well-known figure outside the club for three days before he was killed.

'All I *do* know is that it was the day after I saw 'im when they found 'im face down dead.'

'The very next day? You're quite sure?'

He nodded.

'Well Ratty, that is a very important story, and I think you should go and tell the police at once.'

'Don' like coppers,' repeated Ratty.

'If you go and tell them what you know, then I will see that you have a fine dinner and new clothes and a shilling,' said Frances.

Sarah raised her eyebrows since she strongly suspected who was going to be serving the fine dinner.

Ratty thought about it. 'Two shillin's,' he said.

'Done!'

Tom grinned. 'An' finder's commission!'

Frances could hardly argue with that. 'I hope,' she said, 'that this means that Professor Pounder will be released. I shall hear soon enough if he is.'

A few hours later, Joseph arrived with an invitation for Frances, Sarah, Tom and Ratty to enjoy a celebratory tea at Cedric's lodgings the next day at which they might meet the legendary Professor Pounder, who wished to express his gratitude.

❦

Professor Pounder was a tall, broad man of about thirty-five, with an honest face, short, light brown curly hair and blue eyes. His clothes were worthy of the man, and although he might have felt more comfortable in the garb of an athlete, he wore them well, to do honour to the company. He was quietly spoken and very polite, a man who would not use two words when one would do.

The company sat around an elegant table on which Joseph had arranged the thinnest sandwiches, the lightest cakes, the most delicate biscuits, and scones like tiny white pillows just waiting to be anointed with delicious spoonfuls of jam and cream. He hovered about them wielding the teapot with discreet bravura, and their teacups were never empty.

Tom had been scrubbed and put in a suit and Ratty, whose screams had rung the length of Westbourne Park Road on being introduced to the concept of cleanliness by Sarah, was silent and shocked in his new clothes. Neither let their discomfort inhibit them from sampling every foodstuff in sight.

'I thank you all most humbly,' said Pounder, raising his cup to make a toast. 'To you I owe my freedom, and my reputation.'

'Inspector Gostelow said he was a model prisoner and they were sorry to see him go,' said Cedric, 'but even the force's finest could not find a stain on his character. I am sure they would have him in uniform tomorrow if he would agree to it. Now *that* would be a sight to see!'

Joseph looked wistful, but refrained from comment.

'The Inspector has asked me if I might train his men to defend themselves against criminal types,' said Pounder, 'which I have agreed to do.'

'The Professor,' said Cedric, enthusiastically, 'is the finest exponent of the noble art of boxing that has ever lived. He rivals the best athletes of the Greeks, and can be relied upon to perform a display with such taste and decorum that even ladies do not disdain to attend. Indeed, they are very partial to watching him. The most beautiful ladies in London simply swoon at his feet!'

'That must be very awkward,' said Frances, picturing how the Professor might appear in the roped ring. It was not an unpleasant portrait.

Pounder nodded. 'Some,' he said, 'but I don't take no mind.'

'Do you not admire beauty?' asked Cedric, teasingly.

'I do,' said Pounder, and jabbed a thumb at his chest. 'Beauty of the heart.'

'I agree,' said Cedric, 'and I am happy to say that for beauty of character, of strength, and cleverness and loyalty, of everything that truly counts in this world, we have at our table the finest two ladies in Bayswater! Miss Doughty has a mind that all men should regard with terror – it has killed several to my certain knowledge – and once you have seen Miss Smith crack walnuts with her bare hands you will avow that there is no finer sight that the capital has to offer.'

'That's Jeb Smith's trick,' said Pounder, 'the Wapping Walloper. Best bare-knuckle man in England.'

''E's my uncle!' said Tom, 'or cousin, I c'n never work out which. An' it ain't 'is trick, 'cos it was Sarah what taught it 'im.'

Pounder looked from Tom to Sarah and back again. 'Ah,' he said to Tom, 'well, you be proud of him, lad, however he's related.'

Joseph replenished the teacups and brought fruit tarts.

'I suppose the police have not found the murderer of Mr Horton?' said Frances. 'It may have been a drunken fight with the woman he was last seen with, a robbery, perhaps. You know that I was with his sister when his lodgings were searched and the poor woman was in great distress. I hope, for her sake, that the culprit is caught soon.'

'Oh,' said Tom, eating three sandwiches at once, 'she's not as sorry as she makes out.'

'Whatever do you mean?' asked Frances.

Sarah took a napkin and applied it briskly to Tom's mouth, and it was some moments before he could speak again.

'Well, when I talked to the man at the last place where 'Orton lived, 'e said that when the sister came round she was asking about 'er good-for-nothing waster of a brother what was going to break 'er poor mother's 'eart.'

'That was a little unkind,' said Frances, 'even if true.'

'I bet it *was* true,' said Sarah, grimly. 'Every bit of it. A man who can't respect his own mother can't hardly respect anything else, least of all himself.'

'Oh, how true that is,' said Cedric.

'We are usually more polite about a deceased person than one that lives,' observed Frances. 'We like to remember their strengths and forget their weaknesses. But perhaps they do things differently in Manchester.'

'I don't see how being dead makes a man's life any better than it was,' said Sarah. 'If she said it plain, and meant it, then she was remembering him right. When my grandfather died we all sat down and said he was a mean old grizzler when sober and a worse one when drunk, and then we all cried our eyes out, because we knew it was true.'

'But Miss 'Orton said all that *before* 'er brother was dead,' said Tom.

Frances stared at him. 'Before? Surely not. Miss Horton came down to London after reading about her brother's death in the newspapers. So, when she went to his lodgings she already knew he had died.'

'Oh, well I dint know what she said to *you*. But the man said that she come to see 'im askin' about her brother on the Tuesday mornin' and it was the next day when 'e 'eard about the body found in the area.'

'And did he tell Miss Horton that her brother might be found at the Piccadilly Club?'

'Well 'e dint know as 'ow 'e was a member, but 'e knew 'e'd taken to walkin' up and down an' talkin' to 'imself outside the door, cos 'e'd been up on the Monday an' asked for 'is rent and not got it.'

'And Ratty here saw Horton with a woman that Tuesday night,' said Sarah, 'and they were affectionate and walking arm-in-arm.'

'I have to confess,' said Frances, 'that when Miss Horton came to see me I did not question her story, but I will check to see when the identity of the dead man was first revealed in the newspapers and compare it with when she said she arrived in London.' She turned to Cedric. 'I don't suppose you still have copies of last week's newspapers?'

Cedric raised his eyebrows in mock horror.

'No, I rather thought not, but I do retain them for reference.' Frances rose. 'If what I suspect is right, then I must not waste any time, and Tom will have to take a message to Inspector Gostelow.'

'You see, Pounder?' said Cedric. 'A visit from Miss Doughty is always attended by more drama than the popular theatre.'

'So I see,' answered the Professor.

'And a visit from Miss Smith is often attended by severe discomfort if one is a criminal.'

Pounder nodded thoughtfully, but said nothing.

❧

Later that day, Frances received a visit from Inspector Gostelow.

'Well, I don't know how you do it, Miss Doughty, but thanks to your quick thinking we managed to catch up with Miss Horton before she left London and I have never seen a woman more relieved to confess all. Seems like it was the old story – after their father died the son was the apple of his mother's eye and everything went on his education, while the daughter stayed at home. He gets packed off to London to make his fortune, but they lose touch. When mother gets very ill she wants to see her boy again before she goes, but she tells the daughter that her life policy money will all go to the son and she is relying on him to look after his sister. So Miss Horton goes to her brother's last address and the landlord says he doesn't know where he lives, but he might be found near the Piccadilly Club. That's where she sees him, walking up and down outside, off his head with drink. And probably off his head even without the drink. It soon becomes clear to her that her brother is a wastrel who would spend his inheritance as soon as he gets it. Then he tries to borrow money from her. Final straw is, he tells her he has pawned his late father's gold watch and ring, which were family heirlooms entrusted to him by their mother, and when he staggers against the railing she loses her temper and pushes him over. Regrets it as soon as done, of course, but there you are.'

'And of course, she wanted to find his rooms to look for the pawn tickets,' said Frances. 'But even if her brother had inherited, I am sure that given his unhappy state, Miss Horton could have got control of the legacy, and then she would have cared for him.'

'Ah yes, but she hadn't seen him in a year. He was a bit eccentric before, but his brain had got worse since then, and that night she thought he was just drunk.'

'Poor woman,' said Frances. 'I do hope she won't be hanged.'

'Oh no, it won't be hard to play on the tender hearts of the jurymen. She'll plead the madness of a moment and get manslaughter. I've seen many a bad husband, or brother, or father sent off like that, and the woman reckoning that nine or ten years in prison was a fair exchange for their absence.'

'But she can't inherit from her mother now.'

'No, but there's a cousin who will, and he has said he is willing to give her a home when she comes out of prison, so I expect it will all turn out alright for her.'

Later that day there was an unusual delivery; Joseph arrived with an envelope containing four tickets for a demonstration of the noble art and exact science of self-defence at Westbourne Hall by that unparalleled exponent, Professor Pounder.

'The tickets are for yourself, of course, and young masters Thomas and Ratty, and the other is for Miss Smith,' said Joseph, suppressing a smile. 'The Professor was most particular about *that*.'

'It seems,' said Frances to Sarah, showing her the tickets, 'that you have an admirer.' She was a little cautious about mentioning this, since young men who had previously expressed a tender interest in Sarah's substantial charms had quickly regretted it.

'Stuff and nonsense!' said Sarah, but, unusually, she did not seem displeased.

'But we ought to go, it will be very interesting. I understand that the one minute challenge, which is open to all-comers, can be very entertaining and no real harm is done.' Frances paused, struck by a worrying thought. 'Sarah, I hope you won't think of —'

'Naw – he's in no danger from me!' Sarah stuffed her ticket into a pocket. 'Now, as to admirers, well, I think you ought to look at this.' She handed Frances a copy of *Miss Dauntless in Danger*.

'Oh, are these continuing?' said Frances. She leafed through the pages, which revealed that Miss Dauntless and her companion Sally had moved to commodious apartments in the vicinity of Hyde Park. The enterprising lady detective was portrayed, she thought, in a spirit of rather too extravagant admiration. In one scene of high drama Miss Dauntless, having courageously pursued some criminals through the park, was attacked by a villainous character on the bridge over the Serpentine, and thrown into the water from which she was rescued by a mysterious stranger, who gathered her into his arms and planted a chaste kiss on her lips before disappearing into the night.

'Well, it *is* only a story,' Frances protested.

'That ain't no story,' declared Sarah, 'that's a love letter!'

Frances didn't know what to say.

'You've gone quite red in the face,' said Sarah. 'I'll make a pot of tea.'

❧ END ❧

AUTHOR'S NOTE

The subject of this book was inspired by *Buried Alive* by Jan Bondeson, a fascinating account of the history of the fear of premature burial.

The Reverend Walter Whiter's *A Dissertation on the Disorder of Death*, published in 1819 (downloadable at www.archive.org) is well worth reading for his viewpoint on the signs of death.

For the late nineteenth-century understanding of putrefaction and other signs of death I have turned to contemporary editions of *The Principles and Practice of Medical Jurisprudence* by Alfred Swaine Taylor, edited by Dr Thomas Stevenson.

A detailed account of a visit to Kensal Green Cemetery is to be found in *The Business of Pleasure* by Edmund Yates, published in 1879, and downloadable at www.archive.org.

Most of the people mentioned in this book are fictional. All the streets and public buildings mentioned by name are actual locations.

The General Cemetery of All Souls Kensal Green conducted its first funeral in 1833 and still performs burials and cremations daily. It is open to visitors every day. For details of guided tours and the annual open day see www.kensalgreen.co.uk. A tour of the catacombs is highly recommended!

The Life House is fictional, but waiting mortuaries did exist although not in the UK. The first waiting mortuary, the Vitae Dubiae Asylum, was built by German physician Christoph Wilhelm Hufeland in Weimar in 1792.

William Whiteley's empire with his row of ten shops on Westbourne Grove and new ones being built in Queen's Road (nowadays Queensway) was already a prominent feature of Bayswater life in 1880.

Providence Hall in Church Street was one of the locations where inquests were held in Paddington, often presided over by Dr William Hardwicke, the coroner for central Middlesex.

Reverend Benjamin Day was the curate of St Stephen's Church, Paddington.

The Grand Junction Canal commenced construction in 1793. In 1929 it became part of the Grand Union Canal.

The Paddington Vestry was a forerunner of the Borough Council. Its sometimes tumultuous meetings are very well documented in the *Bayswater Chronicle*.

Dr Thomas Stevenson (1838-1908) was a noted chemist and toxicologist who was often called upon to give evidence at inquests and trials.

In 1877, some of the management and staff of the Hospital for Diseases of the Throat and Chest, Golden Square resigned after the death of a patient.

In 1880, the Aberdeen Hospital for Incurables was in Baker Street, Aberdeen.

On 2 September 1880, 10-year-old James Henry Robinson drowned while bathing in the Grand Junction Canal near Kensal Green Cemetery. The coroner commented that such accidents were all too common.

On 4 September 1880, the Balloon Society of Great Britain organised a number of ascents, one of which took place from Kensal Green.

The Monmouth Club opened at 7 Monmouth Road just off Westbourne Grove in 1877 and its activities were criticized in the *Bayswater Chronicle* from March 1879. In July 1880, David Copping, the club's proprietor, commenced an action for libel against Henry Walker, the proprietor and editor of the *Chronicle*, and publisher George Walters. The case finally came to trial on 22 and 23 October and the defendants were not only acquitted but praised for having performed a public service. The club was closed down.

A 'rum-mizzler' was a skilled pickpocket, expert at making a quick getaway.

ABOUT THE AUTHOR

Linda Stratmann is a former chemist's dispenser and civil servant who now writes full-time. She lives in Walthamstow, London.

ALSO BY THE AUTHOR

Chloroform: The Quest for Oblivion

Essex Murders

Gloucestershire Murders

Greater London Murders: 33 True Stories of Revenge, Jealousy, Greed & Lust

Kent Murders

Middlesex Murders

More Essex Murders

Notorious Blasted Rascal: Colonel Charteris and the Servant Girl's Revenge

The Crooks Who Conned Millions: True Stories of Fraudsters and Charlatans

The Poisonous Seed: A Frances Doughty Mystery

The Daughters of Gentlemen: A Frances Doughty Mystery

Whiteley's Folly: The Life and Death of a Salesman

If you enjoyed this book, you may also be interested in…

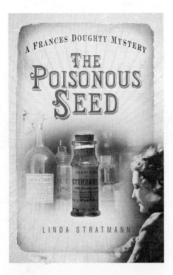

The Poisonous Seed
A Frances Doughty Mystery

When a customer of William Doughty's chemist shop dies of strychnine poisoning after drinking medicine he dispensed, William is blamed and the family faces ruin. William's daughter, nineteen-year-old Frances, determines to redeem her ailing father's reputation and save the business. She soon becomes convinced that the death was murder, but unable to convince the police, she turns detective. Armed only with her wits, courage and determination, and aided by some unconventional new friends, Frances uncovers a startling deception and solves a ten-year-old murder, and, in the process, her life is changed forever.

ISBN: 978 0 7524 6118 2
EPUB: 978 0 7524 6391 9

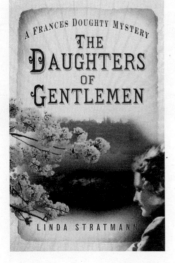

The Daughters of Gentlemen
A Frances Doughty Mystery

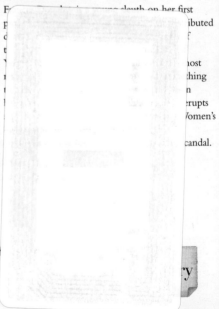

Visit our website and discover the other History Press books.

www.thehistorypress.co.uk